LIKE

OTHER

GIRLS

LIKE OTHER GIRLS

BRITTA LUNDIN

HYPERION

Los Angeles   New York

First Edition, August 2021
10 9 8 7 6 5 4 3 2 1
FAC-020093-21169
Printed in the United States of America

This book is set in DK Garden Gnome/FontSpring;
KG Happy/Kimberly Geswein Fonts/FontSpring; Melior/Monotype
Designed by Marci Senders

Library of Congress Cataloging-in-Publication Data
Names: Lundin, Britta, author.
Title: Like other girls / Britta Lundin.
Description: First edition. • Los Angeles ; New York : Hyperion,
2021. • Audience: Ages 14–18. • Audience: Grades 10–12. •
Summary: "After four other girls follow Mara's lead and join the
football team, she's forced to confront her misconceptions about
gender and her archnemesis"—Provided by publisher.
Identifiers: LCCN 2020016394 • ISBN 9781368039925
(hardcover) • ISBN 9781368044363 (ebook)
Subjects: CYAC: Football—Fiction. • Sex role—Fiction. •
Gender identity—Fiction. • Sexual orientation—Fiction.
Classification: LCC PZ7.1.L849 Lik 2021 • DDC [Fic]—dc223
LC record available at https://lccn.loc.gov/2020016394

Reinforced binding
Visit www.freeform.com/books

For those for whom even stepping foot
on the field takes courage

Last Winter

WHEN MY EYES OPEN AGAIN, IT'S TO THE SIGHT OF MY teammates' worried faces looking down at me. I couldn't speak even if I wanted to, which I don't. I want to sprint down the court, throw an elbow into the Hixon point guard's face, then step back and sink a three over her outstretched fingers.

It's not the dirty shoulder check that bothers me; it's not that the useless refs apparently didn't see it. It's not even that I hit my head so hard on the floor that bright sparks still fly across my vision and pain ricochets around my brain. What bothers me is the look on everyone's faces, like I'm some fragile knickknack on their grandmother's shelf that shatters if you look at it sideways. I'm fine.

"Okay, Mara, shake it off!" Coach Joyce chirps peppily.

Shaking it off isn't going to win this game. I need to make Hixon pay. I check the clock, the stars trailing my eyeline. Three minutes left. My balance lags a second behind my body as I get to my feet. Coach Joyce calls a time-out.

"How you doing?" Coach asks me in the huddle.

"Fine," I say. "Let's do this." But I can feel Carly Nakata's eyes on me like she's going deer hunting and I'm the doe. As if I don't have enough problems.

Coach pulls out her whiteboard to talk strategy as Carly whispers to me, "Are you seeing stars?"

"No," I snap, even as the arrows on Coach's whiteboard swim, crossing and uncrossing. Not that it matters. I don't need a diagram to know she's telling me to attack. I glance over my shoulder at the point guard, who's sucking down water on her sideline. I have five inches on her and three fouls left. She messed with the wrong player. Dark spots form on the edges of my vision. I blink them away.

"You're not focusing," Carly says.

"Because you're talking to me," I growl.

"No, your eyes—"

"Mara, Carly," Coach says. "I need your attention." And now I'm pissed Carly's getting me in trouble, on top of everything.

"Coach, I think Mara has a concussion," Carly says, and right then, I could scream.

"I said I'm fine," I tell Carly through gritted teeth. After I take out the point guard, maybe I need to go after Carly next.

"Look at her eyes," Carly insists, and Coach does. I try to look as unconcussed as possible, whatever that means. Bright-eyed, I guess, alert. No one's taking me out of this game. Not this deep in the season. Not when it's tied up.

I don't know what Coach sees, but she jerks her head toward the bench. "Sit it out," she tells me.

"Are you kidding?" The ref blows her whistle. Time-out's over. I have to get back on the court. I'm not letting that point guard just get away with this.

"Take a seat, Mara."

"Coach, there's three minutes left."

But Coach walks away, turning her focus back to the players still in this game. The Hixon point guard catches my eye as she jogs back onto the court and smirks. My temperature spikes. It's like she's in some conspiracy with Carly to keep me out of the game for the final seconds. A dirty hit I can handle, but what took me out at the knees was my own damn teammate. I turn, searching, and see Carly refilling her water bottle at the cooler.

I'm only dimly aware of the game resuming, the squeak of shoes on the glossy boards, the grunts and breathing of my teammates playing on without me. The only way to win this game is grit and effort, and I can't give that because Carly decided to play doctor. Whose team is she on? I could have won this for us. At least, I could have helped. And instead, I'm standing here with nothing to do but watch the seconds tick down, while Carly's biggest concern is apparently staying hydrated.

"Hey," I say, and she turns, her cap halfway on her water bottle.

It goes flying when I hit her. I was aiming for a kidney, but she's so much shorter than me, I basically hit her in the boob. She staggers backward, her water bottle falling, glugging water onto the floor. Her foot catches on the leg of the water table and she loses her balance, falling into it. I have to hop back to avoid the cooler dropping with a crash, the top popping off, water flowing onto the court. A whistle blows and the game stops. The crowd quiets. Finally, the stars clear from my vision as I look around and see everyone's eyes on me.

Carly sort of grunts and grasps her boob. I look at Coach, and her eyes hold a fury I've never seen before.

"Coach—"

"You're outta here," she says, voice thick with anger, pointing to the locker room.

"Coach—"

"GO, MARA!"

And that's how I get thrown off the basketball team.

WHEN YOU'RE THIS FAR BEHIND ENEMY LINES, THE only way to avoid getting captured is outrunning and outwitting absolutely everyone. In other words, complete dominance, which happens to be my specialty.

I'm keeping low, squinting in the late-summer sunshine, searching every storefront, derelict phone booth, and hidey-hole south of Main Street for the red flag. I'm two blocks into red team territory, and if any of the guys on that team spot me, I'll have to run like hell back to Main before they catch me or I'll be out. As I pass the antique store, a head pops out the front door. I almost take off before realizing it's Quinn.

"What are you, shopping for a nice vase?" I whisper, crouching with him behind the wheel of a pickup parked on the street.

"Checking with the lady inside. You know Wayne's a cheater."

"That's true." The rules say the flags have to be in sight of the road, but Wayne Warren likes to get creative in his capture-the-flag hiding places, to dubious legality. One time we found the flag tied to an actual flagpole, and Quinn tried to shimmy it for five minutes before I thought to lower the flag to our level. Another time they tied it to the parking meter enforcement buggy, and we had to run after it for two whole blocks.

"He probably tied it to a drone that's hovering somewhere over the courthouse," I mutter.

"That would be easy, we just get your brother to throw a football at it. I'd catch it and"—he makes the sound of a cheering crowd—"run it back to our side to earth-shattering applause. Cue makeout sesh with Maria Carpenter."

"Dude, Maria Carpenter is never going to look twice at you."

"Oh, she pines for me, I know she pines." He grins.

"She doesn't even go to your games, dude, she's too busy leading the volleyball team to State."

"Our volleyball team went to State?" Quinn asks, incredulous.

"Twice," I tell him. Our football team hasn't been to State in, well, ever. A fact Quinn does not relish discussing.

"Well, how hard can it be to go to State in volleyball, anyway? That's a sport for girls with weak bones."

I snort laugh. "What does that even mean?"

"Weak bones, you know. You can just tell looking at Maria. She's hot, but her bones are not strong. She needs to drink more milk."

I shake my head. Down the block, someone opens a newspaper box and pulls out a newspaper.

"Now *you*, Mara. You have bones like steel. Ranch bones. Unbreakable."

"Thanks, I guess?" I say, but I'm no longer listening. I'm squinting to see the newspaper box better. The door snaps closed and I see it again. A flash of red.

"They *didn't*." I take off.

"Where are you going?"

I stay low as I run and squat in front of the box for our local paper. Our town is so small, the *Elkhorn Sentinel* is more like a pamphlet, really, but it still costs fifty cents to open the box, and the red flag is sitting primly on top of a stack of papers behind glass. Quinn follows, crouching next to me.

"Those *cheaters*," I growl.

"You got this, Mara, just punch it out," Quinn says jovially. I level him with a look, but he's unfazed. "Pretend the box is Carly Nakata and lay it out, you know you want to."

I ignore the comment. "Do you have fifty cents?"

"Nope."

I keep my eyes on the street, scanning for red-team members. I don't see anyone, but I can't relax until we're back on our side. Wayne could be moments away from turning the corner and pouncing on us.

"Go sweet-talk someone into giving us fifty cents," Quinn says, giving me a shove.

"What?"

"C'mon, try the bakery. Some little old lady's gotta have some change."

"*You* do it."

"You know people don't trust boys. They only give things to girls."

I can't decide whether that's true or Quinn is making up facts again, but it's easier not to fight him when he gets like this.

"Fine. Don't get yourself caught." I duck into the bakery.

A wave of sugary warm dough scent hits me and immediately makes me hungry. I've been hungry a lot this summer, since I started lifting weights in my bedroom. And by weights I mean gallon milk jugs that I've rinsed out and filled with water. I have a routine I printed off the internet. When I started with them, I could barely do one set of ten reps, but now I'm up to three sets. I'm even starting to see a difference when I put on a T-shirt. I'm totally getting a doughnut when this game is over.

I scan the booths of folks, looking for a good target to hit up for change, but the booths are empty save for a cowboy in muddy boots scarfing a buttermilk bar and, in the back booth, River Reyes. Hope surges through me. I don't know River well—she's a weird theater girl who only ever wears black—but at least she knows my name. As I start toward River, she notices me, and then the person sitting across from her follows her look and turns around and I realize to my utter despair that it's Carly Nakata.

"What's up, Mara?" River says around a bite of maple bar.

"Hey, River," I say hesitantly. Then, with a nod: "Carly."

"Mara," Carly says coldly back.

River looks between us with raised eyebrows. "So . . ." she says. "How's your summer?"

"Good, good. Listen, this is weird, but I'm kind of in a hurry. I'm trying to get fifty cents to, uh, buy a *Sentinel*."

"You shouldn't support them," Carly says. "The *Sentinel*'s editorial board sucks." She doesn't look at me when she talks, like she can't even be bothered to acknowledge my existence. I have to laugh. Of course Carly has beef with the *Sentinel* editorial board. Carly has beef with everyone.

"What, are they refusing to print your letters to the editor?" I ask.

"No, they refuse to stand up to the school board, who cut funding for every arts program there is in order to funnel more money to the football team." Now she glares at me as though the school budget is *my* fault. There's an electricity inside Carly that never dies, which is part of what makes her so annoying. As she straightens in her seat, her purse strap falls over her V-neck T-shirt directly between her boobs, highlighting them each individually. To avoid looking at her chest, I avert my eyes to her purse, which is covered in pins for various causes, including a lesbian pride flag, a pin that says IT'S AN HONOR JUST TO BE ASIAN, and a she/her pronoun pin, among a slew of environmental and political messages. How does she get away with being so open about her sexuality like that? It's like we don't even live in the same town.

River makes a face. "Besides, the paper sucks. Nothing ever happens here."

"I don't actually—" I sigh and shift my weight. I have to get a move on. "We're playing capture the flag. The flag is inside the paper box."

"Ahh," River says. "Well, sorry, I can't help you. I don't have any cash."

"Downtown?" Carly says. "Isn't that incredibly dangerous?"

Does she have to take issue with *everything* I say? "We used to play at the park, but it got too easy, so we started playing here. It's not so bad."

"What about cars?" Carly asks dubiously.

"We run around 'em."

"Wow, okay. Your funeral." She shrugs.

Suddenly, I regret every decision I've made in my life that's brought me to this moment in time.

"You know what," I say. "Forget it. I'm just gonna break the glass." Maybe if I wrap my fist in my sweatshirt first I won't get hurt. I'd make Quinn do it but (a) he's too much of a wimp to try and (b) he's too much of a wimp to succeed. This is all me, and the longer I stand here humiliating myself in front of Carly Nakata, the more time I'm giving the red team to get our flag first.

"Oh my god, Mara, don't do that. I got you," Carly says, pulling around her purse and digging in it.

"Seriously?"

"Yeah, whatever, it's just fifty cents. Do me a favor and pull all the papers out and dump them in a puddle, though, will you?"

"Um..."

"I'm kidding," she says as she pulls out one quarter and searches for another.

"Right. Well, I'll pay you back."

"Just don't get yourself run over. It's not worth it."

I want to roll my eyes at Carly being Carly—always knowing better than everyone else what's right and what's wrong. But I can't because she's still digging out a second quarter.

Out the window, Quinn waves frantically at me. Like I'm not already moving through this as fast as I can.

"Stay safe," Carly says, handing me two quarters, her fingers brushing my palm in a movement so gentle I have to believe she's doing it on purpose to draw attention to the fact that the last time we touched, I was punching her in the boob.

I'm feeding the coins into the newspaper box before Quinn can ask any questions. I yank the door open and our hands knock into each other as we both go for the flag. Then he grabs it, even though I was the one to get the box open through great personal sacrifice. He takes off. Before I follow him, I reach in and yank out the stack of *Sentinels*. I glance into the bakery window where Carly is staring out at me with surprised eyes and a slight smile. I toss the *Sentinels* up and let them flutter down into the street before I take off after Quinn down Pine toward Main. If we can cross Main with the flag before they catch us, we win.

Quinn and I have been practicing this since we were kids. At seven years old, sprinting through the pasture to get to the creek before the ram could catch us. At nine years old, playing keep-away with my brother, Noah, behind the barn. I've been running alongside Quinn Kegley for as long as I've been running.

Quinn crosses the street between two pickups, keeping low. Not low enough, though, because Wayne appears from the alley behind us and immediately sounds an alarm to his team—*"They got the flag!"*—before taking off after Quinn. Quinn has two blocks to go and just a half-block lead on Wayne, who is fast enough to play cornerback on our football team, the Elkhorn Elk Hunters. Quinn, a wide receiver, is pretty fast too, but still, Wayne's legs are so much longer.

I start cutting across the street to intercept Wayne, but a Toyota is coming too fast down Pine, and I have to put on the brakes to let it pass. After that, it's a wide-open street. I turn on the speed, slowly gaining on Wayne, who is gaining on Quinn. Over my shoulder, I hear pounding feet and see Stetson Ellison and Curtis Becker rounding a corner and chasing after us, but there's no way they catch up. I bear down.

"I'm comin' home, baby! I'm bringin' home the bacon!" Quinn hollers at Noah and the rest of our team, who are gathering along the dividing line sidewalk on Main. Quinn waves the red flag triumphantly over his head as he runs, which is stupid because it definitely slows him down. Wayne is gaining on him, just ten feet behind him now, maybe eight. But I'm just steps behind Wayne, and I don't think he sees me, he's so focused on catching Quinn.

Noah screams, "Get him, Mara!" which makes Wayne look over his shoulder. There goes my advantage of surprise. Nothing to do now but shove him just enough to slow him down.

I put my arms out as Wayne zags right, and where his body once was, now is just the plate-glass window of Humphries Jewelry. At top speed, I can't slow down even a little bit, and my hands go straight into and then through the window as it shatters around me in a crash you could hear from the highway. I find myself taking a shower in glass shards.

A *WAH-WAH-WAH* alarm sound cuts through the air as Wayne turns to look in horror at the sight of me coming to a skidding stop halfway into the display, somewhere between the engagement rings and the sweetheart necklaces.

Quinn doesn't look back. I lean to keep watching as he sprints easily across the dividing line, cheering his victory, waving the red flag in the air. We did it. We won. Quinn goes for a high five with Noah, but Noah leaves him hanging, rushing toward me. The concern on his face is what makes me finally look down to find my arms streaked in blood, dripping red over the shattered glass and diamonds.

Quinn comes over then, too. "Holy shit, Mara," he says, holding back a laugh. "That is so hard-core."

I don't feel hard-core. I feel like an idiot who ran through a plate-glass window.

As I try to gently disengage myself from the window frame, Carly jogs up with a horrified expression. She's the last person I want seeing me like this.

She looks me over, from my sweat-drenched ponytail to my basketball shorts to my now blood-splattered Brooks & Dunn T-shirt and says, "You don't need to pay me back, I got my fifty cents' worth."

# # #

No stitches; the nurse fixes me up with six butterfly bandages across both arms and directions to take ibuprofen. She finds the whole thing pretty entertaining. She's probably like thirty, and she might be the prettiest old person I've ever seen. I'll bet she would have laughed more if Quinn had told the story instead of me, but he had to go straight home because his parents were expecting him for dinner, so Noah took me instead.

"No long-term damage?" I double-check with the nurse, who smiles at me so nice I nearly swoon, and not from the blood loss.

"You'll heal right up," she says.

" 'Cause I'm gonna play basketball in college, so I can't have anything weird going on with these babies." I flex my arms, then immediately regret it because it hurts like the dickens.

"Worst-case scenario you'll have some gnarly scars," she says.

"Cool," I say.

Mom shows up just as they're releasing me, her face wild with worry. I hold up my arms, showing off my bandages. "Does this mean I get out of chores for a week?"

"Mara Bree Deeble, what in the world were you doing playing capture the flag *downtown*?"

"It's more fun," I protest. Not that Mom places much value on "fun." In her mind, the best feeling in the world is getting fresh gossip from someone else's mom after church.

"You could have said something," Mom says to Noah, who puts his hands up innocently.

"Oh, like you weren't into it," I say to him, and he cuts me a look.

"None of this would have happened if you didn't try to go full swan dive on Wayne Warren," he says.

"Let me see," Mom says, and she gingerly turns my arms over, examining my bandages until she's satisfied. Then she sighs a long sigh. "This is why I worry about you, Mara." She puts her arm around my shoulders, but since I'm so much taller than her, it's not quite comfortable, so she moves it to my waist. We walk toward the doors together.

It's almost a nice moment, and then Mom has to go and say, "Why don't you try hanging around some girls for a change?" And we're right back to where we always are. She can't see that I'm trying to be exactly the kind of girl I want to be.

2

LEROY MAKES ME WEAR LONG SLEEVES TO WORK THE next day so I don't scare off the customers with my Frankenstein arms. Leroy didn't even have to ask how I hurt myself. Everyone working on Main had heard about it one way or another by the end of the day yesterday.

"Did you win at least?" Leroy asks with a squint.

"Oh yeah, we won."

"Well then. Sounds like you were just doing your part," he says, nodding.

"Guess so."

"Like how you're gonna do your part today by stacking the manure for me."

I groan. Stacking the manure is by far the worst part of what is otherwise a pretty good job. But now, at least, I'm glad for the long sleeves. The last thing I need is to rub cow manure into my raw, open wounds.

Manure doesn't smell so much like shit anymore after you've

been stacking it for twenty minutes. It starts to smell sort of earthy and warm. Kind of like how Quinn seems like an asshole when you first meet him, but then after a little while, the stink wears off, and you realize he's a pretty good dude under all that bluster. Not everyone gets to see that part of him, but he and I have been friends nearly as long as we've been alive.

Quinn keeps texting, reliving the glory of yesterday's victory, even though he knows I'm not supposed to write back until my shift is over.

Your injuries were not in vain, Mara, he writes.

Everyone's talking about your valor

Wayne even said if he knew how hard-core you were gonna be, he would have wanted you for his team

Also Curtis says we should play in his family's junkyard next

I risk Leroy's ire by sneaking a text back: *Seems like an idea we probably should have thought of a while back.* But then again, maybe a junkyard isn't any safer than downtown. Maybe that's the point. Either way, I'm quietly thrilled by the idea. *And tell Wayne I'm a free agent now and I'll play for the highest bidder.* Then I stuff the phone in my pocket and get back to work.

Leroy likes the bags stacked two north-south, then two east-west until they're waist-high. At first, every heave feels like it's going to pop my butterfly bandages, but I keep experimenting until I find a way to gently sort of roll the bag of manure into my arms and then tip my whole body to flop it onto the stack. It's not graceful, and I probably look like one of those MIT robots who can only do everyday tasks in the weirdest way possible. But, hey, $11.50 an hour is $11.50 an hour closer to a pickup truck (minus taxes and plate-glass windows).

It was my stacking skills that got Leroy to give me this job in the first place. When I applied last year as a sophomore, he told me he only ever had stockboys, never a stockgirl, and he wasn't sure I could handle the, as he put it, "less savory elements of the job." So I asked him what the least savory element was, and when he said it was the manure, I went over and started hauling until I proved to him I was strong and didn't mind getting smelly. He let me stack the whole pile before he gave me the job. I've seen him hire other stockboys in the meantime. He's never made any of them pass a test to get the job.

My mom had been hoping I'd take the secretarial job at the church, so she was frustrated when I came home with a name tag, sweaty and smelling like manure, but there wasn't much she could say about it once the checks started coming in and I stopped asking her for money.

The cuts sting, and my muscles burn from the stacking, but they're not Jell-O yet, which is a lot better than the beginning of summer, before I started lifting my milk-jug weights. I like that I can notice a difference after just a couple months.

I'm hoping Coach Joyce notices the difference as well. After months of dreading it, I finally called her last week and made my case to her about why I should be allowed back on the basketball team this season. She told me she had to think about it.

While I wait for her to call back, there's not much else I can do except work out. And so I'm looking at my own biceps flex and move under my shirt and hoping I'll be allowed to use them on the court.

I hear Leroy at the register: "What can I do you for, partner?" It's how he greets every male customer he doesn't know who walks in here (which isn't that often—Leroy knows just about everyone).

The voice that follows makes me look up because it's gravelly and abrupt and distinctly female. "Looking for your cement."

I can't take my eyes off her. I've never seen anyone like her in the store before. She stands a bit bowlegged in wide-leg pants that hang loose off her wide frame, her belly blooming in its T-shirt over the band of her jeans, giving her the sort of steady, balanced frame that feels both strong and reliable. Her short hair is nearly buzzed on the sides and just a shade longer on top. Her black T-shirt is faded and old, with some kind of screen-printed band name slowly flaking off after years of use. She's probably in her thirties, but I'm bad with ages.

Leroy trips over his tongue before spitting out, "*Ma'am.* I'm sorry. Ma'am. Aisle three, at the back."

She's already walking away, boots heavy on the linoleum floor, not reacting at all to his continued sputtering apologies.

The cement is just around the corner, so I wipe my palms on my apron to get any residual manure off them and make my way over to her to see if she needs help. She stands wide-legged in front of the cement, arms crossed over her chest, resting on her stomach.

"Can I help you?"

She turns, looks me over, and uncrosses her arms. "Yeah, how much do I need to set four posts?"

"How big are your posts?"

"Four by four, about five feet high."

"Rule of thumb is you want a quarter of the post underground. Times four posts, with a little extra in case you mess up . . . I'd say a forty-pound bag'd do ya."

"You've done this before?"

"I've helped my parents around the farm."

She raises her eyebrows. "Your parents have a farm, but you work here?"

I shrug. "It's a long story."

It's not, actually, but I don't feel like explaining about the bank and the three bad years in a row, and how Stockton Cattle keeps making offers on every cattle ranch this side of the Columbia whether they're for sale or not until finally you take the check they're offering. I don't want to talk about how it's harder and harder for people like my parents to compete anymore, so that's why they took the deal even though Mom grew up on that farm and promised she never would. How Dad wanders the house aimlessly, having nothing to do now that the cows belong to Stockton and Mom's beloved sheep are sold and the bank account isn't scraping empty. And how now Mom does part-time bookkeeping and notary services for the very people she never wanted to sell to, just to keep a little money coming in.

But maybe this woman gets it because she just says, "Wanna help me carry this to the front?" She looks like she could handle it easily herself, but I don't mind. I heave the bag up and fling it onto my shoulder to walk it up to the counter for her, feeling my butterfly bandages straining. Even if they pop, it'll be worth it. I wonder where she got those boots.

"So whatcha building?" I ask.

"Chicken coop."

"Cool. You need lumber?"

"I have some."

"Not pressure treated, I hope?"

"Nah, cedar."

"Good." I want to say more, just to keep her here so I can continue to marvel at her clothes, her hair, her very presence, but I'm out of topics. But what if I never see her again? What if this is it? I walk a little behind her so I can watch her. Her gait isn't quite a saunter, but it's not rushed either. There's an easy confidence about her that feels audacious given how she looks. When we reach the front, I flop the bag down on the counter so Leroy can scan it. He's still tripping over his words.

"You, uh, find everything okay, *ma'am*?"

I cringe. He's overdoing it.

"I did," she says coolly, like this happens all the time. Which it must. Especially around here. He rings her up.

"I can help you to your car if you want?" I ask hopefully.

"Sure."

I carry the cement to the parking lot. She points to a dusty ancient hatchback.

"New in town?" I ask as I load the cement into the back for her. Her car has Oregon plates, but it screams Portland, not Elkhorn.

"That obvious?" she asks.

"No," I lie. "But I would have remembered if I'd seen you around before."

"Been here about a month," she says. "You?"

"Lived in Elkhorn my whole life," I say. Then, maybe I should be embarrassed to ask, but I really want to know: "Do you mind . . . ?" I nod my head toward Leroy inside. "Does that happen to you often?"

"All the damn time," she says. "It's not that big of a deal, but people tend to blow it out of proportion. Honestly, the *ma'am*s are fine, but *partner* was better."

She runs her fingers through her hair, and I'm overcome by the urge to cut my own hair off. She doesn't look beautiful, exactly, more like . . . striking. There's something beyond the clothes and the hair, too. Something less tangible. A confidence. I wish I had it.

"Mara Deeble," I say, putting out my hand.

"Jupiter," she says, and I almost laugh at the name, which is as out of place as the rest of her in the True Value parking lot. We shake hands like adults would.

"Come back anytime. I'll help you with whatever," I say.

"I will, Mara Deeble, thank you."

My cheeks are burning when I get back to the store. I'm terrified Leroy's seen me seeing her and, in seeing, has understood something about me that I don't want people knowing.

I want her boots, and not just her boots, but I want to wear them like *that*, like they are tools and also symbols. Like they will crush you under them, but only if you deserve it. I didn't know T-shirt sleeves could look like that. I didn't know pants could fit like that. I wonder if my hair would do that if I cut it. I wonder how to get my mom to let me.

I guess I knew women could be like that in theory, but I never expected one to walk into my work one day. I never knew it could happen in Elkhorn.

3

WHEN MY SHIFT ENDS, I WAVE GOODBYE TO LEROY and clock out. I have to maneuver my bike out of the stockroom, where Leroy lets me store it so I don't have to lock it up out front where anyone could see it. The bike is hot pink and purple—a gift from my parents when I was fourteen and they didn't understand that I would've loved a boys' bike a hundred times more than one that looks like someone puked unicorn frappuccino all over it. And what do I need a slanted top bar for? I'm literally never going to ride it in a dress. If anyone needs a slanted top bar, it's Noah so he doesn't slam his junk into it when he dismounts. The last time he did that, I offered to switch bikes with him, but he said he wouldn't be caught dead on a girls' bike, which, does he think *I* want to ride that thing? No. But I'm not going to buy a new one since I'm trying to save up for an actual truck. Although now that I have to pay for Mr. Humphries's new window, my truck is on hold for a while. Sometimes it feels like I'll have graduated before I can afford wheels.

So, for now I'm still riding a bike that would be ideal for a bubble-gum-princess cheerleader and keeping it in the stockroom, out of sight. It's not just that it's an embarrassing bike to ride, but also I don't need Quinn seeing it and making more comments than he already does about it. Quinn's a good dude, but there are just some things you don't bring up around him unless you're ready to get into it. That list includes: my bike, the practice of clear-cutting the forest (he's for it), who scratched his brand-new Chevy that one time freshman year (he has a screwdriver and he's ready for revenge), Maria Carpenter's prom dress (could've been shorter), whether Imagine Dragons' guitar licks are better than Blake Shelton's licks (no way), my height (six foot two), Quinn's height (five foot three), or the Elkhorn High School football offensive line (embarrassingly bad).

That last one in particular is a sore subject. Quinn plays wide receiver, and since he's the approximate size of a labradoodle if it stood on its back legs, and like a hundred and twenty pounds in full pads, he goes down if you so much as blow on him, so his main skill comes from being so fast that no one can even get near him. But to do that, he relies on solid blocking from the offensive line to protect the quarterback long enough to get a pass off to him. The Elk Hunters are a medium-to-terrible football team, so sometimes that protection happens, and sometimes it doesn't, and Noah's pass is rushed or short. And sometimes the pass is a gorgeous, perfect spiral and Quinn still manages to drop it. (If you were to ask him, those times are somehow the offensive line's fault, too.)

I've gone to every single football game, partially to support Quinn—especially since Quinn's dad is so busy he doesn't always show up to the games himself—and also partially because Noah's on the team, so going to football games is a family affair. I sit with my parents, a wool blanket strung over our legs and another underneath, protecting our butts from the bite of the cold metal bleachers. I've been watching football this way since Noah and I were kids, and even though the Elk Hunters have never been particularly dominating, I still love it. I love the sharp contrast between the night sky and the day-lit field. I love the malty smell of earth as the grass gets turned up through the game. I love our pep band as they bumble through brassy renditions of pop hits during every time-out. But mostly, I love the game. I always have.

The clouds hang low over the mountains in the distance, and a cool breeze hits my face, because even in the dead of summer in this part of Oregon, it could still rain at some point just about every day.

The highway is only two lanes here, so it's safe enough to bike along, passing the endless rows of pines and the shot-riddled stop signs, hugging the mud-slicked shoulder when logging trucks rumble past with their heavy, oversize loads. It takes about fifteen minutes before I turn onto the long driveway of our house, feeling windswept and rosy-cheeked and warm all over.

I ditch my bike behind the barn. Yes, we still have a barn. My parents sold the farm, which means they sold the land, but they didn't sell our house or our barn or our two horses that I think they keep more to force me to do chores than for any practical reason. I hear the screen door of the house slap closed and the pitter-patter of Delle Donne, our Australian shepherd mutt, running down the stairs. I stick my head out so she can see where I went, and she runs up to me, tail wagging. I give her fifty kisses and a belly rub, then have to pull the fur off my fingers because she sheds like it's going out of style.

"You need a brushing," I tell her, and she wags her tail in response.

Delle Donne Deeble is named after my favorite basketball player (but I'm trying not to think about basketball right now). We also have sixteen chickens, one rooster, and an orange cat who disappears for days at a time. You can take the farm away from the Deebles, but we'll never not be country.

Delle Donne follows me into the house, where it smells like roast chicken. I hope it's not one of ours. Not because I'm sentimental about them, but just because those chickens are old as dirt and stringy and kind of gross compared to the store-bought kind. Dad says my palate is just underdeveloped, but I'm pretty sure the problem is his old-ass chickens, not my palate.

"You do your chores?" Mom yells from the kitchen.

"I will in a minute!" I call back. I want to change out of my work shirt first.

"We'll eat when the boys get home." My mom will refer to people by their gender every chance she gets. It bugs the hell out of me. She comes around the corner now, wiping her hands on a dish towel, her hair swept up on top of her head, still wearing her work blouse and pants. "Oh, and Joyce Handegard called."

Coach Joyce. I freeze. This is it. My basketball fate, delivered.

"She called the home number? What'd she want?" Why did she call the house instead of my phone?

"She just wanted to let me know she'd come to a decision and to have you call her. Personally, I hope she lets you back on the team. I think it's good for you to be around other girls instead of hanging around Quinn Kegley all the time."

"Did she seem happy or mad?"

"Mara, just call."

I rush up to my bedroom. My heart pounds. Forget the manure smell, I can wait to change. Will Coach say I've done my time and I can play basketball again this year? Or will she say I'm too aggressive, too violent, that I'll never be welcome on her court again?

"Hey, Coach Joyce, it's Mara."

"Mara, hi." I can't tell, but I think her voice just changed. Resignation? Guardedness? I prepare myself for the worst. If I'm kicked off the team permanently, that's it. I won't be able to play basketball in college. This height will be good for nothing. My years practicing, playing, spending long nights shooting threes on the hoop over the garage, all wasted. Because of one dumb fight with Carly Nakata.

"I've been thinking a lot about our last talk. It sounds like you're truly remorseful about the fighting," she says.

"I am. I regret it all the time."

I rub my knuckles. After that game, they swelled up. Punching someone hurts a lot more than you think it's going to from seeing it in the movies. Am I remorseful? I regret doing it because it threatened my basketball career, but Noah and I get in fights all the time and Quinn and I used to tussle regularly. I can't help but think that if I had been a boy punching another boy, no one would have thought twice about it. Besides, it's hard to forgive Carly for getting involved in my personal business. Concussion or not, that's between me and Coach. It had nothing to do with her.

Coach goes on. "But the fact is, you were showing aggressive tendencies even before that incident with Carly. If it hadn't been that fight, it would've been something else. You have anger, Mara. I need you to work on it before you come back to the team."

Who *doesn't* get angry once in a while? "I will, Coach."

"It's not that easy. I need you to prove it to me."

"Okay. How do I do that?"

"I have a deal for you. Play a team sport this season. Get through it *without fighting*. Not a punch, not a shove, not a kick. You understand me? I need you to learn to separate aggression from competition. Show me you can do that, and I'll let you back on the team in the winter."

My mind is spinning. Play a sport? That's all? I can do that in my sleep.

"Yeah, totally," I say. "I can talk to Mr. Washington tomorrow."

I find running duller than chores, but I can do cross-country for a few months if it gets me back on the team.

Coach Joyce sighs. "No, I want to see you do a *team* sport. Not cross-country. Something that will force you to work together with your teammates. I've already spoken to Coach Stokes. She's expecting you at tryouts Monday. You'll need to bring your own knee pads."

She can't be serious. *Volleyball?* The volleyball girls are the ones with the long nails who monopolize the bathroom mirrors in the morning before class. They're the ones happily buying the blouses with the voluminous sleeves my mom wishes I would try on at the store. We have absolutely nothing in common. It's a sport with perky cheers from the sidelines, where spandex short shorts are the required uniform.

"Mara?"

"Yeah."

"You'll be there Monday?"

If I want to play basketball this season, apparently this is what I have to do—pull on spandex shorts and put my hair in a high pony and suck it up and be a team player for four months.

"Yeah, of course. Whatever it takes."

"Good. I'm looking forward to seeing your progress."

"Yeah."

We hang up. I kick at a stack of *ESPN* magazines, sending them cascading across the floor. It's going to be a long four months.

MONDAY AFTERNOON, I MAKE MY WAY TO THE GYM with my plastic bag from Fred Meyer with my knee pads inside, tags still on.

A bunch of girls are already sitting around in the bleachers and along the sideline, stretching and chattering with each other about god knows what. Bikinis, probably. Or, like, which body hair they should shave off next to make sure Curtis Becker isn't disgusted if they go to third base.

I take a seat apart from everyone else and change into my gym shoes, hyperaware that the other girls all seem to be friends. I know everybody, of course; we've been going to school together our entire lives. It doesn't mean we're friends. I've always been better friends with guys than girls. When I hang out with Quinn and Noah, it's just easier. No drama.

Maria Carpenter stretches her hamstrings nearby, her long, tan (for a white girl), shaved legs sticking out from her unnecessarily short shorts. She's limber enough that she can fully grasp the bottoms of her feet, her boobs resting on her bare thighs. Surrounding her, a knot of other girls do the same stretch. I imagine each of them looking sideways at Maria, comparing their flexibility to hers, their legs to hers, their blond highlights to hers, none of them quite reaching her ideal.

"On game days," Maria says to her attentive clutch, "I think we should all wear green tanks with white skirts."

"Ooh," exclaims Kelly Wesley, the nearly-as-pretty girl who follows Maria everywhere. "And white shoes."

"With matching socks!" another girl says excitedly.

I want to puke.

Quinn texts me. I'm grateful for the distraction: *Are you gossiping about boys yet?* I stifle a laugh and write back: *They're begging to do my hair, but I'm playing it chill.* Quinn was cool when I told him that I had to play volleyball. After he was done hysterically laughing at the idea of me in spandex, that is. He writes back: *Just don't become a drone, Deeble. I'll never forgive you if you start doing your eyebrows like them.*

He just gets me. I write: *Too late, I already filled them in.*

When I look up from my phone, I notice Valentina Cortez off to the side, chatting with Coach Stokes, chewing gum in a cutoff T-shirt and basketball shorts that make my heart stop. Since when does Valentina Cortez play volleyball? She's not a Maria Carpenter wannabe; she's her own woman.

Valentina's one of those girls who is pretty enough to sit with Maria and co. at lunch sometimes, but she also wears band T-shirts under plaid oversize button-downs with cutoff jeans, and shows up to school with a skateboard under her arm on sunny days. She's a track star, which makes sense because her legs are *ridiculous*. She has these sprinter's thighs, broad and muscled and dominating, that make her look like she could dead-lift a Dodge Ram. She wears this one pair of jeans that have a hole from seam to seam underneath the right back pocket which makes me blush just thinking about. Despite all my fact-finding, I haven't been able to suss out the most important piece of intel: Does she like girls? She has the vibe, but I can't just go up to her and ask her that.

We don't have many out gay kids at our school. Just a handful while I've been in high school—the kids who were more confident than me, or who had more accepting parents, maybe. There are three people out in my grade. Two of them are boys and the other is of no interest to me—I wouldn't date Carly Nakata if she were the last queer girl on Earth. But there must be more queer girls in our class, and I'm just left to guess which ten or fifteen of them are keeping their sexuality a secret like I am.

Valentina is my number one suspect. And not just because I want it to be true. I just get a feeling.

I wouldn't call Valentina and me friends, exactly, but we've been in classes together for years, and she's always been nice to me. As far as I know, she has no idea of my raging crush on her.

I take a breath to center myself and sidle up to her.

"Hey, I didn't know you played volleyball," I say.

"Oh, hi, Mara!" she says, smiling and flustering me with her straight white teeth. "Yeah, I dunno, I thought it might help me stay in shape for track. What about you? You're playing?" Even *she* sounds like she can't believe it. She blows a bubble and pops it.

"Yeah. I guess so. Not sure it's really my scene, though," I say.

"Oh, it's not so bad," Valentina says. But of course she would say that—Valentina's a social chameleon. She gets along with everyone, from the theater kids to the other Latinx kids, to the jocks like me, to supernatural being Maria Carpenter.

Just then Maria calls over to us, "Val, come join us!" Then, almost as an afterthought, she adds, "You too, Mara."

Valentina brushes my arm as she moves to join the other girls. "C'mon."

I try to savor the look she gives me, even as she settles in next to Maria, who touches her back and says something low in her ear. I can just picture Valentina decked out in Elkhorn green and white on game day, adorably matching the other players. She would look cute as hell like that.

Could I do that? Could I drive to Fred Meyer to try on skirts? Could I stand in a dressing room and wrestle a formfitting tank on over my frame? Could I still look myself in the eye after?

I don't know how Coach Joyce expects me to do this.

I sit down with the other girls. "Do you have some lip balm I can borrow?" Valentina asks Maria, who immediately starts digging in her gym bag.

"Of course, girl." I realize Maria is wearing a full palette of makeup to play volleyball in for some reason. I can't help but stare at her eye shadow, perfectly fading before her eyebrow line.

"Here." Maria hands Valentina a little pot of something pink and shiny. "You want some cloud paint, too?"

"Sure!"

"What's cloud paint?" I ask, and then regret it. I don't actually want to know.

But Maria looks me over. "You're lucky. Your cheeks are naturally rosy, you don't need it. But your eyes would really pop with a little mascara," she says, reaching back into her bag and pulling out a black tube. "I have a spare if you want to borrow it."

"Before practice?" I ask. It's hardly the only reason I don't want it, but it's the first that finds its way into words.

Maria shrugs. "You'd be so pretty is all."

Valentina looks like she barely registered the comment, engaged as she is in glossing her lips before we start smacking volleyballs into one another's faces.

"Let's get started!" Coach Stokes says, wheeling a basket of volleyballs over.

I try to psych myself up to bump, set, and spike my way through the next semester, but the psych is just not there.

5

WHEN I GET HOME, NOAH AND QUINN ARE THROWING a football around in the horse pasture, which is a dumb place to throw anything around. Even Delle Donne is smart enough to lie in the grass just outside the fence.

"You're not worried about horse crap?" I call out to them as I drop my bike by the barn. Delle Donne sniffs my ankles as I come squat next to her to scratch her tummy.

"Just makes it more exciting," Quinn says, grinning. Then Noah launches a long one and Quinn takes off running, leaping over horse pies, stretching to get his hands under the ball, elongating his tiny frame. Like this, flying fast through the tall grasses in the high summer sun, Quinn is almost elegant. The ball drops lightly into his outstretched fingers, and he pulls it to his chest as his body gets ahead of his legs and he tumbles head over feet to the ground. He pops back up like a gopher, checking his body for poop.

"All clear!" he cries with delight. I can't help but smile. When Quinn's in a good mood, it's contagious.

"How was your osteoporosis support group?" Quinn shouts. "Sorry, I mean volleyball practice." Then, to Noah, he explains: "They have weak bones."

I drop my bag of knee pads and gym shoes on the grass and climb onto the fence. "I jammed all of my fingers, I have floor burn on my elbows, and I've never heard more about Timothée Chalamet in my life." In other words, I can't imagine going back.

"Hard-core," Quinn says, jogging over to me.

"Quinn, gimme the ball!" Noah yells at him, but Quinn just flips him off.

"Yeah, hard-core not my scene," I say.

Noah comes over, too. "Mara, let's play Five Hundred!"

"Only if we play in the driveway," I tell him.

"You can't dive on gravel, c'mon."

"I don't want to dive into horse shit, either," I say, knocking him in the arm.

"This is Extreme Five Hundred!" Quinn says. "Only for the iron of heart."

"Fine," I say, giving in to Quinn Kegley like he knew I would. "Show me where the crap is."

Quinn just cackles. "Finding it is half the fun!"

Noah swipes the ball from Quinn and scampers away, then turns around and lobs a high, long one, screaming "Fifty!" as it flies toward Quinn and me. We scramble for position under it, the showing-off starting early. Quinn's stiff-arming me away while I'm trying to whack his arm down and get my hip to connect with his rib cage. We're both grunting and slipping in the dew-wet tall grass. Finally, I duck under his arm and get the drop on him, pulling away as the ball begins to fall directly toward my open arms. Quinn must realize I've got him because he uses his last-resort defense, snaking a foot through my legs moments before the foot-ball reaches my hands. I feel the ground rising up behind me, and I barely have time to register the horse crap before I'm landing butt-first in it.

"Mother..." I mutter, rolling out of the pile as Quinn giggles like a volleyball player. The ball bounces away, uncaught. I try to rub the excess crap off me in the grass, but it's going to be impossible to get it all, so I climb to my feet and hurl the ball back to Noah.

"What would your new volleyball friends think of you now?" Quinn asks.

"They're not my friends."

"I still can't believe you're playing volleyball," Noah mutters. "I can't even picture it."

"I'm coming to all your games," Quinn says.

"No you are not!"

"I am, and I'm making signs."

"No you won't, you'll be busy at your little football parties with your big tough football friends," I say. "What would the Kool-Aid Club say if you missed a party to go to a volleyball game?" The Kool-Aid Club is what Quinn's gang of friends named themselves in third grade after they all dyed their hair blue with Kool-Aid and came to school looking like Marge Simpson. When he's not hanging out with me, he's hanging out with them—Wayne, Curtis, Stetson, and Flint Wentworth. We don't cross over much, except when we play capture the flag together.

"Yeah, that's true," he says. "Okay, I won't come. But I'll be laughing at you in your short shorts from afar."

Noah laughs.

"Just throw the damn ball, Noah," I say.

He leans back and hurls another one. "Two hundred!"

This one's even longer than the first one, and I don't even try to catch it as it sails over our heads.

"You could have at least jumped for it," Noah says as Quinn jogs toward the ball.

"Jumped for it?!" I say incredulously.

"Even Kareem Abdul Ja-Mara over here couldn't reach that, dude," Quinn says.

Quinn tosses the ball back to Noah, who gets serious. "Okay then, how about a jackpot?"

Noah fires a bullet with a tight spiral toward Quinn and me, screaming "Five hundred!" as we both lunge for it. Quinn is a few steps in front of me, but the throw is above his head. He reaches up, a sure catch, but the ball shoots through his hands before he can grasp it. Meanwhile, I take the highest leap I can—the same jump I'd take in basketball, going for a rebound, my muscles springy and responsive and doing just what I want them to do. The football sails directly into the diamond I form with my fingers—soft hands, like my dad taught me—and I secure the ball and tuck it against my body. It feels like forever before I start coming back to the ground, but when I do, I land on my feet without even a stumble. I thrust the ball above my head and then spike it. Unstoppable.

Noah shakes his head and says, "Good thing you're not playing for Linkport or we'd be destroyed our first game out."

"Who says you won't be?" I say, and he shoves me.

"I'd tackle you, but you're covered in shit and it's starting to waft," he says.

I shove him back, but what he said sticks in my craw. What if there were another way? What if I didn't have to play volleyball with Maria Carpenter and the rest of the ponytail girls? What if I could play a sport with my best friend and brother instead and still qualify for basketball next season? What if I never had to wear spandex?

"What if I played football?" I ask. As soon as it's out of my mouth, I feel stupid. Even suggesting it feels like I've overstepped some kind of invisible line we've all agreed not to discuss. We don't talk about how Mara is different from other girls. We don't talk about how Mara is gay but no one says so.

And I don't plan on talking about it until well after graduation when I'm off at college in Portland. That way, if everything goes well, great! And if anything goes south, well, once I'm away at school I won't have to worry if my parents get weird about it because I'll be gone. Quinn won't get weird because we're best friends, and he won't let something like my sexuality break us up. At least, I'm pretty sure he won't. Either way, by the time I tell him, we'll both be out of Elkhorn. Everything will be different.

It's been my plan since I was twelve, when I first watched the Hayley Kiyoko video "Girls Like Girls" and had a self-revelation about all the Emma Watson feelings I'd been too afraid to name. After that, I googled some stuff about lesbians, realized it explained a lot of my behavior, and started using lesbian to describe myself. Quietly. In my head. Not in public.

But when I do stuff like this, I worry it gets harder for us all to ignore what's right in front of us. Neither of them says anything, so I go into word-vomit mode to try to shore up my reasoning.

"Coach Joyce told me I have to play a team sport. Football is a team sport. I've been playing with you two since I was in diapers. And I'm, like, bigger than half the guys on the team. I could play. I think I could even be good. And let's face it, you guys could use someone good. Plus, we'd get to hang out all season. I'd much rather spend practices with you guys than with Maria Carpenter and her spare tube of mascara."

Noah frowns so hard he's gonna give himself teenage wrinkles. I look to Quinn instead. He loves an off-the-wall idea. But normally those ideas are his, not mine.

"You serious?" Quinn asks with a hint of smile, and I start to feel just a little less stupid.

"Maybe," I say.

"Will they even let you on the team?" Noah asks, dubious.

"Don't they have to? Isn't it the law or something?" I say. "I heard about a girl in Astoria who did it, so..."

"I don't know why there would be a law about that," Noah says. "That's stupid."

I direct my gaze to Quinn. "What do you think?"

"I think it's fucking genius," he says. A thrill flip-flops around my gut. "I think it'd be hilarious. Imagine the look on Linkport's faces if we show up with fucking Brienne of Tarth on our team. Even if you never play, it would just be dope to have you there to hang out with on the sidelines when I'm not in."

"Well, I'd want to play, obviously."

"Yeah, yeah, totally. We'd put you in and the other team would be terrified to hit a girl. We'd dominate."

"Quinn!" I shove him in his shoulder. He never gets what I'm saying at first. "I *want* them to hit me. I wouldn't want to be treated any differently."

"You don't want to get hit by Linkport, trust me," Quinn says. "Especially Turnip. That dude's a monster, right, Noah?"

Noah just shrugs.

"Oh my god," Quinn says. "Imagine Mara tackling someone. I'd shit my pants if I got tackled by a girl."

"Whatever," Noah says. "I have chores to do." He heads toward the house. He's pissed off and I don't even care. He does things that piss me off all the time. Besides, he doesn't own football.

"I can't wait to see the look on Coach's face when you show up for practice," Quinn says. "He's gonna have a conniption. I should film it and go viral. Make a million dollars."

Coach. Right. I hadn't thought about him. I'll have to figure out how best to approach that. "Am I really gonna do this?"

"Hell yes you are, Mara Deeble. Hell yes you are."

I'm smiling so big I can't believe it. No more volleyball. Yes to football pads and cleats. No more spandex and highlighted hair. Yes to mouth guards and bloody knuckles. I might actually be playing football this season.

6

LEROY IS OUT DEALING WITH HIS TRUCK THAT'S BEEN acting up, so I am at the register when Jupiter comes in.

She walks with a determined stride, like she's running five minutes behind. Today she's wearing a shearling-lined denim jacket that squares off her round edges, broadening her chest and torso, puffing up her shoulders. I've seen a hundred cowboys wear jackets like it, but on her it looks different. Like a choice, not an inevitability. Like a *statement*.

I want one.

I watch her, waiting for a hello, but she disappears into the aisles without a glance in my direction, boots clomping.

I busy myself straightening the flyers on the counter, trying not to look disappointed that she didn't at least smile at me. A man comes up to check out, and by the time I'm done bagging up his mousetraps and Snickers bar, she's standing in front of me, holding out two different chicken-feed bags.

"Which one?" she asks.

"You finished your coop!"

"No," she says. "But the scraps I'm feeding them are making the eggs taste funny."

"You already have the chickens?"

"Yeah."

"And you're not done with the coop?"

"No."

"Where are they living?"

She shifts her weight uncomfortably. "Look, I don't really know what I'm doing here, okay? Can you ... just ... ? Which feed?"

"Our chickens like this one," I say, pointing. "But you can also feed them fresh fruit or vegetables. Just not citrus. And don't give them onions—that's probably what's making your eggs taste funky."

She nods and heads back to the aisle without a word. When she returns, she has three bags of the feed I recommended. As I ring her up, I glance at her out of the corner of my eye and catch her looking at me.

"You know stuff about chickens," she says. It's not a question.

"Had them most of my life."

"You need money?"

"What?"

She gets frustrated and gestures vaguely. "My therapist says I need to get better at asking for help, so here it is: I need help. And you seem like someone I can trust. I can pay you. What do you make, fifteen dollars an hour?" Not even close, but I don't correct her. "I could use you two days a week? Maybe more. I don't know. My partner made this all out to be a lot less work than it is. You interested?"

I'm flummoxed for a minute. I already have a job, but I could certainly use the extra money. I still have two more installments

to make to Mr. Humphries before he's paid off and I can start putting money back in the truck fund. But what the hell kind of work
are we talking about, exactly?

"You know what, never mind," she says, gathering up her feed.
"I got it."

"No, no! Yeah, I'm in."

"For real?" She looks at me hopefully and her gruff exterior
evaporates.

"Yeah. I'm off at four. I don't have a car, though."

"I'll pick you up. Do you need to, like, ask a parent or something?"

Oh. Yeah. Probably. "I'll talk to my mom."

She lets out a long sigh. "Amazing. Thank you. This is so much
harder than I thought it would be. I'll see you at four."

# # #

"I think it's wonderful that you can help a young woman get her
farm off the ground," Mom says on the phone. I don't tell her what
Jupiter looks like, I don't even tell her her name, and she doesn't
think to ask. She *does* ask which church Jupiter goes to and I say
I'll find out.

"All right, just make sure you're home in time to do your
chores," she says.

There's this feeling I get around Jupiter that's just like a nice
long exhale. Like I don't have to constantly watch the language I'm
using or the way I hold myself or the things I like, just to make sure
I don't seem different or weird or *obvious*. I can just *be*.

It's not that Jupiter has said she's gay. Not in words, anyway.
But it feels like she's screaming it with her clothes and her hair
and her body language. And other ways, too. Like when she picks
me up after work, she doesn't roll down her window and call to

me like my mom would, she just honks her horn from across the parking lot and waves with two fingers off the steering wheel. I can't explain it, that's just *gay*. Her hatchback is old, like '90s old, and it's a stick shift, which is definitely gay. And she has attached one of those tractor knobs on the steering wheel so you can turn one-handed while shifting. Those things are the *gayest*.

I changed out of my work clothes into a T-shirt, and Jupiter gives me a look when she sees the scratches and Band-Aids up and down my arms. "You get in a fistfight with a Cuisinart?"

"Just a little capture-the-flag incident," I say, and she nods like that makes sense.

She has news radio on low, but as we pull out, she starts flipping through her presets.

"What music you like?" she asks.

"Oh, um..." I pause because she doesn't seem like a country kind of person, but she asked, so... "Country?"

"I can do country, but not the radio. All they sing about anymore is drinking." She digs around in her door pocket, pulls out a cassette tape, and pops it in. "You know Tanya Tucker?"

"No." I mostly listen to the radio, where it's true they play a lot of songs about cold beer and margaritas and whiskey.

"It's always a good day when you can introduce someone to Tanya Tucker." She hits Play and a mournful voice comes out of the speakers, singing about going to Texas when she dies. Her voice is alluring, almost sexy, despite the lyrics.

After we get out of town a bit, Jupiter turns down Cascade View Road, which gives me pause. There's only a few houses down here, and I'm pretty sure she doesn't live in any of them.

"Where are we going?"

"My place."

"You have a house down here?"

"A house, some land. *Acreage*, if you will." She says it with a funny voice, like she's making fun. I can't read her tone.

It's not that Elkhorn is so small that I know who lives in every single house, but I know Cascade View. Quinn lives on Cascade View. We pass his driveway, which is so long you can barely see his house's roof peek out over the hill.

So if she's still driving, that means...

"Did you buy the Hardys' old place?"

Jupiter snorts. "I knew this town was small, but *damn*."

"They used to go to my church. I came to a potluck here once," I say as we pull into the driveway.

The house looks nice in a fresh coat of paint. It might be a hundred years old, but it's in good shape. Jupiter gets out and jerks her head for me to follow her around back.

Her acreage, as she put it, is beautiful. A long, sloping pasture perfect for whatever livestock she wants to put in there, really, ending at a dilapidated fence falling down into a grove of evergreens bordering the creek.

I can tell from the grade that the lowest part of the pasture will flood in winter from rains, and who knows how high the creek gets, but the house and most of the land are elevated enough that she shouldn't have too many problems. It's a nice plot, and only fifteen minutes from town.

I wonder why she bought it if she doesn't know jack shit about how to run it.

Jupiter opens the back door of the farmhouse and two giant mutts bound out and jump on her before flouncing over to me.

"That's Indigo," Jupiter says, pointing to a brindle pit bull that's wiggling her entire body, "and that's Sleater." She points to a black lab with a white muzzle who looks older. Indigo embraces me with her front paws as Sleater wags her tail vigorously. "You're okay with dogs, I hope?"

"I'm good. I'm very good," I say, tousling Indigo's ears while trying to pet Sleater equally so she doesn't get jealous.

I wipe the slobber off my cheeks. "Hey, Jupiter?"

"Yeah?"

"I don't see your chickens anywhere."

"Oh." She looks embarrassed. "I get worried the coyotes are gonna eat them when I leave them alone." She reluctantly goes over to an external toolshed and unlatches it, then looks at me and says, "Before you say anything, *I know.*"

She throws open the door. Inside the shed, roosting among the garden tools and rusty ancient shovels, are about twelve gorgeous Rhode Island Red hens. They *bok* contentedly. There's chicken shit dripping off all the tools. It's a mess.

I burst out laughing.

"I keep finding eggs in the watering cans," she says.

"You gotta finish your coop!"

"That's what you're here for."

One by one, the chickens flutter chaotically to the ground and wander out of the shed to peck at the grass.

# # #

The coop is half-finished. She already poured the concrete and set the posts like I told her, but the rest of the lumber and wire and plywood walls are still on the ground. She thrusts the printed-out instructions from the internet into my hands and points at the plywood.

"The outside walls are too heavy to hold up on my own and drill at the same time, and I can't build the rest until I get them up. But you look like you have some guns. You hold them and I'll drill?"

She noticed my arms. This summer's been paying off.

"Let's do it," I say.

It feels good to just plain lift and hold plywood. This is work my mom would give Noah if it needed doing around our place, but here it's just Jupiter and me. I hold the wood in place as she gets on her knees to screw the wall into the posts. Once we get the first wall in place, the coop starts to look like a home for something.

In the blankness of physical exertion, my brain keeps fixating on the whole football idea, and one thought bubbles to the surface over and over again: *Ask Jupiter*. As much as it's nice to have Quinn's support, for some reason, I want to know what Jupiter thinks.

"So, I was thinking..." I start. I'm suddenly nervous. What do I know about Jupiter really? She could think it's a dumb idea. I come at it sideways instead. "Did you ever play sports?"

"Softball, basketball. A little soccer sometimes."

"Your school had soccer?"

"Yours doesn't?"

"We used to, but they had to cancel it. Budget cuts. My friend Quinn says it's a good thing because now all the fastest guys play football instead."

"You gotta be kidding me," she says with an incredulous laugh. "So this really is like one of *those* small towns."

"I guess so."

She finishes screwing in the second wall of the coop, and I move to pick up another. Jupiter has long since taken off her shearling jacket. She's just wearing a white T-shirt with the words AS THEY SAY over her broad chest.

I just gotta tell her. Spit it out. "I was thinking I would, too. Play football."

She stops screwing to cock an eyebrow at me. "Why's that?"

"Can you keep going, please? This is heavy."

She goes back to her work and I tell her, as briefly as possible, about Coach Joyce's demands if I want to play basketball.

"Why were you fighting?" Jupiter interrupts.

"Because Carly Nakata can't mind her own business."

"About what, though?"

I sigh and give her the SparkNotes version.

"Hmm" is all she says.

Jupiter keeps working. The sound of the drill is starting to drive me up the wall. "What?"

"Well, it sounds like she was trying to keep you safe."

"Yeah, but she didn't know what she was talking about."

"So you turned to violence."

I can feel this conversation getting away from me. "She wasn't *listening* to me. Whatever, I already got a lecture from Coach Joyce for this when she kicked me off the team. And another from my mom. I don't need one from you." I wince, embarrassed at my attitude. Jupiter's my boss right now, after all, and I really want her to like me. "Sorry."

"No, fair enough," she says. "So, you'd rather play football than volleyball."

"I mean . . . yeah. Obviously," I say.

I feel like if anyone will understand that, it's Jupiter. I mean, she already looks like a linebacker. Put a helmet and shoulder pads on her and she'd look right at home on a football field, but I literally can't picture her leaping to spike a volleyball to save her life. Her feet belong on the ground.

"What's wrong with volleyball?" she asks.

"I mean, you *know*," I say helplessly.

"I know what I think, but I want to hear you put it into words," she says.

"It's just so . . . girly. The spandex, the hair ribbons, the terrible girls at my school who play it."

"Do you have to have hair ribbons in order to play volleyball?"

"It's the whole *culture* over there. Maria Carpenter tried to get me to wear mascara. During *practice*. You know how it is with those kinds of girls. I'm not like them."

Jupiter nods. "Mara, this is your business, so feel free not to answer, but . . . do you like that people see you as a girl?"

It catches me off guard. No one's ever asked me that before. "I mean, I guess so?"

"Because if you'd rather be a boy, or neither, I'm just saying, that's fine. I'll use whatever pronouns you ask me to use."

I push my hair out of my face. It sticks to the sweat on my forehead. "It's not being a girl that bothers me, it's what everyone else assumes about me because of it. I just want to be a girl without everyone expecting me to be so . . . girlish*ish*, you know?"

She stands up and rubs a hand over her buzz cut. "Of course. Nothing wrong with being butch."

I feel a weight lift at the word *butch*. Is that what I am? It feels like too much to call myself. Too real, somehow. Jupiter feels butch, with her boots and her stride and her hair. Can I call myself that if I just like boys' clothes? So I wear flannel and baseball caps. Isn't that just being country? Still, I feel a sense of relief that Jupiter could see me being that way, even if I can't yet, myself. It feels like an open door.

"So what do you think?" I ask. "About the football."

She pulls her eyebrows together. "I think football is a dumb sport that values violence over finesse and brutality over athleticism, and its fans and players have massively misguided ideas of what constitutes masculinity."

I take a step away. "Oh."

"And if you have a problem controlling your temper, it's probably the exact wrong place for you to work on that."

I look down. "Yeah, okay."

I really thought she would come down on the other side of this.

"Also, I think you need to reexamine the reason you think the volleyball girls are not like you. Being masculine-presenting doesn't mean you're better or tougher or cooler than more feminine girls. It took me *way* too long to understand that."

That one blindsides me. "I never said that."

"Just something to think about."

I'm ready for this conversation to be over. I'm ready to never come back to Jupiter's. I thought she would understand me, but she's too... I don't know, too Portland or something. She doesn't get what it's like here. Maybe girls where she's from aren't like girls here.

"But on the other hand," she says, "I also know I wouldn't be caught dead playing volleyball at your age, and if I were in your shoes right now, I'd absolutely join the fucking football team."

My heart flutters. "Really?"

"Really."

"So I should do it?"

"If you feel like you have to, then yeah. Do it. Go in there and show all those dudes how it's done."

"I can do that." I'm smiling now, uncontrollably.

"Take names, not shit, you hear me?"

"I hear you."

"Just promise me, if you get a concussion, you'll stop playing. Football's a death sentence if you play it long enough and you're kind of the only person in this town I remotely like so far. Which is weird, because you're a teenager and I'm kind of your boss."

I'm soaring. She thinks I should play football, and she likes me. Not a ton of people around here do.

"Absolutely. Yes," I say.

We spend another hour building a chicken ladder that leads into the coop and setting up the roost and nests inside, lining the floor and nests with cedar shavings. There's still more to do, like completely enclosing a run for the chickens so they'll be safe from coyotes and they don't have to be locked up in the coop when Jupiter isn't home, but I give her instructions on how to finish the rest of it without me.

Outside my house, Jupiter hands me forty dollars, even though she only owes me thirty. "I only have twenties," she says. "Consider it an advance toward next time." I thank her, and before I get out, she adds, "Good luck. With the football stuff. I assume you know this isn't going to make you the most popular kid in school."

"I never was," I say.

"Neither was I. But it worked out okay in the end. Have fun."

I wave and hop out, already looking forward to the next time I see her.

On the front porch, I stomp the caked-on dirt from my boots, kick them off, and step into the house in my socks. My mom stands at the window, looking out the sheer curtains.

"Who's he?" she asks, nodding out the window to where Jupiter is pulling away.

"That's Jupiter. That's who I was helping."

"*Jupiter?*"

"She bought the Hardys' old place. She needs a hand fixing it up."

"You're kidding. What happened to those kids of theirs?"

"Not everyone wants to take over the family farm."

Mom clucks her tongue and starts back toward the kitchen.

7

"YOU'RE ACTUALLY GOING THROUGH WITH THIS?"
Noah asks incredulously when he comes outside to find me leaning against his truck to get a ride to practice. "You're unbelievable."

"What's unbelievable is how much better this team is going to be once I join," I say, climbing into the passenger seat.

He shakes his head. "You're going to get so much shit from the guys. Like *so* much shit."

"I'm ready," I say. I'm not an idiot. I know there are going to be guys like Wayne who won't like that I'm there, but I know I have the skills. I have Quinn. And whatever I have to deal with, it can't be worse than a season of long bus trips with the volleyball team.

The other players greet Noah as we arrive, but they just sort of ignore me. Maybe they think I'm just here to watch them practice and lust after their virile fifteen-year-old bodies.

I sit down on the grass to start stretching. Next to me, Ranger Sorgaard, a giant Scandinavian viking of a dude with shoulder-length thick blond curls, stretches his quads.

"You're Deeble's sister, right?"

"Yeah. Mara."

"You playing with us this year?" he asks matter-of-factly.

"Yeah," I say, guarded. "Well, I'm trying out."

"Cool," he says, switching legs. "You'll make it. Everyone does. We don't have enough guys otherwise. Plus, you look like you can hack it."

"Thanks," I say, surprised.

He extends a meaty fist, his pinky the size of my thumb. We bump with a smile.

"You get your paws off her, you Norwegian behemoth!" Quinn shouts, darting up to us.

I can't be sure, but I think I hear Ranger sigh. He returns to his stretching.

Quinn grabs my hands. "Get up, I have to make an announcement."

"No, Quinn..."

"Get up, get up! Everyone will be confused if we don't address it."

"What's so confusing?" I ask, but I begrudgingly get to my feet. Quinn hops onto the first level of the bleachers, which makes him about even with me, height-wise. He runs a hand through his light, wavy hair to get it out of his eyes, which makes it fall perfectly against his forehead. I've always been envious of how his hair does whatever he wants it to. My hair, on the other hand, is thin and quick to frizz, which is why I keep it in a ponytail at all times.

"Hey, yo, listen up! I have an announcement!" Quinn says. A bunch of guys turn their heads to look. Down the field, a small group of coaches, including Coach Willis, is standing around in windbreakers. When Quinn starts shouting, they look over as well.

"This is so unnecessary, dude," I whisper.

"Mara's playing football with us this year, and if any one of you has a problem with that, you can take it up with *me*! I, for one, think she's got as much right as anyone to be here, and she could probably kick half your asses, so keep your opinions and your hands to yourself. Anyone got something to say?"

The guys kind of shrug and look around. No one speaks up. Wayne raises his eyebrows and glances sideways at Curtis Becker. Noah focuses on tightening the laces on his cleats.

"Cool," Quinn says, and hops off the bleachers. He claps me on the back. "You're good now."

"Gee, thanks," I say. I can't help but think that the less of a big deal we make out of all this, the less of a big deal it'll be, but Quinn does as Quinn wants.

Coach Willis marches right through the crowd of gathered guys and takes me by the arm, pulling me aside. My pulse ticks up, even though I was prepared for this. I've done my research. I know that girls are allowed to play any boy sport so long as there isn't an equivalent one for girls already. The law says so. We can join football, and wrestling, and baseball. We can play hockey with the boys if there's no girls' team already, and I have the Title IX federal law printed out from the internet in my gym bag in case I need to prove it.

When Coach gets me off to the side, he stops and purses his lips, regarding me. Finally, he says, "Who are you?"

"Mara Deeble, sir." I remind myself to stand up straight. Maybe if I look formidable he'll realize he actually wants me on his team.

"You Noah's sister?" He squints at me. We're just about eye to eye. If anything, I might have a half inch on him.

"Yes, sir."

"Hank know you're here?" he asks suspiciously.

"Yes, sir," I say with confidence. I'm telling my dad tonight, so it's barely a lie.

"And he's okay with it?" He looks skeptical.

"He told me there's no greater test of character than taking to the gridiron and proving victorious," I say. Now I'm just straight-up lying, but it seems like something he'd say. To Noah, anyway.

"And what's your brother think?" he asks.

A burst of anger flares in my chest. What the hell does it matter what Noah thinks? Is he asking because Noah's my brother or because he's the illustrious quarterback?

"Noah! Hey, Noah, come over here, son," Coach Willis calls to him. My stomach drops. Noah jogs over, looking wary. "What do you make of this situation?"

"Sorry, Coach?"

"Your sister wants to play football. What do you think about that?"

I'm snarling on the inside but doing everything I can to keep my face neutral.

"Well…" Noah looks like he wants to say something but stops himself. Maybe it's the ruthless stare I'm giving him that says clearly if he screws this up for me, he's dead.

Coach tries again. "Let me put it this way. Is she going to be a distraction for you?"

Noah looks at me, then back at Coach. "Honestly, yeah, probably."

"With all due respect, sir," I say quickly, trying to keep the anger out of my voice, "I have a right to play football regardless of what my brother thinks. It's the law."

Coach Willis wrinkles his substantial forehead and looks me over. There's an entire wildfire blazing in my gut, and if he doesn't end this charade soon, it's going to consume me. Are boys *that* protective of their dumb sport that they think a dainty little girl can't play? Well, maybe a dainty little girl can't, but I certainly can. One glance should tell them that, but instead we're playing a game of Ask Noah.

"It's fine. She can play," Noah says finally, exasperated. "Let her play, Coach."

"All right, then. Guess we had no choice, anyway." I want to punch them both in the face. Maybe Jupiter is right; maybe this is the worst place for me to be if I'm trying not to get into another fight. We'll see.

Coach looks at me. "You're gonna need some cleats."

"Yes, sir."

"And I'm gonna be watching you. If you think you can just show up and slink around looking for a date..."

"I'm here to play, sir. I'm here to work."

"Uh-huh." The wrinkles on his forehead furrow into even more wrinkles. "And what do you propose we do about the locker room situation?"

The locker room situation? "I can just use the women's, can't I?"

"At practice, sure, but the game field doesn't have a ladies'."

I didn't honestly think of that. "Where do the cheerleaders change?"

He chomps down on the gum in his mouth. "Not my problem."

I don't know what to say after that. He sighs, then, done with the conversation, sticks a pen behind his ear, tucks his clipboard under his armpit, and blows his whistle.

"All right, stop your rubbernecking. The girl stays for now," Coach hollers at the rest of the guys. "Get in the end zone. You're doing lines!"

Eager to finally have a chance to prove myself, I hustle off without even a glance at Noah.

Running lines is a conditioning exercise where you run from the end zone to the five-yard line, touch it, then run back to touch the end zone, then to the ten-yard line and so on, increasing by five yards each time until you get to twenty-five yards. It's exquisitely brutal. And it's that much harder because I don't have cleats yet.

The cardio fills up my lungs and makes my fingers tingle with the thrill of being back out with a team, running drills. I haven't done anything like this since getting unceremoniously booted from the basketball team. It feels like coming home, slicing through the morning mist, my sneakers slipping in the wet green grass, the grunts and breaths of thirty other athletes in surround sound.

Coach Joyce has had us run lines on the basketball court a million times, but a football field is longer than a basketball court and the five-yard intervals add up quickly. Rounding the last interval, I find myself breathing heavy and focusing hard to maintain my position in the center of the group. There's no way I could keep up with Quinn, but I try to focus on the back of Wayne's head and stay even with him. If I can run at the same speed as him, I'll know I belong here. Maybe I should have spent more time this summer running instead of just lifting my homemade weights. As Wayne crosses the finish line, he puts his hands on his head, breathing hard. When he turns around, he sees me right behind him.

"What're you trying to prove, anyway?" he asks.

"Same thing as you."

He coughs out a laugh, then looks from me to Noah. "Your sister's trying to show you up, Deeble."

Noah scowls and looks away, which is dumb because now Wayne knows he's sensitive about it. Wayne laughs again. "This is gonna be good. What if she takes your place as QB One?"

"Maybe I'll take *your* place, Wayne. How hard can cornerback be?"

His mouth hardens into a straight line. "Try it, and I'll put you through another plate-glass window."

"Classy," I say, but when he turns away, I can't help but scratch at my arms where the scabs still rub against my shirt.

The rest of practice is more conditioning—burpees, push-ups, sit-ups, barrel rolls, quick feet, and lines. Lots of lines.

By the end of practice, I'm ready to lie down and sleep for a very long time any old place where no one would bother me. Then Coach Willis hollers that we did great work today and he'll see us again at three for another practice.

Oh right, two-a-days.

The thought of it almost makes me want to cry. And maybe I would if I didn't feel so good about how I did this morning. I held my own around a bunch of guys who've been doing this together since they were six years old. Sure, maybe I wasn't as fast as Quinn and I couldn't do as many push-ups as Stetson, but I wasn't the worst, either.

This might actually work out.

NOAH KEEPS SIGHING. HE'S DOING HIS BEST TO RUIN my post-workout buzz on the ride home. I ignore the first one, then the second one, but after a while, it's starting to sound like he's got something stuck in his nose he's trying to blow out.

"What is it?" I ask finally.

"Nothing," he says.

"All right, in that case, do you mind if I borrow your old cleats?"

He lets out another long sigh that kind of turns into a laugh at the end.

"What?" I ask.

"I just don't know why you're so obsessed with me."

I whip my head to stare at him. "What?"

"You're always copying me. You always want to do what I'm doing. You dress like me. You try to be friends with all my friends..."

He's never complained about how I dress before. "Maybe *you* dress like *me*, you ever think about that?"

"You *stole* Quinn from me. He was my friend first, you know."

"Ha! In kindergarten, maybe!"

"And now you're trying to steal football, too. Why can't you just leave me alone, Mara?"

"Shocking as this may be, Noah, this is a decision I made for me. You didn't even come into it."

"That's the problem!" he yells. "You never consider me at all!"

"Well, which is it, that I'm obsessed with you or I never consider you? Because I'm getting confused."

Noah and I used to be best friends when we were little, running around the ranch, chasing the cattle, playing hide-and-seek in the barn, picking the wild blackberries that grow by the highway in the summer and eating them until our lips turned purple.

We used to get into fights over stupid stuff all the time when we were little. After a good tussle in the dirt, we always ended up tuckered out, no longer angry, feeling even closer somehow. Now, when we wrestle, someone gets hurt. Something changed, and it's not just that we're stronger than we were. We're not the same kids who do everything together anymore.

"Whatever," he says, and clams up again.

"Fine," I say. He can be mad if he wants. I don't need his support. I just need to get through the season without fighting—him or anyone else.

When we get home, I go straight to the barn. I have chores I didn't finish this morning, and I'd rather do literally anything but be in the house with Noah right now, even mucking out horse stalls with tired muscles.

It's not even ten minutes later that I hear my mom yelling for me from the front porch.

"Coming!" I call back.

I wipe my forehead and put the muck rake away. I'm not done,

but I'm happy for the break. My arms are killing me from trying
to do this right after practice.

I can tell something is wrong the moment I see Mom standing
on the porch. She looks about ready to use my own muck rake on
me. My stomach sinks as I realize there's only one thing she could
be so mad about.

I follow her inside. I'm gonna kill Noah.

"Tell us this isn't true," Mom says, standing in the living room.
Dad is standing, too. This is big enough to rouse him out of his book
and get him to engage in the business of the family. Even he looks
gravely concerned. Noah slouches on the couch, watching this all
go down. I shoot him a look so he knows this isn't over.

I launch into the speech I had intended to give at dinner this
evening. "As you know, I have to play a team sport this season..."

"I was under the impression you were going to play volleyball,
Mara Bree."

She only uses my middle name when she's really upset.

"Football is a sport I'm more passionate about." I try to keep my
voice even. "I've been watching Noah play for years. I want to try
it myself. Plus, I *like* it."

"You could get hurt," Dad says.

"So could anyone," I say. "So could Noah."

"You're not like Noah," Mom says.

"You're right. I'm bigger."

"That's not what I mean. You have a very feminine body." She
gestures to my torso.

I gape. I can't play football because I have *boobs*?

"Do you even see me when you look at me?" I look down. I'm
wearing EHS basketball shorts that I wish were longer, a pair of
graying women's size-twelve Adidas sneakers that I bought because
they were my size, not because I liked them, and a Seattle Storm

T-shirt I ordered one size too big so it had a chance of being long enough. These square shoulders don't fit into the blouses Mom wants me to try on at Freddie's. These thighs won't squeeze into any kind of skinny jean.

"I see you. I see my little girl," Mom says.

Little girl? Is she *serious?* "Well, this little girl is going to play football this season. And she's going to be good at it." It's like they never stopped seeing me as their little six-year-old Mara Bree who they could dress up in Easter dresses and curl her hair into perfect ringlets. That's not who I am anymore. That's never who I was. And they can't see me as I am *now.*

"Who else knows about this?" Mom says.

And there it is. Of course that's what she cares about. "Well, everyone at practice, and presumably all their parents now."

Mom looks pale. Dad steps forward. "Mara, don't be cruel to your mother."

"I'm being honest. It's not my fault she cares more about what the church ladies think than my happiness."

"Mara..." Dad says with a warning tone.

This is such bullshit.

"I'm going to Quinn's," I say. "And then I have practice this afternoon and you can't stop me from going." And I turn and walk out. I know Mom is giving Dad a Very Serious Look behind my back, but I don't care.

I go back to the barn, sit down on the bench, and let Delle Donne curl up on my feet while I text Quinn. *You around?* I worry that maybe he's hanging with the Kool-Aid Club and won't answer, but the text comes back right away. *Yeah. Mario Kart?* I let out a breath. At least one person is still on my side.

I grab my bike from behind the barn, slide into my helmet. Just before I push off, Noah calls my name from the front porch. When

I turn, a pair of cleats comes flying through the air at me. I knock them down before they can take my head off. They land in a dirty, smelly heap. I look back up at Noah.

"These stink," I say.

"You want 'em or not?"

"I'm still pissed at you," I say. "This doesn't change anything."

"Whatever." He goes back in. I string the shoes over my shoulder and push off. The wind hits my face like a cold slap as I bomb down my driveway, away from my family.

QUINN'S HOUSE HAS FLOOR-TO-CEILING WINDOWS IN the living room that look out over their acres of grazing pasture, the Cascade Mountains rising dark and vibrant in the distance. A few years ago, Quinn's parents renovated, and in doing so, removed half the walls for some reason. They put in these uneven stone floors, which Quinn's mom told me once she thought added a "rustic chic" element, but which hurt my feet to walk on whenever I take off my shoes.

It's decorated like a house out of *Cowboys & Indians* magazine, with lots of leather furniture and about fifty cowhides scattered around—on the floor, draped across couches, layered on top of each other. It's like Mr. Kegley is trying to send a message to all the cows in his pasture—step out of line and you'll be next. Except he doesn't own any cattle anymore. He hasn't for years, not since he traded his herds for a cushy desk job at Stockton Cattle, where he goes on fancy lunches to the one steakhouse in town and takes a lot of business trips, bringing Mrs. Kegley with him when it's to somewhere exciting, like Seattle or Denver, leaving Quinn all alone to throw parties. Quinn doesn't like mentioning the fact that his dad's not a rancher anymore, but it's hard not to notice. The ranchers I know don't have kitchens like his.

The most important renovation they made is they finished the basement so it's a giant game room that they think Quinn will use to play video games and pool, but instead he likes to get drunk with football players down there and (he says) bring chicks home, but he's exaggerating about that part.

When I arrive, Quinn and I grab a couple Gatorades from the stainless-steel fridge and head downstairs to where he has both a Switch and a PlayStation and all the games you could ever want to play.

"He always takes everything so seriously," Quinn says about Noah as he sets up the Switch. I filled him in already about everything that just went down at home.

"Exactly," I say.

"It's like he can't see how it's not that big of a deal. We don't know anything yet. You could ride the bench all season."

I nail him in the head with a pillow. "I'm not riding the bench all season, asshole."

He cracks up and tosses a controller to me. "Okay, okay. But the point is, Noah's got a stick up his ass, when really, this is the funniest thing to happen to our team in, like, years."

The funniest thing.

"You know I'm not doing this as a joke, right?"

"I know."

"I have to play so I can do basketball this year. I'm in this for real."

Quinn sighs exaggeratedly. "God, I know, okay? You don't have to get Norma Rae about it."

I don't know who Norma Rae is, but I hate letting Quinn know when I don't get his references.

"I'm serious. I'm going to be the best…something this team has ever seen."

"The best something?"

"I'll tell you more when they give me a position."

"Just steer clear of cornerback or Wayne Warren might put a brick through your window." He settles into the other side of the sectional with his controller, throwing one leg up over the back of the couch so I get a full crotch view.

"You know that only makes me want to play cornerback more, right?"

"That's what I like about you, Mara."

"I'm tenacious?"

"You've got a death wish."

"I guess I'll take it."

10

"YOU'RE ELK HUNTERS NOW, AND ELK HUNTERS DON'T quit," Coach Willis insists to us midway through afternoon practice. I wipe at the layer of sweat covering my forehead, my thighs tingling with exertion, my lungs pulling in deep, crisp breaths. As he hollers on about how we're going to make it to State this year, I try not to snort because the Elkhorn football team has never been to State and the only difference between last year's team, which finished last in the region, and this year's is a couple scrawny freshman and, well, me. Coach finishes by telling us we're going to need to shape up and be team players and a bunch of other stuff that sounds like he got it out of a football coach pep-talk thread on Reddit.

"Okay, gentlemen," he says, which gives me a little thrill for some reason, even though I'm not a gentleman. Makes me feel like one of the guys. "Defense, you're going with Gary. Offense, you're with Howard. If you don't know yet, or you want to change what you were last year, stay here."

Guys jog off in both directions, and I stay where I am. If it were up to me, I would like to be a wide receiver like Quinn, racing down the sideline and leaping over my defender's reach to catch the game-winning touchdown, the crowd roaring my name, my parents jumping to their feet to cheer for me. Another part of me would love to be a running back, taking handoffs from Noah and spinning and sprinting downfield, dodging tackles, chewing up grass, racking up rushing yards.

Coach Willis goes down the line of guys, assigning them to offense or defense. When he gets to me, he stops. I get worried we'll have to argue again about whether I belong here or not.

"I got cleats," I say, gesturing to my feet.

Coach looks me up and down in a way that makes me feel like a display in an anatomy class. "Defense," he says, and moves on.

I take the disappointment in stride and hustle over toward Coach Gary. That's it for wide receiver, then. Defensive players never get touchdowns—they don't even touch the ball, unless it's a fumble or an interception. Of course, if Dad were here, he'd tell me that defense wins championships, and maybe he's right. Maybe I can shine here, too. After all, being a cornerback isn't too far off from what I do in basketball—using my size to bat away the ball from my opponent. But being on defense means I'm separated from Quinn, who is cracking jokes with Stetson and Curtis and Noah on the other end of the field.

Then again, none of this matters. I'm only playing football to get back on the basketball team. Whether I score or not is moot. So long as I keep my head down and don't get in any fights, the rest is irrelevant.

Wayne openly stares as I jog up to join them. I've been going to school with these guys since we were kids, but no one welcomes me. Whatever, I prefer dudes who don't smile to girls who smile to your face, then start snarking about you the moment you turn your back, which probably happened as soon as I left volleyball practice. Stares, at least, are straightforward.

Just as I've resigned myself to not having any friends on the defensive side, grizzly-size human Ranger puts a heavy hand on my shoulder. "Good to have you, Mara."

"Thanks, Ranger." At least someone on this end of the field doesn't hate me.

"You ever tackled anything before?"

"A sheep or two."

He grins. "Same principle."

Piece by piece, Coach Gary teaches us how to get in tackling stance—stomping our feet shoulder width apart, squeezing our shoulders back to make our chests into broad tackling surfaces, sinking into a power position so we can explode through our hips, and keeping our hands forward and out, ready to throw uppercuts. It's a new position for me. Stomp, squeeze, sink, hands, stomp, squeeze, sink, hands. Gary has us run it over and over until muscle memory starts to take over. Stomp, squeeze, sink, hands. My brain stops thinking about anything but this. Stomp, squeeze, sink, hands. We run a drill over and over where we sprint downfield and then get into tackle position. Stomp, squeeze, sink, hands. We do everything but actually tackle, and I'm itchy to try it. There's something visceral and primal about tackling. Something satisfying. Stomp, squeeze, sink, hands.

Before I know it, practice is over. My lungs are burning and my legs prickling with exertion. I suck down water on the sideline. Quinn drops down next to me to stretch with me.

"Well?"

"I'm pooped," I say.

"Just wait 'til you have to try to defend *me*!" he says gleefully.

"I'll run you all over this field. Like trying to defend Sonic the Hedgehog."

"Oh, just watch me," I say, laughing.

"Hey, Quinn!" Wayne calls from where he's standing with Curtis and some other guys. "C'mon!"

Quinn hops to his feet. "Sorry, Kool-Aid Club calls."

"Are you guys going somewhere?"

"Probably back to my place," he says. "You didn't want to come, did you?" It's like he has them and he has me, but all I have is him. A few times I've tried to hang out when he's with them, but it's always awkward. It makes me realize how much better I know Quinn than any of those other guys do. He never gets real when they're around. They don't know his secrets, like that he once had diarrhea on a date with Melissa Simpson in fifth grade, or that he's bummed his dad doesn't come to all his games anymore now that he has a new job. That's stuff he only tells me.

"Nah, I'm good. See you later," I tell him, and he scampers off to join the Kool-Aid Club, who are all roughhousing: shoving, punching each other—all the stuff I'm not allowed to do if I want to play basketball this year.

Noah passes by me on his way off the field.

"Hey," I say. "Give me a ride home?"

He pauses just long enough that I think he's going to say no. "I'm not waiting for you," he says instead.

I scramble to my feet and follow him. "I just gotta grab my bike first," I say, and hurry toward the bike racks.

As I unlock my bike, a voice calls out: "Mara?" I turn to see Valentina walking toward me with easy, long strides. She's wearing a T-shirt and a pair of running shorts that slip up her legs on every step, and I think I lose feeling in my extremities for a moment. Those thighs. They may ruin me. I run my fingers over my ponytail to smooth down any flyaways and wipe my forehead for sweat. I hope I'm not cherry red, either from practice or from being in her direct gaze.

"What happened? I saw you that one time at practice and then you just Gone Girled," she says. I glance toward Noah, who's waiting impatiently a few feet away. "I hope it wasn't Maria. I know she can be thoughtless sometimes. She means well."

"I'm not playing volleyball this year." My voice sounds weird. Is that how I always sound?

She cocks her head, and it's the cutest thing I've ever seen. When she looks right at me, all my words flee my brain.

One time in bio freshman year, Valentina and I were paired up for a botany lesson where we had to trek around in the woods behind the high school collecting plant samples. We talked about our parents and how our families were both being courted by Stockton Cattle. I told her I was on the fence about whether my parents should sell or not, because at the time, I wanted to take over the family ranch when I grew up. I was going to go to Eastern Oregon University on a basketball scholarship with Quinn, study business ag, and then come back. She told me she would never go into ranching when she grew up. She wanted to be a musician and tour the world in a band. Listening to her talk about it, I couldn't imagine her doing anything else. I barely even looked at the leaves we collected that afternoon, because I was too enraptured by the thought of her strutting around in front of ten thousand screaming fans, me on the side of the stage, admiring her.

Now I would never stay in Elkhorn. In the two years since that conversation, I've learned a lot about why I was so obsessed with getting Valentina to laugh at my jokes. And why all I wanted to do after that was lie on a blanket in the backyard next to her and listen to her talk about things that interest her—music, cows, skin care, anything that got her fired up. And use my pocketknife to cut slices of apple and feed them to her while she talked so we could stay like that for hours.

Now I know that all that stuff means I have a giant raging crush on her. I also know you're not supposed to have crushes like that in Elkhorn. Taking over the business stopped being an option after that. Staying in Elkhorn stopped being something I wanted to do.

But I haven't gotten over Valentina. I *have* to find out whether she likes girls. Maybe Jupiter can help.

Now Valentina's looking around the parking lot and back at me, furrowing her brows. "Did you...go to *football* practice?" I can't tell if she's impressed or disgusted. PLEASE BE IMPRESSED.

"Oh yeah," I say with this really fake laugh. Oh my god, *who am I?*

"Whoa," she says, her eyes going wide.

I cock my hip to rest my weight casually on one leg, then try to say as nonchalantly as possible, "It's no big deal." UNLESS YOU THINK IT'S COOL, THEN IT'S A VERY BIG DEAL. PLEASE BE IMPRESSED BY MY TOUGHNESS, VALENTINA. I AM STRONG AND I CAN BE YOURS IF YOU WANT ME TO. If she's impressed, it means she's gay. It must. I'm on the brink of knowing.

"Mara, *come on!*" Noah says impatiently, and oh my god, I'm going to murder him.

I look apologetically at Valentina. "Gotta go."

I want to tattoo the smile she gives me on my body so I can keep it forever.

"I WAS GOING TO TELL THEM PROPERLY MYSELF," I SAY through gritted teeth as Noah pulls up into our driveway. I can't believe he's refusing to apologize for ratting me out.

He throws the truck into park, causing me to lurch forward. "Oh, like they would have been any less mad."

I can't believe he's my brother. We may look alike—same round cheeks, same sandy-blond hair. But aren't siblings supposed to support each other? Aren't they supposed to feel like family?

I slam the door closed on my way out and head toward the barn. I don't feel like doing chores, but I feel like talking to Noah even less. I hear his door slam as well as he runs to get in front of me.

"Look, you made your point," he says. "Very funny, ha-ha, you're trying out for football, but it has to stop, Mara. It's not funny anymore."

I draw myself up in front of him so that I'm looking down into his eyes. I have three inches on him and it infuriates him when I make it obvious. The blaze behind his eyes grows. He is itching to get into it, and now so am I.

"I'm not doing this as a joke." I don't know how many times I have to say it before people believe me.

"What is this really about? Do you wish you were me instead of you? I mean, I wouldn't blame you if you did...."

That question is too messy even to try to pick apart.

"Football doesn't belong to you," I say. "I can play if I want to."

"Yeah, if you want to be a freak." He spits the word. It's not the first time someone's called me that. Freak because I'm tall, freak because I don't dress like other girls, freak because I'm too good at four square. But usually it's not Noah saying it. I can't believe he's stooping to other people's level like this.

"Shut it."

"Normal girls *date* football players," he says. "They don't *become* them."

So I shove him.

He shoves me back. And I don't even think, I just stomp, squeeze, sink, hands, and I explode out of my hips and I tackle him.

My first tackle, and I barely have time to congratulate myself on nailing it before Noah wiggles out of my grasp, elbowing me hard in the gut as he does. He scrambles to his feet and I blink the pain away, but before I can fully stand up, he shoves me hard again and I stumble backward. I see the rage clouding his vision. He's not thinking about anything else right now but hurting me. For daring to set foot on his field, for talking to his friends, for being me in his spaces. The fury makes me taut like a bear trap ready to spring.

I launch forward and land a right-left just under his ribs as he slaps me hard across the cheek, which makes me cry out in sharp pain. It's a bullshit move. We've punched and wrestled and kicked and bit, but he's never slapped me before. Boys don't slap other boys. Boys only slap girls. It's the one thing he could have done to make me madder than anything else. I bring my knee up by instinct and connect with his groin and it's over, Noah doubled over in pain, moaning into the grass.

I touch my hand to my cheek and pull away but there's no blood, just pain, and later, probably swelling. I shakily walk toward the house.

"Chores are yours to finish," I say, feeling like I used to have a brother, but now I'm not so sure.

# # #

I've never had a shower feel so good in my life. I scrub the dirt out from under my fingernails and let the sweat melt away under the hot water. I can already feel my muscles strain when I lift my arms to rinse out my hair. I'm going to hurt tomorrow.

My phone is buzzing on my bed when I get back to my bedroom wrapped in a towel.

"Hello?"

"Mara, it's Coach Joyce."

My stomach does a cartwheel. "Hey."

"I heard you didn't show up to volleyball practice today." She sounds tired.

"Yeah. I decided to go a different direction," I say.

There's a pause before she says, "I already told you cross-country isn't going to cut it."

"No, I'm...um..." It's hard for me to say suddenly. Like saying it out loud is admitting something I'm not ready to talk about. "I've been going to...football practice?" I want to kick myself for the way my voice goes up at the end.

"Football," she says.

I wait, but she doesn't say anything further.

"Yeah. It's a team sport, so that would satisfy the requirement, right?"

"It *is* a team sport, yes," Coach Joyce says. "Are you sure that's the right place for you to be? Football can be kind of...aggressive."

"I'd like to try, at least. I won't let anything compromise my chance to get back on your team."

There's another long silence as Coach Joyce mulls it over. "All right," she says, and my heart does a triple cartwheel this time. "But, Mara?"

"Yeah?"

"Be careful."

"I will, I will," I assure her, rubbing a hand over my cheek where Noah slapped me. I can't let what happened with Noah happen again during a practice. That was a onetime thing. I won't let him jeopardize basketball for me.

I've never slept harder than that night.

I WAKE UP WINCING. *OW.* MY THIGHS, MY BACK, MY calves, they're all hollering at me before I even climb out of bed. But my alarm is ringing, and morning practice is approaching. So I swipe my alarm off and gingerly climb out of bed.

I grab breakfast from the kitchen and look around for Noah, but I don't see him. Maybe he's still in bed? I holler up the stairs, "Noah!" Nothing. I check outside—maybe he's doing chores? But his truck is gone, my bike, which had been in his truck bed, is lying in the grass on its side.

He left without me.

I glance at the clock. I only have nine minutes to get to the school and it's easily a fifteen-minute bike ride.

My legs scream bloody murder as I pedal furiously toward the school, cursing Noah the entire way. It's one thing to be pissed at me, but it's another to ghost me with *no warning whatsoever.*

I don't even bother locking my bike, I just throw it over the low chain-link fence around the field and hope that a thief won't be so brazen as to steal it during practice. I might hate that bike, but it's my only set of wheels at the moment.

I run onto the field. The rest of the team is already well into doing their lines, so I join them.

"You're late, Deeble," Coach says. "Double lines."

I'm already sweating hard from the ride, but I yell back, "Yes, sir."

I find Noah in the crowd and shoot him the dirtiest look I can manage. He looks away.

I stumble back to the sidelines for water when I'm done with my lines, and I hear someone cheering from the small bleachers next to the field, "Woo-hoo, Mara!"

I spin around and see Valentina and Carly Nakata waving at me. Through my gasping for air, I feel my cheeks fill with even more heat. What is *she* doing here? Valentina is wearing a faded band T-shirt with cutoff shorts and tall socks and Vans. She looks good. Next to her, Tayley Striker sits hunched over, watching intently. Unlike the tightly coiled power that ripples under Valentina at all times, Tayley is all long, fast strokes. She's thin and tall and looks like the kind of girl who's always cold. I don't have a problem with Tayley, but why the hell would they bring Carly here?

Carly sits with her legs spread wide, elbows on her knees. She sports denim short shorts and a T-shirt she's cut into a tank top that reads RIOTS NOT DIETS.

Quinn sidles up to me. "This is a closed practice, tell your friends to skedaddle."

"They're not my friends."

"Do *they* know that?"

Carly throws her hands in the air as I approach. "Mara, I can't believe you're doing this!" She perches her legs up on the bench in front of her, showing off her socks with Alexandria Ocasio-Cortez's face on them. Her calves look curvy, muscular. I can't tell if she's mad at me or not. I don't know why she would be mad.

"You guys can't be here."

"Okay, totally," Valentina says. I wonder what it means that Valentina is chill being seen in public with our class's lone out lesbian. Does it mean she's gay, too? Or just an ally? Does her being here mean she likes me?

Valentina gets to her feet, but Carly stays seated. "Did you hear there's an all-girl high school football league in Utah?" Carly asks. "I read about it. They have a bunch of teams, no boys allowed. That sounds like the dream right there."

"I don't mind playing with boys," I say. "They push me to be better."

"And girls wouldn't?" Carly asks.

Tayley interjects peaceably. "Are they rude to you?"

"Everyone's been really chill so far," I tell her.

"Well, I think it's cool," Valentina says.

Carly asks, "What made you want to do it, anyway?"

I level her a look. In a way, this is all her fault and she doesn't even realize it. "Coach Joyce is making me do a team sport in order to get back on the basketball team next year," I say directly to Carly, just to watch her face fall. "So I picked football."

"Oh," she says. She pushes her straight, dark hair aside to rub at the back of her neck. Valentina looks nervously between us.

Carly peers at me. Finally, she stands up. "Well, I'm sure none of these football goons will ever stop you from playing with a concussion, so you should be good."

I turn to the other girls. "Bye, Tayley, bye, Valentina, it was good seeing you guys." I don't even care that I look like a complete asshole.

Coach calls us back to center field.

"Dang," Ranger says, lumbering along next to me, "if Tayley Striker was here for me, I think I'd have a heart attack. Can you put in a good word for me?"

"I don't even know her," I say.

"Dang," Ranger says again, rubbing his chin.

When Coach puts us back to work, I'm angry for a while, but after a few drills, I'm gasping for breath. The harder we work, the less I think about Valentina, or Carly, or Noah. The longer we run, the less I think about anything at all except for the burning in my thighs and the prickle in my lungs and my form and my breathing and the rush of air over my ears.

Noah may not be speaking to me, but when we set up for passing drills, he's forced to pass to me. I catch my first one, a beauty that arcs over my left shoulder and into my hands, making Quinn call out, "That's how it's done, Deeble! And by Deeble, I mean Mara!" I can't help but get fired up that I'm doing well finally. But when I look at Coach Willis, he isn't watching.

When I'm up again, I see Coach watching this time, and I'm determined to make just as beautiful a catch. But Noah throws this pass long—accidentally or on purpose, I'm not sure—and even though I turn on the speed and reach for it, the ball slips past the ends of my fingers. My frustrated scream surprises even me. Immediately, I regret it. I learned a long time ago in basketball that public displays of frustration are frowned upon. Our competitive spirit is stoked but only to a point. After all, we're just Elkhorn Lady Hunters. It's not like this is serious, we're just doing this to stay fit. On the court, we are to take our mistakes gracefully and our wins with dignity. The moment you lose your temper or express frustration or feel disappointment at a play, a mistake, an injury, you're gently cheered back to positivity. And god *forbid* you get in a fight. No negative feelings on our court, no, sir, we're just ladies, it isn't real sports, it's just a pastime.

But football isn't like that. Coach Willis doesn't say a word, and no one even registers my frustration. It's almost as if everyone here takes this seriously and understands mistakes are to be mourned and triumphs celebrated. Here, this isn't just a game. It's *athletics*.

And I love it.

I know I'm only playing football in order to get back on the basketball team, but there's something about this game that's infectious. I don't want to just ride the bench all season. I want to do *well*. And I want to prove to everyone—Noah, Wayne, Coach Willis, me—that I am just as capable of playing this game as everyone else on this field. And there's no reason I can't enjoy football while I earn my way back on the basketball team. That's a win-win.

THERE'S A DRESS ON MY BED.

It's new and dark blue with small gray dots on it. Tags still on. Has Mom written all over it.

I haven't worn a dress in over two years, not since I got to high school and demanded my mother let me do my own school and church clothes shopping. School she's fine with, but there's no way to miss the scowl on her face every time I come down for church in a nice pair of slacks and a button-down. So why, after years of this unsteady truce, is there a dress on my bed?

The armistice was tenuous, and I messed with it.

I pick it up like it's roadkill and carry it downstairs to the kitchen.

"What's this for?" I ask. Mom turns around from the stove, where she's stirring a pot of beans.

"Isn't that nice?" Mom says. "I saw it today at Freddie's and thought it looked like you."

She thought it *looked like me*? Really?

"I thought you could wear it to youth group tonight," she says.

I haven't been to a church youth group meeting since seventh grade. Mom knows this.

"I would rather not," I say carefully.

"It's not a request," Mom says, calm as anything.

I look at her for a long beat. She raises the spoon to take a taste. "I could call Coach Willis right now and tell him you do not have permission to play football, Mara. I could do that right now."

"Mom..." I start.

"But you've said this is important to you. Fine. This is what's important to me."

I can't believe I didn't see this coming. Mom needs me to be extra feminine to make up for the fact that everyone in town will be talking about "that Deeble girl on the football team." The only way to counteract the whispers is some good old-fashioned traditional values.

"I'll go to youth group, but please, Mom, don't make me wear the dress."

"Mara, you act like it's medieval torture. It's not the locks, it's just a dress. Millions of women wear one every day."

"I'd rather the locks."

She doesn't get it. She'll never get it. It's not the dress, it's that Mom doesn't even know me. Or care to.

She turns around. "Well, too bad. You're my daughter. And when you forget that, it's my job as your mother to remind you. You're not the same as Noah, or Quinn Kegley, or any of those other boys. You're Mara Bree Deeble. And you'll act like it. Now I think I'm being quite generous, actually. I'm allowing you to continue to play, *so long as* you make some adjustments to your attitude and to your wardrobe. If that's too high a price to pay, then by all means, you can turn right back around and tell Verne Willis that you won't be playing this year after all. It's up to you."

She goes back to the beans without waiting for a response.

# # #

I feel like I'm in drag. What I'm wearing isn't an outfit. It's a costume.

I hate everything about the dress. How it curves under my boobs and drapes gently over my hips, giving me the illusion of a figure. I don't want a figure. I don't want curves, or a butt, or boobs. I don't want to look like a long, sexy giraffe. I want to look like a wolf. Strong, capable, ferocious. I want to be built enough that people don't mess with me, but still soft enough that Valentina wants to get with me. Why should I have to wear this, just because I'm a girl? Why should that have anything to do with anything?

Thank god Valentina doesn't go to the same church as me. I would be humiliated to run into her like this.

I turn around to look at myself from the back. My frizzy hair straggles over my neck onto my shoulders. I've never liked how it just goes wherever it wants. There's probably an elaborate routine I could get into involving goops and creams and the strategic application of heat that would transform my hair into gentle curling waves the way other girls have, but the effort seems hardly worth it. I'd rather sleep. Or stay up late reading WNBA updates. Or get run over by a wheel loader.

I sigh and slip on a pair of oxfords (Mom didn't say anything about shoes) and a cardigan from the men's department at Target (she didn't say anything about sweaters either).

Mom has the decency not to gloat when I come downstairs, but she hands me a hairbrush out of her purse, which I run through my hair as I swallow a sigh.

She drops me off at the door of youth group, telling me she'll be back at nine to pick me up, then calls down the hall to one of the other church moms, "Sheila, how're your sheep doing in this heat?" Mom sweeps off to chitchat about wool and leaves me there.

Inside the youth group room, there's about a dozen plastic chairs optimistically set out, but only five kids there so far. Some of them are just barely in high school, but Wayne's here, and he looks surprised when I walk in.

I really don't need Wayne Warren seeing me in a dress, but if I want to play football, this is what I have to do. I straighten myself up as tall as I can manage and go grab a cookie from the front.

"It seems like everywhere I go, there you are," Wayne says darkly.

"My mom made me come," I say. "Trust me, I don't want to be here either." I take a seat next to some freshman kid with acne. "No offense," I tell the kid. He shrugs.

I have to remind myself to sit with my knees closed.

"Nice dress," Wayne says as River Reyes walks in. "Come to practice in one of those next time and let's see how well you do."

"What practice?" River asks.

River's in the theater crowd, and today she's wearing a very dramatic outfit consisting of a flowy black silk blouse tucked into high-waisted black sailor pants paired with dark, bold lipstick. She definitely doesn't go to my church.

"Football," I say.

"If you can call what she does football," Wayne says.

River scowls at Wayne, which makes me like her a little, then looks back at me. "That's cool."

"Thanks," I say. I'm not playing football to impress girls, but it's seeming to have that effect. Maybe I should have tried to play earlier. Not that I'm interested in River. Honestly, she kind of scares me, with her easy confidence, what with playing Jesus in the school production of *Godspell* last year and all.

"What are you doing here?" I ask River. "You don't go to this church, do you?"

"Maybe I do now," she says with a shrug. "My parents are Catholic, but I'm a little tired of the sermons lately, so I'm branching out. I've tried six churches so far. I heard this one has a good youth group."

"Really." It's my turn to be impressed. "And your parents are cool with that?"

"Oh, no, they hate it, but what can they do? My faith is my faith."

There's a lot they could do. They could ground her. They could forbid her from going. They could force her to wear a dress even though she'd rather kill a man than do that. I wonder what my parents would do if I started going to a different church.

"Which one's your favorite?" I ask.

"Oh, for sure the Universalist Unitarians were the most fun. We went around the group and read aloud selections from Dante's *Inferno* and discussed the concept of hell. Like half the people there didn't even believe in it."

"That . . . does not sound like church."

"Yeah, it was wild. Kinda white though. Then I went to the Church of Latter-day Saints with Tayley Striker. Do you know her?"

"A little."

"She runs the lights for us sometimes in the theater. The Mormons are intense. Services lasted, like, all day."

"I've heard that."

"Some of it was good but some of it was wack. The others have been fine. I liked First Lutheran okay, but they do this thing where they sing *every single verse* of a hymn. Every one. Songs last years.

Who's got the time? I still have, like, nine more churches to see before I make a decision. Or maybe I won't end up going to any of them. But the last thing I want to do is just go to a church because my parents went and their parents went before them, you know?"

"Yeah, I guess so," I say. I always thought that I'd go to my church as long as I lived in Elkhorn. They're not ultra conservative, but not exactly progressive either. They don't do anti-gay sermons, but they also don't do pro-gay ones. It feels like we're just not supposed to talk about it.

But what will I do when I go to college? I don't want to stop going altogether. Maybe River will have tips for finding a church that would be welcoming.

My legs are cold. I press my thighs together and interlock my feet. This is stupid. I wish for the nine hundredth time I could be wearing pants.

The youth minister walks in. I look at the clock. Eighty-six more minutes until this is over.

APPARENTLY, MRS. WICKER TOLD MY MOM THAT I looked very nice at youth group, so Mom is appeased for the time being, as long as I continue to attend. Noah still isn't giving me rides, so I have to wake up earlier to ride my bike to practice. I would ask Quinn for a ride, but he's coming from the other side of town, so it doesn't make sense.

As Friday's afternoon practice comes to an end, my legs are wobbly from the lunges we did around the track between every drill, but I'm running around cleaning up balls from the field and dropping them in a large metal rack on wheels held by Wayne. He and Curtis are letting me do all the work while they stand at the rack and chatter about a party tonight at Quinn's house.

"Lincoln's brother's friend is getting a keg and three bottles of Maker's, so all we need to bring is cups and tonic," Wayne says.

Quinn meets Wayne and Curtis at the sidelines as I jog to pick up the last two balls.

Curtis asks Quinn, "Dude, what *is* tonic, anyway?"

"*GQ* called the whiskey tonic the cocktail of the summer this year," Quinn says smugly.

Curtis nods but then squints. "But what *is* it?"

"All I know is it looks sick under a blacklight," Wayne says. "So let's get a ton of it."

I haven't been invited to this party yet. If it's a Kool-Aid Club thing, I wouldn't expect an invite, but if it's a football team party, then it seems like I should be included. The boundaries with Quinn and me are starting to get blurry. What is our new normal now that I'm also on the team?

I jog up to them and dump the balls into the cart. "So," I say. "Party tonight?"

Wayne and Curtis exchange a look, but Quinn grins big. "You know it. Eight p.m. Be there."

"Cool," I say.

"See you then," he says, slapping me on the back.

I'M FEEDING THE CHICKENS WHEN DAD FINDS ME.

"Mara," he says, startling me. I jump, scaring the chickens, who run away chaotically.

"Dad, hey. What are you doing here?" It's not like him to come find me in the yard. It's not like him to leave his easy chair lately.

"You busy?"

"Just feeding the chickens, then I gotta brush Roger and Angelica," I say.

"Right. Well. I'll be brief," Dad says. "I wanted to talk to you about Sunday. Your mother wants to make sure you have something to wear."

I sigh and toss more feed to the chickens, who are slowly coming back. "And she can't ask me herself?"

"She was worried it would turn into another...situation."

"I'll wear my dress from youth group again, if that's what she's so concerned about."

"She wanted to make sure you had appropriate shoes to wear. She left some on your bed."

"*Seriously*, Dad?"

I stick the scoop back into the feed bucket and walk toward the barn. Dad follows, slower on his stiff knee. He stops in front of Roger's stall and pats his cheek.

"This is hard for her," he says. "But she's not doing so bad. She's letting you play, after all," he points out. "Some mothers wouldn't even do that."

"I'll get her a medal."

"She means well, but she...she just doesn't understand you, Mara."

"What's not to understand? She's known me my entire life."

I head into Roger's stall so I don't have to see his disappointed face. Of course he would take Mom's side in all this.

"Look, she'll come around. Just give her some time."

"And in the meantime, what? I'm supposed to wear dresses and heels every day and go to every church event possible?"

"If it helps."

"You guys act like it's no big deal," I say. "But when I put on a dress, it's like..." I mess with the bristles on the brush. "It's like she's asking me to speak Russian. It's just not in me."

"People can learn Russian, Mara. They do it every day."

I throw the brush down and walk out of the stall, ducking past Dad. I'll brush Roger later.

I'm halfway out the barn before he can take three steps. "Okay, I'm sorry." He puts his hands up. "I know it's hard for you, too. You're very different people."

I turn to face him, pushing my hair out of my eyes. "You could help me out once in a while, you know. Put your book down. Stick up for me."

The old Dad might have told me not to be so mouthy. This Dad shrugs. "This is new for all of us, okay?"

It's weird. It's not that I *want* him to yell at me, but I wish he had his vibrancy back—that special dadness that made him ours. It's like, ever since he sold the farm, he's just been...empty.

"Yeah, whatever."

"So you'll do it?"

I throw up my hands. "Do I have a choice?"

"Just for a little while, that's all she wants."

I shake my head and walk out of the barn.

# # #

The shoes are horrible. Pale blue open-toed pumps with broad white bows on top. I want to gag just looking at them. I stuff them back in the box and shove the box under my bed.

Noah left for the party without offering me a ride, so by the time I ride up to Quinn's house on my bike wearing my least muddy pair of work boots and my softest red plaid flannel over a crisp white T-shirt with a blue bandanna around my neck, the party is already loud, even from outside. The football team is crowded into the living room/dining room/kitchen. I seem to be the only girl here, which is fine by me. I don't really want to watch my teammates slobber all over the ladies tonight.

"Hey, Mara," Ranger says just before he dribbles beer down the thigh of the clean Levi's I pulled on for this. "Oh my goodness, I'm so sorry." He reaches out with a napkin to dab my thigh, then pulls back. "Wait, shoot, sorry. Is it okay if I touch you?"

"Just give it here," I say, and take the napkin from him, which looks like it's partially used already.

"Sorry, sorry," Ranger keeps apologizing.

"It's fine," I say. "They've seen worse, believe me."

I squeeze past a couple freshmen who are nervously clutching their plastic cups and make my way to the kitchen. Someone's playing Luke Bryan over the speaker system. The house smells like sweaty boys and Lit'l Smokies. I'm not surprised. Quinn likes to make Lit'l Smokies every chance he gets. I think he thinks he's cooking, but can you really call it cooking if you're just warming up packaged sausages and adding barbecue sauce? My mom would say no. It might be the one thing in the world she and I agree on.

In the kitchen, about seven guys fight over who gets the next beer from the keg. I elbow past them and sidle up to Quinn, who is stirring his Smokies.

"They're not ready yet, the flavors are still settling!" he says, pushing me away.

I lower my voice and say roughly, "Tiny sausages in a slow cooker. The perfect metaphor for this party."

Seeing it's me, he starts laughing. "Nice, Mara. I thought you were Ranger. I was about to kick your ass."

"Like you could ever kick my ass," I say. "Or Ranger's."

He puts the lid back on. "Five more minutes 'til Flavortown. C'mon, you want a drink?"

I follow him over to the drinks table, where there's about fifteen two-liters of tonic with a few Costco-size bottles of whiskey.

"What's your poison? Beer or whiskey?"

My parents aren't big drinkers, so the only drinks I've ever had before are the beers Quinn and I have stolen from his parents' well-stocked fridge when they're out of town. He knows this, so maybe it's for the other guys' benefit that he's acting like I might know what my poison is.

"Don't you have vodka, bro?" Wayne asks from the keg, where he's shooting beer into his cup. "Chicks drink vodka, not whiskey."

I was gonna ask for a beer, but now there's no way. I look straight at Quinn. "I'll do whiskey."

The corners of Quinn's mouth turn up in amusement, and he reaches for a whiskey bottle, pours about an inch into a plastic cup, then adds some glugs of tonic and hands it to me. I take a sip. It's warm, slightly sweet, with very strong undertones of gasoline and ammonia. In other words, it tastes terrible, and it needs ice.

Quinn's looking at me expectantly, like he really cares what I think of his shitty cocktail. "Mmm," I say as convincingly as possible. "Cocktail of the summer."

"I'm glad you're here, Mara," he says with a smile. "We men can be such brutes sometimes, and having a lady present will sophisticate us, I believe."

I don't know what I ever did that made him think I wanted to sophisticate anyone.

"Who you calling a brute?" Wayne says.

"You, Wayne. Specifically you are a brute," Quinn says, and I can't help but laugh.

Wayne scowls. "Brutally honest, maybe."

"Brutally ugly, Wayne," Quinn says.

I roll my eyes as Wayne walks away. "He has been such an asshole to me all week."

"Ah, that's just Wayne," Quinn says, waving him off.

"Nah, he's, like, seriously pissed at me," I say. "Makes me want to come after his cornerback position."

Quinn shoots me a look. "I already told you. I wouldn't do that."

I shrug like maybe I wasn't serious.

"Mara."

"What?" I protest innocently. "I have to play *something*. What would you have me play?"

"I dunno, kicker?"

I sputter into my drink. "*Kicker?!* Fuck you."

Quinn cackles in delight.

"Besides, then Lincoln would be pissed at me." Lincoln Handel is the world's worst kicker. He's a string bean whose arms and legs seem to be six inches too long for his body, but he always acts like he's so hot, and any girl should want to be with him. His promposal last year was very public and very cringe-worthy and involved releasing pigeons that he had caught himself in the Safeway parking lot, but somehow the girl said yes. I don't get the appeal. "Every position is already taken by someone."

Quinn shrugs. "It's in Coach's hands. C'mon, let's go find a seat."

He leads us to the living room, where most of the offensive line is sprawled out across the country-chic furniture and on the layered cowhide floor. Quinn elbows Curtis Becker to sit up, and he settles in where Curtis's legs were draped over the arm. I post up on the floor, leaning against the side of the couch next to Quinn.

The group is mid-conversation, talking about Linkport, who we'll be playing our second game up.

"I heard Turnip gained a *dollar* over the summer," Curtis says.

"A dollar?" I ask.

"A hundred pounds, dude!" Curtis exclaims. Curtis is enormous. He's our star fullback, who's always blocking the defenders that make Quinn's big runs possible. Curtis looks like he knows his way around a weight room. Even so...

"That can't be possible," I say. I've been doing a ton of weight lifting this summer with my milk-jug weights, and I've only gained about fifteen pounds.

"*I heard,*" Stetson Ellison says deliciously, "he does human growth hormone."

That causes a huge reaction. Everyone oohs.

Stetson is also in the Kool-Aid Club. He has four brothers who all do rodeo, but Stetson plays football instead. He's our second-string quarterback, so if anything ever happens to Noah, he's next in line to take over. But nothing ever happens to Noah.

"Aw, man, come on!" Quinn says. "He's just some guy from Linkport, not the Terminator."

Everyone laughs.

"Still," Quinn says. "I bet he gets a ton of girls."

"A *shit ton*," Stetson agrees.

Quinn stands up to get another drink for himself. "Mara, you want another?" I nod and hand him my cup. The drink somehow got less gross the longer I sipped it, and now my cup is empty.

"I even saw Maria Carpenter hanging on him at some bonfire last year," Curtis says.

Stetson lets out a breath of air through pursed lips. "Damn, Maria Carpenter might be the hottest girl in school," he says.

I pipe up. "But I heard she had to get her appendix out last spring, and now she has a scar on her stomach and won't wear a bikini anymore." I don't know why I said it. I heard that in the girls' bathroom last semester and didn't think about it at all until just now when I repeated it. I don't even know if it's true.

"Sucks," Curtis says.

"Anyway, isn't Kelly Wesley basically the same thing but blonder?" I say. To me, they're almost interchangeable in their perky, girly way.

The boys crack up laughing. "Yeah, she totally is," Curtis says.

Quinn comes back with drinks for me and him. I take a sip—it's way stronger than the last one.

"What'd I miss?" he says.

"Mara's funny, man," Curtis says. "She's like one of the guys, but with insider info."

"Yeah," Stetson says. "She's our man on the inside. She's a spy."

A smile tugs at my lips.

Quinn slaps me on the back. "I told y'all she's the best. She's not like those other girls at all. She's one of us."

Finally, they see that I'm one of them. This is what I've been trying to be all along. I realize what I'm feeling is relief. Maybe this football thing is going to work out after all.

Quinn climbs onto the couch and puts one foot up on the rustic wood arm.

"Hello, comrades!" he says, and everyone turns to listen. Someone turns down the music.

"Oh god," I say. Quinn loves to give a speech.

"I just wanted to say a few words. First of all, thank you for coming to the first Elk Hunter party of the season!" The guys cheer. "We have another exciting year ahead of us. We're going to demolish Gravel Bay. And we're going to State, baby!" At this, the rest of the party lets out a "Hoo-hah" in response. It's a football thing that I've heard Noah do before, but I still don't know when it's supposed to be used, exactly.

"And I want to shout out our new players," he continues. *Here it is.* I bury my nose in my cup, taking another long drink from what really is the worst beverage I've ever tasted.

"To the freshmen, I know this is a big step up from the game you're used to. Welcome to the Elk Hunter crew. And to our other new players who are trying football for the first time..."

I feel eyes turn toward me, and I will my cheeks not to redden. Quinn loves attention and doesn't seem to care that the rest of us might not as much.

"Welcome," Quinn says, raising his cup and looking straight at me. "It's good to have you. It's the things that make us different that also make us strong." I'm embarrassed by the attention, but Quinn's smile makes me feel good nonetheless.

I look around at the other players, who are raising their cups in a toast. Even Noah meets my eye. I can't read his expression, but I give him a small smile anyway. Maybe it's a reconciliation.

Quinn continues, "Let's make this the best fucking season Elkhorn has ever seen!"

"Hoo-hah!" everyone cheers. This time, I join in with them, feeling just a little bit like an Elk Hunter. "Hoo-hah!"

16

MY WHOLE BODY FEELS LIKE A BAG OF MANURE AS I drag myself down the aisles of Leroy's, restocking shelves. I might feel like shit, but it was worth it for the party last night. I stayed 'til past one a.m., laughing along with the team's stories from last season, poking fun at Quinn, and drinking.

There was a moment when Quinn broke out his guitar and started trying to play a Blake Shelton song. And at first everyone ragged on him because it was Quinn being the center of attention like always, but then he reached the chorus, and you couldn't help but sing along with him about the muddy river and the dogs running and how all this around us is God's Country. Ranger slung his arm over my shoulder, and I put mine around Stetson Ellison's, and Stetson didn't pull away, and we all sang together. None of us were particularly good singers, but in that moment, our voices came together, and Noah gave me this look that wasn't exactly warm but wasn't exactly cold either. For the first time I felt a little bit like his teammate.

But then he still drove home without me, leaving me at Quinn's to fend for myself. When it became clear that I was too drunk to ride my bike home, I texted my parents, telling them I was staying over at Quinn's. I rode my bike home early this morning to change clothes and take a quick shower before I had to get to work.

The front door jingles. I hear a pair of boots clomp into the store, and I know it's her without even seeing her.

"Ma'am," Leroy says, and I'm proud of him for recovering from their last interaction.

"How we doing, Leroy?" Jupiter says.

"Oh, can't complain," Leroy says, which is what he says when he definitely could complain, but he just doesn't think decorum allows it.

"Your star football player working today?" Jupiter asks.

"Who now?" Leroy asks. I haven't told him yet.

I stick my head out the end of the aisle. "Heya."

Leroy looks from me to Jupiter and back. "Oh, Mara," he says. "What did you do?"

"Sorry, I didn't realize it was a secret," Jupiter says, and I shrug. He was going to find out sometime. Everyone will.

"I joined the football team," I say, and wait to see how he'll react. Leroy is just about as traditional as my parents, which is the only reason they let me work here, instead of somewhere a little more ladylike.

He's quiet for a moment as he digests it. "This isn't gonna affect your hours, will it?"

"Just on game nights."

He nods. "All right. Well, be safe."

I stifle the little zip of annoyance at that, because it's impossible to know whether or not it's a sexist comment. Does he mean *be safe* because football is a dangerous sport for everyone who plays it? Or does he mean *be safe* because I'm just a delicate little girl? Or does he just mean *be safe* because he cares about me and doesn't want to see me hurt? Maybe some combination of all three. Or maybe it's something else entirely.

Jupiter tells me she wants to repair the perimeter fence around her pasture. We talk about the problem, and then I help her determine woven wire is probably her best option. As I help her pick out the wire, I tell her about the party at Quinn's. She slaps me on the back. "Sounds like a good night."

"Yeah, it was. It's like they finally stopped noticing that I'm a girl and just started treating me normally."

"*Normally* being like a dude," she clarifies.

"Well, yeah."

"Just be careful," she says. "Sometimes guys like that only like you so long as they can pretend you're not a girl. But you are. And eventually something's gonna happen to remind them."

"Okay..." I say. It's a vague warning, and I don't know what to do with it. "But I'm not the kind of girl they have problems with."

She pulls the woven wire off the shelf and nods at me. "That doesn't matter," she says. "But good luck. You'll be by Monday to help me out with this?"

"Yeah, for sure," I say.

I ring up her woven wire, thinking about what she said. The guys know I'm one of the good ones, right? That's what last night was about. We drank together, we sang together. They know I'm not a Maria Carpenter. I'm one of them, they said so.

17

I FEEL LIKE I CAN SEE MYSELF FROM OUTSIDE MY BODY
as I walk down the stairs for church in my dress and shoes. My
hair is smooth, washed, and brushed, falling over my shoulders. I
look like someone else's daughter. The daughter my mom would be
delighted to have. She smiles warmly at that girl from the bottom
of the stairs—at her Mara Bree. She hands me a headband with a
pale blue bow on it that matches the shoes. I don't feel anything
as I put it on.

"Now see how lovely you look when you put in a little effort?"
Mom says, standing at the door with Dad and Noah. I don't say
anything, but as long as she's happy, I can breathe. The only
thing worse than wearing these clothes would be wearing them
and *still* having to quit the team. So long as I give in to all her
demands, she will have no reason to tell me I can't play football. It's blackmail, yes. But it's blackmail I have no choice but
to capitulate to.

Mom reaches into her handbag and holds out her tube of lipstick. "Mom..."

She waves it in my face. Noah snickers. Dad gives me a meaningful look.

I take it with an enormous sigh and uncap it. It's a deep red. I put it on. Smack. Hand it back. Glare at Noah, in his blazer and tie and flat shoes and no makeup. He doesn't even know how easy he has it.

When we arrive, River is sitting at the end of a pew all by herself, but I refuse to say anything to her looking like this. She's seen the dress already, but the shoes and the headband are extra humiliating. I feel like a show pony. I sit next to my mom in our pew, clasp my hands in my lap, and do my time.

# # #

It's starting to get the warmest this part of Oregon ever gets, so for practice this morning, I'm wearing shorts, an EHS basketball T-shirt, and high socks. Stretching on the sidelines with my teammates, I feel like myself again, after the indignity of church.

"Back to pretending to be a boy again, huh?" It's Wayne, just arriving. I had to talk to him for ten minutes after the service yesterday with my mom and his mom yammering away and his little sister running circles around us until I was ready to lose my damn mind. But today Mom's not here to make me be nice, so I shoot back, "Better than pretending to be a football player like you."

Quinn cracks up as he stretches one arm overhead. "*Damn*, Wayne. Roasted!"

Wayne glares at me, but Curtis laughs and slaps his friend on his back. "Relax, man, she's our spy, remember? We need her."

"Yeah, yeah," Wayne says.

"That was an epic party the other night, right?" Quinn changes the subject.

"Yeah, it was cool," I say.

"I'm having another one this weekend." He's moved on to stretching his quads. "We can celebrate our numbers. Whatever number you have, that's how many shots you have to do!"

"Yeah, good luck with that idea, Thirty-Six." I laugh.

We get our uniforms on Friday—the last practice before school starts. It's also the day we find out our positions and depth in the chart, if we don't already know. I've been trying out all the positions on defense, but I'm so sick of Wayne that I decide right then and there I'm going after cornerback whole hog. I glance over at him as I finish off my stretches. He's chatting with Jerry Martinez, the other cornerback. Jerry is six foot six, and there's no way I can outjump him, but I figure Wayne's position is definitely within reach. At some point this week, I need to find a way to prove to Coach that I'd be a better cornerback than Wayne. I'm dying to knock him down a peg or two, just to show him a little humility.

"Sounds boring to me," Stetson says. As second-string QB, he wears number two.

"You can help the linebackers with their shots," I tell him.

"We're *linebackers*," Ranger pipes up. "We don't need help."

"Uh-huh," I say. "I'll keep nine-one-one on hold, then, because you're gonna need your stomach pumped before you make it halfway through fifty-two."

"It's nice having a mom on the team," Curtis says. "I think that's what we were missing."

I roll my eyes as the guys laugh.

"Hey," Quinn says with a sharp edge in his voice. "What are they doing here?"

We all look up. Walking toward us, almost in slow motion, athletic bags slung over their shoulders, are Tayley, River, Valentina, and . . . Carly.

My stomach drops like a quarterback sack.

IT'S BAD ENOUGH THEY'RE HERE, STRIDING TOWARD us with determined faces, but trailing them is a woman in her thirties with thick dark hair pulled back in a ponytail snapping photos with a professional-looking camera. She glances up from the camera and directly at me. I look away quickly.

"What the hell is this?" Quinn asks me.

"Why are you asking me? I don't know!"

"I thought you were our spy," Stetson says.

"I have no intel on this," I say.

The girls set their gear down on the sidelines.

"Hello, boys. Hey, Mara," Carly says.

I drop my eyes.

Coach Willis marches over. "What's all this?"

Carly Nakata, who barely comes up to his armpit, crosses her arms in front of her, feet set in defiance. "We're here to play football," she says.

Are they kidding me?

Carly finds my eyes. "Mara," she says, and jerks her head toward the other girls. The photographer comes around and snaps photos of the four girls standing together in the face of Coach Willis. "Stand with us. For the photo."

She can't be serious. A bright orange flare of adrenaline rises up in my gut. It takes me a minute to realize I'm angry. This is *my* thing. What do they think they're doing here? Do these girls even know how to *play* football? Do they think this is some joke? I'm serious about this sport. Are they?

I look sideways at Quinn, who is raising his eyebrows at me. I shrug like I have no idea what she's talking about—because I don't. Wayne Warren turns to stare at me. Then Curtis Becker, and Stetson, too. Guys who a couple days ago were singing along with me at Quinn's party are now glaring in my direction. I could murder Carly for dragging me into this. I grind my cleats into the grass, gripping down with my toes, ignoring the pain from the blisters that have formed over the last week where the skin on my heels has worn raw. Can't these guys see I'm as pissed off about this as they are?

I shake my head and take an awkward step toward Quinn.

"God, Carly. What a fame whore," I whisper.

Quinn laughs, but it doesn't make me feel better. In fact, I don't feel good about any of this.

Coach looks the girls up and down. "Practice started a week ago."

I feel a shot of hope. Maybe they won't be allowed to join on a technicality.

"We have the right to be here, Coach Willis. We're not leaving," Carly says with a determination I'm familiar with from her.

"You missed your chance, girls. Try again next year," Coach says, turning away.

Carly raises her voice. "You're going to let us try out today, and let me tell you why," she says, pulling up her boxy five-foot-one-inch frame. It's hard to picture this girl on the field, but I've seen her on the court, and I know from experience that what she lacks in height, she makes up for in tenaciousness, for better or worse. Usually worse.

"Because if you don't," she continues, "I'm gonna sue your ass for gender discrimination."

"It's not gender discrimination," Coach says. "I'm letting Mara Deeble play." He points to me, and then everyone is looking at me again. I see the spark in Carly's eye that means she's not going to let go until she gets what she wants, and it scares me. The whole team watches silently. The reporter scribbles notes.

"You'll have to explain it in court, then," Carly says. "Because I can have a lawyer down here in an *hour*."

"Bull," Coach says. "You don't have money for a lawyer." But he looks nervous. He glances at the reporter.

"And *then*," Carly continues as though she didn't even hear him, "Greta here is going to write a story that's going to blow open how sexist you are."

Carly gestures at the photographer, whose scribbling ratchets up a notch.

Coach steps up to the woman. "What the hell do you think you're doing?"

The reporter straightens up. "I'm with the *Sentinel*. I'm writing a story on these girls trying to play football."

I thought Carly hated the *Sentinel*. Or maybe she only loves them when it suits her needs.

I've never seen Coach's cheeks so red. "This is all off the record," he growls.

"No, it's not," Carly says quickly.

"Sorry, Coach, it's fair game," the reporter says.

Coach looks to his assistant coaches helplessly, then back to Carly. He lets out a long breath.

"Fine, girls, you want to play football?" Coach Willis growls. "Let's see how much you like it." He turns to the gathered players. "On your feet. This isn't a tea party. Lines. Double sets." The guys groan and glare at Carly and the other girls as they head to the end zone. Double lines because the girls pissed Coach off? The guys are going to hate them for this.

I keep distance between myself and the other girls during lines, trying to send a clear message: Don't lump me in with them. I'm one of the *boys*. But then, as we finish, and I'm breathing so hard I have to put my hands on my head to try to get more air, Lincoln, our kicker, who I've barely exchanged three words with, catches up to me. "Look what you started," he snaps before jogging off.

I glance around at the rest of the team. Does everyone see this intrusion as my fault?

Why are these girls even here in the first place? Is this just an excuse for Carly to get her name in the paper? River is an experimenter, judging from her church explorations, but I hardly think testing out churches is the same thing as testing out football. Does she realize that playing football is going to be way harder than listening to a sermon? And what about Valentina? Why is *she* here? Does it have anything to do with me? I thought she was playing volleyball.

I find Quinn by the water table.

"Crazy, right?" I say.

"Did you know about this?" he demands.

"No," I say. "I would have told you."

His shoulders relax a little. "Okay, well. You never know. Girl code, and all that."

"Girl code? I barely know them."

"Weren't you on the basketball team together?"

"Just Carly. And look how well that turned out."

After lines, we do agility drills. I'm getting better at quick-stepping, but my spins are still awkward. I hope it gets easier, but sometimes it feels like my body is too big and my limbs would rather fly around uncontrollably than go where I ask them to go with any sort of grace.

I try not to look like I'm watching the other girls, but I can't help but compare myself to them. Tayley skips through the agility drills like a fairy, quick on her toes. Valentina has all the ease of someone completely at home in her body. River looks like she's running through the choreography for one of her musicals. I catch her mouthing "one-two-three-four" to herself. Even Carly is good at them.

The reporter takes notes. What could she possibly be writing down? How good we all are at quickstepping? I try to keep guys between me and her eyeline.

After agility, Coach asks us to pair off for a new drill. I immediately make eye contact with Quinn, and he nods at me. Everyone else pairs off, until there's just one guy left over, Stetson Ellison.

"Deeble," Coach yells at me. "Join the girls."

"What?" I say, incredulous. "I already have a partner." I gesture to Quinn.

"Yeah, Kegley, you're with Ellison. Sorry, Mara, someone has to triple-up."

"I'll triple-up with Quinn and Stetson, then," I say. He can't be serious.

"Go on," he says, his voice hardening. "Unless you want more lines."

Slowly, I turn and walk toward the girls, aware of every step that takes me farther away from Quinn. I pass Noah, who actually looks sympathetic for once. Not that he does anything about it.

I reach the girls. Carly and Tayley are paired off—and I'm not partnering with Carly—so I sort of step over toward Valentina and River, leaving plenty of space between us.

"Hey, Mara," Valentina says.

"Hey," I say. But I can't bring myself to say anything else, or even appreciate that she's being nice to me. I'm too frustrated.

Coach explains the drill, which involves passing the ball back and forth, taking steps backward after each pass so you're throwing longer passes each time. I wonder why Coach is having us do a passing drill when almost none of us outside the QBs will ever pass the ball in a game.

River turns to whisper to Valentina, "Are they going to explain how to throw the ball?"

I cringe, because most of these guys could throw a football before they could do long division. Then I wonder if that's why we're doing this drill—just to humiliate them. I really don't want to have to be the one to teach these girls football as we go, but if no one can throw me the ball, I can't show Coach that I can catch. And if Coach doesn't think I can catch, I'm liable to end up in some bullshit position like kicker. So I grab a football from the ball basket and quickly demonstrate for the other girls: ring finger over the end of the laces, pointer finger spread to give leverage, thumb wrapped around the underside of the ball like you're making a large, open "okay" sign. They examine my fingers like they're studying for a physics test.

Valentina frowns over her fingers on the lacing. "Bring your pointer finger a little lower down," I tell her, showing her with my open hand. Part of me just wants to wrap my fingers over hers and show her that way, but just the thought of doing that makes my breath catch.

"Like this?" Valentina holds it up to show me.

"Bingo," I say, and her face lights up in a way that makes my heart boom.

"Gosh, Mara, if this coach isn't going to teach us anything, I wish you'd give us lessons," she says.

I drop my eyes and think about all the lessons I'd give her if she'd let me.

"I think my fingers are too small for this," Carly mutters, trying to wrap her fingers around the ball. Carly's fingers are wide, but short. The ball looks huge in her hand.

"You might be right," I say. "This might not be the sport for you."

Carly narrows her eyes at me. "That's a rude thing to say."

"Why did you even show up today, anyway?" I ask.

Tayley looks at me with these big, wide eyes. "You really don't know?" she asks.

"What? No. Why?"

"Because of you," Carly says, then adds: "Don't let it go to your head or anything."

I look around, not understanding.

"We saw what you were doing," Valentina says, touching my elbow and causing a sensory wave to shoot up my arm, "and we wanted to be part of it."

Tayley runs a hand over her mousy-brown ponytail nervously. "I always liked watching football, but it didn't seem like something I was allowed to do. But when I saw you join, I was like, 'If she can do it, I can do it.'"

"Basically, Mara, you're a badass," River says. "And we decided we wanted to be badasses, too."

They all look at me expectantly, like I'm their cult leader or something, but I didn't ask for this. "I only joined football so I could requalify for the basketball team," I explain quickly. "I wasn't trying to, like, be a role model or anything."

"Yeah, that's exactly what's so badass about it," River says.

"I'm still not sure I even like football," Valentina says. "But Carly suggested it and it just sounded fun."

I look at Carly. I knew this had to be her idea. Of course it was.

"This isn't some kind of statement," I say.

"Sure it is," Carly says. "Whether you want it to be or not."

"No, it's not," I say sternly. "I'm just here to play football."

Carly cocks her head at me. "So are we."

"You're just here to play football?" I repeat incredulously.

"Yes."

"Then why is there a reporter here?"

I hold her eye for a long time. I don't trust her. She can say this isn't a movement, but she's always the first one in English class to jump down some old white dude writer's throat for not conforming to today's feminist ideals and the last one to let it go in the hallway when some guy makes a rude joke. I *know* her. She's always looking for a place to make a statement, and now she found one, and she's going to try to drag me into it. But I won't be dragged.

"Because they never would have let us on the team otherwise," Carly says. "You know that. Besides, I can play football and make a statement at the same time."

"No you *can't!*" I say.

"Hey, girls, quit your gossiping and start," Coach hollers from the other end of the line. Unreal. It's like they're *trying* to get me on the coach's bad side.

We spread out to start passing. I alternate throwing between Valentina and River. Both of them are horrible, but at least Valentina instinctively knows to turn sideways and step forward with her left foot as she throws, whereas River just stands straight on. It's like she's never played a sport before. Maybe she hasn't. The girl is wearing jean shorts to practice. I wonder if she even owns workout clothes.

River throws a high, wobbly pass that I leap up to catch and just barely grip with the tips of my fingers, and I get a flash of the feeling of playing with Noah and Quinn in the pasture. The pure, full-lunged joy of the sport. When I land and turn to check whether Coach Willis noticed, he's looking the other way. But Valentina claps.

"Nice catch!" she says. "We're lucky we have you here making our passes look good." I feel the blood rush to my cheeks and focus on passing the ball to her—a nice tight spiral that hits her square in the chest. She wraps her hands around it and smiles to herself. Maybe she'll be okay at this after all.

We keep going like that, taking a step backward after each pass so that soon we're throwing ten-yard passes, and then fifteen. Twice, Carly's passes go wide and threaten to take my head off. "Sorry!" she calls after each one, but I wave her off. At least she has power, even though she seems to have no aim. I have to run up to River's passes more often than not, and I can tell she's growing frustrated she's not improving, but it's mostly the fault of the drill. If we had stuck to little five-yard passes, she might be getting a handle on it, but what beginner can throw a twenty-five-yard spiral? It makes me wonder again if Coach Willis is doing this on purpose to punish the new girls. Nobody but the quarterback needs to be practicing passing anyway.

I glance around and see the girls aren't the only ones struggling. Even some of the boys who've been playing since Pop Warner are having trouble completing passes at this distance. And yet we're still backing up after every throw. How far are we taking this? Do we go until Noah's the only one left, because he's the only person on this field who can throw a Hail Mary?

My arm's on fire by the time we reach thirty-five yards. My passes are shaky and inconsistent, and River and Valentina are starting to have to run to catch them when they veer from their targets.

Finally, when my arm muscles start to have the consistency of warm chicken fat, Coach blows his whistle and calls the end of practice. River visibly relaxes. I wonder if this is everything they hoped it would be.

"What time is afternoon practice?" Carly asks loudly, over the chatter of all the other players.

Coach Willis looks at her a long time. "Three o'clock," he says.

"See you then," Carly says, which is possibly the most obnoxious way to let everyone know she's not quitting yet.

In the parking lot, as I'm unlocking my bike and trying to psych myself up for a slow ride home and a long, hot shower, Noah comes up to me.

"Hey," he says.

It startles me, and I fumble my keys.

"Hey."

"That was bullshit that Coach made you stop being partners with Quinn," he says.

I blink at him. "Thanks."

"Did you know they were going to join?"

"No."

He nods okay. Then he turns around and heads toward his truck.

"Can I get a ride?" I call after him.

"No," he yells back. "You'll stink up my truck."

I sigh. At least we're talking.

19

THE THING I NOTICE ABOUT JUPITER'S LEGS IS THAT she doesn't shave them.

At first, I think her legs are ugly. But I'm not sure if I actually believe that. I kind of can't take my eyes off them.

I usually don't shave my legs until basketball season, when I start wearing shorts every day at practice, but since playing football, I had to start shaving early, going through the tedious exercise of removing hair every couple days. But here Jupiter is, flouting the rule.

There's something rebellious about wearing shorts in public with your legs like that. I wonder if I could do it. I wonder if Valentina would think I was gross or badass. I wonder how it would make me feel.

Once we've hauled the woven wire out of the back of Jupiter's truck and down the hill to the fence, I take stock of the situation. The old fence on her property is built from wood, but it's falling apart in places, some of the slats rotted, the rest gray and weathered.

I tell Jupiter the woven wire is plenty to keep sheep in and predators out. We'll have to replace any posts that have rotted, but for the most part, we can just wrap the existing fence in the wire and she'll be good to go. It won't be pretty, but it'll do the job.

It's easier said than done. The wire is sharp and heavy and rubs my hands raw, even through the gloves. It wants to curl, after being wound on its coil for so long. Every hundred feet we have to use a fence stretcher to get the wire taut, ratcheting it so there are no gaps or bows in the wire. It's hard work, especially on my tired muscles, but it's satisfying.

"So, how's the ol' ballsports going?" Jupiter asks as we work.

"You really want to know?"

"Yeah, hit me. This job is boring as hell."

As we work, I tell her about the girls joining the team, and how no one really likes them, and now it seems to have changed how people look at me too.

Jupiter's eyes meet mine as she hammers the wire to the fence post. "How do they look at you now?"

"Like I'm one of *them*."

"Well, aren't you?"

"You don't know them, Jupiter. They say they're there to play, but I would bet you a hundred dollars they're just trying to make some kind of statement. Plus, they barely know how to play football. They're making me look bad."

Jupiter nods and finishes hammering, then stands up and looks at me. "Do *you* think you're making a statement?"

"I'm not trying to, I just want to play the damn game."

"But do you think you're making a statement whether you're trying to or not?"

"Now you sound like Carly," I growl.

"Okay, let's say you play in a game," Jupiter continues, "and some little girl is in the stands watching you, and you make some big play, like a touchdown—"

"Coach wants me on defense," I say.

"Okay, a defensive touchdown, whatever, I don't know football. And she sees you make this big play and then you take your helmet off, and she's like, 'OMG, a girl made that play?' And you're like, 'OMG, girl, yes,' and she's like, 'OMG, I want to play football, too.'"

"That's exactly how I talk."

"Whether you like it or not, you're out there inspiring people," she continues. "You can be there *just to play football* and make a statement at the same time."

I feel like I need a day to figure out how to respond to everything Jupiter says.

"I just...I don't need for it to be this whole production, you know?" I say finally. "Like, when Quinn puts on a helmet, it's not like anyone's like, 'Wow, what an inspiration.' He just does it and that's it. Why does it have to be this big *thing* when I do it?"

Jupiter shrugs and starts hammering the next post. "Because the world's not fair, Mara. Sorry."

"Yeah. That's what I thought."

"Tell me about these girls, anyway. They can't all be bad."

I think about Valentina, and my mouth screws up trying not to smile. Jupiter must see it.

"What, who's that for?"

"No one." I shake my head. "It's not like that."

"Oh sure, it's just that thing where you act like you hate people, but when you think about them, you can't help but smile to yourself. Yeah. Of course."

I roll my eyes. "Okay, so first of all, there's Tayley."

"Uh-huh..." Jupiter goes back to her work, but I can tell she's smiling.

"And she's, like, this really fast runner, so she could be good, but she's never played football before. And then there's River, who is basically a theater nerd who I don't think even owns proper sports shoes because she wears Chuck Taylors to practice. And then there's Carly." Nothing to say about her. "And then there's Valentina, who's like..." How do I describe Valentina? "She's probably the best athlete of all of them. She's a track star. Sprinter, I think, and shot put? So she's got these legs of gold, and she's super powerful. She's better at some of the drills than me, but she's never thrown or caught a football before, so that stuff is all new. Um, what else. Oh, she has a car."

Jupiter pauses, then looks up at me. "So, which one is it?"

"What?"

"Well, you just said five times more about this girl Valentina than the others, but you skated right past Carly. So, which one are you in love with?"

I feel the blood drain from my cheeks. I scoff, but I don't think it's believable. I knew Jupiter could tell I was gay.

"Sorry," Jupiter says, sounding legitimately apologetic. "Sorry, I forget I'm not in Portland anymore. We don't have to talk about it."

My heart hammers in my chest. I've never been able to talk about girls with anyone before. Jupiter is the only one who I know for sure would understand. I want to be able to talk about this stuff with someone. With Jupiter. She seems like she gets it. She seems like she won't immediately go tell my mother, like she can keep a secret.

"No, it's...it's okay," I manage, my heart in my throat.

Jupiter gives me a small smile. "All right, then. In my experience, when I'm into someone, it's either the only thing I want to talk about or the last thing I want to talk about. I'm just trying to figure out what's going on in your head."

"Definitely *not* Carly."

"*Not* Carly?"

"No way. She's arrogant. She's aggressive. She can't take a hint. She makes everything about herself. She came out last year—" Jupiter raises her eyebrows. "I know, but she won't shut up about it. It's like, 'Okay, you have a cool mom who accepts you, stop rubbing it in our faces.'" Jupiter's eyebrows go even higher. *"What?"* I finally ask before her eyebrows permanently join her hairline.

"I didn't say anything."

"You very clearly did with your face."

"Carly's the girl you got into a fight with last year?"

"Yeah."

"And she's gay, but she's not the one you have a crush on?"

"Right."

"And the other girl. You don't know if she's into girls?"

"Valentina. Right."

"Valentina." She raises an eyebrow. "It's a good name. Crush-worthy."

"Isn't it?" I can't help it. I'm gone.

"Well." Jupiter rubs her hands together. "Sounds like a situation ripe for some messy gay drama. I can't wait to find out what happens."

I can't believe I'm talking about this openly with someone, after all this time. And someone as cool as Jupiter. I feel like I've spent my whole life underwater, and I finally came up to breathe.

"If things get messy, it'll be because Carly made them messy," I say. "She can't help it. She's just an asshole."

"Oh, I love assholes," Jupiter says.

"Seriously?"

"Yeah, they remind me of myself. Besides, why do you think I hang around with you?" She laughs and I throw a glove at her.

20

MOM IS WAITING ON THE PORCH FOR ME, HAND ON HIP, watching Jupiter drop me off. And I know that look.

As Jupiter pulls away, Mom asks, "Is that that Galaxy woman?"

"Jupiter, yeah."

"I don't want you seeing her anymore."

"What?" I pull myself up short in front of her. "Why?"

"I got a call from Valentina Cortez's mom, who said she discovered her daughter is trying out for the football team, along with a handful of other girls, and they're all citing *you* as their inspiration."

Wow, the mom telephone network moved quickly on this one. Valentina's family is one of the last that still hasn't sold to Stockton Cattle. Mom and Mrs. Cortez know each other in that way that every ranching family knows every other one, but they're not, like, friends or anything. I thought it might take at least a day or two for Mom to find out, but nope.

"Yeah, that happened," I say. "But I honestly didn't have anything to do with it."

"Mrs. Cortez seems to think you had everything to do with it."

"They just did it on their own, Mom, I swear. I can't stop them! I don't even want them on the team."

"Well, I don't like it. And I don't like this Jupiter person and how much time you're spending with her."

"It's just a job. We're building a woven wire fence like the one in your old sheep pasture," I say.

"Well, she can find some other kid to do her work for her." Mom swats at a fly buzzing around her head. "Maybe she can find someone from her church who will help her out. Which one did you say she attends?"

"I haven't asked," I say, low and angry.

"Well," Mom answers, as though that explains that. "In any case, it's over."

"Mom, please—"

"Enough, Mara." Mom cuts me off. We stare at each other for half a second before she turns and goes in.

I growl to no one and sit down on the steps to figure out what to do next.

Delle Donne comes around the side of the house, curious about the noise. She climbs the stairs and circles me, wiggling and wagging her tail into my side. It makes me feel better but only marginally.

Jupiter and I have never texted. Does she even text?

I write: *My mom says I'm not allowed to work for you anymore*

It sends in a green bubble. I want her to write back immediately, but nothing happens for a long time. I start to get nervous, so I send another one: *She's mad about football*

I wait some more. Nothing.

Maybe Jupiter doesn't care about all that, maybe she just cares about her fence and how she's going to finish it without me. Why would I think she cared about me for anything other than my ability to help her around her house? I shake my head at my stupidity and text: *Leroy has names of people you can call for help finishing the fence. Just ask him next time you're in*

I put the phone down and lean back against the stairs, looking at the clouds in the sky. The phone buzzes. I grab it immediately.

Jupiter: *I'm so sorry, Mara. Do you have someone else you can talk to?*

Yeah, of course, why would she even ask that? It's not like she's the only person I talk to. I write: *Yeah, I have Quinn*

The texts come quickly now. She writes: *I mean someone you can be honest with.*

I'm honest with Quinn

Okay, she writes. I don't know what to say next.

She writes again: *You can always text me.*

Then one more: *I hope your mom changes her mind.*

Me too

I hold my phone for a long time after that, but neither of us texts again. I can't wait to be old enough that I don't need my mom's permission to be friends with someone like Jupiter. One day, I want to have a party with a whole living room full of Jupiters, who are all there not because they need my help with their chicken coop, but because they like me.

How does Quinn fit into that future? I don't know.

I pull my phone out and text my best friend.

Wanna shoot hoops?

I'm worried things are weird with us after this morning's practice, but the text comes back right away: *Totally*

So maybe things *aren't* weird. Boys are so easy.

# # #

Quinn hops out of his sparkling-red Chevy with a gallon jug of water.

"What's this?" I ask, even as a slight memory tugs at my brain— the football players carrying these things around during the season.

"We do it every year. Two gallons of water a day will keep you hydrated. Drink one of these before noon and another before bed."

"Two gallons a day?" I'm incredulous.

"Not counting the water you drink at practice. If you feel thirsty, you're already dehydrated."

I'm almost certain that's not true. "Is this based on science, or . . . ?"

"Hey, do it, don't do it, up to you. But now you have a jug so your only excuse is being a pansy."

"Uh-huh, okay." He didn't have to bring me a jug. Even when he's being an ass, he's still kind of sweet. I reach for the jug and he pulls back, pops the cap, and takes a swig.

"Hey!"

"I backwashed," he says.

"Gross."

"Just a little of that Quinn Kegley mojo. You could use it."

I grab the jug. "Unnecessary."

The basketball hoop over the garage is rusted out from eleven years of wet Elkhorn winters, and the net is long gone, having turned gray and melted off years ago, but the clank the rim makes as the basketball hits it is still just as comforting as ever. We start by just shooting around.

At first, we avoid the elephant in the room and talk about dumb stuff like always. School, and what will happen when it starts. What our schedules will be like. We go back in a week and we find out which teachers we get then. Quinn wants Mrs. Grant for chem because he thinks she's sexy, but I'm hoping for Mrs. Tantlebaum, who Quinn thinks is a dog, but who I think is hot in a no-makeup, goes-on-vacation-to-national-parks, tattoo-for-a-wedding-ring kind of way. I don't say that to Quinn, though.

I sink a three. Quinn retrieves it and says, "You know who's *really* hot? Valentina Cortez."

I pause to take many long swigs from my jug of water to give myself time to think. There is no way in hell I'm going to let Quinn and Valentina become a thing. It would be heartbreaking enough if I didn't get to be with her, but there's no way I catch her in a blue taffeta dress making out with my best friend in the sweaty dark corner of homecoming this year.

"Oh yeah?" I say brilliantly. Way to be chill, me.

"Yeah. Damn, you see that ass? Sorry, of course not. Sometimes I forget you're a chick. Well, just so you know, she has a fantastic ass. I'm sure Carly Nakata has noticed." Quinn chuckles to himself.

There are times I'm sure Quinn knows I'm gay. Like how he never asks me about what boys I like. Sometimes I feel like I'm being so transparent, how could he *not* see? Like when I get tongue-tied at the very mention of Valentina Cortez. Or that time last summer when Quinn and Noah and I tried to stay awake for forty-eight hours straight to see if we could (we could not) and I spent like two of those hours chugging Dr Pepper and analyzing Emma Watson's hair evolution through the Harry Potter movies in exquisite detail. Or the time we drove out to the beach and watched the sun go down while eating cold pizza and then, when it was dark enough we could reasonably take our clothes off without being too embarrassed, we went skinny-dipping in the icy black waves, laughing until we cried, splashing until we were numb all over. Would he do that with a girl he thought was straight? I'd like to think he would. I'd like to believe Quinn could be friends with a straight girl without hitting on her at every turn, but I don't know.

Maybe Carly Nakata can come out to her mom in high school and feel confident that nothing will change, but I don't have that luxury. My parents' reaction is an unknown, which is why I'm going to wait until college to say anything. I don't know exactly how they'll react, but experience tells me it won't be easy. Maybe they'll take a day and get over it. Or maybe a month. Or years, or never. I want to believe they wouldn't kick me out of the house, try to change me. I want to believe they'll love me regardless. But in the absence of knowing, I don't want to risk it right now. I have my coming-out plan and I see no reason to change it.

The only wrench in the plan was meeting Jupiter, who is, after me, the first person I've sort of mostly come out to. Which feels huge and not huge at the same time. It was . . . a non-issue. Which was cool. But it also might be nice if someone would give me a bottle of sparkling apple cider and a loaf of banana bread next time I come out. Just putting it out there.

But now, I remember with a pang of grief, Jupiter is out of the picture. I'm so frustrated with my mom I could squeeze this basketball until it pops. Instead, I take a steadying breath and focus on my form.

The lift, the follow-through, the wrist flick. The ball arcs beautifully and clinks into the hoop. Now I can answer. "But don't you think she's kind of unattainable?"

"For me? No, not at all. Who do you think you're talking to, Deeble?" Quinn shoots a jump shot and airballs it. I rebound it and lay it up. Suddenly, it feels like time to address the elephant.

"What do *you* think of them joining?" I ask.

"It's idiotic," he says. "Carly Nakata is going to play? As what position, the *football*?"

I can't help laughing, even though it's a stupid joke.

"Besides, isn't she supposed to be some big lesbo? What's she doing hanging out with boys anyway? If I were her, I'd be doing all the girl sports, hanging out in all the girls' locker rooms."

"You're sick in the head, you know that?"

"And what's that girl River thinking?" he continues. "We're *playing* in the rain, not singing in it."

"They said...they said they were inspired by me," I say nervously, passing him the ball.

"Well, of course they were. You're a monster on the field. But none of them are like you."

"Exactly," I say, grateful he gets it. "I think all the other guys think it's my fault they joined."

"Oh, it's absolutely your fault." Quinn laughs, dribbling. "But you can't help that."

"I just don't want people thinking I have anything to do with them," I say.

He grabs the ball with both hands and looks me in the eye. "Don't worry what the other guys think," Quinn says. "There's no way those other girls last longer than a day. There's no way the *Sentinel* actually writes anything about them. It's moot. I'll bet they don't even come back for afternoon practice."

I can only hope.

21

THE OTHER GIRLS STAND LIKE SENTRIES ON THE FIELD
as the rest of us arrive.

"All right, but they won't last a full-pad practice," Quinn says
confidently.

Past the girls, piles of pads sit waiting on the sidelines. The
adrenaline hits my bloodstream with a satisfying rush; we get to
hit things today.

Coach Willis gathers us. Then one by one we go down the line
to receive our pads. Defensive Assistant Coach Gary hands me a
set of shoulder pads. I'm surprised by their heft, but I try not to let
it show. Next, Offensive Assistant Coach Howard silently hands
me a pair of yellowing knee-length pants with hip, thigh, and knee
pads sewn into them.

How old is this equipment? How many teen boys have worn
these padded pants before me? Part of me is grossed out by the
thought, but another part of me feels proud to be a link in the chain
of these hand-me-down football pads.

Finally, at the end of the line, Coach Willis hands me a helmet.

"Make sure it fits snug under the chin with no wiggling around. This is the most important thing about football. Your helmet must fit right."

I take the helmet from him, trying to look as solemn as he does, even though my heart is singing. I can't wait to put all this stuff on.

All the other guys are changing into their football pants right on the sidelines, so I guess asking to go back to the locker rooms is out of the question. But the guys seem to all be wearing these long, slick compression shorts under their workout shorts, so they're able to change without showing anything too private. All I'm wearing is a pair of basketball shorts and underwear. I hate to do it, but I look over at what the other girls are doing. They seem to be discussing the problem among themselves. Tayley is sliding her pants over her short black running shorts, wriggling her hand down her pant legs to smooth them out. She looks ridiculous, and I'm embarrassed for her. I don't want to look like that, so I just do what all the other boys are doing—I slip out of my workout shorts, and quickly, but not so quickly that I look like I'm embarrassed, slide into the pants.

When I glance back over at the girls, Carly is watching me with an unreadable expression, but it doesn't matter if she thinks I'm a fool for undressing in front of all these boys. I have my pants on and she doesn't, so who looks foolish now? But then she surprises me by pulling her shorts off right there and then and slipping into her pants, too. She turns around so that her back is to the rest of the players, including me. She wears dark blue bikini-cut underwear that cuts off just high enough that I can see like one inch of butt cheek. I look away. It strikes me that I've never once thought about Carly Nakata's butt in the entire time I've known her, even though we've changed in the same locker room for years. It pains me to admit it, but her butt is very, very cute. I banish the thought, forbidding myself from thinking about it again. Valentina is looking back and forth between Carly and Tayley, trying to decide what to do. Then she drops her shorts, too, and just starts changing into the pants. I immediately avert my eyes because the last thing I want to do is ogle Valentina when she doesn't want to be ogled.

I look away and catch Quinn checking out Valentina with a little smirk on his face and an oven-hot flare of anger burns in my chest. It takes everything in me not to stalk over and smack that look right off him. But I made a promise not to fight. So instead, I take a few steps to the side to place my body in his sight line. Confused, he refocuses his eyes on me, and then he glowers. He takes a step to the left, and I follow, blocking his view. My eyes tell him with no uncertainty: *Leave her alone*. Quinn kind of scoffs and raises his eyebrows like *Watch it, Deeble*, then turns away. Which pisses me off, but not as much as him eye-fucking Valentina pisses me off, so I know I did the right thing.

I pick up my shoulder pads. There are a variety of straps and clips I don't totally understand, but I take my best guess and slide my head through the hole, settling the pads on my shoulders. They're supremely uncomfortable. Like, *oh my god* they hurt. Not just heavy, but they're *digging into* my body.

"Let me help you with that," Ranger says pleasantly, coming over. He easily lifts the pads off my head, turns them around, and puts them back down.

Oh. I had them on backward.

"Thanks," I mumble, heat rising in my cheeks. Much better.

"No problem," he says. "The straps are a little confusing the first time, too. Do you want me to show you?"

"Um . . ." I'd rather not have to ask for help, but since I don't know what I'm doing, I guess I have no choice. "Sure."

"Okay, you want to clip them both in like this, and then you want to cinch them down evenly," he says, clipping the straps in under my armpits, then pulling on them to make them tight. "How's that? Comfortable?"

I take stock of my body. My boobs are pressed flat against my chest, but my boobs aren't big enough that it's an issue. I move my arms around. It's awkward at first, but I could see getting used to it. When I get into three-point stance, I can feel the pads pressing into my body in all the right places. I feel strapped in like a seat belt. Secure. Like I could mow down a wide receiver without a bruise. I feel like a warrior, actually. It's surprising how easily the soldier metaphors start coming once I do something as simple as strap some football pads to my body.

"I feel amazing," I tell Ranger, and he whacks me on the back happily.

"It never really starts to feel like football season until you get the pads on," he says.

I nod. I almost don't want to take them off, ever. I don't care how heavy they get.

"I'm gonna go see if the other girls need help, too," Ranger says.

And there it is—still just one of the girls.

I pull my helmet on, but it bonks against my ponytail, so I shake out my hair and slide it back on. The sounds of the other players fall away and I become aware of the sound of my own breathing. The helmet fits snug against my head and temples. It's musty inside but in a good way. Smells like sweat and hard work.

I imagine wearing the helmet to school, to the first day of class, to lunch. The heavy pads blocking out the sounds of everyone else around me, the taut pressure on my head keeping me focused. The face mask protecting me from any tossed-off comments or sideways glances. If only.

I glance over at Ranger. He's successfully gotten all the other girls in their pads and has moved on to helping them tighten their helmets. Carly's pads reach practically to her ears. She looks like a body builder who got carried away on shoulder day a few hundred times. They must be heavy on her frame. Can she even run in them?

Meanwhile, as the girl with the biggest boobs on the team, River keeps tugging at the pads that go over her chest.

"Is there any way to loosen this?" she asks Ranger.

"You're maxed out," he says.

"This is dumb," River protests. "They must make pads for girls, don't they? We're not the only girls who ever played football. There are others, I've seen them on Tumblr."

I look away, embarrassed that she's turning football pads into a whole rant.

Her pads do look like they've got to be uncomfortable, though. But if she doesn't like them, she should quit. Coach Willis can't be expected to buy girls' pads on the off chance some girl shows up for practice. Right?

I look for Quinn to say something snarky about them to, but he's engaged in some kind of dumb pad-slapping game with Wayne, so I don't go over.

After we're all suited up, Coach has us run lines in our full pads. Halfway through, I'm wheezing for air, and I have to slow my pace in order to make it through. Coach yells at us to stay light on our feet, like a bird, but it's impossible as I clamber through the motions, my shoulders protruding far past where I'm used to, my head heavy under its helmet. Maybe I feel like a bird if the bird is an ostrich. An ostrich with a flamingo strapped to its shoulders.

After a water break, we get started on tackling drills. First, we run through the motions we practiced last week, but it's totally different with pads. We stomp-squeeze-sink-hands our way through the drill, and each time I can feel my muscles growing more comfortable under the weight, more confident in the motions of the tackle. Each time I thrust my hands into an uppercut, I wish they were making contact with a person. I want to use this explosive energy on something worthwhile. I want to start taking some guys down.

There was a time when I thought football was just something I was doing to get back on the basketball team—and it still is, partially—but it's also a whole hell of a lot of fun.

Coach Gary lines us up and shows us how to approach a moving target, how to buzz our feet right before we reach them in case they zig or zag, and how to use our body's leverage to propel through them and bring them toward the ground. We practice the run-up a few times, and I'm desperate to go further. I'm horny for actual contact.

Finally, with thirty minutes of practice left, Willis tells us to line up against someone our same size. We're finally going to do full-body tackling. He points to the other girls and tells them to pair off with each other. Perfect, finally, an acknowledgment that I've got something they don't: size.

My body hums with excitement. I put my hand square on Noah's shoulder before he can pair off with someone else. He's close to my size—well, a few inches shorter, but I don't think he'll bring it up in order to protest. He rolls his eyes when he sees me.

"Really, Mara?" he says, his voice dripping with disdain.

"Be honest. Is there anyone else you'd rather tackle?"

He looks at me for a long minute, then shakes his head. I knew it.

"I thought you weren't supposed to tackle quarterbacks in practices," River says. "I learned that on *Friday Night Lights*."

Coach Howard says, "That comes later. This drill is as much about learning to be tackled safely as it is about practicing tackling." He nods at me and Noah with the go-ahead.

We start five yards apart. My hands are practically vibrating with anticipation. If it feels anything like the one tackle I performed on Noah last week in our yard, then this is going to be my favorite sport in the world. (Sorry, basketball.)

I look into Noah's eyes, and they narrow in concentration as he grips the ball tight between his forearm, bicep, and chest. I sink into ready position. My mind empties of everything but Noah, the ball, and my body. I wait, and focus, and then *wheet*, Coach blows the whistle, and we both explode forward, I buzz, I stomp, I squeeze, I sink, and I throw my hands up and around Noah as my shoulder collides with his torso, as his momentum crashes into mine. I'm sunk low enough that I have the power in my legs to lift him up. We both fly back and then down, and my view through my helmet turns from sky to body to grass. The ground rises up and I land on top of him, every muscle in my body feeling bright and alive from the contact. A smile spreads involuntarily across my face and I want to shout, but I don't have anything to say, so I say, "Hoo-hah!" and finally that expression makes sense.

"Mara . . ." Noah grunts. "You can get off me now."

Oh yeah, sure. "Sorry." I roll off him and help him to his feet.

"How was that?" I ask, not wanting to appear like I need his approval but desperately needing to know if that's what it's supposed to feel like. Because it felt *perfect*.

"Yeah, fine," Noah says, shrugging. Like it was nothing, instead of everything. How many times has he done that in his life? How has he never told me? I can't believe I get to tackle Noah and not only is it completely acceptable, it's school-sanctioned. Incredible.

I can't help but glance over at the other girls to see how they did. Tayley is rolling on the ground in pain with Carly on top of her. "Ow, ow, ow," she says.

"What'd I do?" Carly asks.

"You landed on my arm!" Carly gingerly gets off her. "I guess I'm left-handed now," she mumbles.

"Well, I just got a face full of bosom," Valentina says as River pulls herself off.

"Sorry. That's kind of the idea, though," River says, self-consciously pushing her boobs down.

"No, it's fine, I guess," Valentina says. "But damn, girl, you tackle BOOB FIRST."

Noah flips the ball to me. "My turn," he says, a devious smile growing.

We line up again. I tuck the ball into my body using the five points of contact and squat. I don't love the bloodthirsty look Noah's giving me. Is that the same look I was giving him just a minute ago? The whistle blows, we both explode forward, and unlike last time when everything played out in slow motion, Noah crashes into me and we're both flat on the ground before I even realize he went through the motions. It was fast, but relatively painless... oh, wait, no. There's the pain. Ow. *OW.* That... hurts a lot more than I thought it would. I grimace as Noah rolls off me, his knee connecting with the soft, unpadded part of my torso.

Then I hear the oohing. Why is there oohing?

As Noah stands up, Curtis and Wayne are standing over us, snickering into their fists.

"Damn, girl, he just demolished you," Curtis snorts.

"You got snowplowed," Wayne says.

I look at Noah, who offers me a hand. I ignore it and roll over to push myself to my feet. I brush myself off and go to flip the ball back to Noah, but I realize I don't have it anymore.

"Looking for this?" Curtis asks, nudging our football forward with his foot. *Shit.* Somehow in the tackle, I didn't even realize I'd fumbled. My face grows hot, and I'm hopeful they can't see it under my helmet. I swipe the ball back and toss it to Noah.

"Maybe you'd be better off tackling with the other girls," Wayne says. "Or maybe you guys can have a pillow fight instead."

"Yeah, and we'll watch," Curtis says.

I expect this kind of shit from Wayne, but I'm annoyed Curtis is joining in.

"Let's go," I say sourly. Now I'm really ready to tackle Noah again.

We tackle each other until my muscles are ready to give out, and I'm certain I have bruises all over my body. By the time Coach tells us practice is over, I can barely get back on my feet. I feel like I've been put in the dryer and set to tumble.

I wobbily put my ball back in the basket and make my way to the sidelines to strip off my pads, now heavy with sweat and stained from the grass. My arms are so useless I can barely lift the pads over my head. I don't even think twice before pulling the pants off and sliding back into my basketball shorts. I stay on the sidelines a long time, stretching and psyching myself up to get on my bike to ride home.

The girls walk toward the parking lot in a clump, chattering loudly. Despite Quinn's confident proclamations, they don't look like they're going anywhere.

And despite that, and despite the pain radiating through every part of my body, I have to admit: This was the best practice we've ever had.

22

MOM'S AT WORK WHEN I GET HOME. AFTER A HOT shower, I rummage in the fridge for something to eat to hold me over before dinner. Dad comes in through the back door, wiping his hands on a rag.

"Were you outside?" I ask, weirded out.

"Yeah," he says.

"Why are your hands dirty?"

"Don't worry about it."

That just makes me worry about it more. I don't like him cooped up reading in his den all the time, but he shouldn't be out doing farmwork on his bum knee. I wish he would just take up yoga or something. Like that would ever happen.

"Thought you might want to see this," he says, sliding the evening's *Sentinel* across the counter to me.

Splashed across the front page is the photo of Carly, River, Tayley, and Valentina standing in front of Coach Willis, arms crossed, looking determined. Large, bold letters proclaim: GIRLS ON THE GRIDIRON.

"Where's the photo of you? Now I can't clip it and send it to Grandma."

"Grandma doesn't want to hear about me playing football," I say. "She'll have a heart attack."

"She's already had a heart attack, and it didn't kill her," Dad says.

I snatch the paper off the counter and hurriedly skim the article.

Girls on the Gridiron
by Greta Bradley

Five students are doing what no girl has ever done before in the history of Elkhorn football: They're trying out for the team.

"We just thought, well, why not?" said Carly Nakata, a junior who has never played football before, but who has played basketball and softball for much of her life. "It's ridiculous that there's this boys' club that says that football is a sport that girls can't play. Seriously? Watch me."

Junior Valentina Cortez credits her inspiration for trying out to another Elkhorn student, Mara Deeble. "It didn't even occur to me to play football until I saw Mara try out. Then I was talking to Carly and I was like, 'If she can do it, we can do it!' So we did."

A member of the Thespian Society, junior River Reyes had never played a high school sport before joining the football team. "I played T-ball as a kid, but then I ran smack into my teammate trying to catch a ball and I didn't want to play anymore." She laughs. "I hope I've toughened up since then!"

"I've never been to a football game in my life, but if those girls play, I'd show up," Sandy MacNamara said, standing outside Fred Meyer, a crying baby on her hip and a young daughter

tugging at her pant leg. "And I'd bring my daughters. I want them to know they can do anything."

But the feeling isn't unanimous. John Handel scoffed when he was asked whether he'd like to see girls play for Elkhorn football. Handel was getting out of his truck, adorned with an EHS football window sticker alongside a Semper Fi sticker. "The field is no place for girls," Handel said simply. "It just isn't. They're going to be a distraction for the boys, and they won't be able to handle the pain. It's not sexist. It's just biology." Handel played guard and tackle for Elkhorn High for four years, from 2011–2014.

Elkhorn's first game is in two weeks against rival school Gravel Bay. When asked if they think they'll get to play in the game, sophomore Tayley Striker said, "I hope at least one of us gets to play."

Nakata added, "I'm rooting for all the girls. If any of the Elkhorn Five play, it's a win for all of us."

So, will the Elkhorn Five play? Coach Verne Willis declined to comment on the girls' performances so far, but Mara Deeble made a spectacular catch in the short time we visited practice, so this sports reporter would put the odds at likely.

My fingers curl, crumpling the thin paper, smearing the ink. I want to tear it to shreds. To find every copy and rip those up, too. But what good would it do? Carly wanted her five minutes of fame? Here it is. She wanted something to put on her college applications? Done. She's officially a revolutionary. Congratulations. But some of us are trying to play football here.

"Thanks," I tell my dad, folding up the paper and stuffing it deep in the recycling.

"That's it?" he asks, leaning on the counter to take pressure off his leg.

"Yeah." I take another look at him. "You sure you're okay? Do you need help with something out there? I have time before my chores."

"I'm *fine*," he says. "Relax."

"Okay," I say, but I don't believe him.

I WAKE UP HUNGRY. I SEEM TO ALWAYS BE HUNGRY lately. I go to swing my legs over the side of my bed and *owwwww*. They scream in pain. Every muscle in my legs is stiff and angry. I lift my shirt to examine the bruises that opened up across my body overnight. A mosaic of purples and blues paints my belly. I take a moment to admire them before steeling myself to stand. This morning's practice is going to be rough if these muscles don't loosen up.

It takes forever to wash my hair. A permanent coating of sweat and grime seems to cover it all the time these days. I've never much cared for my hair—too frizzy, too in the way, too blah. But nowadays it seems to bother me even more than usual. Hair dryers aren't really my thing, so I just leave it wet and head out into the fog.

As I pull up to the bike racks at school, I see Coach Willis pacing outside the front doors to the gym, engaged in a tense conversation with his assistant coaches. Gary's holding a copy of the newspaper. Coach looks like someone just ran into his truck. He's raging, finger waggling. The assistant coaches just listen and shake their heads like they can't believe it. I try to eavesdrop on their conversation, but I can't hear them from this distance.

Something flies through the air at me, and I catch it without thinking. It's a wadded-up newspaper. I look up and see Quinn striding across the parking lot, his face a knot of pissed-off-ness.

"Congratulations," he says, his voice bitter and too loud. "The 'Elkhorn Five.' Got a nice ring to it."

"You know I had nothing to do with that."

"Well, you do now."

"Quinn, you saw me, I didn't talk to that reporter. I'm not even in the picture."

"Yeah, but it's the Elkhorn *Five*. That includes you." He sticks his finger right into my chest. "Not me, even though I'm the highest-scoring wide receiver in five years." He doesn't mention that we've also had losing seasons for all five of those years. Not much of a record. "Not Noah, even though he's our QB and captain. *We're* who they should be doing stories about. The players who put in the time, not a bunch of football virgins who haven't even popped their game cherry yet."

"Look, it pisses me off, too, okay? I already told you, Carly's a fame whore. I'm just trying to play football here."

"And yet here you are, getting multiple mentions on the front page. *Above the fold.*"

"'Above the fold'?" I have to scoff at that. "Quinn, it's the *Sentinel*, not the *New York Times*. This doesn't matter."

"We got guys busting their asses out here during two-a-days and the paper doesn't so much as look our way. But as soon as a couple females join up, suddenly they're *noteworthy*. Doesn't matter that they suck at football."

Wow. "What about me? You think I suck at football?"

"You're okay." He shrugs. "For a girl."

That's it. I shove him. A devious smile curls up his lips. "Oh yeah, Mara? You gonna fight me? Because if you do, you don't get to play your precious basketball anymore."

My fingers curl into fists. I envision tackling him and pressing his stupid mouth into the concrete until he stops talking. But I'm not allowed.

"You're such an asshole sometimes," I say through gritted teeth.

He steps up to me and gets in my face, looking up my nose on his tiptoes. "Come on, you know you want to hit me." He taps his cheek. "One good one. Then you'll get kicked off the team and the other girls will follow you and we can go back to having a normal season."

My face burns. "You said I should join. You said it would be fun."

"I didn't realize you were going to be so conceited about it."

I can't believe he's acting like this. But I won't let him goad me into a fight. I set my jaw and spin around to finish locking up my bike.

"You're not invited to my party anymore, Mara," Quinn calls back as he starts toward the field. "Team players only!"

24

I'M ON EDGE ALL PRACTICE. THERE'S NO WAY THE coaches aren't thinking about the newspaper article as they watch us play. I try to keep my focus, but I keep wondering whether Quinn is going to come down off his high horse or not. After I stumble over my feet two times in a row, Coach Gary yells at me to get my head in the game.

Finally, practice ends, and Coach Willis gathers all of us together, sweaty, tired. The sun just begins to peek out of the morning clouds. All eyes are on Coach as he steps up onto the first bench of the bleachers in order to be seen, holding a clipboard. He clears his throat—a dry, husky sound.

"First, I want to say that it's been a joy working with you. As always, the best time of year comes when the summer ends and football season begins. I know we haven't had the greatest track record in recent years, but I have confidence that this season will be different. We're going to go out there and play football—not for the State Championships or for glory, but for each other. For respect of the game." Here he pauses for a "Hoo-hah!" from the team. "We're going to play the best football we know how, because football is the greatest sport in America."

"Hoo-hah!"

"We are all part of a long tradition of athletes in this town, at this school, who make the football program great."

"Hoo-hah!"

Coach holds up the clipboard. "Here is the roster. All decisions are final. When you find your name, meet Coach Gary to get a number. Thank you for showing up and giving it your all."

He bends over to put the clipboard down but then has another thought and straightens up again. "Oh, and one more rule. No one speaks to the press without my explicit permission again. *No one.* Am I understood?" There are nods around the team, and I hold my head high, knowing I didn't talk to that journalist, no matter what people might think.

"All right, gentlemen, I'll see you tonight." The last time he called us gentlemen, I found it a little flattering, but now that the others are here, I don't know, it feels erasing somehow. I wish he'd just avoid gendered terms altogether.

Coach puts the clipboard down on the bleachers, and he and the assistant coaches step to the side to let us at it. My stomach is in my throat. I hear some boys cheering and slapping each other on the backs. Someone cries out, "Are you shitting me?" but I can't tell who. I get closer.

Finally, Ranger hands the clipboard to me with a raised eyebrow. "Well, well, well," he says.

I snatch the clipboard from him and run my finger down it until I see it. *Mara Deeble—Cornerback—2nd string.* Holy shit. I did it. Cornerback. Second string. I scan over. First string is Wayne Warren and Jerry Martinez. I didn't displace Wayne, but I still got the position I wanted. A smile spreads uncontrollably across my face. I look up to find someone to share this triumph with, but the other guys have mostly dissipated. The only people in front of me now are Carly, Valentina, River, and Tayley.

"Well?" River demands. "Are we on there?"

I hand her the clipboard and look over her shoulder as she runs her finger down the names.

They're there. At the bottom. They don't even have positions listed, just their four names, next to *Utility—3rd string*.

"Yeah, utility!" Tayley exclaims, punching the air. "We're all utility!"

"What does *utility* mean?" Valentina asks.

"It's a swing player," I say. "You can be slotted in wherever."

"So it's a fake position," Carly says flatly. "Third string. It's nothing. It's bench warming."

"But we made it!" Tayley says again. "They could have cut us."

"Not after that article they couldn't," Carly says.

"Maybe it's just that we're game for anything," Valentina offers. "Because we're not that good."

"We're better than some of those assholes who don't even try," Carly snaps. "We're out here busting our asses and it seems like some of these bros like Lincoln just join so they can go to the parties."

"If you don't like it, there are other sports you can play," I say.

"That's not going to happen," Carly says.

Carly's eyes sear into mine with sun-bright intensity. I look away, my skin hot.

"Yeah, I figured," I mumble, and head for the parking lot.

25

I CAN TELL SOMETHING IS WRONG WITH MY BIKE FROM the way it leans uneasily to the side. When I get close, I see both rims are sitting right on the pavement, the tubes completely flat. I bend over my bike and finger the tires. Two short, straight punctures—one for each tire, surely made by a pocketknife.

I straighten and look around. Whoever did this must have done it in the last five minutes, right after practice. And even then, they would have done it in full view of the parking lot. Anyone could have seen him.

My stomach clenches. Is this retaliation for the article? What else do they want from me? I'm not the one who called the *Sentinel*. I didn't stand with the other girls for the photo. I didn't even speak to the reporter, and yet, here's my bike, sinking to the ground like a teddy bear with its stuffing pulled out. All because, what, I'm a girl, too?

It's so unfair.

I see Coach Willis wheeling the ball cart back to the equipment room and I shout to him, "Coach!" I jog over on tired legs.

"What's up?"

"Coach, someone slashed my bike tires."

He squints across the front yard of the school at my sad puddle of a bike. Then he looks back at me.

"Sorry to hear that."

I wait to see if he's going to say anything else, but he doesn't. "Aren't you going to do something?"

He cocks his head. "What do you want me to do?"

"Find out who did it and punish them? Someone must have seen him. Do you want somewhere to start? Wayne Warren has been nothing but nasty to me since I showed up. Maybe look into Curtis Becker, too."

"You want me to investigate your bike tires."

"It's a threat," I say. "Someone's trying to intimidate me into quitting the team."

"Mara, you have skill on the field, that's why I'm trying you at cornerback. But I need to know you're going to be able to hack it. If something like that intimidates you, maybe you're not tough enough for football," Coach says. I gape at him, but he just turns and continues rolling the ball cart toward the equipment room.

"You gotta be kidding me," I say under my breath.

"Focus on the sport," Coach shouts. "Forget all this drama."

I didn't even *cause* the drama! I can't believe he's trying to spin this around to blame me for my own bike tires being slashed.

I call Quinn. It rings once, then goes to voice mail. Maybe he's driving. Not that that's ever stopped him from answering before.

I sit down next to my bike, trying to figure out what to do next. I could walk home, but that would take forever. I wish I could call

Jupiter for a ride, but I don't know if she would be okay with that even if my mom hadn't forbidden it.

I sigh and drop my head into my hands, my hair sticking to the drying sweat on my forehead. A loud old car slowly grumbles to a stop in front of me.

"Hey, you okay?" Valentina asks, leaning over Tayley, who sits shotgun. In the back seat, Carly rolls down her window.

Valentina is chewing gum and wearing a 5SOS T-shirt that's been cut into a tank top. The other girls wear street clothes, too. They must have changed after practice while I was moping about my bike.

"My bike..." I say dumbly. "Someone slashed the tires."

"*What?!*" Carly screeches, opening her door to get out.

Valentina puts the car in park and hops out to take a look. "Who?!"

"I have some guesses."

"That's horrible," Tayley says with a stricken look.

Carly's face goes tight as a fist. "I'm gonna make those cowards wish they'd never been born."

"You've done enough," I shoot back.

"What's that supposed to mean?" Carly holds my gaze.

"It means that if it wasn't for that article, my best friend would be picking up when I call him for a ride, which I wouldn't need to do because my bike would be just fine."

"If something like that article threatens your friendship, maybe it was on shaky ground to begin with," Carly shoots back.

"Carly," Tayley says in an admonishing tone, but I don't need her to fight my battles for me.

I stride right up to Carly. "Why is this even newsworthy to begin with?" I gesture around at the group of us. "Five girls join the football team? Who gives a shit? Girls play football all the time. It's not a big deal."

"Of course it's a big deal. If it wasn't a big deal, you would be biking home right now."

I guess I can't argue with that. I wish it wasn't like that, though. "It's just so patronizing, you know? 'Can you *believe it*? A *girl*? Playing *football*?' Like, can everyone just chill out?" I turn back toward my bike.

My options here are limited. I can walk the bike home on my shoulder, but the thought of that is so exhausting I want to cry. I could just leave it and get my mom to drive me back later to get it, but I can't even imagine how she'd react to this.

Valentina lays a hand on my forearm. The heat of it warms goose bumps I didn't even realize had formed. "Mara," she says, low. "I'm sorry this happened. I can give you a ride if you need one."

I definitely need a ride, but do I really want to sit next to Carly Nakata, who I just yelled at, for fifteen minutes?

Besides: "It's out of your way."

"That's okay. I'm giving these guys a ride, too," she says, nodding over her shoulder at Tayley and Carly.

She starts backing up toward her car. "Party taxi is leaving the station in five...four..."

I shouldn't ride with them. I shouldn't be seen with them. My reputation with the team is in jeopardy if I look like I'm getting too cozy with these girls.

On the other hand, someone on the team is already angry enough to slash my tires based solely on my gender. What else can they do? I only have one bike.

"Three...two..." Valentina says, opening her door and stepping up into the doorway, pausing to blow a bubble with her gum and pop it.

Carly watches me like she doesn't care one way or the other whether I ride with them. She picks a leaf out of her silky dark hair and gets back in the car.

"One and a half...one and a quarter..." Valentina says, her white teeth popping against the red of her lips. "You gonna make me do fractions, Mara? One and one-hundredth..."

"Okay, okay."

Valentina and Tayley cheer. Carly gives me a look I can't parse.

Valentina has me stuff my bike into her trunk, the front wheel hanging out, a bungee cord keeping it snug.

"Sorry if I smell," I say as Valentina backs the car out.

"If you smell, that means you were working hard," Valentina says. "Like how you were laying into your brother yesterday. You were killing it." I can feel my ears getting hot, even as I try to will them to stay cool.

"Maybe it was your brother who slashed your tires," Tayley says.

"I don't think he would do that." I don't know that for sure, but I want to believe he wouldn't, despite the way he's been acting lately.

Valentina pulls out of the parking lot through a very narrow gap in the traffic and slams the accelerator to keep up. I grab hold of the door handle and cinch my seat belt tight against my lap.

"I think it was Quinn," Carly says.

"Quinn? No way. He's my best friend."

Carly shrugs. "Not everyone tells you to your face what they really feel."

What is *that* supposed to mean?

I squeeze out a response. "Whatever."

Valentina changes lanes, causing me to grab the handle again.

"Did anyone else really...*like* tackling?" Tayley offers hesitantly.

"Mara sure did," Valentina says.

"Yeah, Mara, you were a beast out there," Tayley says.

"I liked it, too. It was like a juice cleanse but for rage," Valentina says. "Afterward I just feel so…"

"At ease," I finish.

"Yes!" Valentina meets my eyes in the rearview mirror.

"I want to do tackling drills every time I feel like taking some dude out at the kneecaps," Carly says.

Tayley giggles. "It was fun. Football is like all the track and field events, but at once. Like sprinting AND hurdles AND long jump AND shot put… and oh yeah, and this giant dude is comin' at you, so you better look out."

"And it hurts." Valentina laughs.

"Oh gosh, it hurts." Tayley lifts up the side of her shirt to examine her torso. "I'm already black and blue."

"Me too," I say. I want to pull my shirt up, too, but the thought of having Valentina looking at my naked torso is mortifying.

"Your parents are gonna see that," Valentina warns Tayley.

"I know," she says.

"So you'll tell them?"

"I'll tell them."

"Tonight."

"Yes, tonight."

"I hope my parents take it okay," Tayley says.

"What do your folks think, Carly?" Valentina asks.

"My mom straight-up told me it's the coolest thing I've ever done," Carly says. "She always wished I would be more of a tomboy."

"And your dad?" I ask.

"My dad is some white surfer my mom met in Hawaii," Carly says. "He's too high most of the time to have real opinions, but if I asked him, he'd probably say me playing football is 'totally excellent.'"

"Oh," I say, for lack of anything better.

"I just wish I could tell my parents I'm really *good*, then maybe they'd respect that I'm doing it. But I feel like I'm just so *horrible* at football!" Tayley complains.

"Coach Willis is really not doing a very good job of teaching you guys," I say. "I can't believe he didn't give y'all the rundown on the tackling drills we did last week. He just threw you into week two and expected you to know."

Valentina says, "And remember when we did that fire-off-the-line drill? He just kept yelling at us to get into three-point stance and I didn't even know what that *was*."

I cringe. I can't help it.

"I saw that, Mara," Valentina says in the rearview. "But we're not bad at sports. We just need to be *taught*."

"And if he keeps pairing us off with each other, then we're never going to be able to learn from the boys," Carly says. "Isolation isn't helping us here."

"I watched some YouTube videos this afternoon, but it's not as good as someone actually showing me," Valentina says.

"I was gonna check *Football for Dummies* out of the library," Tayley says. "Do you think it would help?"

"Honestly, I think he's turning a blind eye on purpose to make all the girls want to quit," I say. "I told him about my bike tires and he didn't care. He told me to focus on football, not on drama."

Carly growls.

"What?" Tayley yells.

"I shit you not," I say. "If he wasn't such a wet blob of cardboard, he'd actually teach you the basics so you had half a chance of being successful. It's not like we don't need more good players around here." I still don't want them on the team, but they're right that Coach is being unfair to them. And to me. The whole situation sucks.

Tayley turns around in her seat to face me. "Mara, what if *you* taught us?"

"Yeah! You were so good at telling us how to pass that one time," Valentina says.

"Oh, no. I couldn't." I am not really trying to be the person that makes these girls good enough to actually stick with football. That's not my goal.

"But you're actually good. And you're the only one who cares about us," Valentina says.

I mean, I care about *her*. But does it seem like I care about *them*? I gotta reel that in.

"Don't you think Mara should help us, Carly?" Tayley asks.

Carly has her hands fisted into the pocket of her hoodie. She looks at me, then away. "There's no one I would trust more to teach me football," she says, surprising me.

"Seriously?"

"Think about it this way," she says. "If you're waiting for us to quit, you can stop. We're not going anywhere. And if we're less terrible, then people will stop thinking you're bad, just because you're a girl, too." So, she noticed that the guys have been lumping me in with them.

"Maybe if we were better, whoever slashed your tires wouldn't have," Tayley offers hopefully.

"I don't know about that..." I say. But I meet Valentina's eyes in the rearview mirror, and they're sparkling with excitement. Tayley looks at me expectantly.

I sigh. "Okay," I say. "One lesson."

"All right." Carly nods.

Tayley screeches and Valentina screams, "Hell yes! *Secret practice!*"

26

TAYLEY CALLS RIVER AND PUTS HER ON SPEAKER TO plan logistics. We can't hold our secret practice at my house because my mom would have a fit, and we don't want Noah watching us. Valentina's house is out because her mom and my mom talk. Tayley hasn't told her parents she's on the team yet, so we end up at River's house.

River lives in this large craftsman in the nice neighborhood in town. It's so old, it has one of those historical-society plaques on the front of it. Her back lawn is soft and green and perfect for rolling around in. River is a town girl—her parents are both dentists.

"Okay, Mara, tell us everything we need to know!" River says, descending her steps with water bottles for everyone.

The four girls gather around me, and I can't believe that I'm doing this. I have to remind myself that the worse they look, the worse people think I am. If they're really not going to quit, then helping them is only helping myself.

"Okay," I say. "What do you want to know that Coach hasn't taught you?"

"Three-point stance," Valentina says.

"That squatting thing you do before you tackle someone," Tayley says. "And I want to practice catching."

"Can you explain the difference between a halfback and a fullback? I keep getting them confused," River says. "Also every other position."

"Okay, sure," I say. "What else?"

"Are there any fun cheers that we do from the sidelines?" Carly asks. "Like in basketball?"

"Ooh, cheers!" Tayley exclaims, clapping her hands.

I *knew* Carly would derail us. "That's what the cheerleaders are for," I tell them.

"Yeah, but we could come up with some," she presses.

"I think it'll be nice to just focus on the game and not have to constantly try to keep the tone of everything light and cheerful," I say.

"When people are encouraged, they play better. That's science," Carly says back.

She's so *frustrating*. The other girls look like they're watching tennis, heads turning as we volley back and forth.

I unleash. "On the other hand, maybe we'll play better if we don't have to worry what people think of us. I'm sick of pretending I'm here to have fun and not to win. I'm not interested in color-coordinated shoelaces and socks and hair ribbons. I'm not just doing this to stay skinny. I'm here to *play*."

Carly blinks at me. "I can do cheers and wear hair ribbons and still win. Acting like I can't is actually kind of sexist."

Here we go. "Oh, okay. Yeah. Make me into the asshole because I'm sick of people expecting me to look cute while I play sports."

"Look, it's fine if you don't want to wear girly things. But there's no reason you can't be just as much a terrier *with* cute shoelaces on as you are without them," Carly says. "You're pretty tough. I can't imagine color-coordinating would stop you."

I open my mouth to say something back, but I don't have anything. She thinks I'm tough. That's interesting.

"I get what Mara's saying, though," Tayley says, relieving me of having to respond. "It's like my mom is always telling me to bring my makeup with me to my track meets so I can apply it after my races are over. She says she doesn't want me looking like a cherry tomato. It's like I have to overcompensate for being a good runner by being extra feminine when I'm done."

"I thought you were trying to get back *on* the basketball team, Mara," Valentina says. "Did you change your mind?"

"No, I am," I say. "That's why I got into this. But somewhere along the way, I started to really like football, too. I like how no one on the team cares what they look like. No one's apologizing for being a big sweaty mess. No one apologizes at all, actually. Not for wild passes or for stepping on someone's toe with their cleat. It's all just part of the game. No excuses necessary."

"I could stand with just ten percent more apologizing, actually," River says. "I think there's probably a happy medium there."

Carly drills her eyes into my head, brow furrowed like she's trying to solve a Rubik's Cube. It's unnerving, the way she just stares at people like that.

"What?"

"Sorry," she says, looking away. "You're just an enigma, that's all." She lets her dark hair fall over her face as she drops to the grass to retie a shoe I don't think needs retying.

"Okay, well, whatever. Let's get started. Three-point stance.

Start with your feet shoulder width apart," I say, showing them. They jump into position and enthusiastically follow my every instruction. I go around correcting their posture. "Straight back, Valentina. Straight. Straighter."

"It's straight!" she says.

"Straighter... *there* you go."

"Oh god, this is hard," she says. "This is basically a squat!"

"And after today's practice..." Tayley moans.

Carly's stance is perfect. Her broad frame looks like she was meant to be a linebacker—if she could only play other players her size. Like a Pee Wee team, maybe.

We practice dropping into three-point stance and then firing out of it. Then I show them the stomp-squeeze-sink-hands drill we practiced before tackling. Then we pull out the balls we swiped from my house and practice passing and catching for a while. I show River how to hold her feet and take a step as she passes. "Just like passing in basketball or baseball," I say.

"I don't play those sports," she says. "I don't play any sports! Oh my god, why am I doing this at all?" She slumps, letting the ball fall to the ground.

"It's okay, it's okay," I say. "You got this. Everyone was a beginner at some point. Just step and pass. Step and pass." I grab the ball and hand it to her. She steps and passes. The pass is wobbly, but the step is perfect. "You're getting it, there you go!"

It's weird, being encouraging of them for once, but it's a relief not having to wonder who's watching us or who's comparing me to them. To just be together, learning football, feels surprisingly good.

When everyone's exhausted from passing, we sit around the yard drinking water and eating orange slices River cuts up for us and I try to explain everything I know about every football position.

"Have you guys thought about what position you might want to play, if you get the chance?" I ask.

"I'm fast, so I thought maybe running back," Tayley says. "But then today happened and I really hate getting tackled. So I don't know."

"I don't think I'm good enough to play anything," River says morosely.

"This isn't the NFL," I say. "You don't have to be the best in the world, you just have to be willing to dig in."

Valentina picks at the grass. "What do *you* think I should play, Mara?"

I look her over. "You're powerful, especially in the lower body. Maybe a tight end?"

"Yeah, girl!" River hollers. "You *do* have a tight end!" River pokes Valentina in her butt, and they both giggle. I try not to blush at the accidental innuendo.

"What about me?" Carly asks.

"You have a tight end, too," River says.

"No, what position should I play?" Carly asks hopefully.

"I . . . I honestly don't know where I'd put you without worrying you'd get hurt," I tell her. "Kicker, maybe."

She scoffs in exactly the same way I did when Quinn suggested *I* play kicker. "Are you kidding me? No. I want to get touchdowns. I'm fast. If Quinn Kegley can be a receiver, I want to be a receiver."

My face must give away my doubt, because she doubles down. "Watch me, Mara Deeble."

"Okay," I say. I don't know if she can do it, but I do know that Carly won't give up easy.

# # #

Valentina drives me home, my bike still dangling out of the trunk of her car, both of us sweaty and tired, but in a good way. Her driving is less erratic this time. Maybe she's too tired to speed.

"Thank you for today," she says. "That was super cool of you."

"Yeah, it was fun," I say, surprising myself.

"Also, we're having a little party this weekend and we want you to come. Me and the other girls were saying how we gotta have regular get-togethers if we're gonna make it through this season."

"Oh," I say, trying not to sound disappointed. I'd rather just have a one-on-one party with Valentina. Which I guess would be less of a party and more of a date. What I'm saying is I want a date with Valentina.

"We're doing it at Carly's. Her mom works nights and also doesn't care if we drink her wine as long as we pay her back for it. It should be dope."

I would never willingly go to Carly's house in order to drink her mom's wine, much less fork over real money out of the truck fund for the privilege. I'd rather stay home and practice my drop step on the hoop in the driveway.

"You should come. It's on Friday night," she says.

I realize with relief. "Quinn's having a party that night for the team."

"Oh," Valentina says darkly. "We didn't hear about that one. I don't think they really want us there. Are you going?"

"He kind of... disinvited me, actually," I say. "After the article came out."

"Seriously? I thought you guys were friends."

"Yeah, we are. I'm sure he'll change his mind."

"Are you sure you even want to go? After one of them slashed your bike tires?"

This afternoon's secret practice was more fun than I thought it would be, and the girls aren't totally terrible. But when it comes down to it, Quinn's my best friend. And I'm sure he didn't have anything to do with my bike tires getting slashed. These girls are just here for a while, but Quinn and I are forever. Even if he was a jerk earlier.

"Well, if he doesn't," Valentina says, "you should come hang with us. It'll be chill, and no one will lay a finger on your bike, I promise."

I try to read her look. Is there more to that look than a friendly invite? I can't tell. "I'll think about it," I say, looking away before she can see how flustered she makes me.

27

I DIDN'T KNOW MY MUSCLES COULD GET THIS SORE.

Two practices a day is probably plenty. I don't need to be adding a third, secret practice on top of it. Especially not if I'm also going to be shooting hoops and doing my chores and stacking manure for Leroy and riding my bike to and from practice and helping Jupiter with her fence. Even though those last two are done for the moment. Still, maybe I need to take up reading between practices. A nice book never hurt anyone.

I cover my body in a thorough slathering of muscle cream after my shower before going to the kitchen for like six bowls of cereal. Noah's sitting at the counter, glued to his phone.

"Whew, what's that smell?" he asks, screwing up his nose.

"I took a shower. You should try it sometime," I say.

"Did you shower in peppermint milkshake?" he asks as I grab the milk away from him.

I pour my bowl of Frosted Mini-Wheats. "Hey, I know you're pissed at me or whatever, but I need a ride to practice this morning."

"What's wrong with your bike?"

"One of your asshole friends slashed my tires."

He sits up, looks me over. "Why?"

"You'll be shocked to learn they didn't leave a note."

"They slashed your tires?" he repeats incredulously. "How'd you get home?"

"I got a ride."

"From who?"

I sigh. "Valentina Cortez. But it's out of her way, and you and I live in the same house, so maybe you could help me out at literally no cost to you. You have to drive there anyway."

He takes a bite of his cereal. "Fine."

Thank god.

"But we're leaving in fifteen minutes, and if you're even *ten seconds* late, I'm leaving without you."

"Deal." Finally, I can save all my energy for the field. And I don't have to be seen astride that purple-and-pink horror show. It's almost like the tire slasher did me a favor. Almost.

# # #

The rest of the week whips past in a flurry of two-a-days. My muscles adjust to the demanding schedule, and now that I'm not biking twice a day, I can walk onto the field with that much more energy to devote to football.

I try to make things normal again with Quinn, serving up a snide comment about Curtis's foot odor, but Quinn just says, "Sorry we can't all smell like roses like you, Mara."

So, guess he's still pissed.

He does not reinvite me to his party. I think about going anyway, but why do I want to go to a party where I'm not welcome? Quinn will come around eventually, he just needs to work it out of his system. Hopefully sooner rather than later.

And that's how I find myself locking my bike (with its brand-new tubes—another hit to the truck fund) to a street sign outside the Elk Court Apartments on Friday night, wearing my favorite boots. I take a deep breath and get ready to walk into an apartment where a gaggle—yes, a gaggle—of girls is waiting for me, including Valentina. My nerves are a mess wondering what kinds of things go on at all-girl parties like this. Secret telling? Makeovers? I roll my shoulders and walk up to the front door. Whatever happens, I really hope we don't have to paint nails.

28

THE DOOR OPENS IMMEDIATELY AFTER I KNOCK.

"Mara came!" Carly exclaims, and I hear the other girls cheer in the background. I wish I could turn around and call Quinn to see if he wants to play *Mario Kart*, but I know he's probably wheeling in the keg for his own party right now.

"Shoes off, please!" Carly says chipperly. I hate taking my shoes off. It makes me feel trapped. Like I can't leave whenever I want because my boots are being held hostage.

I debated a long time before deciding what to wear tonight. I ended up going with my favorite pair of jeans, which are baggy enough that I don't feel like I'm wearing tights, but also they fit my thighs well—particularly lately, when it seems like my legs get bigger with every workout we do—plus a weathered Chris Stapleton T-shirt that I stole from Noah's closet that he stopped wearing because he recently decided he doesn't like country music anymore. Over it all, I wear a denim jacket I found at the thrift store in the men's department. I like the way it makes my shoulders look broad, but it comes in at the hips, like I'm a big triangle.

I dutifully kick off my boots into a pile of shoes by the door. There's a pretty clear demarcation between Carly's ballet flats and white sneakers and her mom's extensive collection of leather boots. Valentina's skateboard leans against the wall by the door.

"You came!" Tayley says excitedly.

"I came."

"Do you want some rosé?" Carly asks.

When I say sure, she pours me a glass. The color is so soft and Instagrammable, it has to be fake. I take the glass, feeling ironic about it.

Carly has turned all lights in the apartment off except for the twinkle lights that are strung everywhere. The other girls sit around in the living room, all but Tayley sipping wine. Tayley drinks an apricot La Croix and does not look self-conscious about it. Above us are tie-dyed sheets pinned to the wall that look like night skies. The apartment isn't fancy—all '90s wooden cabinets and graying cream carpet—but the Nakatas have made it their own with candles and brightly colored throw pillows on the faded couch. It strikes me that maybe Carly's family doesn't have a lot of money. The thing that looks the most valuable in the apartment is a scratched-up old telescope sitting by the front window, pointed toward the sky.

"Tayley is just about to tell us what happened when she told her mom about football!" River says, gesturing for me to sit down. I take the open couch cushion between her and Valentina, my pant leg brushing Valentina's as I sit.

"I thought she was going to have a conniption fit," Tayley says. "But it turned out that she just doesn't have the bandwidth for conniping. Like, she was *going to* yell at me, but the twins were literally running through the house having a rubber-band fight, and the baby had just woken up from her nap, and dinner was boiling over on the stove, and the phone was ringing with a diagnosis for the dog, who has a thyroid condition. And I was just standing there, waiting for the yelling to actually start."

"Oh my god. Classic," River says, laughing.

"She was like, 'Tayley, if you think—*Cam, STOP IT*—that you're going to play football—*I said let go of your brother*—then you have another think coming—*Tristan, take your finger out of that this instant*—I just don't know where you get these crazy ideas—*Piper, don't lick that, that is for DINNER...*"

We're dying laughing.

"So you can play?" Carly asks.

"Honestly, I think as long as I come home and do my chores, they don't have enough energy to care."

"Woo!" Valentina cries.

"That's awesome, Tayley," River says.

The door opens and Carly's mom comes in. No one moves or tries to hide the wine, which still feels weird, even though I know she's cool with it. Carly's mom is...well, she's hot. For a mom. I've seen her at our basketball games before, the only Asian mom in a sea of white and Latinx ones, but I've never talked to her. She has a pixie cut that frames her face, which gets messed up in a cool way when she takes her motorcycle helmet off. She's short like Carly, so the men's mechanic work shirt she's wearing under her leather jacket is too long on her, but she wears it open with a tight tank top underneath and tight black jeans. She looks a lot like Carly if Carly were ten times more badass and twenty years older. I feel myself staring, so I train my eyes on the carpet in front of me. A greasy paper bag lands in front of us with a thump.

"I brought you heathens sustenance," Carly's mom says.

"Sweet, onion rings!" River says, digging into the bag.

"Thanks, Mom," Carly says. "How was work?"

"Men are scum," Carly's mom says, taking off her motorcycle boots and kicking them into the pile of shoes. "But the tips were good." She comes over, swipes the open bottle of rosé from the center of our circle, and takes a swig from it. "How much have you guys had?"

"One bottle," Carly says like this is something they talk about all the time. "Plus that half you're swigging."

"I'm commandeering this, as is my right as caregiver." Carly's mom counts us. "Five people? You can have one more bottle, but that's it, okay? Did you eat all the spam musubi or did you leave me some?"

"There's two left," Carly says.

Carly's mom's eyes narrow as they land on me. Anticipating something, Carly says quickly, "She's fine, Mom."

"Isn't this the girl that laid you out last year?"

My stomach drops. "I can go," I murmur.

"Don't move a muscle," Carly says. "Mom, it's *fine*. That was a onetime thing."

Carly's mom levels me with a look. I'm, like, twice her size, but somehow I feel like she could still kick my ass. She says, "You lay a finger on my daughter in anger again and you're gonna answer to me, you hear me?"

"Yes, ma'am," I say.

She looks at me a long beat before relaxing suddenly. "All right, you kids have fun."

Carly hops to her feet. "Let's go make a fire. Someone grab the onion rings."

"Bring the shawl basket, Charlie!" Carly's mom calls after her.

We go outside and around the back of the apartment building, where a menagerie of old lawn chairs is set around a poured-cement fire pit. Within ten minutes, Carly has the fire lit and blazing, and Valentina is walking around with a basket containing knit shawls for us to wrap around our shoulders in the chilly night air. Tayley takes three—one for her shoulders and two for her lap and legs. She looks like a mummy.

"Thanks," I whisper to Valentina when she hands me a faded orange one with tassles.

"I'm glad you came," she says with a smile that makes my skin prickle.

Carly brought her telescope down from upstairs and is using an app on an old iPad that shows her where all the stars are to direct it to the right part of the sky.

"Trust me, Mars looks dope as hell right now," she murmurs into the telescope.

River leans back in her shawl and looks up at the sky. "Your mom's so cool. My mom *thinks* she's cool, but she isn't really. Not like Carly's mom–cool."

"Guys, I promise, whatever you think she is, she isn't," Carly says, staring at her cracked iPad with the star map on it.

"Well, she's a bartender and not a dentist, so that's already a step up," River says.

"Not paycheck-wise," Carly says.

"Oh. Yeah," River admits.

"Hey, I've been meaning to ask, why's your mom call you Charlie?" Valentina asks.

"It's my name," Carly says without looking up.

Tayley turns in her chair to look at her. "Your name's Charlie?"

"Yeah."

River passes the bag of onion rings to me, and I take a handful. They're getting cold, but they're still delicious. These days I feel like I can never get full. I take a couple more, then pass the bag to Valentina, who sits down on the other side of me. I hope it's a sign.

"But you've always been Carly," Valentina says.

"I like it better," Carly says. Then she pulls away from the telescope with purpose and looks at us and sighs. "My mom wanted a fun little tomboy for a kid who'd, like, grow up to ride motorcycles with her and drink tequila shots and go to rock shows in her hand-me-down ripped Stones tees. And instead, she got *me*. I like girl-cut T-shirts and banana bread and twinkle lights. I'm never going to be that 'cool girl with the boy name' that she wants me to be. And I think it's kind of bullshit that boyish names make people think girls are more cool anyway. If I could have made people call me Tiffany, I fuckin' would've."

Honestly, I would love to be named Charlie, but it's true it doesn't suit her. How would the world see me if my name were more masculine? How would people treat me if I went by Mo? Or, for that matter, Melissa?

River says, "I'll call you Tiffany if you want."

Everyone laughs, but then Tayley says, "I would, too."

"Whatever. Carly works," Carly says. "Anyway, it's too cloudy to see Mars. I'll look again in a bit." She takes a seat in the circle around the fire and wraps a shawl over her legs. "Okay, let's talk about who likes who," she demands, looking right at me.

My blood immediately runs cold. Does she know? I bring my arms in around my body, as far from Valentina as possible, just in case.

The other girls lean in. This is exactly what I was afraid this party would be. Gossiping, telling secrets, talking about boys. My secrets are mine to keep, thank you.

"I'll go first," Carly says. "I think Quinn likes Valentina."

Everyone squeals. Valentina whips her head to look at me.

"Don't look at me! I don't know!" I lie.

"C'mon, Mara, don't play coy," Valentina says. "I know you're, like, best friends with him."

I can't tell if she's upset by the idea or excited about it. Either way her eyes tell me she's desperate for confirmation. The last thing I want is for her to go after him, but maybe if she likes girls, she won't.

I sigh. "He told me he likes...your ass."

The girls go nuts, howling and slapping their thighs.

"We got ourselves a spy, ladies!" River hoots. Great, now I'm a double agent.

I watch Valentina for her reaction. She looks taken aback. "Is that all he said?"

I shrug. "Yeah."

"Huh." She leans back in her chair and looks into the fire.

"Come on," Carly says, a note of bitterness in her voice. "You didn't expect Quinn Kegley to like someone for their brain, did you? It's all T and A with him."

"That's not true," I say. Even though we're fighting right now, he's still my friend. "He's not some kind of monster."

Carly shrugs. "If you say so."

"It just seems like these white boys only ever care about my ass," Valentina says.

"I hear that," River says, nodding knowingly.

"It is a great ass, though," Valentina admits.

"Well, what other gossip you got, Mara?" River asks. "This is fun. Jock boys I might actually want to get with. The theater boys are all dweebs. Or gay." She pops a cold onion ring in her mouth. "Lovely people. Don't want to make out with any of them."

They look to me eagerly like I'm a scout who's come back with news from behind enemy lines. "I'm pretty sure Ranger is into Tayley." All eyes snap to Tayley, who shrinks into her chair.

"How? We've never even talked," she says.

"Because you're hot, girl!" Carly says.

"I'm not hot, I'm just skinny," Tayley protests, curling into a ball of embarrassment under her shawls. "I hate it." It's true that of all of us, she's the only one who could be considered skinny.

"You're skinny AND hot," Valentina says, and I wonder if it means anything that Valentina called another girl hot.

"He's nice, I think," Carly says. "He's been okay to us. Remember when he helped us with our pads?"

"Well, well, well, Carly Nakata is saying a boy is *okay*. What has the world come to?" I say.

"I'm not anti-boy," Carly says.

I laugh, and so does Valentina. "Sure, you're not," I say.

"I'm not! I think Ranger is good. And that guy Jerry Martinez is nice. He told me he liked my hustle once."

"Thirty guys on the team, and she likes two of them." Valentina laughs.

"It's just that whole group of terrible white boys I can't stand," Carly says. "You know, the ones who follow Quinn everywhere."

"You mean the Kool-Aid Club," I say.

"The what?!" River shrieks.

"The Kool-Aid Club. That's what they call themselves. You didn't know that?"

"I absolutely did not," Carly says, suppressing a laugh. "That's the stupidest name I've ever heard."

I'm so used to it that I never think about it, but yeah. It's the stupidest name I've ever heard, too.

"Okay, what about Noah? He's seeeeexy," River says. I screw up my face. "Oh, don't give us that look, Mara, your brother's hot and he's the QB. That's just facts."

"Facts," Tayley adds, finally relaxing now that the spotlight is off her.

"I don't know who Noah likes," I say. "We don't talk about that stuff."

"All right, then, who do *you* like?" Carly asks, looking me right in the eye, and the things I would do to not answer that question with Valentina sitting next to me approach the homicidal.

"Oh, don't scare her off," Valentina says, stepping in, my princess in shining armor. "We want her to come back next week."

I'm not sure I will if this is what I can expect each time. The fire is nice, the food is good, the rosé is fine, I guess. But it's exhausting talking about everyone's feelings all the time.

"Okay, Valentina," Carly says, turning her sights on her, "your turn. Who do you think is the cutest person on the team?" I can't help but notice Carly says *person* and not *boy*. Does she know something I don't? Or is she fishing, too?

"I don't want to say," Valentina says, shifting under her shawl, in order to tuck her legs up under her on the chair. She looks like a puppy curled up by the fire. I just want to cuddle her and tell her she doesn't have to tell us anything she doesn't want to.

But please, oh please, just give me a sign if it's me.

"You don't have to," Tayley says sympathetically.

River scoffs and stuffs another onion ring in her mouth. "But we'll have more fun if you do."

"Not that our fun should be your top priority," Tayley says, ever the peacemaker.

"Guys, shut up and let her talk," Carly says, and all eyes go back to Valentina.

"I just...I don't think you'll understand," she says, and she looks at me.

My heart skips a beat. Maybe two. Maybe all of them. Maybe I'm dead right now and this is the afterlife. But surely God wouldn't create an afterlife where I have to hang out at an all-girl party, would He? Maybe He would if it meant I got to make out with Valentina at the end of the night.

She looks away, but I'm certain I know what that look means. I know it. I read a book once that said that closeted gay people have to communicate with a series of meaningful looks and coded language. That's exactly what this was. I feel like a top-notch gay for seeing it. The Bletchley Circle of gays, decoding all the secret messages.

Valentina has a crush on me?

Could it be true?

I have to do something to show her she's not alone.

"I have a crush, too," I say, surprising everyone. I glance at Valentina, and she's looking at me expectantly. "But that's all I'll say."

Everyone sighs back into their seats.

"This is some kind of bullshit," River says. "Why's everyone being all *The Americans* about it? I'll tell you all my crush, I don't care. It's Coach Gary." She takes a swig of rosé. Valentina busts up laughing. "I can't help it. It's that dad bod," River says, grabbing her own soft belly with both hands for emphasis. "And his visor."

"Oh my god, and his clipboard." Tayley giggles.

"I like Howard's comb-over," Valentina adds.

Carly sulks in her chair, not laughing, just staring into the fire, her fist grasped around her glass, the onion ring bag torn open in her lap.

"Well, I don't have a crush at all," she says flatly. "Nobody at this school is ready for me."

"If they're not ready for Carly, imagine how not ready they are for Tiffany," I say. Carly shoots me a good-natured side eye, and the other girls crack up even harder. I risk a glance at Valentina, and her face is illuminated, glorious in firelight.

29

HOURS LATER, WE'VE STOLEN TWO MORE BOTTLES OF rosé from Carly's mom, who's asleep on the couch, snoring as the local news plays on the TV. We've also pilfered more La Croix for Tayley, a bag of white cheddar–flavored chickpea fake Cheetos, a bag of baby carrots, and a can of spray cheese, and we're mixing and matching. Apparently, everyone is as constantly hungry as I am these days, which is a relief to know.

Carly finally finds Mars through the telescope. "It wasn't too cloudy after all, it was just in a different part of the sky than I thought," she says, embarrassed.

Everyone dutifully looks through the telescope, but it's clear Carly is the only planet nerd among us. Telescope time turns into whose-house-can-we-see-into-with-this-thing time as River cries out, "I think I can see Mrs. Tantlebaum through her living room window!"

"I *love* her," I say.

"Ugh, so do I," Carly says. "I love her hair."

"Me too!" I exclaim, then, when Carly looks at me, wonder if I'm being too bold with the declarations. Blame it on the rosé.

"I'm going to look for someone naked," River announces next.

Tayley sprays cheese into her mouth and holds the can out to me. "Want thome?"

Valentina stands off to the side, staring up at the stars without the telescope. I'm still thinking about what she said. How can I find out at this party who her crush is? I wave Tayley off and head back toward the fire, passing by Valentina on the way, hoping she'll follow me.

But she doesn't follow me. Carly does.

Carly sits in the chair next to me. Valentina's chair.

"There's something I've been wanting to say to you," she says. She sounds a little bit drunk.

Her legs are too short to put her feet up on the edge of the fire pit like I'm doing, so she stands back up and drags another chair over and puts her feet up on that. Rearranging the furniture to her standards, not caring that someone else will want to sit in that chair again later. Classic Carly. I guard myself against whatever's coming.

She puts her hand out. "I want to bury the hatchet," she says.

"What?"

"I want to move on from what happened during basketball. New leaf, all that. I don't want to fight anymore. What do you say?"

"I don't want to fight, either," I say, which is the truth, but also because if I fight with her, I get kicked off the basketball team again. But it's not quite that easy. "How do I know I can trust you?"

She drops her hand, staring into the fire, really thinking about it. "Mara..." she starts, then reconsiders. Finally, she looks at me. "I guess you can't. But I want you to be able to. So just know that I regret making a scene. I shouldn't have done it in front of everyone."

I've never seen her like this—contrite. "What I don't get is why you were trying to get me benched. We were tied, there were three minutes left in the game. Didn't you want to win?"

"Some things are more important than winning," Carly says.

"Why would you even care if I have a concussion?"

Carly gapes at me like I'm dense. "I'm not allowed to care about my fellow teammates?"

I meet her eye and hold it. Carly came out to the school in the most Carly way possible: an opinion piece in the school paper about the lack of resources for LGBTQIA+ students. It was angry and eloquent and well-argued. She was fifteen years old. By the time I come out to my family, Carly will have been out for at least three full years, maybe more. Is there anything she knows about being gay that I don't just because she's out of the closet? To my knowledge, she's never had a girlfriend. I don't even know if she's kissed a girl. She and I aren't so different, except for the pride flag pin on her bag. But she's living life inside a two-way mirror. Everyone knows what's in her heart, but she doesn't know what's in mine. Can she tell that I'm like her?

"And what about you?" Carly asks. "Anything to say?"

My heart stops for a second before I realize what she's asking. Is it really possible I'd never apologized to Carly for hitting her? "Carly, I'm sorry I hit you." Something releases as the words come out. The relief swirls through me. "Not just because I got kicked off the team, but because it was selfish. I was mad, but that was no reason to hit you like that."

Carly pauses. "Was that so hard?"

I can't help but smile.

"Apology accepted?" I ask.

"Accepted. Friends."

I take Carly's hand, callused from practice, and shake it. Her hand is warm and small in mine, and it lingers a touch longer than necessary, like she's really serious about this truce. I give her hand a squeeze and try to let go. Her hand drops back to her side, but her eyes don't leave me.

A thought alarms me: Here, in the light of the fire, Carly Nakata is kind of hot. I must have had more to drink than I thought. She's not my type at all—girly and too small for me. She belongs with someone more her size, like Quinn, if she were straight. Although she would eat him alive. Quinn needs to be the smartest one in every relationship, and Carly would outwit him by a mile. He's a candle and she's a fire hose.

I have to admit, she's impressive. I know I can be a brick wall, hard to penetrate. But even if it's just to make me mad, Carly knows how to quickstep around my defenses. You have to give her credit for that.

"Friends," I say.

"Cool, but there's actually one more thing I need from you," Carly says.

"What?"

"I need to punch you."

I look at her, trying to decide whether she's being real. She looks dead serious. "You what?"

"It's a question of fairness. You got to punch me. In the *boob*. Not only that, you sent me through the water table. I never got to hit you back. So. To be even, I get to punch you."

"I think we were even when I got kicked off the basketball team," I say. "It's not like I haven't faced consequences."

"Still," Carly says. "It's a question of fairness. Stand up." She hops to her feet, wobbles slightly, then rights herself. "Let's go."

She hops back and forth between her feet, and I can't help but laugh. "You're serious."

"I said let's *go*, Deeble. Stand up!"

I get to my feet and step away from the fire. I don't want this to end with me falling into hot coals.

"All right," I say. "Not in the nose, please."

"I will choose the location myself, thank you," Carly says, putting her fists up like an old-timey boxer.

"What's going on?" River asks, noticing us.

"Carly won't be friends unless she can punch me."

"It's a question of fairness!" Carly exclaims.

"Is this a good idea?" Tayley asks, worried. "This isn't a good idea."

"Can't you die from being punched wrong?" Valentina asks.

"Yes," Carly says. "Mara should be very worried. Her life is in my hands right now." She starts to hop around me so I have to turn in a circle to keep her in my sights.

"All right, let's get this over with," I say.

"Just remember, you can't hit me back," Carly says. "Or you're not allowed to play basketball again."

"Not only that," I say, "but it's a question—"

"A question of fairness, that's right!" Carly says. "Ready yourself, woman!" Then she charges at me. I bring my arms up to protect my face, and Carly slips her punch in under my elbow and hits me just under the ribs.

She doesn't pull it. The breath leaves my lungs in a rush, and I double over. *Fuck*, that hurts.

"Oh my god," Valentina says.

"Do I need to call nine-one-one?" Tayley asks, voice rising in panic.

"She's fine, you guys," River says. "She just got punched."

Carly's feet come into my view as I feel her tentatively touch my shoulder. "Mara?" Her voice sounds worried. "I'm sorry. Was that too hard? Shit. Sorry. Sorry. This was supposed to be fun. Guys? What do I do?"

Breath back, I wrap my arms around her legs and—

"Ahhhh!" I lift Carly onto my shoulder as she screams and Tayley screams and Valentina yells, "Holy crap!" and River laughs hysterically and I run around the fire pit with Carly raining fists down harmlessly on my back before I put her down again.

"You asshole, I was scared!" Carly yells at me, shoving my shoulder. River wipes tears from her eyes. Tayley looks like she might pass out from stress.

Valentina shakes her head and goes back to the telescope. "You guys are so dumb."

"Okay, *now* friends," I say. Carly plops into her chair, and I sit back down in mine. The other girls turn back to the telescope.

I rub my abdomen where Carly's punch still throbs, but the smile lingers. I glance sidelong at Carly.

She tucks her legs up under her and gazes into the fire, smirking. Part of me is jealous that she can get her feet up on the chair. If I tried to do that, I would feel like an orangutan in a high chair. Most of the time, I like being big. I like the power it lends me, and I like the effect it has on boys when I want to remind them that I could squash them. But at times, like looking at Carly now, I'm reminded how the world must feel different for small people.

On the other hand, Carly really probably shouldn't be playing football. She's not just small. She's inexperienced. She might be fast, but one good hit could lay her out for the season. Part of me wants to tell her she should quit this stupid exercise before she gets seriously hurt. But that's exactly what I get pissed at other people for telling me. Is it just because she's a girl that I feel this way? Maybe she's right that I suffer from the same misogyny that annoys me in the boys. But when I think about some giant defender from Gravel Bay smashing his head into Carly's, the preemptive rage fills me up. I don't know what I would do if that happened, but it wouldn't be pretty. Probably, it would involve a lot of punching and some blood. Probably I wouldn't stop until I heard the satisfying crack of bone.

I'm grateful the others are still too distracted by the telescope and the spray cheese to pay attention to us right now, because from the way we're sitting side by side, staring into the fire, they might get the wrong idea about us. Here I am, fantasizing about retribution for some imaginary crime against Carly, when we've barely just become friends again. I'm just glad she can't read my mind.

"What are you thinking about?" I ask Carly to get my mind off it.

"I was just wondering," she says. "Why do you always hang out with them instead of us?"

Not what I was expecting her to say. "Who, the boys? They're my friends."

Carly sighs and slips lower in her chair. "Yeah, but, like, you ignored us for, like, the whole first week of practice. It kinda sucked."

"Because last week they liked me," I say. "And then you guys showed up and I became 'one of the girls.'"

"But being one of the girls is the best! Who wants to be at the boy party when you can be here?"

"I do," I say. "Like I said, they're my friends. Or, at least they were before you started causing problems."

"I'm just shining a light on problems that were already here."

I sigh. "If you want to blast your opinions all over the place, run for student body president. If you want to play football, shut up and play football. It's that easy."

"I know you want what we're doing here to be some kind of apolitical athletic endeavor, but it's not possible. Everything is political. Us playing football. You wearing that bandanna." What about my bandanna, now? "You know what else is political? Your tires getting slashed."

I pull my hair out of my ponytail. The flyaways are bothering me. I remake the pony as tight as I can.

Carly keeps talking. "You realize, don't you, that no one wants us here. Not Coach, not the other guys, not the rest of the town. Doesn't that bother you?"

My anger has been swirling for a minute, or maybe an hour, or maybe it hasn't stopped for the last month. It's always there these days, and right now it's telling me to *shut this down*.

"I don't know. *I don't know.* I just want to play football with my friends. That's it." She does this. She gets in your head until you can't think straight anymore.

"It's not that simple, Mara. It's just not."

I rub my abdomen again, not because it hurts but because I suddenly can't believe I let her hit me like that. Like we could just become friends. Like there wasn't too much between us.

"Everything's always on your terms, isn't it, Carly?"

I don't know what I want. Or, yes, I do. I want her to shut up. I want Quinn to talk to me again. I want everything to go back to normal. I want Carly to never have inserted herself in any of this.

"Hey, guys, let's take five. Who wants chips?" Tayley asks, clearly worried. The other girls have taken notice again. No one wants chips.

"You've never liked me," Carly accuses, pointing a finger. I can see the flint of her dark brown eyes, mad and staring. Her pink lips are turned into a scowl. A strand of her ponytail has come loose and hangs in front of her eye, and she angrily swipes it away. *She's* angry? Good. "I've been nothing but nice to you, and you've never liked me. Why? What'd I do?"

What hasn't she done? She's irritating and she doesn't stop. Can't she see how disruptive that is to the rest of us? Can't she see how that would make me feel? Not all of us can slap rainbow pins on our bags. Not all of us can stand up at the school board meeting and yell about gay rights. Not all of us are as lucky as she is. But I can't say any of that.

"Guys, what happened to friends?" River asks. "Remember? Like, five minutes ago?"

I feel the eyes of everyone on me. I can't bring myself to look at the others. I don't want them to see me like this—ugly, mad.

I stand up and head for the street.

I hear Carly call "Mara!" after me, but the blood is already rushing in my ears, and a new feeling I can't even name is brimming, and whatever the feeling is, it's coming with tears. I rush for the street so the others don't see me cry.

I turn the corner of the apartment building and collapse onto the curb next to my bike. My breath comes ragged and panicky. I try to just breathe deep, but when I let it out, it shakes. I'm a mess. I'm such a mess. See, this is why I hate hanging out with girls. With Quinn or Noah, we could have just fought and then been over it. But Carly wants to talk and talk and talk and *talk* until our ears bleed and our brains are mush and we forget what we were even angry about anymore.

"Mara?" a small voice says from behind me.

Shit. Valentina.

I put my head against my knees. I don't want her to see me like this.

"Is it okay if I sit?" she asks.

I don't trust myself to speak yet. I wipe my eyes as covertly as possible so she doesn't know I was crying.

I hear her sit down on the curb next to me. Her knee peeks out of the hole in her black jeans.

"Carly wanted to come after you, but I said you probably just needed space." She pauses. "I can go if you want."

I let out a long breath. It comes out smooth. I decide to trust my voice. "I just like playing football. That's all."

"I know." There's a long pause, then she adds, "I wish it were that easy."

It's late, and there's no traffic on the street. Valentina's hair is lit from behind by a streetlight, giving her a halo.

"Do *you* like it?" I ask. "Football?"

"I like . . ." She thinks. "I like the running. I like breaking away from the pack. I like it when I catch the ball. That feels incredible. I don't love getting tackled." She laughs under her breath. "I could stand with, like, half as much hitting."

"Is it bad that I kind of love the hitting?"

"I don't think so," she says. "You're good at it."

She meets my eyes. My argument with Carly feels distant, even though I know it just happened. It's like I've been sitting here on this curb with Valentina for hours. I want to stay here all night.

The longer she doesn't look away, the faster my heart beats. This has to be it. It just has to be. There's no other explanation. All my wondering, all my questions. They could be answered right here if I just kissed her. My mouth feels dry. I don't know how to get there from here.

In my hesitation, she continues. "When you joined the team, you know, I thought you were the coolest girl in school."

"You did?" This girl is trying to kill me.

"We all did. It was Carly's idea for us to join, obviously. But when she said it, I just thought... *Yes. I want to do that. I want to be like Mara Deeble.*"

It's like she can see directly into my heart. She's looking back at me. She wants to be like Mara Deeble. Mara Deeble with the boys' clothes. Mara Deeble who plays football. Mara Deeble who can't control her temper, and who isn't very good at feelings. I feel like kind of a mess all the time, and she likes it.

It's now or never, Mara Deeble. Go for the big play.

I take a deep breath... and lean in. Closer, closer. *Please* let this be the right move. I brace myself for her to pull away. But she doesn't pull away.

Our lips meet.

Holy shit, we're kissing.

It feels like the Fourth of July in my chest. My lungs are full of sparklers, my heart is a firework. I can't hear anything over the steady crack of its Roman-candle heartbeat. I can barely think past:

Holy SHIT, we're kissing.

My knee bumps hers. It breaks a spell. She pulls away. I open my eyes. Whatever ecstatic explosions are going off in my body... they're not going off in hers. It's clear from her face. She's shocked.

She stands up.

This isn't happening.

She takes a step back.

Oh my god, this isn't happening. Please. Let's rewind. Let's go back to the kissing, before the kissing, before she told me she wanted to be like me, before she walked up. Let's go back and I tell her to go away and she does, and I'm left alone and this horrifying mistake never happened.

She opens her mouth to speak, but she doesn't say anything.

"Don't..." is all I can say.

"Mara..."

"I'm sorry." I kissed her when she didn't want to be kissed. I thought I gave her time to pull away, but maybe I didn't. I should have asked. "I'm sorry," I say again.

Oh my god, she's going to tell everyone. Tell them what they already know. Mara Deeble is a dyke. I mean, obviously. Just look at her. Everyone knows it on some level already. But now they'll know she tried to make a move on Valentina Cortez. Of all people. Who thought she could ever get with Valentina?

It's my turn to stand up. I walk around her, giving her a wide berth. Making it clear: *Don't worry, I won't come near you again.* I fumble with my bike lock.

"Mara, it's okay," she says. But it's not.

My mom...my mom cannot find out. How could I make a mistake this big? What happened to waiting until college?

"My parents can't know," I say.

She touches her lips.

"Valentina," I say, harder now.

I thought my heart was beating hard before. Now it's a goddamn shoe in a dryer, tossing around, ten seconds from breaking the whole machine.

"Of course."

"I'm sorry," I say again, and I get on my bike and pedal as hard as I can away from her.

30

I DON'T KNOW WHERE TO GO. I CAN'T GO HOME—I'M too hyped up. The only person I want to see is Quinn but he told me to stay away. Well, fuck that. We're best friends. He'll get over it.

It's a twenty-minute bike ride to Quinn's house. I hear the voices and the music from the porch. Everyone inside is supremely drunk. Ranger waves at me, slopping beer over the sides of his cup.

I walk straight into the kitchen and fill up a cup from the keg.

"Whoa, Mara's here and she's drinking!" Curtis Becker yells at the top of his voice. I empty my cup and start filling it up again. The faster I can get drunk, the faster I can forget the feeling of Valentina's lips.

Then Wayne is there. I expect him to insult me, but instead, he goes, "Chug, chug, chug." And then everyone in the kitchen is saying it. Maybe everyone in the party. Maybe everyone in Elkhorn.

My cup is empty again. I try to refill it, but someone takes it out of my hand. "Enough," he says. Fuck that person. Who was that?

Jerry? Someone else puts another cup in my hand. Someone good. I take a gulp, then choke it back up, because it's not beer. It's whiskey. I take a sip. It burns. It's perfect.

Then Quinn shows up, elbowing his way through the crowd.

"I thought I told you you weren't invited," he says.

"Fuck those girls," I say.

His eyebrows go up.

"They're posers," I say.

He looks around to make sure everyone's hearing this.

"They're not football players," I say. "Not like us."

I down the rest of the whiskey.

Quinn slaps me on the back. "Okay," he says. "Mara's back, everybody!"

The whole house cheers.

Ranger finds me. "Are you okay?" he asks, concerned.

"Better than ever," I say. "Where's Noah?"

"He didn't come."

"He always comes to these things."

"Yeah, I dunno."

Whatever. My brother is the last person I care about tonight.

The living room is a dance floor, but the only one dancing is me. "Join me!" I yell at Stetson over a Florida Georgia Line song. He shakes his head. "Come on. Your name is *Stetson*, how are you not two-stepping *all the time*?"

Stetson reluctantly allows me to take his hand and start in a two-step with him. I hear guys cheering. I've forgotten a few of the steps from fifth grade, when we also learned the line dance and the square dance in PE, because that's the kind of town this is. No one seems to care. Stetson is keeping up and pretending to tip a cowboy hat to me between stanzas. He's not so bad. I'm glad I came.

Then Stetson is being pulled away, and Quinn cuts in. "I love this song," Quinn says, and before I know it, his hands are on my waist, and we're two-stepping. He's not quite as good as Stetson was.

I can barely feel Quinn's touch at first, but then his hand drops a little lower, then a little lower.

"Are you touching my ass?" I say. I don't remember *that* from fifth grade.

"What if I am?" Quinn says back.

What if he is?

What if nothing matters anymore? What if everything's already upside down so who gives a shit?

Quinn moves closer. Is this what Quinn looks like when he's putting moves on someone?

His voice is low. "Come on, Mara. You know this day has been a long time coming."

I look down at Quinn, and he has this slow smile on his face. Total confidence that I've always wanted him. I want to recoil, but I don't. Maybe this is fine. Maybe being seen kissing Quinn Kegley is exactly the right thing my reputation needs right now. See? Nothing straighter than this girl right here.

And then it's happening. Quinn is on his toes, his hand squeezing my ass, his tongue in my mouth, tasting like whiskey, the room of guys oohing.

I regret it instantly. I try to pull away, but he holds me firmly. Nothing is worth this.

Then Quinn rolls his hips and I feel his dick, stiff against my thigh, and I shove him. He stumbles back. I wipe his spit from my mouth.

Quinn is laughing. "That why you came tonight?" He readjusts his crotch in his jeans.

I swing. The punch lands square across his nose. He doubles over yelling, "Fuck, Mara!"

The room twirls around me, just once, and then rights itself. This party is too loud, too crowded. I head toward the hallway and guys part for me, staring. This is where walls would be nice. I need the bathroom. There's a line. And I don't need the bathroom, not really. I see the front door and, yes, that's what I need. I book it. The air outside is cool and breezy and feels like an ocean whisper on my face.

An ocean whisper? Oh my god, I might be drunk. That's okay, I just have to get home to my bed. It's not drinking and driving if you're riding a bike, right?

What the *hell* was Quinn thinking?

I spit onto his front lawn. Spit his spit back out.

My fist hurts.

"Mara?" Ranger stands on the front porch, calling to me. He doesn't have his coat on and it's starting to mist. "Are you okay?"

"I'm fine, Ranger. I'm a champ. I'm a star. I'm unstoppable."

"Are you sure?" He doesn't sound convinced.

"Go inside, you look cold." He stands there a minute watching me try to toe the kickstand up. It takes three tries. "Go!" Finally, he goes back in, rubbing his arms.

I straddle the bike and kick off and start coasting down Quinn's wet, sloped driveway, the hubbub of the party fading, and the cool, quiet night closing in. It's dark out ... *too dark.* Shit, I should turn on my headlight. I fumble for the light, but as soon as I take one hand off the handlebars, I wobble, then overcorrect, then veer, slip, crash. It's loud. The light skids away. Then it's quiet again. Wow, the sky is pretty. So many stars tonight. How could Quinn have done that to me?

Ow. *Ow*, oh no, it hurts, ow. My elbow might be broken. No, it definitely is. So long, football dreams. So long, NFL. Oh my god, so long basketball, too. Wow, and I'll have to tell my parents I was drinking, so so long *me*, I guess. Maybe I'll tell them Noah spiked my drink. Noah's fault. I giggle. Ow. It makes my elbow hurt somehow. Where was Noah, anyway?

Fuck Quinn. He's never tried that before. Why now? In front of all those guys? I won't be able to look them in the eye at practice Monday.

Practice. I can't go to practice. I've dislocated my arm. I clearly need an ambulance, but I cannot go back into the house to ask them to call one. I don't want them to see me like this, in my darkest hour. No, I don't want them telling the story of my decline. And I don't want to see Quinn again. Maybe ever.

But what do I do? I can't get home. I can't go back.

Jupiter.

The idea comes from outer space. Like a rocket. A divine rocket idea. Jupiter lives down the road. I'm still flat on my back. Ow. I don't want to get up, but I must. I can't die out here, not like this.

Gingerly, I get to my knees (ow), then to my feet (ow), then get my bike and reattach the light (super ow) and walk down the drive, turn right, and continue down the road until Jupiter's house comes into view. Her lights are still on, thank god. I drop my bike on her front lawn and knock. The rain is coming down harder now. My jeans stick to my thighs where they're wet. I start to shiver.

"Mara? What's wrong?" Jupiter's face turns to panic as soon as she opens the door.

"I need an ambulance. I'll never play football again," I say, holding out my arm so she can see my career-ending injury.

"Are you... *drunk*?" she asks, squinting at me under her porch light.

"I kissed Valentina." My tongue feels too big in my mouth. Is that a thing? Is my tongue growing? "It was bad."

Jupiter pushes the door open. "Okay, come in." She doesn't look panicked anymore. Maybe I wasn't clear enough about the ambulance.

Jupiter's house is warm. My butt feels damp where I fell. I hope it's not blood. I imagine my pants filling up with blood from my butt. Butt blood. Gross. I twist to try to look at my backside and breathe relief. Just rain wet, not blood wet.

"I thought your mom forbade us from seeing each other," Jupiter says.

"She's a dictator," I say. "I don't recognize her authority."

Jupiter has an old faded couch of indiscernible color that looks like she pulled it off the curb somewhere for free.

"What color is that couch?" I ask her, because it's bugging me.

"It used to be green," she says. "Now it's kind of... I dunno, taupe?"

I don't like it. It's not anything. It's just kind of middle color. It doesn't feel like Jupiter. Jupiter is like a vibrant blue. Quinn is jungle green. Valentina is skinned-knee red. Carly is purple pizzazz. *I* might be taupe.

"I hate taupe."

"Okay, well, thanks for coming by to insult my couch," Jupiter says. "This has been fun so far."

"No, that's not..." Shit, I wasn't talking about the couch, I was talking about me. But I can't tell her that. "Sorry. It's a nice couch."

"Sit down."

"My pants are wet," I mumble. "Don't worry, it's not blood."

She blinks and then tosses me a towel from a hook.

"Sit on the dog towel." She runs a hand over her head. "I wish Reese were here. They'd know what to do with you. You want some tea or something?"

"Okay." I never drink tea, but I want to see what it's like, sitting in Jupiter's house, drinking her tea. I sit on the taupe couch, I'm sure blending into nothingness, and look around her living room. Her house has walls, so I can't see the kitchen, but I hear her clink around getting cups out. One wall of her living room is entirely houseplants on wood shelves, and another wall is a mosaic of different-size framed concert posters for bands I've never heard of.

"So, you kissed Valentina?"

Sleater patters into the living room, wagging, and pushes her head up under my hand so I'll pet her. I don't want to talk about Valentina. I stroke Sleater's big soft head and read the concert posters.

"The Butchies," I say, just to hear the word in my mouth, as Jupiter returns with our cups of tea.

"You'd like them," Jupiter says, putting down the cups and stooping over a plastic bin of records. She pulls out an album and puts it on, moving the needle gently into place. Fast guitars come out of the speakers, followed by fast drums and multiple female voices. It's not what I usually listen to, but something about the three women with short hair on the concert poster makes me not want to look away.

"Okay, show me where it hurts," she says, turning back to me, and I point to my heart. She almost smiles. "Where else?" I slip out of my jacket and put my arm out. I had almost forgotten I'd broken it. Red road burn runs angrily down my forearm and over my elbow.

"Oh yeah," she says, "you done this one good. Did you try to ride your bike in this state?" I nod, embarrassed. "Well, you learned that lesson. Don't get on wheels after you've been drinking, Mara. Even bikes. You're lucky it's only this bad."

She pulls out a first aid kit from her hall closet and cleans my arm up. It stings worse than one of Noah's arm burns. Sleater sits on my feet and licks my hand until I pat her, which takes my mind off my arm.

"You don't want to talk about Valentina?"

"She's not gay," I say.

"Did she say that?"

"With her face," I say. "Like this." I make a horrified expression.

Jupiter sucks her teeth. "I'm sorry."

"So then I went to Quinn's. And I might have had a drink."

"You're kidding."

"Or more. And we danced and made out."

"Who? You and Valentina?"

"No, Valentina was earlier. At Carly's. This is at Quinn's."

"Wait, sorry, who made out with who?" Jupiter asks.

"Quinn. Made out with me."

Jupiter finishes putting a Band-Aid on my arm and frowns at me. "How did that happen?"

"We were dancing, and then his tongue was licking my tongue and he was, like, trying to rub his dick on my leg through his pants."

Jupiter drops her head into her hands, then looks back at me. "Mara, I'm so sorry."

"I pushed him away."

"And then what?"

"And then I punched him. And then I came here."

"This *just* happened?"

I nod. My eyes are so heavy I'm having trouble keeping them open.

"Will you get in trouble for fighting?" Jupiter asks.

My stomach drops as I realize what I did. I punched Quinn with about a hundred witnesses. "Shit" is all I can manage to say.

"Okay, don't think about it now. What happens, happens."

I cradle my tea in my hands, feeling miserable. Indigo curls up on top of my feet. I settle into the couch. I don't want to go home. I want this life.

"Will you adopt me?" I murmur.

Jupiter becomes very still. "Mara," she says. "You have to go." She climbs to her feet. "I'm so sorry. You had a bad night, but your mom doesn't want you here, so I have to respect that. Plus, it's—" She checks her watch. I love that she has a watch. It's a gay move, having a watch. "Past midnight."

I don't move. I don't ever want to move. I don't want to go back to my house and my life. I just want to live here and listen to every one of Jupiter's gay records and feed her chickens and never see another person in Elkhorn ever again. Is that too much to ask? "I want a watch," I say.

"C'mon, Mara, grab your stuff. I'm giving you a ride. You're not getting back on that bike in this state. We can talk about me being your Miss Honey when you're sober."

It takes everything I have to get off this gorgeous, incredible, comfortable taupe couch. I take back anything bad I ever said about it.

I reluctantly give Sleater and Indigo kisses on their pillowy ears. Outside, Jupiter starts loading my bike in the back of her hatchback.

"Thank you," I say.

She nods, but she seems off. I shouldn't have come.

The ride home is quiet except for the sound of the windshield wipers. The stoplights in town have already started blinking red. All the stores are closed except the couple bars along the main strip, guys smoking outside, their cowboy hats hiding their eyes from the yellow streetlamps.

The silence is stifling. I press my fists together in my lap and try not to cry. I'm not sure what I did wrong, but I think she's unhappy with me.

A block from my house, Jupiter pulls over.

"You can make it from here, right?"

"Yeah."

"Good." She reaches for her door handle.

"Are you...mad at me?"

She looks at the sky and lets out a breath.

"Just tell me what I did wrong so I can not do it again. I promise. Whatever it is." I can feel the tears threatening to well, and I try to force them away.

"It's not you," she says with an exasperated tone, then catches herself. "Look, you had a bad night. A really bad one. Honestly, I'm sorry about Valentina, and fuck that dude Quinn. I want you to stay far away from him." She sighs. "But this puts me in a weird position. I know you're not thinking about this stuff, and that's fine, but just consider it from my point of view. It's past midnight. You're, what, sixteen?"

"Yeah," I mumble, keeping my eyes on my knees.

"You're underage. I'm thirty-five. I look"—she gestures to herself—"the way I look. That's hard enough for people around here to deal with. But they see me out and about with you after dark? They hear you were at my house? After your mom already put her foot down? Mara, it won't end well. For either of us."

"I'm sorry," I say, feeling bad that I made her feel bad.

"It's not your fault. I just...I don't know if I can be that person for you. The person you call, or show up at their door. I wish I could, but..."

"Yeah, no," I say, reaching for the door handle. "Of course. I won't do it again."

"Do you have other people? Not Quinn."

"Yeah, totally," I lie.

Jupiter rubs the buzzed hair at the back of her head. I'm a terrible liar. And I'm still willing myself not to cry, because I don't want her to know how freaked out I am right now, because I still want her to think I'm cool, even if she doesn't want to hang out anymore.

I get it, though. I'm a kid. That's all I am to her. And she's this adult who knows shit and owns records and I'm just some dumb girl she picked up at the hardware store who can swing a hammer. I'm the taupe one. There's just not that much to me.

I want to forget that this night ever happened.

"Well, okay, bye, then," I say.

"I'm sorry, Mara."

"Yup." I open the door, and I can feel my breath hitching in my throat. *Not yet.* She gets out, too, and helps me get my bike out of the back.

"Walk it, please," she says.

"Yup," I say again, not looking at her. "Thanks for the ride."

"Of course. Sorry again."

And I walk away, the tears rising in my throat with every step.

"Drink water when you get home!" she calls after me, and I don't turn around.

I hear her door close, but she doesn't turn on the car, just watches me until I turn down my road. Once I'm out of sight, I let the tears stream down my face, but crying just makes me feel

weak, and dumb for ever thinking I could be friends with someone like Jupiter. And *why* did I ask her to adopt me? It was a joke.
She should know it was a joke. Why am I so stupid all the time,
especially when it's important? And why did I crash my bike in
the first place? I should never have even gone to that party. Either
party. I should have just stayed home. Nothing good happens when
I go out, or speak, or move.

    I wipe the tears away. *Cowboy up, Deeble.* No one's going to like
me if I'm being a crying wuss all the time. What if Coach drove
by right now? He'd take me off the team in a heartbeat. No crying
in football.

31

SATURDAY, I WAKE UP FEELING LIKE I SLAMMED MY head in Noah's truck door. My skull screams at me when I sit up. I drag myself to the shower and get in, drinking down the shower water to help my dry mouth.

As I soap the night's filth off me, my hand catches on the Band-Aid on my arm, and I remember my trip to Jupiter's with a full-body cringe. Did I really ask her to *adopt* me?

Then I rewind further and remember Quinn's party, and him kissing me, which makes me want to run the soap over my tongue, too. He did that for kicks. We've been friends since childhood and he just tossed that aside for what, to make Stetson Ellison laugh? I nearly gag.

Then I remember Valentina, and it hurts so bad I sit down on the floor of the shower and just let the water hit me. I felt certain she liked me back, but I was wrong. How can I ever trust my instincts again after that? How can I ever show my face to her again?

And almost as bad as that is that now she knows about me. She could tell anyone—Quinn, my mom, Carly, anyone. Maybe she already has. Maybe she went back to the party last night and told all of them. Maybe they told their friends and maybe I'll show up to the first day of school on Monday to hallways full of whispers. And my mom would find out, her worst fears realized. She would take football away from me then, to be sure. And I don't know what else. I don't want to know.

Out of the shower, I put on a pair of basketball shorts and an old, holey shirt I won at the county fair four years ago that doesn't really fit anymore. The only thing that can make me feel better is feeling my body move, so I grab my basketball from its spot in the corner.

I'll never get tired of the sound of a basketball on pavement. I shoot around for a while, getting the blood pumping before lining up to practice free throws. My hair is all over my face, and as usual, I don't have a hair band on me. I'm sick of the way it gets everywhere. I wish I could just cut it off like Jupiter did. I twist it and stick it down the back of my shirt.

The ball feels heavy against my fingertips, the familiar weight of it a comfort. Last night I screwed up a lot of things. I screwed things up with Valentina. I dig my toe into the imaginary free-throw line. I screwed things up with Carly. I make a T on the ball with my thumbs. I screwed things up with Jupiter. I drop into a squat. And most fucked-up of all, things got screwed up with Quinn—that one's not my fault, but it hurts more than the others. And I threw a punch. The one thing I wasn't supposed to do this season. I push up through my legs, straightening my arm and following through, popping my wrist, letting the ball roll off my fingers, making its clear perfect arc toward the basket. The ball whirls the rim, then drops through. *God, that feels good.*

The screen door slaps closed as Noah skips down the stairs,

Delle Donne on his heels. He sits on the bottom step and puts on his shoes while watching me. Delle Donne bumps her wet nose into my knee. I scratch her on the butt where she likes it.

"Heard things got frisky at the party last night," he says.

I snatch the ball and shoot him a look. "Where were *you*?"

"Didn't go. Didn't feel like feeling like shit today."

"That's never stopped you before."

"I didn't know you and Quinn were a thing. Mom'll be thrilled you're marrying into a ranch family." Noah finishes his laces and pops up, taking the ball from me and laying it up. What would have happened if Noah had been there? Would Quinn have dared to do what he'd done with my brother watching? Would Noah have punched him so I didn't have to? Or would it all have been a joke to both of them?

"We're *not* a thing. Quinn stuck his tongue down my throat. He was drunk."

Noah turns to look at me slowly. "Seriously?"

"Yeah."

"That's messed up."

I don't know why him saying that makes me want to cry, but it does. I didn't even tell him about the rest of it, the crotch grabbing and all that. He's already on my side.

He's just standing there holding the ball like a chump, so I steal it out of his hands and shoot a jumper over him. He doesn't even try to block me. "Yeah," I say.

"Mara, I know he's your friend, but—"

"He's not," I say. It's clear to me now. "Not at the moment, anyway."

Noah nods.

The door slaps again as Mom steps out. "Let's go, Noah."

"Back-to-school shopping," he says to me by way of explanation.

Mom had wanted to take me shopping, too, but I said no straightaway. I don't need her handing me more flowery blouses and dresses over the door to my dressing room. As a compromise, she gave me fifty dollars to take myself shopping with. Fifty dollars won't go very far at Freddie's, but I can get a couple whole outfits for that much at the thrift store.

After Noah and Mom leave, I go back to shooting baskets, feeling the old, asphalt-roughened ball between my fingers, paying attention to the way my muscles move under my skin, the way my shoes scrape across the blacktop.

I've spent the last few weeks being torn between the boys and the girls. Now, none of them want me. And maybe I don't need any of them. Maybe it's fine if they hate me. I don't need Quinn or Carly or Valentina or Jupiter. I don't need any of them in order to play the best football I can and then the best basketball I can. All I need is to believe in myself and to work harder than anyone else. If I focus on that, instead of all the petty drama and little fights, I know I can unseat Wayne from his first-string slot. If I put myself first, who knows what I'm capable of. No more trying to pick sides. From now on, I'm just going to be Mara, solo.

I line up another free throw. This one goes in without a sound. Perfection.

# # #

After hoops, two Advil, and some more water, I feel more like myself. I lift my milk-jug weights in my room for a while, but I grow frustrated that what used to feel like a full-body workout this summer no longer has the same oomph. I try to hold two milk jugs in one hand. It hurts my hand, but I lean into it. The pain is clarifying. The workout starts to make me sweat again. I gulp from the gallon jug of water Quinn gave me and help myself to a whole package of turkey cold cuts, slice by slice. From the kitchen, I grab a bag of rice and work on my grip strength by opening and closing my fist inside it. It gets difficult quickly, but grip strength is what helps cornerbacks snatch balls and hold on to them, so I keep going. I remember the look on Wayne's face when I plucked a ball out of the sky during our drills last week. I picture that and push through the pain.

My hair falls into my face for the umpteenth time, and I swipe it away. I'm so sick of my hair, but if I cut it off, Mom would lose her mind. That might be the last straw for her, actually. The thing that makes her pick up the phone and call Coach Willis and end this all for good.

Unless there were some way to make her feel better about it.

The idea comes to me fast, and I start moving before I have time to overthink it. It's a solid plan. A way to make us both happy at the same time.

My bike feels good under my legs, and I fly down the highway, trees whipping past, my quads powering me toward town.

I hit the thrift shop first, heading straight past the men's section, where I usually shop, and into the women's. The back wall is where the tall rack is, the one with dresses. Without even stopping to look at the styles, I scoop up every one in my size and take them to the dressing room.

The first one fits perfectly. Bright, multicolored floral fabric falls to just below knee length. A row of perfect white buttons extends down from the lace-trimmed V-neck collar. I absolutely hate it. I put it in the to-buy stack.

The next dress is a pleated floor-length number covered in blue-and-teal paisley print, with oversize fabric buttons and a built-in gold vinyl belt. This one is less pretty than the first, but it's the right length, it covers my body, and most importantly, it's very, *very* feminine.

In the hat section, I find a hideous-to-me but lovely-to-my-mother white hat that covers my entire head. In the shoe section, I travel to the very end of the rack and pray they have some in my size. I try on a towering pair of heels, but I feel like I'm walking on a tightrope, and I don't want to break my ankle in church and lose out on the rest of the season. I downgrade to the lowest heels they have. Finally, I take it all up to the front. It comes out to fifty-three dollars. There goes my back-to-school money.

Carefully, I fold the dresses and pack them with the shoes into my backpack. The hat I attach to the outside so it doesn't get crumpled.

There, that's done. Now it's my time.

Across the street from the thrift shop, a barber pole spins lazily. Three chairs inside sit empty. I've never had a haircut here, but Noah started coming after he got too old for Mom's kitchen haircuts.

The barber looks up at me from one of the chairs. "Help you?" he asks.

"Yeah, uh . . . yeah." This feels like just a huge moment, but also totally normal. "Yeah, I want to cut my hair off."

The barber's eyes wander from my hair down to the rest of me and back to my hair, appraising me.

"How short?"

"Like a man's."

He pauses. "You sure you want to do that?"

"I'm sure."

"It will take a long time to grow back," he says.

"I'm sure," I say again.

"Okay." He gets up at last. "What kind of cut do you want?"

I pull up a picture on my phone of the tall guy from that show

Quinn likes, the one whose arms and chin and legs I always admired as he swings swords and tilts at armies. "Can you make me look like this?" I ask. He squints at the picture.

"If you say so," he says, sweeping the cape over me and fastening it at my neck.

When the clippers turn on, I get goose bumps. He sweeps them over the back of my neck, switching to scissors for the top. It takes less time than I thought it would. Ten minutes to fundamentally alter my appearance. There's no changing my mind now. He hands me a mirror.

I'm startled to realize how much I look like Noah. I never thought we looked that similar before, but now the resemblance is obvious. When I run my fingers over my head, I marvel at how the hair just...ends. My entire face looks different: older, maybe. I imagine how it will feel to pull my helmet off. No more ponytail getting in the way. No more tangles, no more endless washing and brushing. No more hair bands and bobby pins.

"If you don't like it, you can come back in six weeks and I'll help you grow it back out in a decent way."

"I like it," I say quickly.

"All righty."

I wish I could show Jupiter this.

The barber sells me some pomade to put in it if I want to style it a different way. The container is black and gray with a thick, heavy font designed for men. I give him a good tip and tell him I'll see him for a refresh in a month.

When I walk out, I'm touching the back of my head, feeling like a different woman entirely.

The road flies by under my tires on the ride home.

32

MOM'S CAR IS IN THE DRIVEWAY WHEN I GET TO THE house, so she must have come back with Noah while I was away. I stow my bike behind my barn and then dart inside with my helmet still on in case anyone happens to be looking out the window at that moment. I don't want to ruin the big reveal.

In the barn, Angelica nickers, and I pat her as I take off my shorts and T-shirt. I slip the dress on over my head, and it falls just as it did in the store—easily over my hips, showing off my waist. I lay the lace flat across my clavicles and smooth the wrinkles out. This is the kind of dress my mom used to stock my closet with when I was younger, before she started listening to me about what I wanted to wear. Between the darts, the lace, the soft floof of the fabric over the butt, it's my mom's dream dress. The cut of the neck makes me uncomfortable—it's not low, but anything lower than a T-shirt crew neck makes me feel weird. But this is for the greater good.

I step into the low white patent-leather heels. The dirt floor of the barn is not the ideal place to walk in heels, but I'll manage. They're the ugliest shoes I've ever seen, and my mother is going to love them. My feet are gnarly from football practice, covered in blisters and calluses. In the heels, you can't tell. The heel changes everything, lifting my calves so that they extend prettily, giving my butt a boost, forcing me to stand up straighter. They're not exactly comfortable, but I look perfectly dainty.

Finally, the hat. It's a molded white wool hat with a small brim and a large red bow, matching the red in some of the flowers on the dress. I run my fingers through my hair first, feeling the soft waves of the short hair on top and the prickly buzz over my neck. Then I touch it again. Then one more time before I'm ready to cover it up.

There's no mirror in the barn, so I have no idea what I look like, but I feel like I belong in *RuPaul's Drag Race*. I look down and everything seems to be in place. It's all I can do. There's something about wearing this dress that I picked out myself—knowing that it's not who I am—that's more tolerable than wearing the one Mom picked out for me, hoping it could be who I was. I know this dress is just a costume, and it's the knowing that makes it feel like it has less power. I put it on, and I can take it right back off whenever I want.

I give Angelica a good rub and then Roger so he doesn't get jealous. "Wish me luck," I whisper. Roger sniffs in response.

The walk from the barn to the house is the longest I've ever taken. Noah is texting on the couch when I walk in. When he sees me, he bursts out laughing.

"Shut up," I say, which just makes him laugh harder. "Where's Mom?"

There are tears in his eyes as he points to the kitchen, then swings his feet to the floor to follow me. I motion at him to keep his distance.

Mom is doing dishes at the sink as I enter the kitchen. I clear my throat. "Mom?"

She looks over her shoulder, and her eyes go wide when she sees me. She turns off the sink and wipes her hands on the dish towel before turning slowly to face me.

"Well," she says. "This is a surprise."

"How do I look?" I ask.

"Like a lovely young woman," she says carefully. She looks like she's waiting for me to reveal that I'm pranking her.

"This is what I'm going to wear to church tomorrow," I say.

"I would love that," she says, looking me over bit by bit. Finally, her eyes land on the hat, and just under the hat, my hair. Her brow knits.

"Also, there's this," I murmur, and slowly pull off my hat. I touch my hair to make sure it's not sticking up funny.

"Oh my god," Noah says in low awe from just outside the kitchen.

"Shut *up*, Noah," I hiss.

Mom stares at my head with this sort of stricken look that fades to exhaustion. "Oh, Mara," she says, reaching for my head and lightly touching my hair, pulling it out and letting it fall. "Oh, what have you done?"

She sounds like she's in mourning. Maybe she is. Mourning the kind of daughter she doesn't have.

"I cut it," I say, trying to sound light but firm. "But don't worry, I have this lovely hat! I'll wear it to church. And I'll wear dresses. I have others. I have heels. You don't have to worry about what people will think. Lots of girls have short hair. Jennifer Hansen!" I name a girl two years above me whose family Mom knows.

"Jennifer Hansen had a pixie cut," Mom says. "This..." She

trails off, but I know what she means. This is not a woman's hair-cut. Not the way Mom sees it, anyway.

"This is what I want," I say.

Her eyes look sadder than I've ever seen them. I thought she might get mad or frustrated. I thought she might storm over and pick up the phone and call Coach Willis. But instead, she's falling into herself. A tear runs down her cheek.

"Mom?" I've never seen her like this.

"Why do you want to be a boy? You're such a pretty girl." Her voice sounds so small, fragile.

"I'm still a girl," I try to tell her. But that's not what she means.

"You're asking me to accept this, but I don't know how, Mara. I don't know how your life looks if you keep going down this path. I don't know what to do with you. First football, now..." She shakes her head. "I can't accept this, Mara. This isn't who we are." Never mind this is who *I* am. "If this is what you want to do... then I don't want you coming to church at all."

"What?" A breeze winds its way around my legs, reminding me I'm in a dress. I squeeze my legs together, feeling foolish suddenly.

"There's no point in making you go if you're going to make a mockery of it." She gestures from my outfit to my hair. "Play foot-ball, don't play football... I don't care. But I can't support it, and I certainly won't be there Friday."

"Mom!" Noah exclaims from the doorway. "You always come to my games."

Mom just shakes her head, turns away from the sink, and leaves the kitchen, pushing past Noah.

I watch her go in shock. On some level I must have known she wouldn't react well, but telling me not to go to church? I thought she'd try to make me go three times a week, four, five. Never did I think she'd just give up.

I should feel free—I never loved going to church, and I certainly wasn't looking forward to going out in these outfits. But something about being denied it makes me feel like I just lost something important with my family.

Noah glares at me. "Way to go, dipshit."

"What are *you* pissed about?"

"Mom loves football. Now she's not coming because you're stressing her out. It's not always about you, Mara."

Noah leaves and I'm the one left standing in the kitchen feeling like an idiot in a dress.

The back door opens, and Dad walks in, sweat sticking his thinning hair to his forehead. He stops short when he sees me. "What's all this?"

Suddenly, I'm angry. Where has he been? At least when he was spending hours in his study, I knew where to find him. Now he's just flat-out absent. "Where do you *go* all the time?" I ask, louder than I mean to.

"What?" He looks taken aback. "What are you wearing?"

"Ughhh," I say. I actually stomp my foot, I'm so frustrated. But I forgot I'm wearing heels, and my ankle wobbles. "Forget it." I storm out as forcefully as I can in these stupid shoes.

# # #

The next morning, I lie in bed, examining the cracks in my ceiling. I hear Mom's good church heels clacking on the wood floor in the kitchen, then Dad's nice polished shoes clomping around behind her, his gait heavier on one leg than the other. The dishes clink as they eat. Noah clatters down the stairs in his ashy, cracked oxfords that he doesn't take care of. Low voices at the bottom of the stairs that I can't make out. The front door opens, then closes. Mom's car starts up, the gravel crunching under her tires as she pulls away. Finally, it's quiet. It's the first time I've missed church for something other than being sick in years. Maybe ever.

I'm not sure whether I believe in God or not, but just in case, I close my eyes and pray in a low whisper. "I apologize for missing church. I would be there if I could." But if going to church means I can't cut my hair, well...I bring my hand up to touch my head. I can't believe I actually did it. As badly as it all went down, I still feel proud of myself for making it happen. My hair is mine alone. I whisper the end of my prayer: "I don't think you care about hair, but if you do, I hope you can see this makes me happy."

33

THE BEST THING ABOUT SCHOOL STARTING IS THAT two-a-days are over. I like football practice but not *that* much. The second-best thing is I got Mrs. Tantlebaum for chem. I look forward to not being able to concentrate at all on learning the difference between DNA and RNA because Mrs. Tantlebaum's DNA and RNA have made her the hottest teacher at this school.

I show up to school on the first day wearing the same old navy button-up shirt with octopuses on it I wore all last year because I spent my back-to-school money on a dumb failed scheme. But the shirt looks different on me now, after my summer lifting milk jugs and these couple weeks playing football, the rolled-up sleeves tugging over my arms. The pomade the barber gave me calms down my frizzies and gives the whole thing volume. I'm surprised how good it looks. Even Noah asked me how I got it to look like that when I saw him in the morning, so I showed him the pomade.

I'm assigned a locker on the second-floor hallway because I'm finally an upperclassman. When I locate it, I discover it's right next

to Ranger's. He points to his head with a dopey smile, then points
to my head. "Your hair!" he says.

"My hair."

"It's shorter than mine." He sweeps his shoulder-length blond
waves back and gives his hair a shake. "We're like opposites."

"And locker neighbors," I say, stepping in front of my locker.
The door has a paper taped to the front covered in glitter glue and
puff paint. In bright, multicolored letters, it reads:

ELKHORN SUPPORTS

OUR TEAM

DEEBLE #22

A little of the glitter has fallen off onto the floor below my locker.
I've seen the football players' lockers decorated by the cheerleaders
for games and big days like the first day of school, but it's a very
different thing to actually see a locker with your name and number
on it. There's a cheerleader out there whose job it was to do this.
She gathered with the other cheerleaders on a weekend to make
it. Then she came to school early with tape and a locker list to find
mine and decorate it. There was forethought and effort that went
into this god-awful, ugly sign. There were good vibes.

"Pretty gaudy, huh?" Ranger says. He slams his locker closed.
He has the same sign but with his name and number.

"Kinda, yeah," I say. "But also kinda cool."

Ranger laughs to himself. "Gotta love a rookie. So full of enthusiasm. So happy to just be here." He punches me lightly on the
shoulder and heads off to class. The first bell is about to ring. I
hurriedly work my lock combo until it opens and start sliding my
books onto the shelf. I take the time to tuck a photo of Elena Delle
Donne into the edge of the locker so I have at least some kind of
decoration. It's one of my favorite pictures of my favorite basketball
player. She's even taller than me—six foot five—and in the photo,

she has on this badass clear plastic face mask she wore during games after she broke her nose. I know it's just standard medical equipment, but there's still something gay about that mask. I can't explain it except to say that it's not a thing any girl at this school would wear even if they were supposed to, except maybe me.

I close my locker and turn to go to class, but a very short girl steps into my path.

"Hi," she says. "Mara Deeble?"

She's wearing a backpack that's bigger than she is, so I can see it on either side of her, dwarfing her. She has on an Elkhorn cheer tank top and skinny jeans and the whitest all-white sneakers I've ever seen in my life. Either she just bleached them, or she bought them literally this morning. She's so tiny, I find myself looking down on the top of her head. The part in her hair is perfectly straight.

"Uh, yeah," I say.

"I'm Ichelle Martinez," she says, putting out a tiny hand confidently. "Your cheerleader."

There's nothing else to do but shake it. "Hi, Ichelle."

"I'm a freshman," she offers. "That's why you don't know me. But you might know my brother, Jerry?"

"Jerry Martinez is your brother?" There's easily a foot and a half difference between them, but now that I'm looking closely, I see they share the same gently rounded nose, the same soft brown skin.

"Yeah." She shrugs. "Anyway. Anything you need on game day, I'm supposed to help you with. Also, I'll be making you cookies? So, um, like, do you have any food allergies?"

This is so weird. Football players get a personal cheerleader who's like basically their servant and who makes them cookies on game day? Football really is unlike any other sport. The girls' basketball team doesn't get this. It's not like there's a male version of cheerleaders who stand on the sidelines to root for the lady sports and bake us treats on game days.

"No allergies," I say.

"Cool," she says, then pulls one of her arms free and swings her massive backpack around to her front. There's so much centrifugal motion I worry she's going to fly into the locker bank on the opposite side of the hallway, but she stays put. She scrawls a number on a notebook paper. "Text me if you need anything."

I take it. "Thanks, Ichelle."

"Okay," she says with finality, then turns to go. I look down at her number. I have a cheerleader. She turns back a few steps later. "I think you're cool!" Then she scampers to class.

I watch her go for a long time before starting to walk to my own class. Until now, I've only ever been playing football for myself. But now, I don't want to let her down.

# # #

Mrs. Tantlebaum looks tan and relaxed after her summer driving around to national parks with her husband in their converted van. Quinn's an idiot for thinking she's not hot. Quinn's an idiot for many reasons. I haven't seen him yet today, but I know I'll run into him at practice, no way to avoid it. I can't help but wonder if he's told anyone about me punching him. Anyone who wasn't at the party to witness it, that is. My stomach clenches just remembering it.

Valentina sits one table over from me in chem. I can barely stand to look at her, but I know we need to talk. She's too much of a risk.

After class, I catch her eye as she puts on her backpack. "Can we talk?" I ask.

"Sure," she says pleasantly, like we're gonna chat about the homecoming theme instead of something life-and-death like our ill-fated kiss.

"Not here," I say, jerking my head toward the chem supply room. We duck in. I close the door as she picks up an Erlenmeyer flask and starts playing with it. I didn't realize being alone with her would freak me out more than being in public. I want to get this over with.

"Your hair looks good," she says, and it stupefies me. I came here to apologize for my unwanted kiss and now she's complimenting my hair? This girl is a head trip.

"Thanks. Look, I'm sorry I kissed you the other night."

"Oh, um. Yeah. That's okay," she says, and stacks the Erlenmeyer flask with the others, taking care to line it up just so.

"I thought we had a . . . vibe going, I guess? Anyway, it doesn't matter. I'm sorry. But I guess what I wanted to talk about was, well . . ." I'm weirdly out of breath. All the bike riding and cardio I've been doing and *this* is what gets me winded?

"No one knows?" she guesses.

"Well, yeah. Except you, now. So, like, I'd appreciate it if you didn't tell anyone."

"You don't have to worry."

I scoff. She holds my future in her hands. She holds my relationship with my parents in her hands. She holds my reputation in her hands. The trajectory of my last two years of high school is basically up to her. How could I not worry? "I do, actually, have to worry. It's important."

She swallows. "What I mean is, I won't tell anyone. I'll keep my mouth shut."

My heart rate slows down, but I don't really feel better. Maybe part of me hoped that she would take this opportunity to tell me how wrong she was for pulling away Friday night. Until this moment, there was still the possibility that she would grab me around the back of my head, my fresh haircut under her fingers, and pull me into a deep, mind-blowing kiss. She could tell me that she had been afraid before, but now she wanted to give us a try.

I didn't realize how much I was still hoping for that until it didn't happen.

"You haven't told anyone already, have you?" I ask. My voice comes out flat, bitter.

She tips her head to the side like she's looking at an injured bird. That's not how I want her looking at me. "No," she says. "No one."

"Thank you."

She rubs a knuckle across her eyebrow. "I do like you, Mara. You're not...Like, you're not wrong about that. It's just that I'm... I don't...like girls like that."

This conversation specifically should be banned under the Geneva Conventions, because it is torture. I gotta get out of here.

"But if I did..." Valentina says. "You'd be the first girl I'd tell."

"Okay, well," I say, not knowing what to do with that information. "I should get to class."

"You should talk to Carly, though."

She's exploring some dot of grossness on the floor with her toe. "What?"

"I won't tell her, but maybe you should. She'd be a good person to talk to. 'Cause, like, she's been there."

She might be gay, but it doesn't mean we're the same. "I'm good."

"She has a club, you know. Like a secret club for...people like you."

She can't even say it, which just adds insult to injury. But maybe I can't say it, either. All of a sudden, I hate that I'm having this conversation in an actual literal closet. I hate that Carly's club is some underground thing. I hate that I have to have this conversation with Valentina. I resent everyone in this town who has made me feel like all of this has to be secret.

"Queer people," I say, feeling my heart pound as I say it out loud, maybe for the first time ever.

"Yeah," she says shyly. "She invited me once, but I told her the same thing I told you. I'm not like that."

"Yeah, you don't have to keep saying it." Or non-saying it, as the case may be. "But I'm fine. Thanks for not telling anyone. Especially Carly." I hike my backpack up. "I gotta go."

34

SINCE WE'RE HAVING PRACTICE AFTER SCHOOL FOR
the first time, I have to go to the locker room after last bell to change
clothes. Which means I have to see the other girls. Including Carly,
who I haven't talked to since the party.

I get there early to try to miss them. Maria Carpenter is already
in there with some of the other volleyball girls getting ready for
their practice. Maria looks radiant in overall shorts with a tank
top and cowboy boots—what I think of as popular girl sexy farm
chic. Maria is slipping her overall straps off when she sees me.

She smiles a perfectly lip-glossed, white-toothed smile.

Maria Carpenter and I, despite being in classes together for the
last ten years of our lives, have nearly no relationship whatsoever. I
remember once playing four square with her in third grade. Another
time I think we traded friendship bracelets at Erica Farmer's ninth
birthday party. That's about it. We are different classes of people.
She is lovely and small and beautiful and boys like her because

they want to get with her. I am too big for her crowd—soft in places I should be hard and hard in places I should be soft.

Despite all this, Maria comes over and touches me on the arm. "I'm rooting for you, you know."

"Sorry?" Maybe she doesn't recognize me with my new haircut.

"I just think it's super cool that you joined the football team," she says. "I mean, with your height, I wish you had stuck with volleyball. I think we've got a good chance at State again this year. But it's okay. You're gonna kill it out there. I hope you crush Gravel Bay next Friday."

"Thanks?"

She floats back to her team. Suddenly, I feel bad telling all the boys about her appendix scar.

# # #

Carly and Tayley come in as I'm slipping into my shorts.

"Hey, Mara," Tayley says breezily, then stops. "Oh my god, look at you!"

Carly, interest piqued, apparently, despite our fight, turns to look at me.

"Carly, doesn't she look cool?" Tayley says excitedly.

I feel weird under Carly's evaluating gaze. She says, "You style your hair different or something?"

Tayley laughs.

"Yeah." I bring my hand to the back of my head impulsively.

"I like it," she says sincerely, which catches me off guard. "You look like Megan Rapinoe."

I mean, Megan Rapinoe is extremely hot, so I don't even know how to take that.

I guess I just stare for a minute because Tayley whispers, grinning, "Just say thanks."

"Thanks," I mumble.

Carly drops her stuff and starts dressing. Tayley beams at me as she opens a locker.

I remind myself that it's okay to be pleasant to the other girls, but it doesn't change the fact that I've decided to go solo. I'm not on their side. I'm not on the side of the boys. I'm just Mara doing Mara.

Valentina and River come in, and Valentina and I exchange the briefest of glances, but I look away. I won't be distracted. There's just two weeks of practice left before our first game against Gravel Bay, and I need to show Coach Willis that I'm worth putting in the game.

Coach splits us into two groups on opposite ends of the field so more people can scrimmage at the same time. Still, the rest of the girls stand on the sidelines. They don't even have positions yet. As soon as I slip on my helmet and pop my mouth guard in, I feel huge again. Like I'm not Mara Deeble anymore, but the Hulk, unfathomably strong. Unstoppable.

Wayne lines up as right cornerback, and I take left. We meet eyes across the field. I am going to have to play my heart out if I'm going to beat Wayne at the position he's been playing for years.

Coach Gary calls for man-to-man coverage and my heart sinks, seeing that I'm lining up against Quinn. We haven't connected since the party. It's hard to see his face through his helmet, but he looks like he has bruising around his nose. It doesn't look cool, like a Hollywood black eye. It just looks like he has weird red lines on his stupid little face.

On the snap, Quinn ducks right, and I follow, trying to stay on him, reading his movements. He cuts across the field, so I assume they're running a slant passing route, but at the last second, Quinn cuts out and four feet opens up between us in a blink as I struggle to adjust course. The ball is already landing in his arms by the time I even realize it's happening. Now it's just me and Quinn and thirty yards of open field between us and the end zone and it's my fault he has the ball because I was out of position. I focus the power into my legs, trying to catch up to him, but Quinn is fast, and no matter how much I give it, I can't gain on him. Then a green streak crosses my vision and plows into Quinn from the side, sending them both hard to the ground. Wayne hops to his feet, picking grass out of his mouth guard.

"That's how you tackle, Deeble. In case you were confused."

There's nothing to say to that. Quinn puts his hand out for help up. For a second, I forget I'm mad at him and reach to help him, but he pulls his hand away from mine and redirects it toward Wayne.

Right. Fine.

On the next play, Noah fakes a handoff to Curtis, but I spot it from a mile away. I'm on Quinn exactly like we've practiced it. So is Wayne with his receiver. Noah ends up dumping to a tight end, who gets nailed by Ranger.

As we walk back to the line, Quinn says, "You're lucky it's not broken, or I'd be pressing charges."

"Oh, come on."

"I'm serious. You could have killed me."

I dig my toes into the grass and drop into position, feeling the adrenaline course through my limbs. I'm ready for him when he launches off the line and runs a post route. I'm in position as the pass comes our way. Quinn snatches the ball and tucks it to his chest in the same moment that I slam into him shoulder-first, feeling the impact of my hit travel down my body, then the impact of the two of us slamming into the ground. I climb off him and look down on him. For a minute, he looks stunned. Maybe I rang his bell.

"Dang, Mara," he moans. "Watch where you put your giant fucking knee next time, huh?"

"Don't ever kiss me again." I walk back to my team.

"Deeble!" Coach Willis says, and Noah and I both look at him. "Twenty-Two," Coach clarifies, waving me over. I jog up. "That was a beautiful tackle."

"Thanks, Coach."

"But you gotta go easy. Quinn's on our team," he says.

Should I be playing the best football I can or not? "Okay, Coach," I say without meaning it.

Coach then calls out to Wayne and tells him to switch sides with me. I'm relieved I don't have to cover Quinn anymore today.

On the next play, Valentina comes jogging onto the field to try out for free safety.

She gives me a big grin and I know I'm supposed to be flying solo right now, but I can't see the harm in shooting her a thumbs-up. But on the next play, Quinn goes long and shakes Wayne. Valentina has the chance to stop him, but Quinn spins around her right into the end zone.

Valentina looks crushed as Quinn does a stupid victory dance. From the sidelines, Tayley and River clap. "It's okay, Vee!" Tayley calls. "You'll get him next time!"

Valentina slinks back to the new line of scrimmage, and Noah comes over and pats her on the back, saying something low I can't hear. Her shoulders straighten.

"Bullshit," Wayne says, crossing in front of me. "If Coach plays any of you girls in a real game, we're screwed."

"You were out of position," I say to Wayne. "That's just as much on you as her."

He shakes his head and says again, "Bullshit."

The extra point is the easiest kick in football to make, but somehow Lincoln pings it off the uprights and misses.

"Fuuuuck!" Lincoln screams. The other guys slap him on the back and the butt, and tell him next time, but the fact is, if he can't make a simple extra-point kick, how can we trust him when we need a field goal from the forty-yard line with eight seconds left?

I don't know why Wayne would think the girls are the worst thing about this team when Lincoln Handel is right there, sucking in full view.

I can't handle them right now, so I break my own rule by walking up to Tayley and River. "Either one of you guys play soccer before?"

"Literally never," River says, one hand on a cocked hip. She's actually wearing dark wine-colored lipstick at football practice.

I turn to Tayley. "Seven years," she says.

"This team needs a kicker. You want to play, that might be something you should practice."

Tayley nods, eyeing the uprights. "Pretty big target."

I walk away quickly, just so they know we're not friends again. I'm still just Mara, solo, but the thought of Tayley taking Lincoln's position makes me smile inside my helmet.

# # #

The next day, Coach Joyce intercepts me after classes on my way to the locker room. "Keep up the good work," she says. She watches our practice that day, and I feel the extra eyes on me all afternoon. Not only do I have to perform better than perfect just to be considered worthy by Coach Willis, but I also have to impress Gary and Howard if I have a hope of ever starting in a game. Not to mention keeping my temper for Coach Joyce, who apparently hasn't heard about the punch Saturday night, thank god. I guess Quinn has been too ashamed to bring it up. Still, how much longer can I take this pressure?

The rest of the week feels like an endless grind of school and football, and the intersection of the two. One day in the hall, I see Valentina chatting with Noah. As I get close, Valentina walks off.

"Since when are you guys friends?"

Noah cocks his head at me. "You're not the only one who gets to talk to girls." He slips away, leaving me with questions and a sour feeling.

The shine is starting to wear off Mrs. Tantlebaum. She may be hot, but she assigns a *lot* of homework. Although, she is very nice about it on Thursday when I get a charley horse in my calf in the middle of class, and fall off my stool onto the ground trying to rub it out. Everyone stares at me, but once I'm done writhing, Mrs. Tantlebaum explains the biology behind what causes muscles to seize up and how stretching and water can help prevent it. Some of the volleyball girls write down her suggestions.

That night, I take an ice bath. My calves aren't the only muscles giving me trouble. It seems that since I started football, every single one of the 650 muscles in my body hurts at one time or another throughout the day. Football truly is a full-body sport. I'm using muscles I didn't even realize I had. Every time I sit down, and stand up, and laugh, and load the feed for the horses, and bend over to pet Delle Donne.

My phone goes off at 5:00 a.m. so I have time to get my weights and a run in before morning chores. Every time that alarm rings, I have to remind myself that the reason I'm doing this is because I have to work harder to be better than these boys who have been playing longer than me. And I have to be better than them just to get the same amount of respect.

The purple blooms appear in various places around my body depending on where I hit or got hit the day before. One day, I wear my favorite pair of camo cargo shorts to school and three different people ask me what happened to my leg because of the T-bone steak–size blue smear across my shin. One girl even asks if I've been in a car accident. No, just football.

But the injuries don't bother me. If anything, the pain reminds me that I'm working hard. The harder I get hit, the more I know I deserve to be on the field. The harder I hit someone, the more proof it is that I can play this sport. No one can doubt me with bruises like these. No one can question my commitment or my tolerance for pain. No one can tell me girls can't handle football if they see what I go through just to be here. It's an armor against the attacks that I know they're thinking.

I'm not the only one getting hurt. Curtis Becker dislocated his shoulder in practice one day. He ran to the sidelines, clutching where it bulged at an unnatural angle. Coach Howard popped it back in, slapped his butt, and sent him back out. I heard he went to see the doctor that night after practice, but if they told him to stop playing, he didn't listen, because he was right back at practice the next day, talking about the sound it made when it popped out and grossing everyone out with the delicious details.

The pressure mounts as we get closer to our first game against Gravel Bay. The buzz among the other players grows. It's all anyone's talking about. Who will start? Who will play? How is the other team looking? They have a strong offense this year, someone's dad heard. What has Gravel Bay heard about us? The unspoken question hanging in the air: Do they know about all our girls?

Does it make us look weak? Do they think they can slaughter us because of it?

Tensions run high during scrimmage. After one particularly intense passing play that results in an incomplete pass, Curtis Becker screams at Coach that I was holding. I wasn't holding. Coach tells me to watch the holding, that the refs wouldn't go easy on me for that. I wouldn't expect them to.

As for the other girls, the coaches have dumped Carly on special teams, the squad that's used only for punts and kickoffs, where she's a blocker for the punt returner. Mostly she seems to get mowed over. It's not a particularly glamorous position, but Carly doesn't complain.

River's so terrible at football in general that for a while, it seems like Coach is just cycling through every position trying to find something she won't trip over her feet trying to play. She keeps her attitude up in an annoying way. Each time she completely fails at whatever position Coach puts her in, she laughs and shrugs. Once, after completely whiffing a tackle of a wide receiver when she was playing strong safety, resulting in a touchdown, she cocked her head and said, "This all looks a lot easier on Wii." The guys grumble at her because it seems like she doesn't take any of this seriously. I wouldn't be surprised if she sits the bench the whole season.

For several practices, Tayley works on the sidelines, kicking into a practice net. I thought it might take weeks for Coach to try her at kicker, but after one of Curtis's touchdowns, Lincoln jogs onto the field and drops to one knee behind the center to receive the snap. He doesn't look happy about it. Half the defensive line comes up out of their stance when they see Tayley take three long strides backward and one stride to the left behind Lincoln. Only Valentina, who Coach is trying on special teams, stays in position.

"Back to work, fellas," Coach Gary yells, and the guys find their way back into their stances.

From the sidelines, I hold my breath. I want her to do a good job. Not just because her playing well will reflect well on all the girls, but also because we need a good kicker, and Lincoln ain't it. On top of that, Tayley is chipper and friendly and I am a little bit rooting for her.

Trying to be solo isn't as easy as I thought it would be.

Tayley takes a deep breath and nods that she's ready. The snap comes and Lincoln catches it as Tayley begins her approach. It's a delicate, perfectly timed dance the holder and the kicker must perform together, and everything has to unfold smoothly and quickly for a kick to go well. That doesn't happen. Lincoln bobbles the snap, can't get it set up in time, and yanks the ball back so that Tayley whiffs entirely. He hops to his feet, trying to salvage the play by running or passing, but he's immediately tackled by Valentina.

I watch it all go down from the sidelines. There was something weird about that bobble from Lincoln, combined with the look on his face when he came out onto the field. I don't have any evidence, but part of me wonders if Lincoln bobbled that ball on purpose, so Tayley couldn't kick it, so he could run in himself, so she'd look like an idiot and him like a hero. It didn't turn out that way. He just looks like he can't kick *and* he can't hold. Where does he think that leaves him?

Lincoln gets to his feet, spitting a huge loogie on the ground right at Valentina's feet. All that, and then he got tackled by another girl. He's staring at Valentina with these wolf eyes that make my skin crawl. I tense up, but they just exchange low words and he stalks off. As Valentina and Tayley come off field, I stop them.

"What'd he say to you?"

Valentina has a snarl on her lips as she repeats it. "He said he would knock me down for that, but he liked it too much."

My anger flares. Lincoln walks off the field, leaving the ball for someone else to pick up. I want to hit him so hard his helmet flies off. But, of course, I don't. *No fighting, Mara.*

After practice ends that day, I see Tayley continue honing her kicks long after everyone else has begun packing up to go home.

COME GAME NIGHT, NOAH AND I BOTH TROT DOWN-
stairs in our football jerseys carrying our giant football bags. Dad
meets us at the bottom of the steps with his green-and-white wool
blanket and team sweatshirt. Mom sits in the living room, watching HGTV.

"Mom, are you really not coming?" Noah asks. I can't believe
she's being like this.

"Have a great game, Noah. I'll hear all about it when you come
home."

Noah shakes his head and storms out the front door.

I want to say something to Mom that will make her see how
hurtful she's being, but I don't have the words.

I follow Noah out to the truck, but Dad takes longer to come out.
When he does, his mouth is set in a grim line.

We arrive early with the other football families. Dad grabs his
blanket, wishes us luck, and heads for the stands. This is usually

where I would go with him to scope out our seats and get a couple Cokes and hot dogs for us from concessions, but tonight I peel off with Noah and head for the locker room, my chest a tangle of nerves. I'm excited but also anxious. Will I get to play? Will I play well, if I do? With all these people watching? It's one thing to say you want to play football, but it's another to actually do it in front of everyone. Tonight's about proving myself.

Coach told us yesterday that the girls would use the team's one locker room first, then the boys when we're done. The other girls and I change quickly, because we know the boys are piling up in the corridor, waiting their turn. It makes me self-conscious.

We're quiet as we dress. Maybe the others are as nervous as I am. The muffled sounds of the pep band warming up filter in.

"Everyone ready?" I ask before I open the door to let the boys in.

"One sec, Mara," Carly says. "Huddle up."

And maybe it's stupid, but it's kind of nice to circle up with just these four before the whole mass of guys comes in.

"River, are you wearing lipstick to a football game?" Valentina whispers, and sure enough, she's reapplying her dark, dark red.

"What? It goes with the uniform," she says. I sputter out a laugh. "See? Mara likes it."

"I like that it's going to piss the other team off," I say.

"Okay, listen up," Carly says. She speaks low, almost a whisper. But there's an urgency to her voice. "Listen to me. We did this. We made it to this point. No one thought we could do it. No one rooted for us. But we came together and we did it anyway. Now we're going to go out there, and Willis might play us or he might not. But if he plays us, you can guarantee, we're going to play as hard and as well as we goddamn can. Because no one is going to tell us we can't play football. We're going to prove everyone out there who hates us just because we're girls wrong. We can play, and we don't have to apologize for it."

"Hoo-hah!" I say. It's almost ironic—the whispered speech doesn't call for a *hoo-hah*, but there's something about claiming it for our space that feels right. It's not their cry to keep. It can be ours, too.

"Hoo-hah!" the other girls respond.

And the smile is stuck on my face. God, I hope Coach puts me in. And maybe after he puts me in, he could put Tayley in, too. She's been working extra hard for it.

"Okay, *now* we're ready," Carly says, and we all slap each other on the back as we head for the door.

The boys take forever getting ready, to the point that I start to worry about the clock. Kickoff is rapidly approaching. I look at the other girls, scattered around the hallway. Valentina listens to music on her headphones. Tayley might be praying, her eyes pressed closed, her lips barely moving. I get close to the door and listen in. A voice is speaking. Coach's voice?

"Guys, I think Coach is talking," I say. I listen harder as the others move closer.

"Did they forget to get us?" Tayley asks.

"Yeah, I'm sure they 'forgot,'" River says with air quotes.

"They just fucking left us out here," Carly says angrily.

"Do we go in?" Valentina says.

"Hell yes," Carly and I say in unison, then look at each other. We push through the door, ignoring Tayley's protests that they might still be naked in there.

We just catch the tail end of Coach's speech, his impassioned voice filling the locker room. Some guys are on one knee, other guys sit around on benches. Some have their eyes closed, taking in what Coach is saying. Quinn sits on the far side. He doesn't look up when we come in. I can't believe these assholes started without us.

"You came all this way, gentlemen. Don't hold anything back now," Coach says. "You gotta leave it all on the field tonight. I want you guys to believe you can win, because you can. And you only got one shot at it. You came here tonight as brothers, and you're going to leave as champions."

At the beginning of this season, I might have liked being called brothers, being treated as if I'm just one of the guys. But now it feels more like a deliberate dig.

We hoo-hah and make a circle, putting our hands in. I'm on the outside, and my arm doesn't quite reach.

Noah counts us down. "Three, two, one."

"Bull's-eye!"

As we run onto the field, I try to put my annoyance about missing the speech out of my mind. After all, we're about to play football. Night has fallen, but the lights are brighter than the sun, shining on this patch of grass and nowhere else, making the football field feel like the only thing in the world.

The stands are almost full. That early-season optimism is here. Elkhorn hasn't had a winning run in seven years, but every year is full of new potential. Tonight, the stands are so full, it feels like the whole town must be here. Except I know just who's missing. Dad looks on, bundled under his blanket. I can't help but feel a pang of disappointment that Mom's not here, too.

"Go, Mara!" someone shouts. It's Ichelle, cheering for me from the sidelines with the rest of her squad. She does a kick and a punch with her pom-pom and I wave. At least *she's* rooting for me.

Coach doesn't start me. I didn't think he would, but I had hoped. I've worked my ass off in practice, and I feel like I'm doing okay. But I guess okay isn't good enough. I still might get to play if Jerry or Wayne gets injured or tired or we run certain plays that require more backs. I stand anxiously by the water cooler.

A woman approaches me. It's that reporter Greta again. "Mara, hey. How does it feel to suit up for a game?"

"I'm not supposed to talk to the media," I say, and turn away to fill a cup of water.

"*I* feel incredible," Carly says, coming over.

The reporter brightens and turns to Carly. "Coach Willis isn't starting any of the five girls on his team. How do you feel about that?"

"I think it's bullshit," Carly says, and I feel my whole body go rigid. "Look, I know I'm not starting material, but this one is." Carly gestures to me. "It's absurd that Mara's not starting. No one here wants to recognize her talent."

"Can I talk to you?" I hiss at Carly, and pull her away.

"What? You know it's true," she says once we're out of earshot.

"First of all, it's not true. Jerry Martinez is way better at cornerback than me. Not to mention Wayne."

"That meathead loser? He's got nothing on you."

"He might be a shithead, but he can play."

"Yeah, and you're a shithead and you can play better."

"Carly..."

"Mara, shut up and take the compliment. This isn't personal. You're *good*. You should be on the field right now."

"Even if that were true, *which it is not*, you're not allowed to talk to the press. Coach said so."

"Oh, since when are you such a rule follower?" Carly says. "The Mara I know used to say screw the rules and pick fights whenever she wanted."

"I'm here to play football, not get my name in the paper, remember?" I say.

"I'm here to play football *and* get your name in the paper," she says, and turns back toward the reporter.

I throw my cup in the trash and walk to the other end of the sideline. I don't want to be associated with her. If she wants to talk to the media against Coach Willis's direct orders, fine. But I won't be part of it.

Lincoln kicks off and it goes out of bounds at the forty-yard line. He comes off the field shaking his head and swearing at himself. It's not a pretty sight. Tayley pats him on the back, but he shrugs her off and sits down on the bench with a *humph*.

Every fiber in my body wants to run out with our defense as they take the field. I watch helplessly from the sideline as our defense falters, then falters some more. Gravel Bay is kicking our asses up and down the field. My legs itch to go in. I start to pace. The Sea Lions go up by seven, then fourteen, then they score a field goal. Quinn gets plastered all over the back half of the field. He and Noah can't put together a play to save our lives.

Finally, at 17–0, Coach calls for a post route, and Noah bombs a long ball to Quinn, who gets tackled at the twenty-five. They bumble the next three plays, but still, we got ourselves into field goal position.

"Striker, get in there," Coach says. My heart stops.

Tayley's going in first? Tayley looks so surprised, she freezes, but jumps into action when Coach hollers, "Now!"

Tayley gives me a quick grin as she slips her helmet on and jogs out onto the field. "Lincoln, no screwing around," Coach says, and Lincoln begrudgingly jogs out after her.

The announcer calls out her name, and just like that, Tayley Striker becomes the first girl to play football for Elkhorn High. There's a moment before the crowd realizes it, but when they do, there's a huge cheer, bigger than any so far in the game.

I can't believe it. I know what I should be doing is rooting for my team no matter what, but I can't help the resentment bubbling up. That was supposed to be my cheer. I hear some boos in the cheers, too. Those should have been my boos. Instead, I have to stand here and watch.

Tayley takes her paces and line up the field goal with her arm. She takes a deep breath. Ready. The crowd quiets.

The snap, the kick. It sails easily through the uprights.

Field goal. 17–3.

The crowd loses their minds. The announcers breathlessly declare that Tayley Striker is not only the first girl to play in a game for Elkhorn High, she's also the first girl to score.

Wow.

I want to be happy for her, but instead I deflate like my slashed bike tires. Tayley is the first. Tayley went in. She scored. And I'm here standing on the sidelines like a damn cheerleader. No, not even a cheerleader—they at least have a job to do.

As Tayley jogs off the field, she gives a little wave to the cheering audience. Then she holds her hand up for me to high-five her. And even though I'm jealous, I still feel happy for her. I do. She nailed that field goal. Beautiful form. Reluctantly, I high-five her.

At halftime, it's still 17–3. Tayley could have scored another field goal with a few minutes left to go in the half, but Lincoln bobbled the snap. Tayley looked frustrated when she came off field, but there's nothing she could have done.

Coach's pep talk at halftime is pretty forgettable. A lot of "leave everything on the field" this and "you didn't come this far to fail" that. We hoo-hah at the end and head back out there. On the way to our sideline, I end up jogging next to Quinn. I risk saying something, even though we've been on rocky ground lately.

"That was a nice catch you had earlier."

"Didn't turn into much, did it?" Quinn grumbles.

"Field goal's not nothing," I say, trying to stay positive. "We got a whole 'nother half to catch up."

"Our linemen are going to have to pull their weight, then." There he goes, blaming his blockers for the fact that he's outmatched by Gravel Bay's defenders. "Otherwise we're going to find ourselves at the end of this game and the only person who scored any points is a damn girl."

I slow down, then, letting some space open up between us.

"No offense."

"The girls are as much a part of this team as you are," I say. "And if you want to blame somebody for screwing up this game, stop blaming your linemen and start following your blocks. You have to quit getting happy feet and start hitting the hole. And you should be *thanking* Tayley. If we had Lincoln kicking, we'd still be scoreless."

As I pull away from him, I accidentally catch Carly's eye. She gives me a look that lets me know she heard the whole thing. And I should probably feel embarrassed about that, but part of me is glad she heard. I can't remember anymore why I used to ever think Quinn Kegley was best friend material.

It's deep in the third quarter when Jerry plucks a pass out of the air, spins through three tackles, and skips into the end zone. Finally, a break.

I see Tayley talking to her special teams coach, who in turn talks to Coach Willis, who doesn't look happy but nods his okay. When it's time to send Tayley in, Coach points at River and says, "You too." To Lincoln he says, "Handel, take a seat."

"Are you kidding me, Coach?" Lincoln protests as River runs for her helmet. "Are you seriously kidding me right now? *Her?*"

Finally, Coach turns to him, and growls, "I said take a seat, Handel."

Lincoln stomps back to the bench and harrumphs as he sits down.

The announcers call out that River Reyes is officially the *second* girl to ever play in an Elkhorn High game.

River shouts at the announcer's booth, "And first Mexican girl, bitch!" She hoots and high-fives Tayley as she reaches the middle of the field.

River's excitement is contagious. I'm happy for her, and there's a certain pleasure seeing Lincoln sit on the bench, but I can't help but feel my heart ping a jealous note that with every second that ticks down, I'm less and less likely to play in this game. Less and less likely to make history with Tayley and River.

I was the first girl to play football for Elkhorn. This was my idea. They only joined because they were inspired by me, after all. And yet, at this rate, it feels like every other girl is going to play before I do.

River kneels in the grass, pointing at the ground with her right hand where she'll hold the ball as she holds her left up to where she wants the snap. She's practiced this. That must be what she and Tayley have been up to at the practice net while I've been running drills on another part of the field.

Suddenly, I'm anxious twice over. This is a totally standard extra-point kick. It should be simple, but if anything goes wrong— if Tayley's pacing is off, if River bobbles the snap, if the snap is too high or too wide, if River doesn't spin the ball properly when she sets it down, if the ball hits Tayley's shoelaces wrong, if everyone does everything right but slightly out of time with each other—we could miss out on the extra point. And even if River and Tayley act perfectly, sometimes kicks go poorly. Sometimes it's the wind, or the inflation of the ball, or a bump in the grass. Sometimes shit just happens. But no one will see it that way. Everyone will assume that it was because they're girls. Because everyone knows you can't trust us. Not with football.

And as much as I want to be my own player, I will always be seen as one of them. If they screw up, it's my screwup. If they succeed, well, it's one less mark against us. We have to be perfect just to be acceptable. And if any one of us is less than perfect, we're all tainted.

The snap flies. It's on target. River catches the ball. She sets it, spins the laces away, pulls her left hand back, and holds it with two fingers as Tayley finishes her approach and . . . it's a beaut. The ball sails through the uprights. The crowd erupts in cheers. It's 31–10. We're losing by twenty-one points, but I'm grinning anyway. We didn't give them a reason to doubt us today.

River and Tayley run back to the sidelines, Tayley pumping her fist and River literally singing "Oh Bless the Lord" from *Godspell* as she whips her helmet off. I high-five them both this time.

"Beautiful kick," I tell them.

"Hell yeah, hell yeah!" Carly yells at the top of her voice. "Girls gonna rule this game!"

I want to wince that she's over-celebrating in a game that's still a blowout, but at the same time, I feel exactly the same way. As much as I really want to be in this game, I'm also so excited that Tayley and River got to play, and *score*. It's complicated.

By the fourth quarter, I'm convinced I'm not going to get any playing time. But then the Sea Lions find themselves in a third-and-long situation, where a passing play is all but guaranteed, and Coach Gary calls for a nickel defense, which involves adding an additional defensive back. Coach Willis nods at me, and that's it,

I'm running in, snapping my helmet, swinging my arms to keep them warm.

The announcers must call my name, but I don't hear it. The crowd might even be cheering, but the only thing in my ears is the beating of my heart. The only thing I see is right in front of me.

I'm covering their weeniest receiver, a guy who hasn't gotten more than a handful of passes all game. There's nearly no way they pass to him now, when they need a first down. I'm just covering him so that the other backs can cover the better players. But this might be the only fifteen seconds of game I play all night, so I'm going to give it everything I got. I stare the weenie receiver in the eye as I get into my stance, and breathe.

I can do this.

The snap comes, we both start moving. I get my hands on him, and he bats me away. We're going deep. The receiver might be weenie, but he's fast, and I turn on the heat to stay close to him. His eyes lift up, which only means one thing.

The pass is coming this way.

I keep one hand safely on his shoulder and look back to trace the ball, arcing through the sky. The pass is leading us. If I can reach out far enough, I can intercept it . . .

I leap. Stretch. I'm sideways to the ground, at my longest. I've never wished for another inch until now. Even if I can't intercept it, if I can just block it, I will save this play.

The ball brushes the tips of my fingers. It wobbles. The weenie receiver catches it.

And I fall. I don't feel the impact at all. The receiver is already five yards, then ten away by the time I can scramble back to my feet to go after him. It's already a disaster and getting worse by the second.

No one can catch him. He crosses the goal line. 37–10.

I want to keep running, past the end zone, past the uprights, past the locker room, away from the lights, into the night.

But I stop. And turn around. And go back to the sidelines. And hope I get another chance.

Noah doesn't look at me. I don't blame him.

Then there's a slap on my back. It's River. "You got some serious air out there, dude."

I drop my head. It wasn't enough.

Then another slap. Tayley's voice: "Mara, you almost had it! Did you touch it? It looked like you touched it."

"Yeah."

"I could tell. So close!"

"Next time you'll intercept it for sure," Valentina says.

And maybe she's right. If there *is* a next time. If Coach ever trusts me to go in again after that. But I did almost block the pass. I was right there.

I pull my helmet off, finally. I rub my hand over my sweaty hair.

Carly steps next to me. "Sorry," she says. "That probably sucks."

She's the only one not drowning me in optimism. When I look at her, she shrugs. "I'm guessing."

"Yeah, it does."

Carly holds her helmet—she hasn't put it on once, even though Coach likes all the players to wear them, even when they're on the sidelines, just in case they get put in. He says it makes us look more professional. Without her helmet, I can see the dark eyelashes that line her eyes, which are looking at me with sympathy. Her eyes are a deep brown—dark and forceful. But they also have a ring of green around the very outside that I'd never noticed. Maybe I've never really looked at her eyes before.

"I heard what you said to Quinn," she says. "Thanks for sticking up for us."

"Yeah, well. If they're going to clump us together, I guess we're together, whether I like it or not, huh?"

"Guess so."

# # #

We lose 41–10. We would've lost with or without the touchdown I gave up, but that doesn't make me feel any better about it.

The boys swarm the locker room first, everyone forgetting or not caring that we're supposed to take turns. I wait in the hallway with the other girls. It takes forever before they finally vacate and we can go in and change. By the time we emerge in our street clothes, the stands are empty and the parking lot has only a few scattered cars left. If there's a party tonight, no one invited us.

I'm searching for my dad's truck when I hear a small voice: "Excuse me, Twenty-Two?" It's coming from a girl, maybe nine years old, clutching a football to her chest with one hand and a Sharpie in the other. A few parking spots away, a mom with a baby on her hip watches with a smile.

My heart stops for a second as I realize what she's here for. "You want my autograph?"

"All of you. All the girls," she says.

The other girls are scattering across the parking lot, headed to their cars.

"Hey! Guys!" I call out for them, and they turn around and look back.

I take the ball from the girl with a smile and sign my name and number across its bumpy surface.

"Oh my god," Carly says when she realizes what's happening.

"She wants our autographs," I say, barely believing it.

"This is the greatest moment of my life," says River. "We're being stage-doored!"

Valentina puts her hands on her knees and gets on the girl's level. "What's your name?"

"Summer," she says.

It turns out Summer loves football. She plays center in her Pop Warner league, but she wants to be a quarterback. She's not sure her coach will let her play anything but center, though.

Carly looks her right in the eye. "There are men in this town who will do anything to uphold the white cisheteropatriarchal power structure. But you can disrupt that just by going out there and being yourself."

I laugh. "Seriouly? Cisheteropatriarchal?"

"It affects her, she might as well have a word for it. She can google it later."

"Just keep playing," I tell Summer. "Show them that when they try to hold you back, it only makes you stronger. You got this."

When we're done signing, Summer asks for a picture. Her mom snaps a photo on her phone.

"We have fans," Tayley says, tears welling in her eyes.

Well, one fan.

But it's still pretty cool.

# # #

When I get back to Dad's truck, Noah's already taken the front seat, so I wriggle into the jump seat in back. Before he turns on the engine, Dad turns around to look at me.

"You looked great out there."

Noah snorts and I don't blame him.

"Dad, I played one play and gave up a touchdown."

He waves a hand at me. "Ahh, forget that. I don't mean the play, I mean..." He grasps for words. "You looked like a football player."

"She *is* a football player," Noah says, sounding confused.

"Yeah, but she looked *real*. She's really doing it."

"I'm really doing it," I say, and there's a little swell of pride in my chest. I think I know what he means. I've felt it, too. Once I put on the pads, the uniform, the cleats. Once I step out onto the field, I don't feel like some girl playing football anymore. I just feel like a football player. I feel like I belong there.

"I'm proud of you," Dad says. "I'm sorry your mother wasn't here to see it."

And I stare out the window, the swell in my chest turning into a knot.

"Me too."

36

I PLAYED PRECISELY ONE PLAY IN THE GAME LAST night, and I've now been made to watch it nine times. Coach Gary is using the tape as an example for all the defensive players—if she'd gotten a better jump off the line, if she'd been faster here, if she'd watched his hands, if she'd stayed on her feet instead of jumping, if she'd kept her hips on a swivel, she could have intercepted, she could have batted the ball away, she could have tackled him right away. But instead: touchdown.

These Saturday morning practices are meant to curb any wild partying we might be considering taking part in after games, but from the red-eyed way my teammates shuffled in this morning, it doesn't seem like it made much of a difference. If Coach Gary has noticed that half his defensive line is falling asleep in the dark room watching tape, he hasn't said anything. He just keeps showing me giving up a touchdown over and over again.

As we wrap up, one of the hungover linebackers toward the

front snorts loudly at his phone. He shows it to Lincoln next to him, who says, "Those *bitches*."

My body tenses. What *about* those bitches?

I want to know, but I don't want to ask Lincoln. Back in the locker room, Carly is already holding court, standing on a bench. She whirls around when I come in, looking sheepish.

"What?" I ask.

"Don't flip out," Carly says.

"Show me."

"We're front page," Tayley says with a tentative smile. "Again."

River holds out today's *Sentinel*. They ran the photo of the five of us after our game standing with Summer above the fold, under the headline "Elkhorn Five Inspire Next Generation."

"How'd they get this photo?"

"I guess Summer's mom gave it to them," Tayley says.

Mom's gonna be pissed my haircut's on the front page of the paper, but damn, I still love the way it looks. The article starts with quotes from Summer talking about how she wants to play quarterback when she grows up. It goes on to talk about the game and that three of us played, and then there's the quote from Carly about how no one on the team recognizes how talented I am.

I slap the newspaper down on the bench. "They used your quote."

"I was just telling the truth," Carly says.

"You're gonna get yourself kicked off this team, can't you see that?" I'm so flabbergasted I can barely see straight. "You're in here criticizing the coach, insulting the rest of the team..."

"When did I insult the team?"

"When you said no one wants to recognize my talent."

"That's only insulting to the rest of the team if you think a girl having more talent than a boy is insulting."

"I just watched game tape for an hour of me flubbing a play that resulted in a touchdown. Would a quote unquote 'talented player' have done that?"

"You just need more chances to get on the field and prove yourself. What I said was true. You only played one play last night. That's *absurd*. You should be playing the whole damn game. The reason you're not is because they don't want to acknowledge that you're actually good."

Her eyes are fiery. She has to look up to meet my eyes, and it gives her this puppy-doggish look that would be adorable if she wasn't being so stubborn.

Does she really think I'm that good? Or is she just saying it because it's convenient to her cause? The way she looks at me when she says it makes me think she isn't lying, but what's real and what's not with her? I have no idea.

37

"HEY, KID, CAN YOU POINT ME TOWARD THE AERATORS?" some cowboy asks me when I go back to work Saturday afternoon.

"Back wall," I say. As soon as he hears my voice, his eyes cut up to mine. He glances down my body. My voice gives me away—I'm not the boy he thought I was.

I still love my hair. I don't have to worry if it's too frizzy. I don't have to spend an hour drying it or styling it. I left all my hair ties on a table in the locker room for other girls to use. It's short, it's out of the way, and it feels good when I touch it. When I look in the mirror, I love the girl I see. But that pride falters when I think about what people like Leroy see when they look at me, or the cowboys who are in and out of the store all day. I've been called *boy* twice already today and a third time a guy called me *bud*, which, while technically gender-neutral, is something I've never been called before. I wish we could go to Jupiter's suggestion of just calling everyone *partner*. Why does literally everything have to be about gender, anyway? Can't we just give it all a rest?

My phone buzzes with a text from Noah. *Everyone's climbing the hill tonight to do the E if you wanna join.* The E is the giant letter on the hill above Elkhorn formed from little white rocks. Every year the football team hikes up the hill and cleans up the edges to make it look fresh again. I know the hike will involve lots of drinking. I know Quinn will be there. I really don't want to be on a dark, deserted hillside with him and a bunch of his friends while everyone's drinking. *I have a test I need to study for,* I text back, and stuff my phone in my pocket.

The door jingles and Jupiter enters.

"Hey!" I can't help the big smile that takes over my face.

"Oh my god." Her eyes widen at the sight of my hair, and she puts her hands out as though she's about to cradle the sides of my head. "You look sick as hell, Mara! Can I touch it?"

"Yeah, it feels cool."

She touches the buzzed sides. "This is a great fade. Did you get this done in town?"

"Yeah, the barbershop. He was weird about it, though."

"Yeah." Jupiter turns my head this way and that so she can see the whole thing. "He did a great job, though."

Maybe she won't bring up the last time we saw each other. Maybe that's for the best. We left things on a weird note. I'd rather everything went back to normal.

"Did your mom freak out?"

"Kind of the opposite, actually. She just...shut down."

"Oh, damn." Jupiter drops her hands. "You're not the daughter she ever imagined raising."

"I guess not." I chew my bottom lip. It's too much to talk about in the aisles at work. "Whatever. Anyway. Whatcha looking for?"

"I need more woven wire. I'm almost done with the fence, but it's a pain in the ass finishing it without you."

I lead her over to the woven wire. "What do you plan to put in that pasture, anyway?"

"We were thinking...sheep?" She looks at me like she's hoping for confirmation that it's a good idea.

"Awesome."

"You ever had sheep?" she asks hopefully. "My partner said they're easy."

Her partner again. "Your partner is right. If you'd said goats, I'd be worried. Goats are assholes. Sheep, on the other hand, have a pleasant disposition." I pull a ream of wire off the shelf for her.

"Okay, cool." She sighs in relief. "They're better at all this stuff than I am."

"Where is this partner, anyway?"

"I didn't tell you? They're a musician. They'll be back from tour in two weeks. You should meet, I think they'd really like you," she says, then shuffles her feet as she remembers. "Or, I guess...if your mom would say it's okay. Which..."

"Yeah." A touring musician from Portland who uses they/them pronouns and who knows things about sheep? I absolutely have to meet this person. How am I going to get my mom to change her mind about Jupiter?

"So, sheep, okay," Jupiter says like she's psyching herself up. "Do you, ah, know how I go about getting some?"

"Huh." My wheels turn as I start to put pieces together. "What if I were able to get you some sheep *and* smooth things over with my mom at the same time?"

Jupiter cocks her head. "What do we have to do?"

"You got church clothes?"

WHEN I COME DOWNSTAIRS FOR BREAKFAST IN THE morning, I'm wearing the soft yellow cotton dress that drapes lightly over my body. Of the dresses I picked out at the thrift store, it's the least obvious, but in some ways, it's the most feminine. The cotton is light, and there's a tiny white ribbon bow on each cap sleeve. I'm getting better at walking in the pumps. I sit down in the kitchen with Noah, Mom, and Dad, and scoop myself some oatmeal out of the pot Mom made.

Mom stares at me.

"What are you up to, honey?" Dad asks.

"I thought I'd go to church," I say.

Noah watches as he shovels oatmeal in his mouth.

"We talked about this," Mom says.

"Mom, it's church. I'm going. You can give me a ride, or I'll ride my bike. Either way."

Noah cough-laughs into his oatmeal. Dad raises his eyebrows.

Mom's eyes go to the yellow dress, to my shoes, to my hair, then back to my face.

"You're wearing the hat" is all she says.

\# \# \#

When we arrive, I pray none of the milling parishioners try to talk to me. I don't want to waste time gossiping this morning when I have business to get to. Plus, my feet already hurt. Wayne outright laughs when he sees me, but I walk right by him and into the chapel. Jupiter is sitting exactly where I told her to sit. Fourth pew, center. She looks cool as hell in a nice navy blazer, with a white patterned shirt and a bolo tie. She even brushed her cowlick down.

Dad stops to make small talk with another ex-rancher, but Noah and Mom are right on my heels. When we reach our pew, I say to Noah, "Did you see Mrs. Lewis's cookies are set out already?" He perks up and starts weaving his way to the back of the church to snag a cookie before things begin. I slide into the pew next to Jupiter. Mom sits next to me.

Here goes nothing. "Oh, hi!" I say with fake surprise.

Mom looks over, confused.

"Hi, Mara. That's a nice dress," Jupiter says, and I shoot her a look. No need to go overboard.

I gesture to Mom. "Jupiter, do you know my mother?"

"Hello, Mrs. Deeble. Jupiter Douglas." Jupiter puts a hand out, and Mom looks at it for a beat, as though checking for some kind of trick before delicately taking it. Even though she can tell she's being set up, she can't allow herself to let someone's hand hang without shaking it. Manners are manners.

"Well, hello, Miss Douglas. What a *coincidence* to run into you here," she says, hitting *coincidence* with all the subtlety of a pile driver. I watch Mom examine Jupiter's outfit and it's pretty clear she doesn't think it's as cool as I think it is. What I wouldn't give for a blazer right now. "Jupiter. Is that your given name?"

I cringe. This is painful. But Jupiter doesn't skip a beat.

"It's a chosen name. Do you like it?"

"I can honestly say you're the first Jupiter I've met," Mom says, folding her hands in her lap.

I'm worried the conversation is stalling out, so I step in to keep it going. "Jupiter moved into the Hardys' old place."

"So I heard," Mom says. "And where are you from, Miss Douglas?"

"I'm from the Bay Area, but I've lived in Portland the last fifteen years."

"Ah, a Californian," Mom says with practiced evenness, but I know the word *Californian*, to her, means something specific— an interloper, a person with skewed values, someone inauthentic. Lately more and more Californians have come north, seeking cheaper houses, maybe, or somewhere with water. Still, Elkhorn has largely escaped the influx. It's too small, and it's not on the coast, bordering one of Oregon's pristine, moody, gray beaches. But mostly? Elkhorn is just deeply, fundamentally uncool.

So far, a poor start.

"We knew the Hardys well," Mom says with an edge to her voice. "Saw Tyler grow up into a fine young man. And Theresa a lovely young woman, though she was always a bit of an odd one. I was surprised they didn't keep their parents' land, but I suppose Elkhorn isn't everyone's first choice." Mom pauses, then considers Jupiter. "What brings *you* here?"

"Just needed a bit more space," Jupiter says. "I'm thinking about raising some sheep, actually. Leroy, he said you're the one to talk to about that."

Jupiter's pulling it off exactly how I coached her. I can see the doubt on my mom's face—she dislikes everything Jupiter stands for. And yet, she loves to talk about sheep.

"Is that so?" Mom says carefully.

"Yeah." Jupiter surges onward. "I have about two acres, so I was thinking maybe five or six sheep. But I'm not sure what sort to get, and where around here to buy some."

Mom is legitimately torn. Who in town has what kind of sheep is her favorite topic in the world. She looks from Jupiter to me and back. The longer she waits, the more concerned I become. What if she turns a cold shoulder to Jupiter? What if services start before she can come around?

Finally, Mom says, "Milk, meat, or wool?"

The corners of my mouth start to turn up, but I fight the smile. It's not time to get cocky yet.

Jupiter says, "I'm thinking wool. I want to learn to make my own yarn."

We didn't get this far in the strategizing, but it was the right thing to say. My mom made her own yarn until we got rid of the sheep. Every pair of mittens I owned for the first fifteen years of my life was knit from our sheep's wool.

Mom nods thoughtfully. "Clark over there, in the blue suit? He has about a hundred head of Columbia. Usually has a few he's looking to sell at any given time. *Great* wool."

"Okay, good," Jupiter says.

"If you're looking for long wool, the Ericksons keep Leicesters, but sometimes"—she lowers her voice as though sharing the juiciest of gossip—"they can be a little on the thin side."

"Good to know," Jupiter says seriously.

Mom goes on like that, pointing out who has what sheep and how many, and how they treat them, and Jupiter listens. Jupiter decides she might like some Merinos, and Mom promises to introduce her to the Vasquezes after the service.

Jupiter thanks her profusely for her help. "Now I just need a good set of hands to help me transport them back to my place," she says, and I hold my breath. Mom looks between us, registering the question behind the comment.

"Maybe Noah could help you out," she says.

"Mom," I say, jumping in. "I know how to do it, and I could really use the money for my truck fund."

"She's a hard worker, ma'am," Jupiter says, laying it on thick. I almost laugh at *ma'am*, but my mom loves it.

She sighs and looks down at the hands clasped in her lap as though she's praying about it. Maybe she is. I glance at Jupiter. I really want this to work.

Finally, Mom raises her head. "Don't let it interfere with chores. And I want a full update on the sheep at all times."

My smile stretches ear to ear. "You got it."

Noah and Dad find their way back to the pew just as things are about to start.

Jupiter leans over and whispers, "Do I have to stay for the whole thing now?"

I mouth, "Yes," and she stifles a groan.

ON MONDAY, ALL ANYONE CAN TALK ABOUT IS HOW off the hook the E party was. Apparently, they stayed on the hill until five in the morning. The whole offensive line puked in the trees. The running backs streaked in full view of the city lights. And most importantly, there were *girls* there.

Usually, the E thing is just for football players, but apparently some volleyball players and cheerleaders showed up this time around. Kelly Wesley climbed up the hill wearing a miniskirt. And if whispers are to be believed, Maria Carpenter made out with Quinn Kegley in full view of the whole team.

I wonder what she likes about him. Is it that he's skinny? Cute? Is it that he's good at football, or quick-witted? Why *Quinn*?

"Why *Quinn*?" Carly sneers in the locker room, echoing my exact thoughts.

"He's funny," Maria says with a shrug. "I don't know. All the other boys in this town suck. Why *not* Quinn?"

Maria wriggles into a tank top as the volleyball girls look on.

"He's a known asshole," Carly says. "He's been a jerk to us from the moment we joined the football team."

"Mara's friends with him, why aren't you going after her?"

I have one foot into my pants when they all look at me. Of course Maria knows I'm friends with him. It's Maria's job as popular girl to know who all the political alliances are in the school so she can move seamlessly among them.

"Not so much anymore," I say, yanking my pants up.

"No?" Maria says, interested in the new gossip.

"I just want to know one thing. Did you *want* to make out with him?"

Maria cocks her head at me. "What do you mean?"

"I mean, was it consensual?"

Heads turns from me to her.

"Yes," she says forcefully. "Is that so hard to believe?"

I shrug. "It's just not a given with him."

Carly examines me. "What'd he do?" she asks, hard.

Everyone's looking at me now. I've been friends with Quinn since I was what, six? Eight?

"Quinn..." I start. "It's true that he's funny and charismatic, and he can make you feel like a better person than you are." I pause to pull on a sweatshirt. Is my oldest friend a good person? Would I trust him with a girl? I've spent a thousand hours with him playing *Mario Kart*, but would I tell a friend to date him?

Quinn is an offside kick. Bouncing around. You never know what he'll say or do next. I've seen him be the most sensitive guy in the world, like the time he cried during *Homeward Bound* and when we got to the end, he insisted we start the DVD over again from the beginning. But other times, he's the most selfish person I know.

"I just don't trust him anymore," I say.

Maria raises her eyebrows. "Okay, interesting. How about Stetson Ellison?" Maria asks. "He went to second base with Kelly."

Ew. Kelly smiles demurely. "He was a gentleman."

"And Valentina was making out all night with your quarterback," Maria says.

My stomach drops. "Noah?" I ask, almost a whisper.

Valentina shoots me an apologetic look as she tries to keep the smile off her face.

"Is that true?" Carly asks.

Valentina shrugs, then nods.

"Damn, girl!" River cries, and slaps Valentina on the back. "He's a fox!"

"Tell us everything!" Tayley squeals.

"What were you even doing there?" Carly gapes at Valentina.

"Maria invited me," Valentina says.

I can't look at them anymore. The air rushes in my ears. Not Noah.

This whole time I thought she might have been crushing on me, when she was secretly into my brother? It's so humiliating.

I grab my shoes and make for the exit. I'll put them on outside. I can't be here anymore.

At practice, Coach Willis works us harder than he has in a while, but I welcome the work. It turns my brain off. Our next game is against the Linkport Orcas, which has an okay defense, but it's their offense that shines, led by their star fullback, Turnip. We practice tackling and getting tackled all day, focusing on how to take down a beast eight times your size. It's an exhausting day, and I know tomorrow will bring fresh bruises spreading across my torso and legs like spilled blueberry milkshake. But it's better than thinking about Valentina snuggling up with my brother.

# # #

When we get to Linkport, their coach tells our coach that they've designated the equipment room as the girls' changing room, which is simultaneously insulting—we have to get changed between racks of footballs?—and also better than what our own team provided for us. As we disembark the bus, Noah gets off with Valentina. Just looking at the two of them makes me want to gag.

Noah says, "I'm gonna make sure you play today, okay? You deserve it." He runs his hand down her arm and peels off with the boys.

"Gross," Carly says, out of earshot of Valentina.

"You're telling me," I say.

When we get to the locker room, there's a piece of paper taped to the door that says in thin, shitty boy handwriting: WELCOME ELKHOE FIVE. Carly tears it down and balls it up.

"I feel so accepted," River says drily.

The Linkport field doesn't feel so different from our own. The squint-bright lights making the yard lines pop in the darkness of the October night, the smell of the freshly cut grass, the ocean-vast buzz of the crowd waiting for kickoff, it's all the same whether we're at home or away. But I know, when we look up in the stands, we'll see a town come out in Linkport Orca blue and gray to support their sons, not Elkhorn. As we take the field, I look at the away bleachers, where there are a few white-and-green-clad figures clapping and cheering for us. A banner held over three heads reads, in broad, green, hand-painted letters: PLAY THE ELKHORN FIVE.

I drop my eyes, my cheeks burning. Will the guys on the team blame this on us somehow? Probably. Do I care?

I lift my head again and raise a gloved hand to wave at the stands.

Quinn sees me. "Your doting fans."

"Jealous?"

"Nah. Just weird that we have fans who would rather see the girls play than have the team win."

Never mind that "the girls" scored in the last game and he didn't. I turn toward the field and watch Noah go out for the coin toss. "Heard you were making out with Maria Carpenter last weekend."

"Now, that's a woman," he says. "We had a lovely time and she didn't even feel the need to punch me after."

"You needed a lesson about boundaries," I say.

"You need a lesson in how you're not as hot shit as Carly Nakata makes you think," he says.

"What's that supposed to mean?"

"You know she wants to fuck you, right? The way she's always blowing smoke up your ass. You're not as good of a football player as she says you are, Mara. You're *okay*. But from the way she talks about you, it's like the two of you are married or something."

"Dude. Carly does *not* like me that way." There's literally no chance. She can't stand me. That's why we're always arguing.

Quinn scoffs. "Relax. God, you're so uptight all the time. You can cut your hair off, but I know you're not gay. You've been in love with me for too many years."

My jaw falls open. Is *that* what he thinks? I can't even form a response before he wanders over to Wayne and Curtis.

I'm so dumbfounded I barely register Noah winning the coin toss. But apparently he chooses for Elkhorn to kick, because before I know it, Tayley is trotting out onto the field.

Tayley kicks a beautiful one, high and arching, landing right in the arms of the returner at our ten-yard line. He's a little squirrely guy, and he ducks and spins his way to midfield. Then he's past our guys and they're on his tail, but he's too fast, and just like that, there's nothing but open field between him and the end zone until a streak of green sideswipes him into the sidelines as they both go down, tumbling end over end. The streak of green stands up, a 99 on her jersey.

Tayley got the tackle.

Our stands go nuts. I smile inside my helmet.

That guy just got bulldozed by a girl, and he doesn't look happy about it. I can't hear what he's saying, but there's clearly some trash talk happening between them. The ref comes over and pushes him away as Tayley jogs toward our sidelines.

As the cheers die down, something else takes their place. A chant, the words slow to come into clarity, but when they do, they hit me like a blindside tackle. *"Put her in. Put her in. Put her in."* Is the *her* me, or one of the other girls? Or is it intentionally vague as to be any one of us, or all of us? Is this what they drove two hours to do? Chant for the girls? I steal a glance at Coach Willis, who stalks the sidelines, ignoring the crowd.

Wayne crosses behind me, murmuring under his breath, "Put it *in her*, more like." I would like someone to give me a trophy for not whirling around and sticking an uppercut just below his pads. Instead, I lift my helmet, spit on the ground, and ignore him. But I feel the rage build in the back of my throat.

Linkport has a hell of a passing game. With Turnip defending their QB, no one can get through. It's not long before Coach calls for a nickel defense to cover their slot receiver and I'm running onto the field. I hear the cheers, but I stay focused on finding my man and getting my body into ready position.

As I squat, feet apart, hands ready, I hear Wayne, who's lining up behind me, mutter, "What a view."

My fury flares, but I redirect its attention to the only man I need to care about right now: my receiver.

I stick to my guy like we're handcuffed. The pass goes to Wayne's receiver for a six-yard gain. The slot receiver stays in, so I stay in. Wayne doesn't say anything this time. What can he say? I'm doing my job.

Another play. I run with my man. The pass goes another way again. Incomplete. My blood is pumping now, after a few sprints downfield. I feel the sweat cooling my arms in the light evening breeze coming off the ocean. The sun has just set somewhere over the Pacific. The lights are the brightest thing in town, and they're shining on us.

It's third and four, and this is their last shot at a first down before they have to punt. We gotta hold them. The snap comes. I race with my man. He cuts, and I follow, just a few steps behind. The pass goes up, this time to my receiver. I pour on the speed. I've been doing those wind sprints in practice for just this moment. I feel unstoppable. His arms go out, I reach, too. For a moment, it seems like anything could happen, and then I swat and make contact with the ball and it tumbles to the ground. Incomplete pass. They have to punt. I feel eight feet tall. Like a giant that the villagers best not fuck with.

As I run off field, I jog next to Wayne. He says nothing, and I should probably keep my mouth shut, too, but hey, trash talk isn't fighting, right? "You hear those cheers? Those are for me."

"You wish," he says, but they *are* cheering for me, and we both know it.

I allow myself to glance at the bleachers. They're screaming their heads off. Hell yeah they are.

It's 7–7 just before halftime when Tayley flubs a field goal. Maybe it's because the wind picked up, or maybe it was the other team getting into her head—they haven't stopped trash talking her since she made that tackle—or maybe it's just because sometimes kickers miss, but her field goal went wide, and we went into the half tied instead of up.

On the jog to the locker room, Wayne mutters to me, "Told ya girls can't play."

My fist clenches and all it wants to do is connect with his stupid jaw, but I can't, so instead I cut across his path, forcing him to stumble over his feet.

How dare he suggest that just because Tayley missed a field goal, somehow I can't play cornerback? Would I ever tell Curtis Becker that he'll never play college ball because Noah threw an interception? Would I ever put Angelica to pasture because Roger broke his leg? But no one ever expected brilliance from Wayne Warren.

Coach Willis frames his halftime pep talk around being able to bounce back from mistakes. It makes me angry, because we've all been playing really well, aside from that one flubbed kick. All it serves to do is focus everyone's attention directly on Tayley, who looks like she wants to sink into the floor.

When he's done with his speech, Noah goes up to him and quietly speaks, gesturing at Valentina. He's asking Coach to put her in, just like he said he would. Coach waves him off, but I can't tell if he's going to do it or not. Valentina catches me watching and I look away.

Sometimes I remember how it felt to kiss her, in that moment before she pulled away. Her lips, so soft. My heart, full, feeling like I was finally being seen. Feeling like I wasn't alone. But apparently, I was wrong. Apparently, I was pushing myself on her. And when I think about that, it all sours again, and I can barely touch the memory with a five-foot stick.

The game stays tied through the rest of the third quarter. In the fourth, Linkport kicks a long field goal that barely makes it over the crossbar. 10–7 Linkport. Every time Coach puts me in, Wayne says something snarky, which only makes me madder, which only makes me play harder, fiercer, more focused. I'm playing better than I've ever played. I'm tackling guys faster than me. With my hair and my pads, I don't even think half these guys can tell I'm one of the girls, which on one hand is sort of a thrill, but on the other hand, I want them to know when I make a tackle or block a pass that a girl just did that. I want us to get the credit.

We need a touchdown to win it, and there's just six minutes left in the game. We're trying to hold Linkport, and it's third and six. If we can make them punt here, maybe our offense can put together a drive to the end zone. Coach sends me in, and I'm guarding the same slot receiver I had earlier in the game. He scowls at me, no doubt remembering that bat away in the first half.

"You're gonna eat grass, Twenty-Two," he growls.

I smile at him. Who needs trash talk when you have game?

We take off at the snap. The pass is fast and tight, and I barely have time to register it's coming before it's in my arms.

Holy shit, it's in my arms.

40

MY LEGS START MOVING ON THEIR OWN. I TRANSFER the ball to my right arm, tucking it tight, the way I learned. I try not to think about the fact that this is my first interception ever and try to focus on the eight huge-ass dudes barreling at me. But I got this. It's just like when Noah's chasing me around the barn with a Super Soaker. I turn on the speed, spin out of a linemen's arms, then stop short and cut right, letting another lineman hurtle in front of me. There's a gap up ahead that two of my guys are blocking out for me, and I power up to make it through before it closes. I have no idea who's behind me. A tackle could come at any moment, but it doesn't. And then I'm through the gap and the field is wide open and all I have to do is run. I don't look back, I just put all my remaining gas into my legs and power my way down the thirty, the twenty , the ten, the five, and then a Ford F-350 slams into me from behind, helmet-to-helmet, and I hit the grass, face-first.

For a moment, the pain is so sharp, I don't feel anything else. Then I become aware of the grass sticking up through my face mask, tickling my nose, then the ball, still safely tucked under me. Then the screaming from the stands. My neck hurts, and the pain reverberates down my entire body like a guitar string that just snapped.

But was it a touchdown?

I push myself onto my knees. There's grass stuck in my face mask. I pull my helmet off. Nothing but green. It's when I look down that I see the end zone line running right under my shins.

I got a fucking touchdown.

I look up in time to see the score change from 10–7 to 10–13. I did that. That was me.

The F-350 shadows my face as I look up at him. Turnip. I just got tackled by Turnip.

"You do that again, the medics will have to pick up the pieces of you," he says, low and intense. I definitely do not want to run into him off the field anywhere.

Then the ref ejects him. Head-to-head contact is called targeting, and it's an automatic ejection from the game.

He stares at me his whole walk back to the sidelines. It gives me the creeps.

Finally, I climb to my feet and stretch out my neck. It feels okay. I hand the ball to the ref and jog to the sidelines. Tayley is running on the field at top speed to kick the extra point, and she's coming straight for me. She leaps at me and encompasses me in a full-body hug.

"Oh my GOSH!" she screams.

And then River is there, too, and she's whacking me on the back in triumph, and I realize I haven't even celebrated my touchdown.

"You're a MONSTER out here, Deeble!" River cries, and then they continue onto the field and I keep going to the sidelines, where Carly is grinning and holds up a hand for a high five, and yeah, she's Carly and whatever, but I got a goddamn touchdown and I deserve a high five from *somebody*, so I slap her hand with everything I got and she hoo-hahs, a little bit ironically but maybe a little bit not. Valentina even comes over, but thankfully she just smiles and nods at me, and doesn't try to touch me, because I don't think I could handle that right now.

I hear the cheerleaders screaming my number and I wave at Ichelle, who is beaming at me and shimmying her pom-poms. And then Ranger tousles my hair, and Noah even comes over and swings an arm around me and says, "I taught you everything you know, don't forget that." And I still have three inches on him, and I'm still semi-pissed at him, so I wrap *my* arm over *his* shoulders and give him a noogie, because I'm so conflicted he's finally acknowledging my existence on the team that I have to react with violence, obviously. He squirms away. I look back to the field in time to watch Tayley kick a magnificent extra point.

Quinn is grabbing more water, not even looking at me. I can feel our friendship slipping away, bit by bit, and I'm not sure I care to rescue it. In some parallel universe, Quinn isn't such a dumbass, and he didn't try to force himself on me that Friday night, and he's not being a whiny crybaby right now. In that universe, he's slapping me on the back and making some joke about mashing Turnip like a potato. But instead, we're in this universe, and it sucks.

Now that we're up with just a couple minutes left, Coach must feel pretty confident, because he points at Valentina and goes, "Okay—you. You're in. Don't blow it." And Valentina looks briefly at Noah, who gives her a double thumbs-up. Then she runs onto the field.

Wow, they must have made quite the connection at the E party. It twists my somach up in knots to think about it. Still, I want Valentina to do well. The thing about playing safety is, you gotta know when the motion changes the play and how to read the QB to see where he'll throw before he even knows himself. You're the last line of defense. You're using your brain first, and your body wisely.

Valentina gets this. And she's studied the game tape and knows Linkport's plays, so she knows where to go when she sees them running a slant route. When Wayne's receiver catches the ball, Wayne tries to tackle him, but Wayne can't get him down. Valentina sprints toward him and delivers the blow that brings the receiver crashing to the ground in a crunch of pads and helmets. I look to Coach—did he see that?

We think of football players as nothing more than meat sacks, but in reality, playing football is as much a mental game as physical. And playing safety is more about speed, agility, and smarts than about meat. And Valentina's smart.

I watch her pick herself up, shake off the hit, and jog back to the line of scrimmage, but then Flint Wentworth goes back in and taps her on the shoulder and he's taking her place. One play. That's all she got.

Still, she's smiling when she comes off. Noah claps her on the back. She just became the fourth girl in Elkhorn history to play in a football game.

I look around for Carly. She's standing by the water dispenser, sipping from a paper cone, watching Noah and Valentina, just like I was. She's the last one. I wonder how badly Carly wants to play. Is this all just about the press coverage to her? If so, she might be just fine on the sidelines, wearing the uniform and never getting it dirty. But if she actually cares about football, if she actually likes the game itself, she would be aching to be put in. I know I was. I still am.

With less than a minute left in the game, the Orcas are forced to punt.

Noah sidles up to Coach and tilts his head toward Valentina. Coach nods his okay, and Valentina stuffs her helmet on to go in again. I feel a zip of excitement for her, even though this is probably a nothing play. It's basically the end of the game; since we're up 14–10, we can just let the clock run out and walk away with it. All we have to do is catch the punt and take a few knees.

But instead of waving a fair catch, Quinn decides to run the ball. Maybe he's out for glory, or maybe he just wants to have fun in the final minute of the game before we have to all load onto the bus for a long journey home. He catches it around our own twenty-yard line and starts running in his signature way: zippy, zaggy, and impossible to catch. He crosses the fifty and looks like he might go all the way.

Part of me is jealous. Quinn gets his shot to be a star every time he sets foot on the field. That's how it goes when you're a wide receiver and a punt returner. When I was running the ball back after my interception, the rush was huge. That must be how Quinn feels all the time. No wonder he loves football. And then I rub my neck, remembering how Turnip steamrolled me right at the end. How does Quinn handle hits like that?

And then it happens. Quinn's crossing the thirty and Valentina is gearing up to block a Linkport player to give Quinn a hole to run through. But the guy gets lower than Valentina does and runs straight through her. Then he plasters Quinn, too. They both hit the grass and the ball tumbles away. Fumble.

"No," I say under my breath.

"No!" Coach shouts as a Linkport player scoops the ball up. I eye the field. It happens so quickly, no one on our team has time to react. There's nothing between this guy and the end zone. He runs it all the way back, scoring a touchdown. It's 16–14 Linkport.

Their stands go wild. Our whole team groans. Valentina crawls to her feet, looking shaken and embarrassed that she let that Linkport player past her. Quinn rolls onto his side, gripping his left arm and moaning. Coach runs onto the field to check on him as the rest of our guys make a circle around him. I'm too far away to see what happened, but I can hear his wails of pain. Valentina pulls her helmet off and brings her hand to her mouth. She looks horrified.

The medics pull Quinn to the sidelines and let Linkport kick the extra point. Game over.

41

ON THE BUS HOME, QUINN SPREADS OUT, TAKING AN
entire seat to himself. His arm is wrapped up in an absurd number
of bandages and strapped to his chest. I'm in the seat directly in
front of him, attempting to read my history textbook. Every bump
the bus hits makes him moan. It's incredibly annoying. I wheel
around and glare at him.

"It can't possibly hurt that bad," I say.

"What are you, the pain police?" Quinn shoots back. His legs
are curled up so that his entire body fits on the bench seat. "Why
don't you tell your little gal pals their help is not needed for the
rest of the season? Thanks, but no thanks."

"You're blaming this on Valentina?" I say, incredulous. "If you
would've just called for a fair catch, you'd be fine right now. And
we would have won."

Plus, I would have had the winning touchdown, I think but
don't say.

"Fair catch is for pussies," Quinn says.

"Whatever." I get up and grab my bag. I can't sit in front of him for the next two hours.

I storm toward the front of the bus. Two rows up, I pass Valentina, who's sitting next to River. River's rubbing her back. Valentina meets my eye. "Don't listen to him," I say. "This is *not* your fault."

The only other free spot is next to Carly, but her backpack is on the seat next to her. I step up to her, but she doesn't move it right away.

Maybe I'll just sit in the aisle.

Carly tips her head to the side. She's really going to make me ask. I sigh.

"Do you mind?" I manage, gesturing at the seat next to her.

"Oh, do you want to sit here?" she asks innocently.

I nod. She furrows her brow like she's really concerned. "Are you sure you want to be seen sitting next to another..." She looks over her shoulder exaggeratedly, then drops her voice and says, *"Girl?"*

All right. "Never mind." I start to walk away and Carly laughs.

"Sit down, Deeble. God. Do you ever lighten up?" She hauls her backpack onto the floor, and I reluctantly slide in next to her, keeping my butt as close to the aisle as possible.

She's wearing her post-game clothes—a pair of short green athletic shorts that were issued to us in middle school that I can't believe still fit her and an oversize gray sweatshirt that has the bottom cut off so the hem curls right around her belly button. A white tank top sticks out underneath. The shorts reveal basically the whole length of her legs, which I absolutely do not look at. If you overlook the well-earned blue-gray bruises sprayed across her legs, she could be in a magazine for active women, holding a brand-name water bottle and talking about her fitness regimen. Me, on the other hand. I'm wearing EHS sweatpants and a hoodie from the feed store. I didn't think at all about my "after-game look." I just put on some comfortable bus clothes.

"Good game today, touchdown-getter," Carly says.

My cheeks warm, and I'm thankful that the bus is dark so she can't see it.

"Thanks." I can't think of anything else to say.

Dark trees whip past the windows as we leave Linkport. We have a long two hours of travel ahead of us. Two hours sitting next to Carly.

As if reading my mind, she says, "We don't have to talk."

It catches me off guard. Since when does Carly not want to talk? "Oh...okay."

"I plan on sleeping."

"All right," I say, reaching into my bag for my earbuds. I line up a Tanya Tucker album I bought after Jupiter introduced me to her and hit play, then immediately hit pause and rip my earbuds off again. "I just want to know one thing."

She looks up in surprise.

"I want to know why you keep rooting for me even though we're always fighting. It's like, one minute we're at each other's throats, and then the next, you're going for a high five." She stares at me, mouth slightly open but silent. "It's confusing," I clarify. "I never know what's in your head."

"Mara, I root for all the girls whether you like it or not." She shrugs. "I mean, unless you wanna tell me you're not a girl."

"What do you mean?"

She lowers her voice, "Like if you told me you were trans or something. That would be fine with me, and I would still root for you as a not-cis boy."

"I'm not trans."

"Okay. Then I'm rooting for you because you're a girl."

"But *why*?"

She stares at me. It feels like we're talking past each other. Like we're both saying the most obvious things in the world, but to the other person, they're not obvious at all.

"Because, Mara, to them we're all the same. If they're going to make one of our mistakes all of our mistake, then I'm going to claim one of our successes as a success for all of us. When you're out there playing well, it's good for Tayley and for River and for Val and for whatever girls are in the stands thinking maybe they want to play someday." Like Summer, that girl from the parking lot after last game. "So, yeah, I'm gonna root for you. Because it's bigger than just us, you know?"

I'm quiet for a while after that. Because I've been thinking the same thing, but I don't want to tell her. After a bit, I just put in my earbuds and turn the Tanya Tucker album up and try to ignore it ever happened.

Just past Beaver, I glance over, and Carly is asleep, her deep brown hair falling over her eyes, her dark eyelashes long enough to brush the tops of her round cheeks. Her head is tipped toward the window, and her breath makes fog on the glass every time she breathes out. Her butt is scootched toward me so she can have a better sleeping angle, and we're nearly touching at the hip. I can almost feel the heat coming off her body.

Somehow, she's like two-thirds my size, but she's also taking up two-thirds of the seat we're sharing, which is exactly the kind of logic she would say makes sense, but it doesn't once you think about it.

I could nudge her awake to try to get some of my seat back, but I don't. I just lean back and close my eyes and wonder what forces in this world made Carly Nakata the specific brand of person she is, because she's not like anyone else in Elkhorn I've ever met.

42

"YOU HAVE TO HIT YOUR MARKS, DEEBLE!" QUINN hollers at me from the sidelines after I fall out of position on a simple hook route. I know this, but it's a pain in the ass to hear it from Quinn instead of one of the coaches. Ever since Quinn found out his arm is broken, he keeps showing up to practices every day but doesn't participate in any drills. He just stands around with the coaches and hollers encouragement or—more commonly—ways to improve. Like *he's* a coach now. And the real coaches just let him do it. It's annoying as all hell.

I'm done with my milk-jug weights. It's too hard to hold two in one hand. Instead, I find myself more and more in the school weight room. If I get my chores done early enough, I can get a solid forty-five-minute session in before I have to change and get ready for class. Using real equipment is so much nicer than sitting in my room lifting plastic containers of water, but the effect is the same. There's something about lifting that pushes all the other thoughts out of my head. I don't have to think about Quinn and how we barely talk anymore. Or about Noah, and how we used to hang out every day, and now we just take silent rides to school in his truck. Or about Valentina, and how she kept her promise not to tell anyone, but how now everything's weird between us.

Or about Carly. And how that ride back from Linkport was actually kind of okay.

But all of those thoughts disappear when I lift. The whole world shrinks down to just me and these dumb heavy things that I'm repeatedly moving through the air. It's stupid, but these days it's the only thing that makes me feel calm or normal.

As the season progresses, the sun sets earlier and earlier until we're finishing practice in the dark, muddy and wet from incessant drizzling, muscles tired but less sore than at the beginning of the season. Three more games pass. Coach doesn't make eye contact with me when he plays me, just keeps his eyes on the field, points, and says, "Deeble."

We lose all three games, which puts us at 0–5 for the season with just two games left. We're not going to State. We're not attracting any scouts. No one's going pro after this. We're just hoping to win a game.

One day, I bump into Coach Joyce in the hallway outside the weight room after I finish my workout. She smiles warmly when she sees me, which is the first time in a long time she's done that. She wears her usual outfit—an Elkhorn Basketball T-shirt tucked into khakis and athletic shoes.

"Mara, hi. I've been talking to Coach Willis, and it sounds like you're doing a great job on the football team."

I wipe the sweat off my brow with my T-shirt. "He said that?" It's not that I don't think I am, I just can't believe Coach Willis said so. He's always been so gruff with me.

"He did. And he said you've been staying out of trouble. Keeping to yourself mostly." Coach Joyce tucks a strand of her no-nonsense hair behind her ear.

"That's true."

"I hope you're also having fun?"

I take a drink from my water bottle to buy a minute to think. When it comes to the drama off the field? No, I'm not. It's distracting. But when it comes to the game on the field? "Yeah, I am. I think I'm actually made for football. I like it."

"Really?" She sounds surprised. "Not more than basketball, I hope?"

"Never," I tell her, even though it might not be true. I still love basketball, but nothing quite feels like football.

She smiles at that, then looks me over. "You look different. You been hitting the weight room?"

"Yeah," I say.

"Keep it up and I'll be happy to have you on the basketball team this year."

Those are the words I've been waiting since last winter to hear her say.

"Thanks, Coach." I hit the showers with a little extra zip in my step.

I'VE NEVER SEEN JUPITER NERVOUS BEFORE, BUT IN her truck on the way to her house after my shift at Leroy's, she's babbling.

"Anyway, sorry for not stopping by earlier. It's been busy with Reese back and the sheep and the dogs and the chickens, and we're thinking of planting a winter crop in the raised beds, and Reese thinks we should do kale, but I was hoping we could do something a little less obvious, like garlic or Walla Wallas." She looks over at me as she navigates off the highway onto Cascade View Road.

It seems like I should probably say something to help her feel less anxious. "You can never have too much garlic," I offer.

"See? Yes!" She slaps her steering wheel. "That's what I said. Whereas you can *definitely* have too much kale. Easily."

When Jupiter texted me to see if I could come over after work today, I was surprised. Over the last week, between work and practice and school, I've been by her place twice to finish the fence and prep the pasture for sheep. She told me one of the Vasquez kids would help her load them in, so this visit isn't to work, she just wants me to meet Reese, her partner, who is finally done with their tour.

Reese steps out of the house as we pull up. They wear a dark blue corduroy jacket over dirty black work overalls with a pair of beat-up cowboy boots sticking out. They have on the same black felted cowboy hat with a silver buckle Mr. Hardy used to wear to church every Sunday back when he used to be alive. And that's when it hits me. I *know* Reese. They're one of the Hardys' kids. Only, when I knew them, they were a surly teenager trailing behind their parents to church in a floral dress and Mary Janes. I was always scared of them because they seemed like the type to never smile. But right now, Reese's got a huge smile, their round apple cheeks popping, their ear-length hair framing their face as they step off the porch.

I barely know what to do, but then Jupiter reaches over and unclicks my seat belt. "You better get out and say hi or they're going to climb in here."

So I climb out and Reese is right there. "Do you mind if I hug you?" they ask. I shake my head, and they envelop me in a really good hug, the soft corduroy of their jacket rubbing against my cheek. They smell like animals and hay, like my dad used to before he sold the cows and the sheep. It's way more comforting than I thought.

"It's real good to see you again," Reese says. "I've heard a lot about you."

No shit? We pull away and I look back at Jupiter, who finds something interesting to look at in the Doug fir nearest her. Reese laughs. "She won't admit it, but she's fond of you. Come in. I'm just about to pull out the chicken."

And when Reese turns around to lead me into the house, I see that their jacket is a Future Farmers of America jacket, just like the one I got a couple years ago, before I dropped out when we sold the cows. Mine's hanging in the back of my closet. I thought I'd never wear it again, but seeing Reese wear theirs makes me want to pull mine out. I remember they came in men's cuts and women's cuts, and my mom pitched a fit over me wanting to buy the men's cut. I had to put on Maddy Listhoffer's one to prove that a women's would be too short on me before she'd let me buy the one I wanted. Now, seeing Reese in a men's-cut jacket, with the big yellow OREGON spelled out over their shoulders, above the giant FFA logo, I feel weirdly emotional. I've never seen this dumb jacket on anyone who didn't look like... well, like everyone else in this town.

Inside, the house is looking homier than ever. Indigo and Sleater go wild when they see me, wagging their tails and stretching in excitement. Every time they remember me it makes me feel like someone worth remembering. Jupiter brings me to the back window and points at the six gorgeous Merino sheep grazing inside our fence, the fading autumn sun casting long shadows over the pasture. I'm proud that something I helped with is being put to use. Closer to the house, the chickens roam inside their enclosure. I see the raised beds Jupiter is thinking of planting garlic in.

"This is starting to look like a real farm," I tell Jupiter approvingly.

She shrugs in her leather jacket and ripped band tee. "Who'da thunk?"

Reese pulls the roast chicken out of the oven and starts carving it. It smells amazing. Even Jupiter swoons a little. "I've been surviving on squash soup, beer, and turmeric tea for the last six months," she says.

"It's really pathetic," Reese says. "She can barely keep herself alive when I go on tour."

"Where all have you been, anyway?" I ask.

"See for yourself." They nod to the wall with all the framed music posters hanging on it. I look over and see their face smiling out from one of them under the band name As They Say, with a long list of tour dates under it for cities all over the country.

"Cool." It's so weird that someone who grew up in Elkhorn could do that. Not just play music, but actually tour. With posters. And a band name. Cool is an understatement.

Reese brings the chicken from the kitchen to the table. "It *is* cool. But it's nice to come back home, too. Can you grab those plates?"

I set out the plates as Jupiter puts out a jar of iced tea. "But, like, *why*?" I can't help but ask.

"Why what?"

"Why is it nice to be back? Didn't you live in Portland? What's so great about Elkhorn?"

Reese and Jupiter share a look like they're amused by the question, which annoys me. Portland is huge, and there's an actual gay community there, and music and bookstores and interesting people. Here we just have cows. And some of us don't even have those.

"I left Elkhorn when I was seventeen, vowing never to come back," Reese says, sliding into their seat. "First time I had vegan food was in Portland. First time I had sex with a woman." I find myself blushing, but I try to play it cool. "The queer culture in Portland is just like..." They wave their hands, trying to find the words. "It's just, there's so much of it, you know? I knew I would find lesbians there, but I didn't know about the rich diversity within the dyke community. Trans women and nonbinary folks and butches and femmes and everything in between. It wasn't until I moved to the city that I let myself think that I could be anything other than a girl. That's the joy of a vibrant queer community. Suddenly, your options are more than just lesbian, bi, or straight. You realize you have *choices*. There are words for the way I feel, and there are other people who feel that way, too."

I'm nodding so vigorously I feel like my head's going to bounce off my neck. I want that. I can't wait for that. To kiss Elkhorn goodbye and go live my life with other people like me.

"So why the hell are you back?" I ask. It doesn't make a lick of sense.

Reese shrugs. "I missed the cows."

Are they serious? Then, a quirk of their mouth. "I dunno, Mara. I didn't realize how much I'd miss it until I left. You can see the stars out here. The commute isn't terrible. The dogs are happier. I don't have to live in an apartment the size of a tofu box. Besides, no matter how long I lived in Portland, it never really felt like home. Elkhorn is my home. I shouldn't have to leave it just because I turned out nonbinary and queer. I should be allowed to waste my life away in this podunk place just like everyone else I went to high school with. They're not special."

I have to smile at that.

"But you're not…afraid? Living here, like this?"

Jupiter swallows a long drink at that. "Well, yeah. But Reese knows Krav Maga, so…" she says.

Reese touches Jupiter's hand. "The way we look together, we're in danger anywhere we go. Yes, even Portland. Being unsafe is part of the deal when you're visibly queer. But at least I know the people here. Went to the same school as them. They knew my folks. We shared a church. It's something."

"Let me know if anyone gives you any guff," I say. "I know how to tackle now."

Reese laughs. "Thank you."

"And you?" I ask Jupiter. "You're not even from here. You like it here?"

"Portland was getting old anyway. Too clean. Too many tech yuppies. It's not the dirty art town it used to be. Copywriting wasn't paying the rent the way it used to. I was thinking of getting out anyway, but then Reese inherited the place from their parents... a change seemed good." She looks at me. "I knew I would like the space, but I didn't think the youth element would be so bad." I laugh. "Also the food! Where is the great takeout?"

"We have Las Hermanas Bonitas."

"Yeah and ten places that serve both burgers and pizza and that's *it*. Where is the Vietnamese? The Szechuan? The Mediterranean?"

I lift my eyebrows. "What's Szechuan?"

"Oh my god!" Reese and Jupiter both react in pain.

"We need to get you to a city for college," Jupiter says. "Somewhere with food."

"And then come back if you want," Reese says.

"But try Szechuan first."

"Is it spicy?" I ask. I can't do spicy.

"*Yes*, and that's the point." Jupiter pounds her fist on the table. "Start getting your tolerance up now. In fact..." She rises and goes to the fridge to pull out a jar of some kind of red chili oil with chunks of crispy garlic in it. "Here. Start now. Tonight."

They make me try the sauce on my chicken. I end up liking it better than just regular chicken, although by the end of my dinner, my mouth is on fire and my eyes are watering. Reese pours me a full glass of milk, like the farmer they are. We finish the night playing Scrabble and the two of them soundly beat me and it makes me want to practice until I can be as good as they are. Before the night is over, Jupiter takes me out to say hi to the sheep and check on the chickens. I give Sleater and Indigo full-body hugs and kisses before I go and I think, *Yeah, I'd like to see the city.* But it's true that there's something about life out here that's also nice. Maybe I don't want to live in Elkhorn my whole life, but also maybe I want the choice. Jupiter and Reese make me think maybe it *is* my choice.

Jupiter gives me a ride home through the dark, cool night, and I feel warm and tingly from a nice night at their house. The thought crosses my mind that Carly would have really liked this night. Nothing would make her happier than seeing a queer couple thriving in Elkhorn.

"Hey, Jupiter, next time? If there is one, I mean . . ."

"Yeah?"

"Do you think it would be okay if Carly came?"

Jupiter glances at me, then back to the road. She looks like she's trying not to smile, but I don't know why.

"Yeah, of course."

"Cool," I say, and I don't know what's wrong with me these days, but I can't wait to tell Carly about this.

44

"DAMMIT." THE TOILET PAPER COMES AWAY BLOODY. It was supposed to be a quick halftime pee, but now I have to figure out what to do. I didn't bring any pads. And my pants are white.

During basketball season, Coach Joyce used to carry around period supplies for us, and we could always go to her if we needed something. Somehow, I doubt Coach Willis does that.

Hixon's way of giving the girls changing space is actually the most forward thinking of any of the schools so far—they strung sheets up in the locker room, barricading off the final bank of lockers, creating a private area for us. The lights don't quite reach, so it's dark, and the cacophony of the boys roughhousing while they get ready is a lot, but at least it feels like we're part of the team.

I make my way from the bathrooms through the tangle of boys and duck behind the sheet to our dark hole, where our clothes and bags are strewn all over the benches. I try Tayley first, because she seems the most prepared for things. Something to do with her umpteen brothers and sisters.

"Hey, Tayley," I whisper. "Do you have a pad?"

Her face falls. "Oh, sorry, no!" she says louder than I would like. I don't want the whole team hearing about this.

"I have a tampon," Carly says, fishing them out of her bag. "You don't want a pad anyway, with these pants, do you?" She holds out a rainbow array. "Regular, super, or super plus?"

I've never used a tampon before. I'm not about to admit that, especially to Carly, but it's true that a pad would feel like a diaper on the field, and I can't have that.

"Two minutes!" Coach Gary calls out. I grab a super and head back to a bathroom stall.

With the door closed, I close my eyes and focus. It goes in easier than I thought, and I can barely feel it. Is that really what it's supposed to feel like? I pull up my pants and tie the waist strings as fast as possible and make it back just in time to join the rest of the team on the jog onto the field.

"Pays to have ladyfriends after all, huh?" Carly murmurs as we join the pack.

I don't say anything, because the answer is yes, and I don't want to have to admit it.

The game is 30–6 Hixon going into the second half, and I've never seen Coach look so grumpy. Hixon's defense is a solid wall that our running game can't get through, and Noah's been intercepted three times. Their offense dominates, too. Coach's halftime pep talk was a miserable pick-me-up that no one was feeling. Aside from Tayley's two field goals that River held for her, he's barely been playing the girls. I've only gone in twice. It's hard to get pumped up to go out and stand on the sidelines, hoping not to bleed through my pants.

The third quarter goes about as well as the first two. Before long, Hixon's got two more touchdowns, and we're facing a 44–6 game. Quinn stomps around the sidelines like a bull in the ring, just looking for someone to yell at. He's never been good at losing.

In the fourth quarter, Coach looks at me and jerks his head in, then does the same to Valentina. Finally. The game is such a blowout, he's putting in the girls. Shows how much he trusts us. There's no way to come back from this, so he's just accepting the loss.

My period cramps flare as I jog out there, and I press a hand to my pelvis, pushing the pain down. It almost feels good, like a manifestation of how spectacularly shitty this game is going so far. My cleats dig into the grass. The lights gleam off everyone's helmets. My fingertips are pink from the cold. My mouth guard tastes briny against my tongue. I look at the clock. Twelve minutes and sixteen seconds left. That's twelve minutes and sixteen seconds to prove to Coach that I belong here.

But no matter how much I buzz or sprint or reach, the Hixon offense just keeps making gains. First down, then another, then another. My receiver, number 47, is a tall, ropy, muscly guy with three inches on me, and even when I leap for the ball, he can leap higher. Every time he catches a pass, he growls some kind of insult on his way to the line of scrimmage. "How's that taste, girly?" or "Afraid to chip your nail polish, honey?" Every time, I get madder.

I want to intercept him. I want to run it back and show him he isn't hot shit just because he's a boy. But he *is* hot shit. *And* he's a boy. And maybe those things aren't related or maybe they are. But the fact is, he's just better than me. And it's infuriating.

They score again. Valentina and I return to the sidelines with the rest of the defense, exhausted, and defeated, while the O-team heads out to make another go of it.

Quinn passes me, grumbling, "So much for equality, huh?"

"You got something to say, Quinn?" I spin on him.

"Whoa, Mara. What are you, on your period?" He puts his hands up, as much as he can, with one in a sling.

"As a matter of fact, *yes*," I say back. He looks thrown.

"I'm just saying, it's not so much fun playing when you get trounced, is it? Equality goes both ways."

I can't even tell if he's being an asshole right now or not, but between the score, my inability to make any moves on 47, and the smirk on Quinn's face, my rage snakes up my gut and into my arm. All I want to do is throw one, single, beautiful punch into Quinn's face and watch him hit the grass. But he's injured. And I'll be benched. And that would be the end of basketball, a thing that is finally feeling within reach after my conversation with Coach Joyce.

A whistle blows. We failed to get a first down, and we're punting.

I clip my chin strap on and turn my back on him, the anger simmering in my stomach like a Crock-Pot of his precious Lit'l Smokies.

I go in. Number 47 catches the ball, then goes out of bounds, but the adrenaline and fury in my veins need somewhere to go, so I tackle him anyway. It feels good, landing pads to pads, our muscles crashing into each other. My knee hits the grass with a cold thunk that sends a missile of pain shooting up my leg, but it's delicious. My receiver is furious. I regret nothing.

"How's *that* taste, little boy?" I snarl through his face mask. He shoves me off him.

The ref calls unnecessary roughness for a late hit. It's a fifteen-yard penalty, but I barely care. I just want to hit him again. Because I can. Because I can't hit Quinn. Because this, at least, is acceptable.

I don't even try to intercept the next pass. I just hit 47 the second the ball touches his fingers, driving him into the ground. We land in a painful heap as the ball dribbles away. Wayne picks it up and starts running, but the ref whistles the play dead for an incomplete pass. Wayne never even had possession.

I drill my eyes into 47's. "How'd that one feel, hot rod?" He pushes me away.

The next play, 47 hesitates off the line, and I'm on him the whole play. He doesn't get the ball, and he doesn't say anything on his way back to the line. The shine has come off his cocky exterior.

The next play they run it.

The play after that they run it.

The next play is a passing play, and I'm on 47 like glue. His eyes rise, and I know the pass is coming our way. I buzz my feet, ready to drill into him as soon as the ball comes, and when I do that, the most incredible thing happens.

He flinches.

The ball bounces out of his hands and onto the ground. Not even close to a completion.

Part of me is disappointed I don't get to hit him, but it was a success anyway. We just held them on third down for what feels like the first time in the game. They get ready to punt it. I knock shoulders with 47 as we go in opposite directions. He doesn't say anything. I can see his coach starting to yell at him before he even reaches the sidelines.

I don't feel like hitting Quinn anymore.

The game ends 51–6, with just seven of those points coming in the fourth quarter. Everyone else is miserable, but I feel pretty damn good. I found something that worked on 47: hit him so hard he's scared to be hit. I keep replaying that flinch again and again in my head. I feel like every defender I go up against automatically assumes that he can outrun, outjump, and outhit me. Well, 47, spread the word. That's not necessarily true.

Still, every other Elk Hunter on the field is hanging their head. We slap hands with the other team after the game. They're in bright spirits. One Hixon player snarks over his hand slapping, "Next time try fielding a full team."

They're not saying it, but they're saying it. Loud and clear. *This is what happens when you let girls on your team.* Curtis Becker shoves one of their guys, and he shoves back, and the coaches leap into the fray to pull everyone apart before it can become an all-out brawl. The hand slapping is over. We're all sent back to the locker rooms.

Coach Gary intercepts the girls. "Why don't y'all give them a minute," he says. I can hear slamming and shouting from inside the locker room. I don't really want to go in there, with all that anger coursing through the team, looking for somewhere to land. It just might land on us. A sheet hung between lockers suddenly doesn't feel like enough protection.

"Sure thing," I say. Before long, it's just us left, leaning against the wall, watching the stands empty, the sun long gone, the night cooling briskly.

"That was pretty intense," Valentina says.

"Which part?" Carly snorts.

"The almost brawl, I guess?" Valentina says.

"Also the part where someone spit on my shoe," Tayley says.

"Wait, that happened?" Carly asks, straightening.

"Yeah, after the second field goal. He said something, too, but I didn't catch it. I was too busy watching my kick go in."

"Nice." I smile at Tayley. "You kicked ass tonight."

"What'd that receiver say to you?" Valentina asks me. "I saw him getting in your face."

"The same old stuff. Nothing interesting."

Tayley tugs on her jersey. "I wish we could go in. I'm sweating in these pads."

"Me too," I say. Then we go quiet again. There's something nice about the silence. I'm sure they're just as tired as I am, just as low-key worried about the bus ride back. It didn't feel safe on the field, and it doesn't feel safe in the locker room right now, but in this moment, just the five of us leaning against the scratchy wood building, with the lights bouncing off our hair and shadowing our faces, I feel okay. Our team lost the game, but we at least played well. This little group, this subteam of Elk Hunters. We're still here.

"Hey, guys?" I say, before I have time to overthink it. I close my eyes and feel the breeze on my face.

"Yeah?" says River.

"I just want to say . . . I'm glad y'all joined," I say.

There's silence. I open my eyes to find them all glancing at each other.

"Seriously?" Carly says. "The *great* Mara Deeble? Is happy to play with other girls?"

"Hey!" Tayley says, whacking Carly on the arm. "Don't make her regret it."

"Yeah," River says, pulling out her phone. "I gotta tweet this before she takes it back."

"No!" I say, grabbing at her phone. "No tweeting!" For all I know, it'll end up in some *Sentinel* headline. But River just cackles and hits send.

"Too late!"

"I'm retweeting!" Valentina giggles, pulling out her own phone.

"Oh my god." I hide my face in my hands. "You guys are the worst."

"Don't listen to them," Tayley says, stepping in front of me and putting both hands on my shoulders. "We're honored to be on a team with you." Then she pulls me into a hug, even though we both smell like drying sweat. The kindness of it almost knocks the wind out of me.

"Thanks," I say. I don't even know why I'm welling up.

Just as soon as Tayley pulls away, River pulls me into another hug, pads to pads. "You're a fucking rock star, Mara."

When River lets go, she goes to hug Tayley. I look at Valentina, who steps up and wraps me in a hug, too. There was a time when the physical connection of that would make me feel too many feelings to process, but not anymore. "Thank you for being you, Mara," she says.

"Thank you for being you more," I tell her. She smiles as she lets go, then turns to hug River and Tayley both.

Then it's just Carly and me. She looks like a gerbil in an over-size '80s blazer in her perfectly pristine football pads. It makes me smile. "You don't have to hug me," I tell her.

"*You* don't have to hug *me*," she says, the three feet between us suddenly feeling loaded in a way it wasn't before.

"I don't mind hugging you."

She takes a step toward me, and I reach for her. Her arms wrap around my waist as mine go around her shoulders. If they weren't covered in four inches of plastic pads, her head would be pressed right into my chest.

"Thank you," she says.

"For what?"

"For taking no shit."

I feel like *taking no shit* describes her better than me. "Friends? For real this time?"

She pulls away and looks up at me. "Really?"

"I'd like it," I say.

"Okay. Friends."

We actually shake hands. A truce, finally. Friends.

Tayley, River, and Valentina literally cheer. Then the Elkhorn Five is hugging, all pads and elbows and sweat-slicked hair.

Finally, the boys start filtering out of the locker room in their street clothes, making their way to the bus. They don't look at us or talk to us. A lot of them have earbuds in, eyes on the ground. After a bit, Coach Gary sticks his head out and tells us it's okay to go in but to hurry up because we gotta hit the road soon.

We get inside the locker room and duck behind the sheet to our corner. I open my duffel bag, but my clothes aren't inside it. I spin around, looking for them. I don't see any clothes anywhere. When I look up, the other girls are doing the same thing.

"Where's my shit?" Carly asks.

Slow panic unfolds in my chest as my brain begins to understand what happened.

"My clothes are gone," River says.

"Mine too," Valentina says, digging through her duffel.

"Maybe they got taken by mistake?" Tayley goes out to check the boys' side of the curtain, but she comes back shaking her head.

Carly and I lock eyes. The others, they're too optimistic. Too kindhearted to jump to the worst conclusion. But not Carly. She knows what I know.

Our own team.

45

SILENTLY, CARLY THROWS HER BAG DOWN AND marches out. I'm right on her heels. She shoves through the door, pushes past the coaches who are outside loading gear into the luggage compartment, and climbs straight aboard the bus, where thirty smelly, loud, angry boys are impatiently waiting to go home. Someone on this bus plotted to screw us over tonight, and Carly and I are going to find out who.

Carly steps up onto a seat. "Here's what's going to happen," Carly hollers over the hubbub, and the boys quiet down and turn to stare at her. "Someone here is going to point to the guy who did it. And then he'll give them back, and we'll get changed, and we can all go home."

Tayley, River, and Valentina rush breathlessly onto the bus. Behind Valentina, Coach Willis stands in the doorway, looking pissed off. "What's going on here? Why aren't you dressed?"

I glare at him. He has never been there for us—not when my tires got slashed, not after any of the many shitty comments directed at me, never.

Valentina pulls the door lever, and the door slams closed in his face. I can see him raging, but his shouts are muffled.

I turn back to the boys, scanning the faces for some hint of a weak link. The bus is quiet. No one giving anyone up.

Carly continues from her soapbox. "Look, we're not happy. You're not happy. We're all sweaty and tired, and we all want to go home."

I start walking up the aisle, slowly, looking everyone in the eye. I look at Curtis, who stares out the window. I look at Ranger, who shrugs—he doesn't know. I look at Noah, who drops his eyes the moment mine hit them, but it's unclear whether it's out of guilt or something else. Finally, I meet Quinn's eyes, and he's staring straight back at me. A dare.

I stop in front of him, meeting his gaze.

"Where are our clothes, Quinn?" I say, so low it's almost a growl. He shrugs in this infuriating way that either means he definitely knows where our clothes are or is pretending to know because he thinks it makes him look cooler. "That's really pathetic," I say. "You're pathetic."

I pass by him, but as soon as my back is to him, I hear him complain under his breath, "At least I can play football."

I spin back around. "Get up."

He looks taken aback, at least.

"Get up, Quinn."

"No." He's tucked casually back into the corner of his seat in this way that makes him look thirteen again.

I grab him by the front of his sweatshirt and haul him to his feet. It's easy to do—he only has one good arm, and he's like twelve pounds. The other guys ooh, but no one tries to stop me. I almost like that I'm still in my full gear for this. I know I look formidable. He scrambles to get his feet under him. "What the fuck, Mara?"

Once he's standing in the aisle, I put my whole hand around his bicep. My thumb and middle finger can almost touch on the other side. That gets a laugh from the guys. "You're gonna tell me that *you're* the pinnacle of strength? Get outta here." I shove him and he takes a step back, then gets right in my face.

"It's not about how tall you are," Quinn snarls. "It's about how well you play as a team. And you don't belong here. None of you do. We were a brotherhood before you arrived, and now we're just a joke. If not for you, this would be a regular season, but instead, it's...this." He waves his hand around to gesture at me and the other girls. There's a few grunts of agreement around the bus. "This isn't a football team, it's a mockery."

"Quinn, you were there when I had the fucking idea. I only joined because you encouraged me."

I can tell a lot of the other guys didn't know that from the way they murmur to one another.

"I thought it would be *funny.* I didn't know it would turn into this," he shoots back. "If I did, I would have told you to suck it up and put on your knee pads because volleyball is where you belong."

I thought I could earn my way onto this team by playing well and keeping my head down. I thought if I was strong enough or fast enough, eventually, I would thrive here. But maybe that was naive. Maybe they were never going to accept me, no matter how well I played. Maybe Quinn and the rest of these guys really are the assholes Carly says they are. Maybe I should never have done this.

"Who here agrees with him?" Carly says then, her voice ringing out in the quiet. No one moves. "If you don't want us on the team, I'd rather you say it to our faces than have you quietly talking behind our backs or taking our shit. Stand up if you agree with Quinn. If you think you'd be better off if the five of us left the team."

I kind of wish there was at least a long pause, but guys start standing almost right away. Wayne Warren, of course. Lincoln, shooting a glare at Tayley. Curtis Becker after them. A bunch of guys on the O-line, broad and angry. Stetson Ellison and Flint Wentworth. Practically all of special teams. Heads start turning to see who's left.

Jerry remains sitting, his arms crossed over his chest. "I got no problem. They can stay," he says. I nod at him and he nods back.

About half the D-line, scattered around, remain sitting. I've been practicing with them all season, and they've been decent to me.

Ranger's still sitting. The lineman next to him kicks his shoe, and Ranger shakes his head. "Mara's good, man. So's Tayley. Sorry, Lincoln, but it's true." Lincoln narrows his eyes at him, but who could fight Ranger? He's built like a wall.

Then my eyes find Noah, and a hopeful little spike goes up my spine to see he's still sitting, too. Maybe, for all his barbed comments, he really is on my side.

But his eyes look tortured. He glances around the bus before rising to his knees in his seat, a pathetic middle ground.

"I don't want anything to do with this," he says.

Does he think *I* want anything to do with this? I'm exhausted from the game, sweat drying in my hair, muscles tingling as they cool down, but even in this state, I'm practically vibrating with the desire to pull him off this bus and have it out in the parking lot. Not because he's the worst of them—he's far from it. But he's my brother and staying neutral isn't enough. I need him to stick up for me. I need him to *care.*

"Noah," Valentina says from the front of the bus, where she still holds the door lever closed as Coach Willis claws at the doors from the outside. "Don't be a loser."

Noah looks scared, torn between Valentina's gaze and the pissed-off looks of all his standing teammates. Finally, he drops to his butt. "Fine. Stay. I don't care."

Wow. He won't stick up for me, but he'll take a stand if the girl he wants to get with asks him to?

Carly touches my elbow. "Mara...let him go."

"He doesn't even give a shit," I say, fingers tight in a fist. "None of them do." Finally, I look at her. "What are we doing here?"

"Come on," she says, tugging at my arm, pulling me away.

Valentina relaxes her grip on the door handle and Coach Willis pries it open, storming in like a bull, hollering. I don't hear him.

We end up pulling off our pads and riding back in our uniforms, tacky with dried game sweat.

I sit next to Carly again. She pushed me into a seat and sat down next to me, and I didn't fight it. It's good to have someone between me and the aisle. A level of protection.

Two towns later, I'm still too angry to sleep.

Carly's voice comes low, just over the rumble of the bus. "We're not doing this for them. We're doing this in spite of them."

I'm looking out the window. It's raining outside, the cold causing the window to fog up. It's not much of a view, but I keep looking. "I thought if I played well enough, they would come around. But the better I play, the more they hate me."

"They resent you. They're white and they're boys so they're used to having all the power, and then you showed up and you're better than a lot of them. That's threatening. Because if you can beat them, and Tayley and especially Valentina and River, then they're going to have to reckon with their assumption of white male supremacy."

"I really wanted to hit Quinn. And Noah. All of them."

Carly laughs. "As someone who's been on the receiving end of that, I don't envy them."

I look at her then. It feels like a rare pleasure to see her smile.

"I don't get you," I say.

"What's not to get?"

"Most of the time it feels like you hate me. And then sometimes you're, like . . . really nice."

"Are you kidding?" She looks like I just hit her again.

"What?"

"You think I hate you?"

"Well . . . yeah. Sometimes. *Don't* you?"

"I think *you* hate *me*."

I'm flabbergasted. "Sometimes . . . I get frustrated. That doesn't mean I hate you."

She doesn't say anything else for a minute, but she keeps playing with her jersey. She seems nervous. Her fiddling makes her shoulder rub against mine. She looks cool in her loose uniform and football pants. At school, she's always in her pastel V-neck girl shirts and jeans and flats. She loves a stud earring. Her prettiness is so natural and easy it's almost frustrating. She's a *girl* girl. But in her football uniform, she looks like me. Boyish, in that way that shouldn't have a gender at all but does. Her broad frame is made even broader with the pads. Where I look like an emu, she looks like a bulldog on a skateboard—fast, low, and cool.

"What I don't understand," I say slowly, "is why you even care so much."

"Is it a crime to care?" she asks, defensive.

"You can never just leave stuff alone. You're like my dog when she sees a bird she wants to chase. You just keep howling."

"It's how shit gets done."

"But *why*? Why do you care?"

"Seriously, Mara?"

"Why do you care if the football players are rude to me? Why do you keep inviting me to your house even though you know I don't do parties? Why, when you *know* we're just going to fight again. Why do you keep trying to be my friend?"

"You're such an idiot, do you know that?" she says, her face turning red.

"What?"

"You just don't see what's right in front of your face, do you?" She grabs her backpack, shaking her head, and stands up.

"Where are you going?" I ask, baffled.

"I can't with you," she says, and she goes and sits next to Valentina, who shoots me a look that I can't decipher.

MY FAVORITE HOODIE WAS ONE OF THE THINGS THAT
went missing. I wake up still mad about it.

In bed, I lie thinking of Carly standing on the bus seat, hollering and pointing fingers at the boys, in her full football gear, her
hair falling out of its ponytail and drifting down her neck. I think
about Noah, shirking back, refusing to stick up for me. How do
we come back from this? A few months ago, I had both Noah and
Quinn on my side. Now, in their place, I seem to have Tayley, River,
Valentina, and, of all people, Carly. Carly, who's had my back even
when I ignored her. Even when I punched her for the crime of looking out for me. That's who she is—the kind of person who will do
the right thing, even when it sucks. When her anger is pointed at
me, she's terrifying, but when we're on the same side, there's nothing better. I like being on the same side.

Oh my god.

It's not possible, is it?

Could I... *like* Carly?

It's absurd.

But the way she looks in a football jersey...

No, it's absurd.

I flash back to the night of the party at her place, how she looked staring into her telescope, trying to get us to pay attention to the stars and planets. I think about when she punched me in the gut, and I can't help but smile remembering the look on her face when she thought she might have actually hurt me. I remember Jupiter asking me who I liked more, Valentina or Carly. At the time, the thought that I would like Carly seemed so ridiculous it was laughable. What happened? What's wrong with me?

She got so mad at me just last night when I tried talking to her. Something about me just pisses her off. There's no way she would ever like me back. We're magnetic poles. Everything we do repels the other. It's something in our chemical makeup. The best thing I could do would be to pretend this moment never happened. No use dwelling on someone who has such a natural aversion to me.

Maybe throwing myself into morning chores will help. I get up to feed and water Roger and Angelica.

Noah's already up and outside, washing his truck. Seems early to be doing that. But as I come around, I stop short. Soft pink paint the color of the azaleas my mom loves drips and pools off the truck onto the wide gravel driveway. It's splashed across the body and windshield in thick, violent strokes and there are dribbles spattered in a ten-foot arc. They pepper the front bushes, even my mom's car.

On the side panel, a finger has dragged seven ragged letters out of the paint: TRAITOR.

"Noah..." I start, but I don't know how to finish.

Sweat sticks to his forehead as he wipes at the paint with a rag, wringing it out into a bucket full of water. "Just keep walking, Mara."

I'm still mad at him from the bus last night, and he clearly doesn't want me to be here. But if he doesn't get the paint off before it dries, it'll be there forever. So I go back into the house, come out with dish soap, and squeeze it over the hood, then grab another wet rag and get to work.

My fingers are freezing and red, but we keep soaping and rubbing. "Do you know who did this?" I ask after a while.

"No." He rubs at the crack in the window. "But I can guess. Probably the same people who stole your clothes."

"And slashed my bike tires."

"And poured coffee in my locker."

"What?" I stop rubbing but he doesn't meet my eye. I didn't know that happened.

"Yeah, my textbooks were ruined. I have to pay for them."

"Oh my god."

"Also probably the same people who put gum under my truck handle so that I'd have to touch it when I opened my door. And the same people who stole my shoelaces while I was at practice so I had to wear my cleats home."

"Seriously? You didn't tell me any of this."

"Oh, so you could make a whole scene about it? Pick fights with guys?" He takes the dish soap from me and squirts it along the side panel. "Why do you think I stopped going to the parties? They think I can get you to stop. They want you to quit football. At first, I did, too."

"You made that pretty clear."

"Well, I don't particularly like having you on the team, honestly.

But I don't like the way the other guys are being such assholes, either."

"You didn't stick up for me on the bus last night," I point out. "You haven't stuck up for me at all."

"If I said something, it would just make things worse."

"But when Valentina asks you to..."

"I didn't know what to do, okay? I just...I didn't know what to do." He sounds so pathetic, but I don't feel bad for him. He might feel like he's the one in a tough spot here, but he's not, really. He's not the one out on a limb. He's not the one trying to do something that hasn't been done here. He's just trying to find the path of least resistance through it.

"There's no middle ground here, Noah. You can't support Valentina and not me or the others. We're all going through the same shit."

He sighs and straightens up, cracking his back. "Can I ask you a question? Why *don't* you quit?"

"Because I like football. And I need to play it to get to play basketball. And I'm good at it. But mostly, because *fuck them*."

He nods but doesn't say anything.

I help him finish his truck in silence. And look at that, we made it through a whole conversation and not a punch was thrown.

47

MONDAY, VALENTINA'S NOT IN SCHOOL. SHE WASN'T in English in the morning, and after, Tayley finds me at my locker and asks if I've seen her. She isn't responding to texts.

By lunch, we're worried. River finds me in the library, where I usually eat, and almost literally drags me to the courtyard, where Tayley and Carly are waiting at a table. No one's eating much. I sit in the empty seat next to Carly, but it's weird, being near her, after my, well, *realization* over the weekend.

"Maybe they had a . . . cow issue?" Carly says, screwing up her face in an adorable way. Oh my god, what is wrong with me?

"A *cow issue*?" I can't help but make fun of her.

"I don't know!" Carly throws up her hands. "I don't know what cows need!"

"But if it's a cow issue, why wouldn't she text back?" Tayley asks.

"Did anyone else have anything happen over the weekend?"

Carly asks, looking at Tayley and River, but not at me. She's been weird ever since our conversation on the bus.

"Noah had paint thrown on his truck," I say. They turn to me, wide-eyed. I tell them what happened.

Then Carly says she had her mailbox vandalized—busted clear off its post and dented like it'd been struck with a baseball bat.

"Those dickheads," I say. Carly catches my eye, and I have to look away. I can barely look at her anymore.

When we get to practice we find that Quinn is out, too. It's not a huge deal since he hasn't been playing after breaking his arm, but it's weird he's not there stalking the sidelines and telling the rest of us what we're doing wrong.

"You know where Quinn is?" I ask Noah after lines.

"He wasn't in pre-calc," Noah says.

Tuesday neither of them shows up again. By Wednesday, we're worried.

"If she's not in school Friday, she can't play," I say at lunch. I've been eating with the others at the courtyard table all this week. Today even Noah sets his lunch down to eat with us. I raise an eyebrow at him but don't say anything. He's risking something by being seen eating at our table, and I'm not going to do anything to discourage him.

"I just don't understand why she's not responding to our texts," Tayley says.

"I hope nothing happened to her property," Noah says, sending us all spiraling down a what-if hole.

On Thursday, Quinn shows up to practice, all smiles, like he hadn't even been missing.

When I hear Curtis ask him why he was gone, he says he had mono. The kissing disease. It makes me wipe involuntarily at my lips. Ranger tells him to go home if he's sick, and Quinn just says, "I'm not contagious. Unless you're trying to kiss me." Then he makes a bunch of kissy sounds at him.

"That's homophobic, bro," Ranger says, and Quinn rolls his eyes but stops.

Practice this week has been rougher than it has been all season, partly because we're gearing up to play Linkport again, and everyone's afraid that Turnip might be on the warpath. Remembering his tackle still sends a splinter of pain down my spine. I'm not looking forward to matching up against him again.

But the worst part of practices this week is that that aside from Ranger, Jerry, and the girls, no one will meet my eye. The team is in pieces, and I don't know if Coach even realizes it. He pushes us harder, yells at us louder, but it won't make us play better if our fundamental problem is we don't respect one another. Our magic, if we ever had any, is broken, and everyone knows it. Friday night is going to be a disaster. We're hurtling toward an iceberg, and no one's raising the alarm.

After practice Thursday, Carly huddles us up in the girls' locker room.

"What are we going to do about Valentina?"

Carly positions herself across the huddle from me. But then Tayley realizes she left her phone plugged in and goes to get it and when she comes back, she finds a place in the huddle on the other side of Carly, which pushes her toward me. Elbow to elbow. I get that feeling like when someone holds a finger in front of your face without touching you and all the blood feels like it's flowing to that point. There's an electricity in *not* touching. It would almost be better if we did touch. It would release the pressure. Am I the only one feeling it?

I take a tiny step to my right and our shoulders brush and she nearly jumps out of her skin. Interesting. I wish I knew what was going on in her head.

"We should check on her," River says.

"I can't tonight," Tayley says. "Family home evening." Tayley's family does one night a week where they all spend the evening together discussing the Bible. It *cannot* be skipped.

"The rest of us, then," Carly says. "I know where she lives. We should make sure everything's okay. She *has* to come to school tomorrow or she won't get to play."

"Actually, I have to babysit my brother," River says.

"It was your idea!" Carly protests.

"I forgot my dad's working tonight."

"You two go and report back," Tayley says.

I look at Carly, who avoids my eye. "I can just do it," Carly says, staring at my shoes. "If you have to get home and, like... do horse stuff. Milk the cows. Or whatever."

I'm terrified to spend the afternoon alone with Carly but also thrilled. Will I give myself away? Will I make a fool of myself? Or will it be more of a chance to spend time with someone I only recently figured out isn't as horrible as I thought? "It's okay, Noah can do the chores," I say. "I'll go with you." I feel a tingle building in the back of my neck. She keeps avoiding my eye. "Unless you'd rather go alone..."

"It's fine," she says abruptly in a way that seems like it's *not* fine. Then she tries again, looking at me this time. "If *you're* okay coming."

"Yeah."

"Cool."

"Great."

Her dark lashes make her eyes pop, especially when she directs them right at me.

Then, as quickly as she looked at me, she looks away and grabs her bag.

"Let's go, then."

"Great," River says. "Text us immediately when you know something."

"Annnd break," Tayley says, breaking up the huddle.

# # #

Carly has to move a stack of *Bitch* magazines off her front seat so I can climb into her dirty VW Golf.

"Don't mind those, that's for a project for US History."

"When'd you get a car?"

"It's my mom's. She lets me borrow it on days she takes her bike."

"Cool."

After that, she drives in silence for a while. Halfway there, she plugs her phone into her radio and opens her music.

"You like Hayley Kiyoko?"

My stomach lurches. *She's only the reason I realized I was gay* is what I want to say. But I don't. "I listen to country mostly."

"Oh, okay."

She puts her phone down.

Then, after a pause, I say, "You hate country, don't you?"

"I really do," she says, laughing, and I laugh too.

"You can play Hayley Kiyoko. I, uh, I like her, too." I try not to turn red, hoping she didn't hear my stutter.

"It's just . . . it's *fine*," she says. "It's not country music itself. It's that it's hard to love a genre of music that doesn't seem to love me back."

"Yeah," I say, because I get that. There are artists I don't listen to because they seem like the type who would yell at me for using the wrong bathroom. "There's a lot of Wayne Warrens. But not all of it's that."

"Does country have any queer Asian women?"

I say carefully, "If there are any, I'd listen."

"I might, too."

I chew my lip, feeling guilty. Here she is, telling me exactly who she is, but I'm not doing the same thing.

The dirt kicks up as Carly turns down Valentina's long drive-way. She pulls up to the house and turns the car off. I have the urge to tell her, right then and there. I'm gay, just like her.

"Carly . . ." I start, but before I can finish, she's already unclick-ing her seat belt and climbing out of the car. I scramble to fol-low her.

She knocks on the front door. "There's no one here," she says. She sounds desperate, but whether because of Valentina or what we were just talking about—or *not* talking about—I'm not sure.

"Maybe she's in the field?" I suggest.

Carly looks at me in horror. "I'm not going near cows."

I have to laugh. Townies, jeez. Can't take them anywhere. "Just follow me."

I go around the house, past the cattle gates, to where the pas-tures extend far into the distance. I climb up the metal fence and hook one leg over, squinting against the sun hidden somewhere behind the bright white overcast skies, scanning the horizon.

"What are you going to do if you see her out there? I'm not walk-ing in pasture. I've seen cow poops. They're like *frisbees*."

"Would you relax? I don't see her."

I climb down and start walking toward the barn.

"Is it weird there's no one here? You got paint, I got a messed-up mailbox. Maybe Valentina got something worse and they just... left."

We get to the barn. A couple horses chill quietly in their stalls.

"They're not gone," I say. "They wouldn't leave their horses."

"Hello?" a voice calls out from inside one of the stalls.

Valentina steps out. Instead of her plaid-and-ripped-jeans pop-punk getup she's usually in, she's wearing a bleached-out gray sweatshirt with the sleeves pushed up under knockoff Carhartt overalls. Her hair's up in a messy ponytail with strands coming loose and sticking to her neck. She looks so pretty it's almost enough to make my breath catch, but not quite. She'll always be pretty, but my crush on her seems to have lifted when I wasn't looking.

Valentina wipes her forehead with her wrist because her hands are gloved and covered in dirt and probably some horse shit. She's holding a muck rake and looks exhausted.

"What are you doing here?" Valentina says flatly. Maybe this was a mistake.

"You haven't been at school," Carly says in a timid voice that's not at all her.

"Or answering our texts," I add.

Valentina looks at me. "*You* haven't texted me."

"Well... everyone else said you weren't responding."

"We had a problem at the ranch. The cows had to be moved to the other pasture, and my parents didn't want me going to school until we finished it."

That's *an* explanation, but it doesn't feel like *the* explanation.

"So that's it?" Carly asks. "It really *was* a cow issue?"

"It's getting colder. If we didn't move them off the mountain, they could have died from exposure," Valentina snaps at Carly. "Just because you don't understand it doesn't mean it's not a real problem."

"Okay, all right," Carly says defensively. "We were just worried about you."

"Why?"

"Well, Mara and Noah and I experienced some...vandalism after the last game. We were worried something like that happened to you."

"Oh..." Valentina's brave face falters. She pulls her gloves off and leans the muck rake against the wall. "After we got off the bus Friday night, Quinn found me by my car and asked me if I was dating Noah." Her eyes go to mine, then away. "I said we hadn't defined anything yet, but he still got pretty angry about it. He said Noah was a pussy and I could do better. It seemed like he was going to try to kiss me, but I kinda shoved him on his broken arm and got in my car before he could try anything."

"Oh my god, Val, I'm so sorry," I say. I could hammer Quinn.

"Anyway, yeah. Then, later that night, I was sleeping and I heard a sound, and I woke up and looked out the window and saw Quinn and some other guys scratching something into my car."

"They did *what*? What was it?" Carly straightens.

Valentina shakes her head. "I don't want to repeat it. It was... a slur." Her eyes flick to me. "For lesbians. It's in the shop getting repainted now. My parents were *piiiiiiissed*. They called the school and got Quinn suspended. I didn't see the other guys or they would've been suspended, too."

"Oh my god," Carly says.

"I'm sorry," I say again. "Those assholes."

"It is what it is," she says. "Is Noah okay?"

"He's fine. Some paint on his truck; no lasting damage."

She looks relieved. I wonder if she really likes him. It wouldn't be the worst thing, I guess. She'd be good for him.

"These fucking *boys*," Carly says with gravel in her voice. "I wish we could just play without them."

"We can play without them, but we'd have to be playing volleyball," I say.

Carly sighs deeply. "It's so stupid. Why is football a boys' sport anyway? Why can't we have girls' leagues? I might actually have a chance of playing if we were lining up against the ladies of Linkport."

"Are you coming back to school?" I ask Valentina before Carly can go off on a tangent. "If you're not there tomorrow, you can't play."

"Coach isn't going to let me play anyway. I've missed a week of practice."

"You don't have to come," Carly says, and I look at her in shock. "If it's going to be weird for you with Quinn being there and all."

"We all have to be there," I say. "This is our last game. If we're not together for this, then we'll never be together again. And then they'll have won."

Valentina and Carly both look at me, then at each other.

"Mara Deeble, did you just say the girls have to stick together?" Valentina asks.

My cheeks burn. "Well...yeah. If not now, when?"

"Wow," Carly says. "Never thought I'd see the day."

"I'm writing this in my diary," Valentina says.

"Tell the historians to mark this day, this hour, as the hour that Mara Deeble went to the mat for the Elkhorn Five."

"Okay, okay," I say, but they're just getting started.

"Carve the words into stone!" Valentina cries.

"Write them in the sky!"

"If we're not together Friday, the boys will have won!"

The smile cracks across my face and once it does, I can't stop a laugh from forming. Before long we're all laughing. The horse nickers and stamps her feet.

"So, you'll come?" I ask.

Valentina brushes the hair out of her face and takes a moment before answering. "I'll come. But, Mara, it's not going to be pretty. You know that, right?"

"We'll manage. As long as we stick together."

Valentina nods, then opens her arms for a big three-way hug. I wrap my arm around Valentina's shoulder, Carly's arm around my waist. We stand pressed together for a long time.

IN OUR MATCHING UNIFORMS, WE LOOK LIKE A TEAM, but we're not really. You can slap green and white on us, but it doesn't make us a unit.

They line us up by number to run into the gym for the pep rally, where the student body cheers—or doesn't, depending on how much they care about high school athletics. Because of our numbering, I'm squeezed uncomfortably behind Curtis and Wayne. I stand up as straight as I can to show them that they don't have anything on me. They're tall—I'm tall. They're strong—I'm strong. They're pissed off—I'm pissed off. And I have as much right to be here as they do.

If Quinn was involved in the vandalism spree last weekend, I'd put good money that the Kool-Aid Club was all in on it. I don't trust any of them as far as I could throw them.

Valentina lines up behind me. She wears an oversize white collared shirt, tucked in at the front and hanging long in back over loose black ankle pants and boots. It's the kind of outfit that would have made my heart jump out of my chest a few months ago, but now I can appreciate it without losing my mind.

"I like that look," I tell her.

"Thanks. I like your shirt." I'm wearing a dark blue button-down, tucked into my nicest pair of black jeans. I wanted to wear one of Noah's ties. I even got so far as to steal it out of his bedroom, and when Noah caught me, he just nodded instead of threatening to tell Mom. When I put it on in my bedroom, I looked in the mirror and thought I looked like the kind of girl I would want to go up to at a party. I looked like the hottest version of myself. But I also looked like the gayest version of myself. So I took the tie off. If I'm going to stick to my coming-out plan, some looks have to wait until college, no matter how hot they are.

"Thanks," I say, and wonder what the other girls would have thought of the tie.

Carly lines up behind Valentina in a green dress with a large white floral pattern. "Your hair looks cool today, Mar," she says.

I rub the back of my head nervously and try not to blush. She's never called me Mar before.

"Thanks. Your dress—it's team colors."

Valentina coughs out a laugh.

"I don't think she likes it," Carly says.

"No, I do, I do!" I protest.

Valentina laughs. "Not even a *Nice dress*, just *It's team colors*."

"Hey, Valentina," Carly says. "Your outfit..."

"Yeah?" Valentina cocks a hip and puts her hand on it.

"It's on your body," Carly says, and they both crack up.

I throw my hands in the air. Okay, it's make-fun-of-Mara time.

"We're just kidding, Mara," Carly says. "It's okay, we all know you can't give or take a compliment. It's charming." This is a thing she talks about when I'm not around?

"It's a nice dress," I say. "I don't know how to compliment dresses, but it...looks good on you."

Carly holds my look. "Thank you."

I hear the principal getting on the microphone in the gym to hype the crowd up.

I rub my head again. I stopped by the barber again for a fresh-up. The number-two buzz feels prickly on my fingers. I assured him I still liked it. He told me he saw me on the front of the newspaper and he told his wife he gave me that haircut. He almost looked proud.

Through the gym doors, I hear the principal tell everyone to put their hands together for their Elk Hunters. Two cheerleaders throw open the double doors, and we start running into the gym, led by our captain, Noah. The fluorescent lights beam down on the bleachers, full of students on their feet, clapping and cheering as the pep band sways and crashes through our fight song.

The balloons Ichelle taped to my locker are popped by the time the pep rally is over, and the motivational poster she painted has an anatomically optimistic dick drawn on it. I pull out a Sharpie and turn the dick into a football before opening my locker to dump my stuff. I won't let it bother me, but I can't let Ichelle see her hard work vandalized.

At lunch, Valentina, Tayley, Carly, River, and I are at our new usual table in the courtyard. Noah sits next to Valentina. There's a light drizzle happening, but we've pulled the table under the overhang to stay dry. Ten minutes into lunch, Ranger comes out and sits with us.

"Mind if I join you?" he asks before sitting down next to Tayley and dumping out his brown bag with two very tall, loaded turkey sandwiches, an apple, a banana, a pickle, a baggie of carrots, a container of olives, and a pudding cup. He looks up at us taking in all his food, then shrugs. "Takes a lot to keep this figure," he says, rubbing his tummy—the same tummy that's kept my brother from getting sacked all season.

It's weird, though, because Ranger usually sits with the other football guys at the tables outside the weight room. Then, a few minutes later, Jerry comes out the doors with his lunch and joins us. Now I'm suspicious. What's going on? There's not enough room at our table, but Tayley tells them to drag another one over, while Carly and I exchange looks. Finally, because she's a loud-ass who isn't afraid to say stuff, she asks, "What the hell are you boys doing out here?" And I love that about her.

Jerry leans back in his chair and says, "The other guys are dicks. We don't want to eat with them anymore."

And that's basically that.

FOURTH PERIOD, MRS. TANTLEBAUM TELLS ME TO GO
to the office. I go, hoping this doesn't have anything to do with the
game tonight. Coach Joyce is waiting for me there, and she doesn't
look happy. She pulls me into a meeting room and sits me down.

"Mara, I wish I didn't have to ask you this, but I've heard one
side of the story. Now I'd like to hear your side. Is it true you got
into a fight this season while on the football team?"

My heart rate spikes. Somehow, she knows about Quinn at the
party. He must have told her. I'm going to kill him. Still, it was at
a private party. That shouldn't count! "I'll be honest, I've wanted
to. A bunch of times. You have no idea how much I've put up with.
But I never hit anyone on the field or at a practice."

"What about off the field?" Yup, she knows. *Damn it.* It's not
bad enough he had to throw a grenade on our relationship, but he
has to blow up my basketball season, too? I didn't realize the depth
of his assholery. If he was going to do this, why did he wait until

now? He could have gone straight to her after the party. Maybe his rejection by Valentina left him stinging. Or maybe he thought an October surprise would hurt the most.

"If it's Quinn you're talking about..." She watches me intently. "That wasn't at practice, it wasn't even on school grounds. It had nothing to do with football, it was just a dispute between friends." My tongue stumbles over the word *friends.*

She's shaking her head like it doesn't matter. "Quinn is still on the team."

"Coach, the reason I hit him—" Maybe she would understand if I could just tell her, but the words get stuck in my throat. I don't want to remember it, much less tell it again.

"The reason doesn't matter, Mara. You have to learn to navigate conflict without violence. That was your challenge for the season, and you've proven to me that you can't do it."

I try a different tactic, easier to talk about. "The only reason Quinn told you about this is because he's pissed off that girls are playing football," I fume. "He and his friends are going out of their way to harass me and the other girls and my brother. They've been trying to make us quit all season, and since that didn't work, now he's coming to you to try to ruin basketball for me, too."

Doesn't she see how unfair this is? How personal he's made it?

"But you admit, you *did* fight him?" she insists.

"You can't listen to him on this, Coach. This is bigger than just me and him. This is about who is welcome on the field."

"Mara..." Coach warns me.

"I punched him because he kissed me," I say quickly before I can lose my courage. "We were at a party. He was drunk. He wasn't listening to me. He kissed me and wouldn't stop. And he kind of... rubbed up against me. So I punched him." I feel icky at the memory.

"Mara..." She rubs at the hairline above her eyebrow, concerned. Her eyes find me over her glasses. "I'm sorry that happened to you."

I slowly unclutch my pant legs, which I didn't realize I had been doing, and rub out the creases that formed there.

"If you want to report Quinn for an unwanted sexual advance, I will go with you to the vice principal. I have to warn you, though, that if you do that, there might be other consequences involved for being at a party with alcohol and presumably taking part yourself..."

I dig my heels into the ground to try to stabilize myself against the rising swell of anger. Quinn's the one who attacked me, drunk, and I can't report it because there was alcohol at the party? The unfairness of it threatens to overwhelm me.

"And I understand why you did it, Mara. In other circumstances, I might even say he deserved it." I don't like the tone in her voice. "But I needed you to show me I could trust you and you haven't."

"Coach..." I'm pleading now.

"I wish you the best in football, but I can't in good conscience let you back on the basketball team this year. I'm sorry."

It feels like the floor drops out from under me. Coach Joyce tells me to go back to class. I walk there in a daze and don't hear anything Ms. Tantlebaum says for the rest of the period.

If I'm not playing basketball, what was any of this for?

It's Carly who finds me in the weight room.

"Mara, why are you working out? We have a game tonight."

I don't trust myself to respond without breaking down, so I don't say anything, I just keep doing my set.

"What's wrong?" When I don't answer, she comes over and literally takes the weight out of my hand. "Tell me."

So I tell her.

When I'm done, Carly stares at me in horror. "That. Little. Weasel."

I throw up my hands. "What can I do?"

It's rhetorical—there's nothing I can possibly do—but Carly doesn't take it that way. "You're gonna go out there and play the best football of your life and you're going to show that shitstain that he's not worth licking the dirt on the bottom of your cleats."

I shake my head. "The only reason I played football in the first place was to qualify for the basketball team this year. Now there's no point."

"So you're just gonna leave us dangling? Me, Tayley? River? Valentina? What about us?"

"Play, don't play. It's up to you."

"We're the Elkhorn Five, Mara, not the Elkhorn Whoever Shows Up. Those boys are throwing everything they can at you to get you to quit. Don't let them win."

It suddenly all feels so exhausting. Quinn and I were friends for so long. All those summers chasing chickens and winters trudging through the rain to the school bus, telling gross stories to make each other laugh. Quinn and Mara. And now here we are. This is how it ends?

But, I remind myself, our friendship hasn't been all beatific pastures and easy memories. There's the time in fifth grade when Quinn stole my shoes after we went wading in the river because he was mad I had newer Chuck Taylors than him. After I got my first bra in middle school—a sports bra with straps as wide as my wrists—he would point out to me every time he could see one peeking out through the neck of my T-shirt. He never let a joke about his dad's job slide without a jab back. You're absolutely not allowed to comment on his singing voice or you're dead. When my family sold our farm, he didn't even call. As far as friends go, he's the late-night Dairy Queen hamburger version—warm on the outside but cold on the inside. How had I managed to forget or ignore all of this until now? Did he ever really care about me? Or was I just a convenient companion? An enthusiastic sidekick in the story of his life?

The thought of never being friends with Quinn again feels like grief. Like going to a funeral and hearing the eulogies and realizing you never even knew the person you thought you loved. Or maybe I *did* know Quinn all along and I was just overlooking the parts I didn't like.

I look at Carly, standing in front of me. "How did you know I was in here?"

"You left chem, and then you didn't show up to fifth period. I got worried."

"So you came looking for me?"

She hesitates. "I can leave, if this is weird. I'm not trying to stalk you."

"Don't leave."

Would Quinn have come looking for me? Probably not. Maybe this is what friendship is. Noticing when someone doesn't show up to fifth period and then going looking. Would Carly have called after my family sold the farm? I'm starting to believe that, yes, she would have.

"Well?" Carly says. "Are you coming?"

"I'm coming."

50

QUINN'S MOM ANSWERS THE DOOR WHEN I RING THE bell. Her hair looks like a bell, perfectly smooth and rounded, curled out at the ends. "Quinnie's in the basement," she says.

He looks shocked to see me, at least. He pauses his game. I loiter near the door.

"Deeb! Hey. What's up?" I can't believe he's trying to play this like nothing weird has happened between us in the last couple months. Does he think I'm just going to plop down and take a controller from him like everything's normal?

"I talked to Coach Joyce today," I say.

"Oh yeah?" He keeps the faux-friendly act up, which is infuriating.

"She said I'm off the basketball team." He doesn't even have the decency to flinch.

"Sucks," he says. I can feel the rage building inside me, no reason now not to let it out. Nothing to keep me from beating the shit out of my former best friend except, maybe, the fact that he has a broken arm. Even so, I'm not feeling much sympathy.

"I know it was you," I say, and his face hardens, the act finally dropped. "And I know the paint was you. It took us an hour to get it all off, you know."

"It was supposed to have dried before you woke up," he says casually, turning back to his video game. He has to keep the controller in his lap in order to push the buttons with his arm in a cast.

"Well, it didn't. And Carly's mailbox and Valentina's car, and our missing clothes, was that all you, too?"

"You would have found your clothes if you'd just checked the dumpster," he says, shooting some baddies in his game. "Instead of pitching a whole fit."

"What about my bike tires? You slash those?"

"That was Wayne. He started it. Drew that dick on your locker, too. He really hates you," he says to his video game. Finally, I cross the room and stand in front of the TV. "Hey!"

"We used to be friends," I say. "Best friends."

"For you, maybe," he says. "I've always had the Kool-Aid Club."

"So, all those years hanging out, what? They meant nothing?"

"You tell me, Mara," he says. "I thought we were building something, but as soon as you kiss me, you freak out and stop talking to me."

"I kissed *you*?" I laugh incredulously. "You practically stuck your tongue down my throat. Not to mention everything you tried to do..." I gesture to his general crotch area, not wanting to put words to it.

"That's not how I remember it."

"Then your memory is lying," I say coldly. "I have never wanted to kiss you and I will never want to kiss you. God, is that the only reason you ever hung out with me?"

"Nah, you're chick bait. Girls love to know a guy can be friends with girls. Maria loved that about me. Ate that shit up. And you're, like, the least *girl* girl I can be friends with, so you make it easy. Or you did, anyway. Until this year."

I'm stopped momentarily. That's not the only reason he was friends with me. I know it isn't. That doesn't explain the years of good times we had together. The endless games of capture the flag. The bike rides. Still. "That's a really shitty thing to say. Even if I know it's not true."

He shrugs and reaches under the coffee table for his brand-new Nike Air Maxes and starts putting them on.

"I can't believe you'd let football ruin our friendship. After everything. And then go out of your way to sabotage basketball for me."

"Oh, you deserved it. After you sabotaged football for me," he cries.

"What are you *talking* about? You still have football. We have a game tonight."

"People used to show up for the Noah-and-Quinn show. Now they just come because of the girls. I've seen the signs. 'Play the Elkhorn Five!' What, just because you're girls you should get to play? The paper seems to think so. They're falling over themselves writing articles about you. Front page. Mara Deeble. Never played football in her life, and here she is with four other random chicks who can't even take a hit. Meanwhile, what about the rest of us who have been training for this for practically our whole lives? What about me, Mara? I need newspaper coverage if I'm going to get noticed. You think I can just get a football scholarship on my own? No. And certainly not with a broken arm I got because Valentina doesn't know what she's doing out there. She's a hazard to all of us when she gets on the field."

"You know that's not true."

He waves his cast at me. "Look at it, Mara!"

"So that's it, then. Our entire friendship is over because our stupid little newspaper put me on the front page." I no longer feel like kicking his ass. I just feel sad.

Quinn doesn't say anything, just finishes tying his shoes, awkwardly. He stands up. "Are we done here?"

There's a knot the size of a walnut in my throat. It's really that easy for him to just walk away from this. "Quinn," I say. It feels important that I'm clear in this moment. "I can't just forgive this."

"God, Mara. No one's asking you to. Just do what you gotta do already." He crosses to the stairs.

"Okay, then. You've been an asshole to my face, an asshole behind my back, and an asshole to my friends. Just so we're clear: We're not friends anymore."

"See yourself out," he says, and goes upstairs. I hear the front door open and close. I look around his basement—this room where we've hung out so many times, playing video games, talking. Was our friendship ever really real? I feel like I'm mourning the death of a dog who didn't die, he just ran away to live a different life without me. I take a last look. Then I go.

51

THERE'S ONLY ONE THING I HAVE LEFT TO DO BEFORE tonight's game. Mom's in her bedroom, combing her hair at her vanity. I almost never go in here, but it feels like she's hiding, and I only have fifteen minutes before we need to leave for the game. I'm already suited up, wearing everything but my shoulder pads and my cleats. I want her to see me like this.

She looks at me through the mirror. "What is it?"

"Tonight's our last game," I say. "Noah's last high school game ever. I know it would mean a lot to him—to us both—if you came tonight."

She puts her brush down carefully, her lips a flat, grim line.

I continue, fast before she can say no. "I know you don't agree with what I'm doing. I know you don't like my clothes, or my hair, or me playing football. If it were you, you'd do it all differently. But this is *me*, Mom. This is who I am. I'm your daughter. And this is what I look like."

"You're confused..."

"I'm not," I say.

"And it's okay to be confused. We were all troubled as young people. You grow out of it."

"I'm not growing out of it, Mom. And I want you to love me for who I am right *now*."

"Of course I love you," she says, turning in her chair to look at me directly. "Do you think I don't?"

There's a knot in my throat that makes it hard to swallow. "It doesn't feel that way lately."

"You're a challenge. You've always been a challenge, since you were a baby."

"This is not about your parenting. It's not a reflection of you at all. It's about me. Can you love what you see here?"

I gesture to my body, standing in my socks in her doorway. My hair is freshly cut, slightly tousled. My head almost reaches the top of our old house's low doorjamb. I feel like I fill this doorway, with all my height and breadth, all my fat and muscle, all my strength and fear. I'm not the baby she knew. I'm not the child she raised. I grew up, in both senses of the word.

Mom's eyes drift down and up my body. They linger on my hair. What does she see when she looks at me? A monster? A sinner? Her daughter who she raised?

She's quiet a long time. Her eyes tell me she can't do it. At least, not right this second. Maybe it's a journey.

"Just come to the game tonight," I say. "Start there. Please."

# # #

We can hear the roar of the crowd even from inside the equipment room. I look at Carly, who looks at Valentina, who looks at River, who looks at Tayley, who looks at all of us.

"How many people do our stands hold, d'you think?" Valentina asks.

Tayley guesses five hundred at the same time that I guess three thousand.

River breathes out. "We sold out *Godspell* every night. The theater has *ninety-four seats.*"

"So this is more," I say.

"This is a lot more." She looks shaken.

"Bring it in," Carly says. We huddle up. "It's the last game of the season. We've come a long way since August." That's for dang sure. "Now we're going to go into that boys' locker room and Coach is gonna call us all gentlemen a couple dozen times and we're gonna get side eye from more than a few of the guys. But we're not going to let that slow us down, are we?"

We answer no, no way.

"I don't know about you, but I remember a time not that long ago when Mara was showing us how to hold a football because Coach didn't bother." God, did that happen? That feels like ancient history now. "And I know we've had some rocky periods, but damn if we aren't a team now. And we're gonna show those dudes that we have every right to be there. Valentina, you're gonna go out there and cover that field." Valentina smiles at her and nods. "Tayley, you're gonna get us so many field goals, the other team's gonna need to use their fingers to count 'em up." Tayley laughs. "River, you're gonna . . . hold that ball better than anyone ever held a ball."

"It's a lot more complicated than that, actually," River says.

"And that's why you're the pro at it and not me," Carly says. "And, Mara? You're going to demolish the Linkport receivers, and you're gonna get so many interceptions they'll have to check your gloves for superglue."

"And you?" I say.

"Oh, we both know I'm not playing tonight."

"Nah, girl, it's the last game, they have to play you!" River exclaims.

"The people want to see the Elkhorn Five!" Valentina says.

"We'll see," Carly says, but she doesn't sound convinced.

I clear my throat. "I, um, have something to say before we go out there." Everyone turns to me. "I just want to say that I know you guys joined because of me, and it took me way too long to embrace that. I was a bit of a jerk to you guys when you first showed up—"

"A bit of?" River says.

"Okay, a giant jerk," I say. "But I'm happy you did. We are so different in some ways, but we're all in this together. I wouldn't have made it without you."

"Would you say," Valentina says with a pleased look, "that in the end it was *we* who inspired *you*?"

"Aha!" Tayley exclaims.

"Can the great Mara Deeble even be inspired?" asks River.

"Yes, I would say you inspire me," I say, and everyone cheers.

"I've never been someone's inspiration before," Tayley says with awe.

"I'm putting it in my college application," River says. "Right after International Thespian Society. 'Mara Deeble's inspiration.'"

"Okay," I say, trying to get things back on track.

"I think you should get it tattooed on your arm," Valentina says to me. "WWEFD? What Would the Elkhorn Five Do? Just to remind yourself of how inspired by us you are."

I catch Carly's eye, and for once she's not joining in the roasting, she's just watching me. For a moment our eyes connect. She smiles like she's proud of me. When I look away, the other three are watching us. I suddenly feel warm.

"Thank you all for your contributions to this pep talk," I say. "I love everyone in this equipment room. We have one game left. Let's go out there and win one. Go, Elkhorn Five!"

Carly offers up a "Hoo-hah!" And they all reply, "Hoo-hah!" And I repeat, "Hoo-hah!" And they shout back, "Hoo-hah!" And then we're all slapping each other's backs and cheering, and I feel like this is my team, and I wouldn't want to be anywhere else.

# # #

The rain can't diminish the deafening cheers as we burst through the damp paper banner the cheerleaders hold for us. The pep band blasts our fight song as loud as they can play it, and we leap around and smack each other's helmets, spraying water, as we run across the field to our sideline.

My dad waves to me from the stands, the green-and-white wool blanket draped over his legs and my mom's, sitting next to him. She decided to come at the last second. I don't know what it means for the future, but I'm just really happy she's here. For my sake and for Noah's. I wave back.

Toward the top of the stands, Jupiter stands in an army surplus jacket next to Reese. The two of them hold a sign above their heads that reads GO FIGHT WIN. I have to laugh at the joke, even though it's all moot now. I can fight all I want tonight. But I don't feel the urge to do anything but demolish Linkport.

Leroy's also in the stands, cheering—as much as Leroy actually cheers—alongside Ranger's parents, Fritz and Sonja, who have their PLAY THE ELKHORN FIVE sign as well as cardboard cutout letters that read 51 for Ranger's number. And in the front row, the Elkhorn High volleyball team is lined up cheering their heads off. Maria Carpenter waves vigorously at me.

I go over to Valentina. "Is that the volleyball team?"

"Oh yeah, they love the Elkhorn Five," Valentina says. "You didn't know? Maria Carpenter is, like, obsessed with us."

"Huh," I say, looking back at them.

"They're actually super cool," Valentina says. "I called Maria after Quinn tried to put the moves on me to warn her. Then she called him and broke it off with him. Whatever 'it' was at that point."

"Whoa," I say. "Wait, when was that?"

"Thursday."

That explains why Quinn called Coach Joyce when he did. It wasn't until he was dumped by the hottest girl in school that he was finally humiliated enough to lash out at me.

I regret every bad thing I ever thought about Maria or any of the volleyball girls. I wave at them, and they cheer louder. They look rosy-cheeked; I wonder if it's the brisk air or the cloud paint.

On the sidelines, there's actually a news camera and reporter for the Portland local news station. I think, briefly, that maybe they're here because Turnip is probably going to go pro one day, but then the camera pans across the Elkhorn players and stops on my face.

Of course they're here for the Elkhorn Five. Should've known. Instead of turning away this time, I look down the barrel of the camera and run my hand through my hair, then slip my helmet on. That should make some good B-roll for them.

We win the toss and choose to kick, so Tayley runs onto the field with her tee, and she kicks a gorgeous one that lands at the Orca ten. Despite the soggy field, Linkport manages to run it back almost forty yards, thanks to Turnip bulldozing a path for their punt returner. Turnip is playing more than just O-line this time. I guess the Linkport coach realized he had a real specimen on his hands and is playing him wherever he can.

"Deeble." I snap my head to look at Coach, and he jerks his head toward the field. I'm going in.

Not only that, I'm *starting*.

I can't help it, I glance at Wayne. He's absolutely *stewing*. I blow him a kiss.

My cleats struggle to find grip in the soupy grass. I attempt to get into ready position, but as soon as I hear the snap, my legs slip and I struggle to steady myself. Luckily, the exact same thing happens to my receiver. We find our balance at the same time and take off, but by then the timing is off with the quarterback, and the pass goes long by five yards.

This is gonna be some game.

We force a punt. I'm jogging back to the sidelines covered in mud, wet head to toe, and grinning. By the time this game is over, you won't be able to tell our jerseys from Linkport's; we'll all be mud brown. It's *great*.

Coach sends Lincoln in as our punt returner, telling him, "Fair catch, son." He's been playing the position ever since Quinn broke his arm. On the field, Lincoln dances around, warming his body as the kick goes up. He catches it on our fifteen, but instead of waving a fair catch, he starts running. He can't escape Turnip, though, who nails him. Lincoln flies backward, bobbling the ball, then dropping it. The ball bounces this way and that before Ranger throws his body on it at our own eight-yard line. Coach looks so frustrated he just might cuss. "What'd I tell you? What'd I say?" Lincoln hangs his head.

Anyone watching from the sidelines may not realize our team is cleaved in two unless they looked closely. The bulk of the team stands on one side of Coach, while the girls and our allies stand on the other side. As we make our way down the field on offense, the entire group slowly shifts with the chains, but we don't cross the invisible barrier created by Coach Willis.

Noah fights his way against the ruthless Linkport D-line, run by run, pass by pass, putting together first downs and yardage gains little by little, until finally he throws a messy four-yard pass to Curtis, who snatches the ball out of the air, spins out of his defender's arms, sprints the remaining twenty yards, and strides across the end zone like it was nothing. We cheer from the sideline, and the pep band goes into "Life Is a Highway," and for a flash, we almost feel like a team again. But then Lincoln scowls and spits on the ground by Tayley's feet as she's heading out to kick the extra point, making her jump back and glare at him. Maybe it was the wet ball, or the soggy field, or maybe it was Lincoln getting in her head, but her kick goes wide, and all our enthusiasm from getting the first score dissipates in an instant. It's 6–0 Elkhorn.

The rain starts really coming down in the second quarter, fully saturating the field. It makes defense nearly impossible—it's hard to stay upright when the ground beneath you is slowly churning into mud pie. I've seen beef stews with thicker consistency than this field. The only upshot is that Linkport's offense is having just as difficult a time. Passing the wet ball with cold fingers becomes unviable, so Coach calls running play after running play. He tells everyone who will listen to keep to the sidelines, where the grass is marginally more intact.

It's impossible to run any play more complicated than "hand off the ball and go." It's like we're playing capture the flag again. No plan except don't get caught. Just try to get the ball over the line before someone reaches you. That's it.

Quinn looks itchy on the sidelines. I'm sure he's thinking about how he could have dominated in this kind of a running game. Too bad he messed himself up.

Turnovers are a play-by-play reality. First, Curtis lets the ball leap right out of his fingers after a handoff, like it was a cat that didn't want to be picked up. Then the Linkport QB fumbles a snap. Then Ranger forces a fumble by tackling a Linkport running back from behind, causing the ball to fly directly into Wayne's hands, who runs it a good ten yards before fumbling the ball himself when he is knocked flat by Turnip, who scoops it up and hustles toward his own end zone. I cut an angle toward him. When I wrap my arms around his massive body, my feet slide out from under me. Turnip easily wriggles free of my grasp as I hit the mud. He crosses the goal line and roars like a lion as I pick myself up and look for somewhere on my pants to wipe my hands. Their kicker makes the extra kick and it's 7–6 Linkport at the half.

We limp into the locker room wet, cold, and hurting. My thighs chafe where my pads rub against them when I run. My heels are rapidly developing fresh blisters from my wet socks. I've slipped so many times I can't tell which aches are from tackles and which are from falling. I'm grateful my hair is buzzed because when I take my helmet off, I can shake my head like a dog after a bath and feel the sweat and rain fly off. Insta-dry.

We grab towels from a pile on our way into the locker room, but they're pointless. Instead of trying to get dry, I wrap my towel around my shoulders for warmth and peel my shoes off to put Band-Aids on my blisters.

The locker room is eerily quiet as guys engage in self-care—wiping the mud off their faces, changing their socks if they're lucky enough to have a second pair. The assistant coaches hand out screwdrivers for us to pry the grass out of our cleats.

Coach Willis clears his throat and steps in front of us, speaking low: "Gentlemen," he begins, and Carly's eyes cut to mine from the bench next to me. I almost laugh, despite the bleak atmosphere in the room. Carly is soaking wet, but her jersey remains sparkling white, barely a splatter of mud around her ankles. She's like the single dime in jar full of pennies. We gotta get her in the game.

Coach talks a lot about how we're gonna make our running game better—routes to run that will maximize the less muddy places of the field, focusing on small gains over big plays. "Stay low, and stay upright," Coach says. "Going slower but keeping going is better than falling on your behind." When it comes time to talk about defense, he just says, "You guys keep doing what you're doing." And I swear when he nods at us in approval, he's looking right at me.

This coach, who's barely said twelve words to me since I joined the team, who I've never known where I stand with, just gave me his approval in the last game of the season. And yeah, I'm soaking wet and covered in mud and my tailbone is killing me from where I've landed on it a million times, but I'm ready to get back out there and do it some more. I share a smile with Valentina, who's been playing safety off and on through the first half to give the first-stringers a chance to towel off and recover. It's a brutal position, but especially tonight. Her face is smeared with dried mud where it splashed in through her face guard.

A scoff sounds from the back. Quinn sticks his chin up in the air defiantly. He's the only one not wrapped in a towel because he's wearing a warm raincoat over his jersey and jeans.

"How come you got three thousand tips for the boys, but you're not gonna say anything about the girls?"

I exchange a glance with Carly, and we both sit forward, ready for whatever's coming.

Quinn stands up. "Striker and Reyes might have lost us the game with that missed point and Deeble"—he looks right at me—"fell on her ass rather than tackle Turnip when it counted." Other guys murmur in agreement.

Everything else aside, he's right that I should have had Turnip. I could have stopped that touchdown, but the mud got the best of me and he powered through my grip. I have no excuse for it.

"Okay, Kegley, that's enough," Coach says. "It's a mud bowl out there."

Noah stands up. "We're here to support each other despite our mistakes, Quinn. That's what being a teammate is."

I look at Noah in surprise. This is the first stand he's made all season, but is he doing it for me or for Valentina?

"Someone's getting laid," Wayne says under his breath.

"Don't lash out at me just because Mara's starting instead of you tonight," Noah says. "It's not my fault she's spanking you in the stats."

An "Oooh" goes up from some of the guys at that, and I feel my cheeks warm. In profile like this, I almost see the resemblance between Noah and me.

Quinn barks back, "I'm just saying, if this were a normal year, maybe we'd be winning this game right now instead of being made a mockery."

Now I'm fully pissed. I rise to my feet and stand next to Noah. Carly joins us. Valentina and Ranger rise out of their seats, too, then Tayley and River.

"Okay, settle down, everyone," Coach says. "Ladies, take your seats, please." I don't move, and neither does anyone else. There's no reason to focus on us instead of shit-stirrer extraordinaire Quinn Kegley, who is also standing.

"You can make this right, Coach," Wayne says. "Bench 'em all."

"I'm not benching anyone except for the *next person who*

speaks," Coach says in a tone he usually reserves for giving some-one extra lines. The room quiets down. "And I said *take a seat*," he hollers. I reluctantly lower back down onto my bench, and the others follow suit. Quinn waits to sit last as some kind of power move.

The tension in the room makes me feel hot, despite my wet clothes. It feels like the tiniest spark will start a riot. I wonder if things could have been different if I'd acted differently from the beginning of the season. If we'd been more accommodating maybe, or deferential to the boys. If I were better at making jokes. If I hadn't cut my hair. If Carly hadn't talked to the press. What would have happened if we didn't make the team? Would Quinn still be my friend? Would my mom and I have ever fought? Would I have kissed Valentina?

Coach says some platitudes about how we're a team and teams stick together, but no one's listening. He calls for us to put our hands in, and I stand on the outside with the other girls, arms firmly at my side. It's the weakest "Hoo-hah" I've ever heard.

On the run back to the field, I jog next to Carly. Lincoln stops abruptly in front of her on purpose, causing her to bump into him and fall onto her hands and knees, mud splattering up the front of her jersey and onto her face. I help her up gingerly, but when she stands, I see she's laughing through her face mask.

She breaks free from the group, sprints fast, then drops into a perfect softball slide and shoots across the muddy field like it's a Slip 'N Slide, cackling with laughter. I look down at my uniform, which is more mud than fabric at this point, and barely drier than it was before I went into the locker room, and I chase after her and do the same thing. On me, you can barely tell, but on Carly, there's a perfect, gorgeous, muddy streak down her torso and right leg. Finally, she's no longer clean.

The third quarter is scoreless. The rain finally slows down, but the field remains soup.

With eight minutes left in the fourth quarter, Noah strings together a drive that takes us to Linkport's forty, then their thirty. Finally, the momentum is slowed when we find ourselves at fourth and eight on their twenty-five-yard line. Any other game, this would be an easy field goal, but I can see Coach Willis nervously approach Tayley on the sidelines, where she's kicking warm-up kicks into the practice net.

"You think you can make it, Striker?" he asks her.

She stands straight and nods her head. "Yes, Coach."

"Because we can chance the conversion."

"We can do it."

Coach looks at River, who stares back confidently. "We got this, Coach."

He chews his lip and nods. "All right, then. Take this game back."

I slap Tayley's shoulder, and Carly hoo-hahs as Tayley and River take the field.

River dries the ball with a towel she has duct-taped to her belt, then dries Tayley's shoes with it. Nothing is staying dry out here, but they're doing their best.

I glance over at Quinn, who paces the sidelines. It's hard to think that he might be rooting *against* Tayley in this moment. How twisted did he get that he might be hoping we *don't* win this game?

River gives the ball to the ref, who places it. Immediately, it begins to dampen with drizzle.

Our center snaps the ball, River catches it, spins it, places it. Tayley is already into her approach. Our line has collapsed into theirs, but one Linkport player somehow finds traction enough to leap above the others, reaching his arm up high. Tayley's foot connects, and the ball flies barely over his fingertips, toward the uprights...

It's good.

Tayley barks out a quick "Alch!" River hugs her. I realize I'm screaming. Carly next to me is screaming. I embrace her. We're jumping up and down. Ranger wraps his huge, wet, muddy arms around us both, then Noah, too. Then I realize I'm trapped in a hug burrito with Carly Nakata. My heart speeds up and I try not to overthink it.

It's 9–7 Elkhorn. Six minutes left in the game.

As I take the field, I tell myself that all we have to do is hold them, then run the clock down. They only have one time-out left. We can win this game. After everything, we can end the season on a win. It's up to the defense now.

Linkport has Turnip playing all sides. He seems to be the only one on either team immune to the mud. Maybe it's his size, or his slow speed, but he can plow through defenders, mud or no mud. Linkport gets a first down on the first play. My legs are exhausted, shaking every time I try to get into position. My pads feel like they weigh twice as much as usual. My helmet makes my head droop. It takes everything not to think about what a hot shower and sweatpants will feel like. Even the stands look thinned out. Is it possible people have left due to weather? I squint up and see my parents sticking it out. Reese and Jupiter are enjoying some nachos from the concession stand, their hoods up, knees pressed together.

Four minutes left. My receiver looks exhausted, too, but he has the adrenaline of needing to score on his side. The pep band plays on. The cheerleaders, just as wet and cold as us, cheer. I can't let Ichelle down. She would want me to keep playing 'til the bitter end. I won't let us lose this. I summon the strength to keep going.

On third and eight at the fifty, I slip coming off the snap. When I look back up, I see that Linkport has risked a fake to Turnip. My whole team seems to be following him up the outside, but the ball is actually in the hands of a fast, skinny guy picking his way up the middle and toward the opposite sideline. I chase him, focusing on finding my feet beneath me. He's determined to make it those eight yards to a first down, and all I need to do is stop him at seven. I gain on him and squat-grab-lift-hands into him, just like always. The crash is satisfying as we both land in the mud with a splat, sliding another three yards together before coming to a stop. We pop to our feet and look at the chains. My teammates are waving their arms—no first down, no first down. The Linkport players are screaming it is.

The ref takes the ball and sets it down around where we started our slide. The chains come out. Both teams look on, stressed, as the chain gang put down the first marker, then stretch the chain . . .

Three inches shy of a first down.

Hell yes. Turnip looks ready to kill a man. Or me.

Forty-two yards is a long kick for any kicker to make, but in these conditions, it's near impossible. They could go for a first down, but if they don't make it, we have the ball at midfield. Linkport does the safe thing and decides to punt. It might be a mistake, but in a game with so many turnovers, punting doesn't seem like that big of a deal. They're betting they'll get the ball back with enough time to score.

Lincoln toes the sideline ready to go in to return the kick, but Coach mumbles, "Sit back down, son," and looks around at the players he has left—all of us exhausted, wet, muddy, and frustrated.

Except one. There's only one player on this team right now fresh enough to keep the ball in our possession.

"Play Nakata," I say.

Coach looks at me. Carly looks at me. I'm not sure which one is more surprised.

"She's got the speed, and she's fresh," I say.

Coach looks at Carly suspiciously. She pulls herself to her fullest height. "I'm ready."

He looks her over. "You afraid to be hit?"

"No, sir."

"You gonna hold on to the ball no matter what?"

"Yes, sir."

The clock's ticking, Coach has to make a call.

"If you have space to run it, run it, but don't get cocky. I'll be happy so long as you keep possession. Don't be afraid to signal fair catch." Carly hops back and forth on her feet, excited. "Okay, show me what you got."

"Okay!" she says, and looks at me.

I grin big at her. "Get in there!"

Valentina, River, and Tayley slap her on the back as she struggles to find her mouth guard and slip it in. She does a couple fast jumping jacks, then ducks her head and runs onto the field.

52

THE NOISE DOUBLES WHEN THE CROWD REALIZES who's going in. The pep band launches into "This One's for the Girls." I'm smiling so wide my cheeks are pressed against the inside of my helmet. An arm comes over my shoulder—it's Valentina. Tayley's arm wraps around me from the other side, River's arm around her. We watch Carly jog to the end of the field, then get in ready stance. She looks focused, alert. The only player on the field with any white left on her jersey.

I wonder if she's scared. Or if she's able to feel the joy of it. Or if she's just numb, focused on her one job—catching the ball and running it back as far as she can.

Lining up on either side of her are the rest of our special teams—a bunch of wet, exhausted boys, including Wayne and Curtis. Their shoulders sag as they grind their cleats into the mud, looking for purchase. If we can just hold on for a couple more minutes, we can win this game.

I look from their drooping helmets to Turnip on the Linkport side, who, despite the conditions, looks as dominating as ever. Does he not get tired?

Someone snorts, and it's Quinn. He looks positively gleeful. I start to get a bad feeling. The only thing standing between Carly and certain mowage is a line of guys who hate her guts.

The kick flies, everyone moves. Turnip lumbers downfield; Carly positions herself underneath the ball.

The crowd hushes in the moment before the catch. Or maybe it's that my heart is beating so loud I can't hear them anymore.

Carly puts out her arms and the ball drops right into them. She clasps it to her chest, then takes off, repositioning the ball into five-point contact just as she learned that afternoon at our secret practice. Our Elk Hunters clash with their Orcas. Turnip powers through the initial line of blockers. Carly hurtles forward, fast on her feet, lightly skipping over the mud on her fresh legs like it doesn't affect her. She looks like a deer out there, fast and sprightly. She should have been playing this entire time.

Flint Wentworth closes in on Turnip and gets low for a block, but Turnip powers right through him, sending Flint sliding, mud caking in his face mask.

Carly spins out of the arms of a potential tackle and zips past the fifty-yard line. It's already a hell of a punt return. She could go out of bounds at any time and it would be respectable. But she flits forward. Turnip closes in. The only defender left between him and her is Wayne Warren. I watch Wayne take an angle on Turnip that would knock him out of bounds in time to make a path infield for Carly. Wayne runs his approach, but a second before he makes contact, the mud beneath him betrays his footing, and he slips. Turnip barrels past him. Wayne's slip sends him sliding toward Carly, who has to jump to avoid him. Turnip slams into her at the height of her jump.

The crunch is sickening. Carly's head snaps back and she drops. Carly lands on her back in the mud.

The crowd grunts, then falls silent. Carly doesn't move. I don't breathe. Turnip backs up.

I'm steps ahead of Coach Willis, running onto the field. I slip in the mud and push forward. Carly isn't moving. As I get closer, Turnip puts his hands on top of his head, looking worried. Shit. If *Turnip* is worried...

If anything happened to Carly, I'm going to murder someone. I can feel the old, familiar rage growing in my gut.

"Carly!" I fall into the mud next to her.

"Mara," she moans, and relief floods through me that she can talk. "Ow."

"Don't move, don't move."

The medics crouch next to her, pulling out a neck brace.

"I told you, one play," Carly says.

"You kicked ass," I tell her as Coach Gary pulls me back. All I can do is watch desperately from behind the coaches, catching glimpses of her body as the medics strap her to a backboard.

Then I hear it. A snicker. Wayne.

I look at him in disbelief, rage roaring in an instant. He nudges Quinn and whispers, "Like a sack of dirt." And Quinn is shaking his head and smiling.

Are they *enjoying* this? Carly got hit because Wayne missed his block. Could it have been intentional? He slipped—people have been doing that all night. But this slip came at the exact wrong time. For Wayne, was it the exact right time?

I'm marching forward before I realize what I'm going to do. No one hurts Carly on my watch. No one *laughs* about it. Not in front of me.

When he notices me, a flicker of fear flashes across Quinn's face, before he hides it. *Good.* Be scared. There's nothing stopping me from throwing a punch anymore. My basketball season is already tanked because of Quinn. I can fight all night long and it won't change Coach Joyce's decision. This whole season has already been for nothing.

The distance between us closes. He squares off. Like he can do anything to stop the rainstorm of pain that's about to hit him. My fist closes, my muscles tingle with the need.

"Mara!" a small voice calls out from the stands. I keep marching. "Mara!" It comes again.

I'm two feet from Quinn when he flinches.

"Mara, is she okay?"

I look toward the voice. It's Summer, the girl who plays Pop Warner. She leans over the banister in the stands, decked out in green and white from head to toe. My number painted on her cheeks. Her eyes huge and watery. Her mom stands behind her, concerned.

"Is everything going to be okay?" Summer asks.

And I can't look into her face and tell her it is, because I don't know that it will. It already isn't okay.

And I can't hit Quinn in front of her. I don't want her to ever do what I'm about to do.

I look back to Quinn, who is raising his chin defiantly, his good hand poised to fight back. "C'mon. What do you have to lose?"

I have more to lose than just basketball. I take a step backward. Quinn shakes his head like *I'm* the pathetic one.

Then a muddy brown smear comes from the sidelines and takes Quinn out with one swing. Noah.

Quinn hits the mud with a splat right on his broken arm. He wails out.

"You're a piece of shit, Quinn," Noah says.

Wayne looks on in shock, then straightens up and hits Noah. Noah grabs him around the waist and they both go down, scrabbling in the mud.

Curtis tries to kick Noah while he's down, but Valentina rushes in and shoves him, sending him flying backward, mud spraying out from under his ass when he lands. Tayley scuffs her shoes through the mud, sending a spurt flying into Wayne's face. He spits brown.

Then Jerry Martinez is there, throwing a punch at Stetson, who slips his mouth guard in and tackles Jerry. Coach Howard tries to pull them apart, but he can't do it in the mud. I take a step away from their flailing legs and bump right into River, who's slapping Lincoln with a muddy towel and calling him every Shakespearean insult she can think of. "This is for treating Tayley like scum, you saucy lackey! I wish we were better strangers!"

Two guys from the D-line head toward the tussle and Ranger clotheslines one and Tayley stiff-arms another right into the ground. Coach Willis gets a stray fist to the ear, which only makes him holler more than he already is. Coach Gary slips and falls in the mud, landing on his back in his windbreaker, struggling like a flipped turtle. The Linkport players stand near their sideline, stuck somewhere between shock and amusement.

Noah is still scrambling around on the ground trying to pin Wayne when Flint Wentworth flies into them both off a shove by Valentina. Quinn is moaning on his hands and knees. A referee stops blowing his whistle long enough to help him up, but as soon as the ref turns around, Tayley says, "I don't think so," and kicks Quinn in the back of the knee. He buckles to the ground.

And I realize, watching my friends fight side by side...I don't need to take on every fight myself. I have allies. Friends, who are willing to protect me, stand up for what's right, so that I don't have to do it alone.

Eventually, the coaches and refs gain some control over the situation. They have Wayne and Noah separated. Ranger is holding three guys back on his own. One ref is seeing to Curtis, who has blood flowing out of his nose. Valentina, River, and Tayley are being cornered off by Coach Gary. They shout at the boys over his outstretched arms.

The Elkhorn Five have given everything in order to play football. It's time for me to take a stand for them.

I find Summer in the stands again. She's watching the fight wild-eyed. "Summer!" Her eyes find me. "Yes. It's all going to be okay."

I take another step backward, then another. Then I turn and take off running the opposite direction, away from the fight, toward where I know I need to go. Somewhere I can really make a difference.

As I run, I look over toward Carly. They've got her on a stretcher. The ambulance is pulling onto the field.

I stop in front of the TV lady. "Let's go. Let's talk." She looks at me in surprise. "I mean it, get your microphone out."

She scrambles to get ready. When she's got the microphone under my chin and the camera woman has the big black lens pointed at me, I start. "My name is Mara Deeble, and I'm one of the Elkhorn Five. What do you want to know?"

"Mara, there are some that say that having girls on the team has been disruptive to the game. What do you say?"

"Disruptive? Hell yeah, it's been disruptive. Some institutions need disruption."

She asks about my experiences. I tell her honestly. That some boys on the team have been welcoming, but many others have been hostile, belligerent, even menacing. I tell her about the nasty signs, the clothes incident, the vandalism on Noah's truck, the slashed tires. And about the coaching staff's complete lack of leadership all season.

"And what's it all led to? One girl's on her way to the hospital and the rest of the team..." I point over my shoulder at the Elk Hunters football team, bloody, muddy, and spitting mad.

"Is there anything you want to tell girls out there who might be thinking of playing football but who are put off by the stories you just told?"

I wipe my forehead and look at the mud for a minute. Is this a path I would recommend to other girls? Maybe other schools are better than mine. Maybe for another girl at another school it would be simple. Maybe it would be worse. Maybe it would be easier for the boys to accept me if I had been the only girl. Or maybe it would have been lonelier. It's impossible to tell another girl what she should or shouldn't do. Except that if she wants to play football, she shouldn't let anyone tell her she can't.

I look back up at the reporter. "I guess what it comes down to is, after everything, do I regret it? No. I don't."

53

THE REFS EJECT SO MANY PLAYERS THAT THEY HAVE no choice but to call the game a forfeit for Elkhorn, even though we were up. All we had to do was make it to the end of the game and we would have had a win this season, but we couldn't do it. The trudge back to the locker rooms is silent. I don't even change, I just yank off my shoulder pads and throw on a sweatshirt and tell the rest of the girls to meet at the hospital.

Noah is right on my heels as we get to the car at the same time my parents come out of the stands. They check him over for injuries, but Noah insists he's fine. Just some bruises.

In the car, it's quiet, no one quite knowing how to address what just happened. But then Mom says, "I didn't know you were starting, Mara."

"This was my first time."

She clears her throat. "You, uh . . . you looked like a natural out there."

It's the last thing I expected her to say. A rock in my throat makes it hard to swallow. I lean forward and put my hand on her shoulder. "Thank you for coming," I say. She nods once and looks out the window.

We pack the waiting room—Carly's mom, Valentina, River, Tayley, Ranger, Noah, Jerry, and me. Quinn is there for a while but only to get a stitch in his eyebrow where Noah socked him. Lincoln comes in to get checked for a broken wrist where River knocked him down, but it's just sprained. They don't stick around. The nurses try to send us home, but Carly's mom won't let them. She says, nonsensically, that we're all immediate family, and the nurses let it go.

We watch the eleven o'clock news together, and they use almost all of my interview, interspersed with footage of the brawl and a few cool shots of our mud bowl. Everyone cheers when they use the B-roll shot of me running my fingers through my hair and slipping on my helmet, but I just feel tense. I don't know if it will change things, but I'm glad I finally told my side of the story.

Around midnight, Reese and Jupiter show up with burgers for everyone, which is perfect because I am ravenous. We eat over our laps, squeezed into the waiting-room chairs. We're so hungry, we don't realize what we're eating until Noah scowls at his halfway through and says, "What's wrong with this beef patty?"

"It's lentils and beet juice," Reese says. "It's vegan."

It doesn't matter; we're starving. And no one's in the mood to make jokes when who knows how Carly's doing.

Most of us are in sweatpants and hoodies, but mud still dots our faces, sticks in our hair. We haven't showered. We're tired. But none of us will leave until we hear.

The doctor comes in after midnight with news. The tackle

caused Carly's neck to fling forward beyond its normal limits, which tore ligaments in her neck and caused the muscles to strain. She then landed on the ground and hit her head again, which caused a concussion.

"What's that mean?" I ask. Everyone else is being quiet. It's freaking me out.

"She's going to be fine," the doctor says. "But she can't play football for a couple months, and she has to wear a neck brace for three weeks."

The relief fills me up. I drop my head. Tayley puts an arm around my shoulders. Valentina laughs. The room changes color with everyone's sudden relaxation.

"I had to wear a neck brace once in seventh grade. You feel like the Terminator in it. It's cool," Ranger says.

The doctor tells Carly's mom that she can see her, but the rest of us really do have to go home. We make plans to come back in the morning if she's still there. We hug, first together, then individually, in every permutation. We've been through something together. Not just tonight, but this season. We're different than we were.

Just as I'm about to leave, Carly's mom calls my name from the hallway. When I go over, she tells me that Carly is asking for me. My heart skips a beat. Out of everyone, she's asking for *me*?

I tell my folks I'll be five more minutes, and I follow Carly's mom down the hall. "Go on, I'll wait here," she says. "No punching, no matter how infuriating she gets."

"Understood," I say.

Carly doesn't have a whole room, just a bed with a curtain around it. I duck behind it. She's sitting up in bed, a neck brace swallowing her from chin to collar. She looks so fragile like this, but I know she's not.

"It's okay, you can laugh," she says.

"I wasn't going to."

"I look like an idiot."

"You look like a badass."

"Mara..."

"Ranger said when he wore one, he felt like the Terminator."

"I don't feel like the Terminator. The Terminator can move his head. I feel like someone in a neck brace."

I sit in the chair next to her bed. "Does it hurt?"

"A really hot nurse gave me drugs."

"Mariposa?"

"Yes!"

"She fixed me up after the plate-glass window. Soft hands."

"*Excellent* bedside manner." Carly smiles, then says, "I heard everyone got in a fight because of me."

"There was a fight. Was it 'because of you'?" I use air quotes.

She raises an eyebrow. "Mom said everyone was fighting to avenge me."

"That can't be right," I tease.

"I can't help but notice you came out unscathed."

"Oh, me? I didn't fight. You know I'm not allowed unless I have a *really* good reason."

"And me lying on the ground near death wasn't good enough reason?"

"Nah," I say. "I could tell you weren't hurt that bad."

"Okay, and did you come to that understanding before or after you rushed to my side, crying my name?"

My heart zips. She registered that? I don't have an answer right away.

She continues, serious this time. "My mom showed me the interview you did. I'm really proud of you, Mara." Her hand is doing this weird grabbing thing.

"What are you doing?"

"I'm trying to reach for your goddamn hand, but I can't move my goddamn neck," she says.

"Oh." I take her hand. Her fingers lace through mine. I look at them a long time before getting up the courage to look at her. She's watching me, this small smile stuck on her face like an idiot.

I can't believe this is happening.

"I'm proud of you, too," I say.

"For what?"

"For..." It takes me a minute to be able to put it into words. "For not letting anyone keep you from being who you are."

She squeezes my hand and holds my look. I have the sudden feeling that if I kissed her, it would go a lot better than with Valentina.

"Carly?" her mom's voice comes from the other side of the curtain.

If Carly could have slammed her head back into her pillow, she would have. Instead, she just kind of sinks and looks at the ceiling. "What?"

"We gotta go, babe. They're kicking us out."

"Two more minutes!"

"You can see Mara tomorrow. Let's go get some sleep," she says.

Carly gives me this look that's a little wild. I don't want to leave, either. In this little hospital curtain bubble, it feels like anything is possible. What if we leave here and everything reverts back to how it was?

"I don't want this to be goodbye," she whispers to me.

"You can't stay here forever."

"No, I mean... football is over. We never have to see each other again if we don't want to..." She trails off.

She's right. No more practices. No more divided team. No more reporters sticking microphones in our faces. We could go back to how we were before.

I stand up and hold her hand in both of mine. "That's not going to happen," I tell her.

"Promise?"

"Promise."

"Carly." Carly's mom pulls back the curtain. I put Carly's hand down.

"Bye," I say, and duck out, heart pounding.

54

I'M PUTTING ON MY BOOTS BY THE FRONT DOOR TO get ready to do morning chores when I hear my mom's voice from the dining room. "Mara? Would you mind joining us?"

Tentatively, I pull my boots back off and go to the dining room. Mom and Dad are both sitting at the table, hands folded in front of them. What is this? This isn't normal. This is concerning. "Yeah? I was about to do my chores."

"Have a seat," Dad says sternly.

Now I'm really freaked out. I go around and sit. Mom takes a sip of tea.

"Your father has something he'd like to tell you."

Cancer. He has cancer. Heart disease. Diabetes. Frostbite. Fuck. What.

"I want to thank you," Dad says.

"What? What for?"

"I know I've been a little...blue. Lately."

Okay, not cancer, maybe. But my mouth feels dry anyway. Dad's sadness has been a constant in this house. We've never talked about it.

"Okay," I say.

"After we sold everything, I needed..." He searches for the word. "Purpose." He levels me with a look. "I looked at you and I saw a girl who knew exactly what she wanted and went after it. I loved seeing that. But I can't help you be a better football player. I can't even teach you about the farm. That's all over now. I didn't know how to be a father to you. And I'm sorry I haven't been around."

"That's okay," I say even though it's not, really. This is the most he's said in a long time. I'm trying to listen hard so I can remember it back later.

"Anyway," my mom prompts, and Dad gets back on track.

"Anyway, you know Fritz Sorgaard? Lives over out by the old dump road?"

"Yeah. Ranger's dad." What's this got to do with the Sorgaards?

"Well, he needed a riding mower, and I had that one out back we're not using anymore, and he offered to buy it off me at the last 4-H meeting, but I said I had a better idea and was he still in need of his Ford now that Felix made it off to college and he said no and so we traded."

"Dad..." Is this story going where I think it's going? Did Dad trade for a truck for me?

"Well, trouble was, that old Ford burst a head gasket and didn't run anymore, and it takes about two grand to replace."

"Oh," I say, deflating. Never mind.

"How much you got in your truck fund?"

"Three hundred and forty and change."

Dad nods. "Not quite enough, is it?"

"Not even close."

"Hank," Mom prods again.

Dad nods to Mom like *okay, okay* and turns back to me. "Come with me," he says, standing up.

He leads me to the front door. Before he opens it, he says, "Hold on to that three hundred and forty, because you're going to need it for your insurance."

"Insurance for what? For a truck that doesn't run?"

"Oh, it runs," Dad says, opening the door.

In the front driveway is a bright blue late-'90s-era Ford Ranger. The wheel wells are rusting out. The bumper is dented. There's heavy scratching on the back bed from years of sliding gear in and out. And it's absolutely beautiful.

"Took me a couple of months, but I got a new head gasket in there, plus new tires, a fresh set of spark plugs, and all new air filters. Even filled up the windshield wiper fluid for ya."

I look back at Dad in awe, afraid to say anything in case it's all a mistake.

"Go on. It's yours. Go check it out."

I leap down the stairs and slowly circle the truck. Noah leans against the passenger door. "Just washed it. Let's take her mud bogging."

I run my finger over the hood, the squared-off headlight wells. I open the driver's-side door and haul myself up and in. The front seats are covered in a worn brown wool blanket. I gasp when I see that the wheel has a steering knob on it, just like Jupiter's car.

I run my fingers over the stereo. "No CD player; you'll have to learn to make tapes," Noah says.

I can't wait to make a hundred mix tapes. I look up through the windshield at Dad and Mom standing on the porch.

"Thank you," I mouth at them.

Mom smiles at me. Dad nods.

# # #

"I was at the game this weekend," Coach Joyce says from the door of the barn.

I finish pouring the feed for Roger and Angelica. "Coach, hey. What are you doing here?"

"I wanted to talk to you," she says, watching me carefully. "I saw your behavior."

I put back the feed and wipe my hands on my jeans. "Okay."

Coach continues. "You had every reason to join in on that fight...but you didn't. That says something, Mara. That says you've grown. So"—she straightens her body toward mine—"if you would like to come back to basketball, I would love to have you."

Huh.

"So, punching Quinn? It just, what, doesn't count anymore?"

"I believe people can change. And you've proven yourself. Besides, he sounds like he deserved it."

"What about the others?" I ask.

"What others?"

"Carly Nakata. Valentina, Tayley and River, too, if they were interested in going out for the team."

She hesitates. "Valentina, Tayley, and River...they were all involved in that fight, which means they'd be disqualified."

"And Nakata? She wasn't fighting."

She hesitates even longer, trying to read my face. "I'm confused, Mara. Do you *want* her on the team?"

"Yeah, I do."

"It would depend on her injuries. I would need a doctor's note, but yeah." She opens her hands, palms out, a big smile on her face. "So. Can I count on you this season?"

I would have killed for this option in August. Being courted to play basketball, a sport I love—that I'm good at—with Carly potentially off the team for injuries. Just me and the game—no distractions, no drama. Now it just seems... *boring.*

"I'll think about it," I say.

She lowers her hands in bewilderment. "Okay. Anything you want to talk about?"

"I have to discuss it with Carly and the rest."

She looks at me a long beat. "All right."

55

"EWWWWW," RIVER SAYS.

"He did not." Valentina covers her gaping mouth with her hand.

Tayley insists. "He did! And they didn't even look away. They just stood there on the front porch with their arms around each other."

I can't believe it. "You had your first kiss with Mr. and Mrs. Sorgaard *watching*?"

Tayley blushes again.

Carly shakes her head and pokes at the fire. We're all sitting around Carly's building's fire pit. "I have never known any human obsessed with his parents as much as Ranger is."

"So, it's going well, then? You like him?" Valentina prods.

Tayley nods, her smile threatening to take over her whole face.

"Well, hopefully the *next* kiss is more private," I say.

"And the kiss after that, and the kiss after that..." Carly teases as Tayley turns red.

"What about you, Valentina?" River saves Tayley by redirecting us. "How's romancing the quarterback going?" Valentina has been over to the house no less than once a day since the end of football practice. I would be fine with it if it didn't mean Noah keeps slacking on his chores, leaving me to fill in for him. He's been flouncing around the house. His snark levels are way down. He even offered to give me a ride the other day, which I didn't need now that I have my own truck. Still. It's adorable.

Valentina just smiles, her cheeks reddening, and wraps her shawl tighter around her shoulders. "Good," she says simply. Everyone cracks up.

"Very demure," Carly says drily.

"What about you, Maria?" Valentina asks Maria Carpenter, who has joined us tonight, along with Kelly Wesley. They share the bench, a wool blanket tucked around their legs. When Valentina first suggested inviting Maria, I was unsure, but they're fresh off a loss in the quarterfinals at State and she said they needed cheering up. Besides, she says, Maria and Kelly came to every single home football game that didn't conflict with a volleyball match. They love the Elkhorn Five.

Maria sighs a long sigh. "The era of Quinn Kegley is blessedly behind us," she says. Then she looks into the fire. "I don't really trust my instincts right now. I think I'm just gonna focus on school for a little while and see where that gets me."

Carly says, "Oh my god, even *homework* is better than Quinn Kegley."

Everyone laughs.

"It totally is," Maria says.

Carly rubs her neck. She's had her neck brace off for about a week, but she's not supposed to strain it. She reaches to put another log on the bonfire, but I jump up and grab it from her.

"Stop it, let me help," I say.

The nights are getting colder and rainier as we head toward December, but Saturday night bonfires at Carly's are still a staple. We're wearing layers under layers under rain jackets and eating the tiramisu River made between sips of Carly's mom's pinot noir (she says rosé is for summer months).

"So, I had something I wanted to talk about..." I start. My heart picks up because I know there's the potential for this to be a fraught conversation.

"Ooh, is Mara kissing someone, too?" River jokes. Valentina looks intrigued. Carly looks at me sharply, which almost makes me smile.

"No, no. Not that. I wanted to talk about football."

Everyone groans. River says, "What about it?"

"Are we going to play next year?" I ask. The question has been weighing on me. It's not that I welcome more abuse from the Kool-Aid Club and associates, but when I think about my life without football in it, a sadness clutches me. I wish I didn't have to choose between playing a sport I love and getting harassed, but that's why I'm bringing it up with the other girls. "I want to do it, but I won't do it without the rest of you."

The Elkhorn Five look between each other. River says, "I don't know, rumor is, they're doing *Spring Awakening* next fall." Valentina boos. "What?"

"I liked playing," Tayley says, "but I'm not sure I can handle another season of Quinn Kegley vandalizing our personal property." A chorus of *mm-hmms* follows.

"Are we even allowed to play again after fighting?" Valentina asks.

Tayley snorts. "Oh, come on, I barely even pushed a guy!"

Maria swivels on her. "Didn't you chip Flint Wentworth's tooth?"

"That was an *accident*! And he was punching Ranger in the pancreas!"

"I remember that!" River cries. Everyone dies laughing. The night of the brawl was once scary and dangerous, but over time, the retelling of what everyone did or did not do during that fight has become a source of revelry.

"And then we all got corralled by Coach Gary," Valentina says. "And I thought Mara would be right with us, but then I turn around and she's running toward the news cameras!"

Everyone laughs some more. This is how it always gets told.

River mimes holding a guy in a headlock and punching him with considerable effort. "Hey, Mara, can I get a hand with Wayne Warren?" She mimes looking up. "Mara? Where's Mara? Oh, there she is . . . *ON THE ELEVEN O'CLOCK NEWS.*"

Everyone dies laughing again.

"How're your fans doing, Mara?" River asks.

"I got three more DMs just today," I say. After my interview went minorly viral, my messages started filling up with girls asking me if they should join their team, girls asking what position they should play, girls asking for advice or encouragement. "It's so weird."

"I'm just so glad you haven't forgotten the little people now that you're famous," River says.

"Everybody's little next to Mara," Tayley says, pretending to crane her neck to look up at me.

Carly stares into the fire.

I nudge her. "What do you think?" I ask. "About football?"

"I'm gonna grab some more wine," she says, rising from her chair.

"I'll help you," I say, and when she shoots me a look: "You're not supposed to carry things." So she has to let me.

In the kitchen, Carly pulls out another bottle and spins around looking for where she left the bottle opener last. I hand it to her. "You okay?"

"Yeah," she says. Her hair is falling out of its bun and onto her neck, which is a thing I can't stop looking at.

"You don't look okay," I say.

She opens the wine, then sighs.

I rub the back of my head where I just got my hair cut again. It prickles satisfyingly under my fingers.

"Carly, what is it?"

"I have an idea, but I don't know if it's going to work," she says, not looking at me. I wait it out. I know her well enough to know she hates to be quiet. She'll tell me eventually.

Finally, she looks at me. "Are you going to play basketball this year?"

Not the question I was expecting. "Um, well, Coach Joyce said I could, but I haven't given her an answer yet." I pause, then ask, hesitatingly, "Are you?"

She rubs her neck. "Doc said I can play as long as I tell him if I start to feel pain."

"That's great!"

"Yeah..." She doesn't sound so sure. She turns to look at me, wet shoes squeaking on her kitchen floor, her rain jacket sprinkled wet, her hair flying everywhere. She's unbelievably cute in this moment, but her face is making me nervous. Does she not want to play basketball anymore? Does she not want to play with *me*? Maybe that moment we had in the hospital was just a moment that passed. Maybe she wants to take it all back.

"It's just... *Mara*." She levels me with a look. "You remember what happened last time it was just you and me on a team."

"Well, yeah."

"So...the other three girls can't play. What's gonna happen if it's just us again? What if we turn on each other? What if we need them around as, like, buffer?"

I stare at her. *That's* what she's worried about? "You think we need buffer?"

"I don't know. Do you?"

"No."

She looks up at me and leans against the corner, her eyebrows pulled together in a worried knot.

"I don't know if I've been clear enough about this, but I'm never going to hit you like that again. I don't want to hit anyone like that, but especially not you. I'm so sorry that happened. I don't want to be that person anymore."

She chews at her thumb, so I keep talking. "As for the others, I like having them around. I like Tayley and River makes me laugh and Valentina is fun. But when it's just the two of us"—I swallow—"that's good, too."

I feel suddenly warm in my layers. The kitchen steams with the rain evaporating off our shoulders.

She doesn't look away. "So, you're saying," she says carefully, "you want to play basketball with me?"

"I'm saying..." My breath feels shallow in my throat. "That I like being alone with you."

"I like being alone with you, too." Carly shuffles her feet and lets out a weirdly long breath. "Mara, you know that I've had a crush on you for, like, ever, right?" She lifts her eyes to mine.

My heart thuds in my chest as I remember her hand reaching for mine that night. "Since the hospital?"

"The *hospital*?" She barks out a laugh of disbelief. "No, dummy, since, like, freshman year."

"What?"

"Oh, come on. I was so obvious. I was, like, hanging all over you."

I can't do anything but gape at her. "What?"

"Why do you think I was such a stickler about you not concussing yourself during basketball?"

"Because... Wait. What?"

"I had to practically *beg* Valentina to ask you to come to my party for me because I couldn't bear to do it myself and have you reject me."

This whole time? This whole time I thought she hated me? "You said at the party you didn't have a crush."

"I was *lying*, come *on*! How many times do I have to make that reporter write about how talented you are and how tall and strong and cool you are before you'd pay attention to me?"

I can hardly breathe. *This whole time.* She's right. I *am* a dummy. "I kept asking you why you cared."

She shakes her head. "The thing is, you don't even realize what a heartthrob you are. You're like an elk, all statuesque and shit. All full of swagger."

"I always thought I was like an emu."

"Oh my god!" Carly buries her face in her hands.

I need to kiss her right now. Like *right* now. "Carly..." It comes out raspy, barely a whisper.

"Yeah?" she says into her hands.

"Can I kiss you?"

She looks up fast. "Took you long enough."

When our lips meet, it's a hundred times better than with Valentina because she wants it and she's kissing back.

"Ow. Ow, ow, ow, sorry, ow," Carly says, pulling away and

rubbing her neck. "I'm sorry. You're just so tall and I'm not supposed to bend my neck for another week."

"How about this?" I lift her from her hips and set her gently on the kitchen counter. Eye to eye.

She smiles slowly. "I've never seen you from this angle."

I feel giddy with adrenaline. All I want to do is kiss her again. "And?"

"Perfect."

She wraps her hands around my elbows and pulls me into her. This time we kiss until we run out of breath, and then we kiss some more. Her hair is soft and full. Her hands find their way to my neck, and I feel the tingle all the way to my toes in my boots.

I can't believe it took me this long to do this. I can't believe how much of my life I spent trying to define myself as being the opposite of Carly, when we could have just existed alongside each other all along. When I could have been in her arms. It feels silly now.

"I can't believe I'm kissing Mara Deeble," she says breathlessly when we separate. My heart zings.

I sweep rain-wet hair out of her eyes, marveling that she's letting me touch her. "This doesn't mean I'm coming to your gay club meetings, you know," I say.

She gasps. "But we need a treasurer so bad!"

I hold up a finger in warning, and she nods. "I know, you're not the treasurer type."

"But now will you tell me who all's in the club?"

"Nope!" Her eyes twinkle. "You have to show up to find out. Those are the rules."

"Anyone on the football team?"

She gives me a coy smile. "Maybe."

My jaw falls open, but she just shrugs. Maybe I'll have to re-examine my coming-out plan. I'm already out to Jupiter, Reese, Valentina, and Carly. Maybe there's wiggle room enough for Carly's club, too. I'll think about it.

"Hey, what was the idea you wanted to tell me?" I ask.

"You have to promise to keep an open mind," she says.

# # #

When we rejoin the others, Tayley asks, "Where's the wine?" and Carly stops in her tracks because we forgot it upstairs, and I look at her and nearly snort laugh because her hair is a mess in back and she looks flushed. Valentina narrows her eyes but doesn't say anything.

I run back for the wine. When I return, Carly refills glasses and says, "So, you know how we all love football, but we don't like playing with the boys?" A general murmur of affirmation. "What if I told you there was another way?"

Carly refused to tell me the idea until we were all together. I don't understand what she's trying to say yet.

"If we wave a magic wand and erase Quinn Kegley and his friends from existence?" Valentina asks.

"Close," Carly says. "We play without him."

"There's no way those guys don't play football next year," River says.

"They'll play boys' football," Carly says with a satisfied smile. "We'll be playing *girls'* football."

River looks at me like I have any idea what she's saying. *Girls' football?*

"Is that a thing?" Valentina asks.

"There's a league in Utah with over five hundred girls playing in it," Carly says. "We don't need to start with that many, we just need a couple teams."

"Can we convince that many girls to play?" Tayley wonders.

"Who's the most popular girl in school?" Carly asks. Suddenly, it clicks. I know how she's going to do this. And it might be brilliant.

Everyone looks at Maria, who fakes humility, but she knows it's true.

"And who's the best football player?" Carly asks.

"Mara," River says.

With Jerry, Noah, and Ranger graduating, this time it might actually be true.

"And who are the most famous football players in the state right now?"

"The Elkhorn Five," Kelly pipes up.

"Exactly," Carly says. "Imagine: We rally the girls at our school. Mara encourages all the girls at the other schools in the state, all her fans. I annoy the school board for funding until they're sick of the sight of me. Guys. *We can do this.*"

"Imagine having shoulder pads that actually fit," River says.

"Imagine lining up against a team the same size as us," Tayley says with a note of amazement.

"Maybe I'd play more than special teams," Valentina says.

"I could get the cheerleaders to join," Maria says. "Half of them dumped their boyfriends after the brawl. They don't want to cheer for a sexist team, anyway."

"Any of them that don't want to play can cheer for us," Carly says.

Tayley looks at me. "You on board with this? You're good enough to play with the boys."

I look around the circle of us, our faces lit by fire. It's late, we're all a little sleepy and a little tipsy, but right now anything seems possible. Could we actually do it? I'm not sure, but I'd like to find out. All we can do is raise our cups and try.

"I wouldn't have it any other way." I say the only thing left to say: "Hoo-hah!"

"Hoo-hah!"

Acknowledgments

AS A KID, I WAS THE ONLY GIRL ON MY FLAG FOOTBALL team. I remember the pride I felt when they turned on those bright, bright lights just for us; I remember the cool, damp grass under my fingers when I got into my three-point stance; most of all, I remember the cold shoulder of every one of my teammates. I loved the game, but it felt like no one wanted me there but me. I played flag for two years, and when it came time to graduate to tackle football, I didn't try out. I realized that as I got older, bucking the gender norm stopped being perceived as precociously cute and started being seen as weird, even threatening.

I remain proud of that tiny Britta—it takes courage to sign up for a sport that marks you as different. These pages are my attempt to honor her.

There are many others who helped bring this book to fruition. Most importantly, my endless gratitude to Aya and Eliot for the love, care, and laughter that filled my well while writing.

To my agent, Jim Ehrich, for being not just good at his job, but a good dude. A deep thank you to my editor, Kieran Viola, as well as Cassidy Leyendecker and the entire team at Hyperion who ushered this book to existence. A book is a team sport. To Marci Senders, who designed the book, and Ana Hard, who illustrated the cover, thank you for making this story into a beautiful object.

I want to thank all the girls and women who shared with me their past and present experiences playing football including Kennedy, Michaela, Bella, Rylie, and Claire. And to the fellas who shared their high school memories, Greg, Brian, Joe, and Shepard. Also thank you to Sydney, Jenni, and Britni, who helped put me in touch with football players.

Thank you to Julia for sharing her extensive knowledge of cattle ranching. Everything I got right was thanks to her, and everything I got wrong is my fault alone.

Thanks to Mikayla and Sage for being my youth advisors and keeping me relevant, always.

For being early readers and cheerleaders, thank you to Bree Barton, Bridget Farr, Molly Shalgos, Greg Murray, Sarah Enni, Malinda Lo, Carrie Lee, Avalon Gordon, Amy Spalding, and Zach Gonzalez-Landis. Your notes, encouragement, and hollering got me here.

And, of course, to the Astoria capture-the-flag crew. We really did play capture the flag downtown and Josh really did put his hand through the plate-glass window of a jewelry store.

Finally, thank you to those who gave care during a pretty challenging few years, including my family, my writing friends, my regular friends, Laura, Tali, and, first and last of all, Aya and Eliot.